RIFT VALLEY

REEVE ABRABEN

outskirts
press

Dedication

To my beloved children: Lane, Lindsay and Logan

Acknowledgements

Sometimes you get rewards that aren't deserved. My children, Lane, Lindsay and Logan are just that to me. I love you dearly.

To my friends and office staff, thank you for sticking with me through my darkest times. I hope that I live up to your faith in me.

To my editor, Ellis Amburn, thank you for taking a great story and making it roar. I wish you were here to see my dream realized.

Contents

CHAPTER ONE

1957

In the normally bustling operating room of the Palm Beach Good Samaritan Hospital, two surgeons, mentor and protégé, friend and associate and both handsome, albeit a generation apart, assessed the merits of a fine double-barrel shotgun. Being a Saturday, the suite and its skeleton crew were kept on the ready for emergencies only, which at present involved Ruth Bliss, a doyenne of Palm Beach society, who in an opiate daze wondered just what the hell was going on. The younger of the two surgeons, Doctor Paul Bennett, bounced the buttstock of the unloaded gun on the counter and pulled the trigger.

"Gordy, you stole this gun." Paul grinned as he handed the shotgun back to its new owner. "A Browning Superposed for a hundred bucks, and the only thing wrong with it is the inertia block's sticking. You finally hit one out of the park, my friend."

Taking the gun from the young associate, Doctor Gordon Williams studied his new prize. "Do you think you could put that in terms that maybe I could understand? What's an inertia block, and how can you be so sure that's what wrong with it?"

"These guns have a mechanism that resets and shifts a trigger when the gun recoils. If it gets stuck you can fire each barrel independently with the selector button, but it won't do it automatically," Paul answered authoritatively. "It could be some dirt or rust. Or maybe a bur on one of the metal parts. Either way, it's probably an easy fix."

Nurse Grace Wilhelm was dividing her attention between a newspaper article on the newly enacted Civil Rights Act and the goings-on just outside the nursing station's glass enclosure. She paid little attention to the gun clinic behind her. A seasoned Navy nurse during the Second World War, she was quite familiar with weapons *and* the havoc they dispatched. Her tour of duty in the Pacific had left her exceptionally qualified as a nurse and battle hardened as an individual. She had earned her stripes and didn't kowtow to anyone, surgeon or otherwise. She was the operating room supervisor and everybody knew it.

"Will you guys get that thing out of here? I think it's upsetting this patient," she snarled over her shoulder while observing patient Bliss through the window. "You're probably breaking a dozen rules," she added for effect, even though hospital rules were fairly inconsequential to her.

The patient, Ruth Bliss, had started the morning as she had for years with a breakfast laden with lard, fruit in Devon cream, buttered croissants, eggs Benedict, and café con leche, but today it had caught up with her, and her gallbladder had said, "Enough!" In her morphine fog she was struggling to make sense of the shotgun-toting surgeon while simultaneously trying to follow the jabbering of hospital orderly Gil Davis. Even in a drug-induced disorientation, the double-barrel Browning just didn't fit in the setting.

She had been introduced to Dr. Bennett shortly after the ambulance attendant wheeled her into the emergency room but was in far too much pain to grasp much about him or what he said to her eldest son, Carl. The exchange, she gathered, concerned gallbladders and surgery, but despite her distress, she did get an impression that for a man of his seemingly young age, Dr. Bennett appeared highly self-assured, perhaps even cocky. His speech revealed a proper Southern upbringing, but he seemed to orate to, as opposed to conversing with, the hospital personnel.

Obviously smitten with him, the nurses went out of their way to accommodate him, almost to the point of overindulgence, suggesting to Ruth that he was probably a very desirable eligible bachelor, which was, in fact, the case.

Paul Bennett was certainly good looking enough, in an unrefined sort of way. He had a dazzling tan that was punctuated by gentle blue eyes and sunglass-shaped, raccoon-like pale patterns produced by hot breezy weekends spent rigging baits, checking lines, gaffing fish, and occasionally mopping up anglers' vomit aboard Cap's boat. His tan contrasted with his tousled, short, sandy-blond hair, and his build was such that his scrubs hung on his body like a parachute in a tree, barely concealing the sinewy muscles on his lanky frame. He looked the part of a well-to-do surgeon, except for his hands. They had the chalky, cracked, salt-cured texture of a weathered mariner's, hardly what you'd expect to see on a surgeon whose skill relies heavily on tactility and nimbleness. He was a fishing mate not for the money but for love of the sport and his adoration of *The Lucky Brake's* helmsman—his dad, Cap.

The touch of Paul's hands, rough as they were, felt like a caress to Ruth Bliss as he poked and prodded her abdomen. She found herself longing to be forty years younger so she could have had a shot at him.

Later as she lay awaiting surgery, Gil, the orderly, was trying to sound knowledgeable about her imminent procedure, but she was unimpressed, dismissing him as one of those delinquent youths in jeans and black leather jackets who raced around town in noisy hot rods, being disrespectful and causing trouble.

"Excuse me, young man," she ventured, fully expecting the fellow to make some smart remark or ignore her altogether. Instead he came right to her side. "Can I help ya, ma'am?"

"You see that gentleman over there?" she asked, pointing her pudgy finger at Paul.

"Yes, that's Doc Bennett. You need me to get him for ya?"

"No, don't bother him. He's going to take out my gall bladder, you know."

"Well you ain't got much to worry about; Doc as sharp as they come."

Deciding he'd found a rare opportunity to show off his medical knowledge, the orderly said, "Mrs. Bliss, I seen folks bowed up something awful from them gall bladders. What happens is this: the duck gets plugged up and bile makes it swell till it bursts."

Feeling more empowered by his illusory rhetoric and diagnostic expertise, Gil mapped out his course of action. "We go in there and do somthin' called a colo-selectomy and—"

"How very interesting," she said, cutting short his graphic analysis of her malfunctioning organs. "What I'd like to know, however, is why he has that gun in there."

"Hmmm, looks like a nice little over-n-under scattergun. Its okay ma'am, Doc knows how to fix them things. Even had him mend an old pump gun of mine a while back. Doc's an expert on about everything."

A rap on the glass got Gil's attention, and he knew who it was without even having to look. His immediate superior, Grace Wilhelm, was trying to inform him that the surgical case in operating room one, a traumatic leg fracture caused by a collision between a motorcyclist and a stray dog, was wrapping, up and he was needed to dump linens, wipe the room and mop the floor.

"I got to get to work now, Mrs. Bliss, he said. "They're needin' me in surgery. We'll be comin' to fetch you soon. Don't worry."

Inside the nursing station, Dr. Paul Bennett turned his attention to the head nurse. "Why don't you leave Gil alone, Grace? He's doing his job."

"That's because I *don't* leave him alone," she countered. "Left on his own, you'd be operating on a floor with a sheet of dried blood two inches thick. I don't know why you doctors always stand up for him. It makes him think he can get away with anything."

"I like the kid and feel sorry for him. He wants to be a doctor so bad it's killing him, and you know what his chances are—zero. He'd probably be a damn good one if it was just cut and sew. Have you ever seen his taxidermy? It's beautiful, and I don't have to remind you that he probably saved a couple of those kids' lives after that bus accident."

Standing next to them, Dr. Gordon "Gordy" Williams felt compelled to jump in the fray. "I know for certain that at least one little girl benefitted from his quick thinking, and as far as his taxidermy's concerned, he did a fine job on a pair of quail he did for me."

She remembered the bus incident vividly but still wanted to tell him to shut up about his totally irrelevant quail. She was peeved that once again Gil Davis was jeopardizing her authority. "The kid's a moron. I can't believe you persuaded him to apply to medical school. He dropped out of school in the ninth grade, for Christ's sake. What did you think that was going to accomplish, having him apply?"

"At least he'll never wonder if he could've gotten in," said Paul. "Just leave him alone. This is as far as he'll ever get so don't make it miserable for him,"

Turning to Gordy, Paul resumed their discussion of the shotgun. "You don't deserve this, Gordy. What's the story?"

"The guy at the pawn shop said it wouldn't fire both barrels, but if I'd take it as is, two hundred. I offered him one and he grabbed it."

Gordy had the worst judgment of value Paul had ever seen; the gun was worth much more.

"You're way out of your element on this one, Gordy. Unlike every other 'prize' you've ever gotten, this one's actually got internal parts. Just so you don't break tradition, you better let me have it. Two and a half, cash right now."

"I finally get a nice one, and you want to steal it from me, you Shylock. No thanks, I'll just keep it. You can fix it for me, though."

The telephone rang and Grace picked it up. Outside the room Gil was wheeling the old woman toward the operating room.

"Bring it by the house tomorrow, Gordy, and please . . . please promise me you won't try to fix it yourself. I couldn't stand to see the screwheads burred up, and you *know* that'll happen if you mess with them. I've seen your handiwork before."

Gordon smirked. "The old man should have spent less time teaching you hobbies and a little more on diplomacy."

"You know what he once told me about burred screws on nice guns? He said it's like slingin' shit in the Sistine Chapel, and he's right, I've seen some beaut—"

"Paul," interrupted Grace. "The E.R.'s on the phone. They've got Cap down there and he's being admitted. It sounds like it might be pretty serious."

Paul chewed the inside of his cheek. "Grace, do you always have to be an asshole?" he snapped

"It's not a joke, he's really down there."

Tossing the gun on the countertop, nicking the stock and unwittingly leaving the muzzle pointing at Grace, he raced out of the room. Everything else in his world ceased except Cap.

Someone else would have to extract Ruth Bliss's gallbladder.

The architects that designed the hospital undoubtedly had spent little time in Florida, or they wouldn't have placed the emergency entrance on the east side of the building. The result of this error was evident every morning as the rising sun burned through the wide glass doors, turning the area into a greenhouse that strained the air conditioning system. Once the area heated up it never really cooled back down until late evening. It wasn't actually hot, but not far from it—hardly the temperature for such an emotionally charged venue. Paul's scrubs were already sticking to him when he burst into the room.

He knew immediately that the flurry of activity around his adoptive father meant Cap was having a serious medical emergency. Paul's knee-jerk reaction was to jump in and help, but someone grabbed his arm. He jerked free, prepared to pounce on the offender, but caught himself when he realized it was Dr. Kenneth Margolis, a squat, cherubic, semiretired internist.

"Paul, can I have a few words with you?"

"I'm busy, Ken," Paul said, his eyes irrevocably fixed on the gurney ahead.

Ken's hand clamped down on his arm and the pressure increased until it was impossible to ignore. "Paul, that Negro over there brought your dad in about a half hour ago." He pointed to an elderly man sitting somberly by the entrance.

It was Sheldon, and the sight of him plunged Paul into even deeper gloom. Cap and Sheldon had been cronies since the Great Depression, so close that the loss of either would have left the other devastated. In an era when it was customary to treat Negroes as second-rate citizens, Cap had always dealt with Sheldon evenhandedly.

"Can you give me a second? I've got to talk to him," Paul said, already in mid stride.

Sheldon stood and wiped his eyes. "Ol' Cap fixin' to leave us, Mr. Paul?" he asked, his fingers worrying the rim of his battered bowler hat. "He looks terrible sick."

Lacquer lines formed anew down his rawboned anthracite cheeks. His body displayed the ruggedness common to those who suffered decades of brutally hard labor in the steamy snake-infested timber camps of Florida's Gulf Coast. Only after years of suffering in the hands of tyrannical overseers had Sheldon and his wife Clorsese been rescued from their wretched existence. Cap liberated them and made them part of his family.

Paul said, "Sheldon, I can't tell you anything about Cap right now, cause I just don't know. Give me a couple of minutes to find out, and I'll be back," he added, fighting to conceal his own distress.

Motioning with his head, Sheldon asked, "Where they carryin' him now, Mr. Paul?"

Paul turned to see the stretcher being wheeled down the hall. "Shit! Just wait here, okay?" He assumed that Cap was being taken for an x-ray, and he was getting frustrated that things had progressed so far without his involvement. Desperate to talk to Cap, he pursued the departing team.

Dr. Margolis, who had been joined by Gordy, intercepted Paul and confided, "It looks like your father's either got acute pancreatitis, a perforated ulcer, or in the worst case, an aneurism of the descending aorta. We're getting films of the abdomen and chest, and they're running some bloodwork. He's complaining of pretty severe abdominal pain, which I'm afraid points in the direction of an aneurism." He waited a few seconds for it to sink in. "Just to be on the safe side, Paul, does he have any immediate family besides you that we need to call?"

"I'm the only one he's got besides him," said Paul nodding his head in the direction of Sheldon.

Paul could handle the diagnosis of an ulcer and pancreatitis, but an aneurism was something else. Those unfortunate enough to have that type of large vessel condition were not likely to survive, and those who made it long enough to undergo the risky operation still had a survival rate of less than 50 percent.

He closed his eyes, ran his fingers through his hair, and then locked them at the back of his neck as he struggled to wrest a strategy from his brain. "Who's the vascular guy this weekend?" he asked Gordy. "Is Sternberg on?"

"They just called his wife; he's out of town until Tuesday."

"Christ! What else can go wrong? You know that leaves that asshole Kevin Kalen covering for him, and I'm sure as hell not letting him anywhere near Cap."

"Paul, if it comes down to it, you haven't got a choice," Gordy argued. "Kevin's our best bet, and you know it."

"If you're thinking about moving him to Miami, I wouldn't advise it. If he's bleeding, the movement will make it worse and the trip will kill him," Dr. Margolis added.

An orderly handed several large x-rays to Margolis, who took a quick glance, using the ceiling lights, and then slapped them on a viewer. The three men stood studying the images, and finally Margolis rendered his diagnosis. "I'm not seeing any free air under the diaphragm, so we can rule out any perforations. We'll have to wait for the labs, but in the meantime, you ought to prepare for a laparotomy. Either one of you have any thoughts?"

After pondering Margolis's suggestion, which would involve going into Cap's abdomen for a look, Gordy said, "I think we should try to get a hold of Kevin."

"Look, you guys, Paul admonished, "Kevin Kalen's an overrated jerk who's only claim to fa—"

"Stop right there," Gordy said. "Don't you dare start that crap with me. I won't stand for it. Kevin gets nothing but the toughest cases, and you know damn well that's why his morbidity is higher than the rest of us. Period."

Paul knew he'd stepped into dangerous waters with Gordy, and it was a place he'd found himself in with ever-increasing frequency. Backing off, he said, "I was just trying to—"

"We're wasting time here," Margolis said, reaching over the counter for the directory. "I'm going to give Kevin a call. The sooner we get a hold of him the better."

"No, wait . . . I'll do it."

"That's better," said Dr. Margolis, shoving the register toward him. Bracing himself for the eruption that was sure to follow, Paul said, "No, I mean the surgery. I'm going to do it."

Both men stared at him in disbelief, Gordy's face turning crimson and Margolis fingering his watch chain.

"Have you lost your mind?" Gordy asked. "This could turn out to be a nightmare, even in the best of hands, and besides, you're too close to Cap to open him up."

Having heard as much as he cared to, Margolis remarked, "You might give this a little more thought, Paul. Now if you'll both excuse me, I need to see if I can get those labs sped up." He hastened off, shaking his head.

"I owe this to my father," Paul told Gordy.

"What you owe him is to let Kevin take over, should it be vascular. Have you given a moment's thought to how you'll feel if Cap dies in your hands?"

"Yes," said Paul, but he was lying. He hadn't thought at all about it and couldn't bear to. "I'm sure the two of us can handle the surgery," Paul said

"Oh no, you're not dragging me into this, sonny, I don't want any part of it."

"If it's an aneurism, I'm doing it, Gordy, and that's it. I'm perfectly capable of handling anything vascular, especially with you there."

From a technical standpoint Paul was right, Gordy reflected. Dr. Paul Bennett was as capable as anyone in the operating room. He took chances and expected a lot from himself. As a result he had a pretty good record of getting patients out of the hospital and back to their homes. Together they were as proficient as a pair of surgeons could be; however, this was going to be different—a close personal relative and a potentially tough high-risk surgery created a recipe for disaster. If things went badly, he doubted Paul could distance himself sufficiently to make the correct split second decisions, but Gordy relented. "I'll assist you, but I want you to get this loud and clear, son. I won't accept any responsibility for what happens. Do you understand?"

Venturing a guarded smile, Paul said, "Yes, Gordy, I understand, and thank you."

Resigning himself to the task ahead, Gordy set things in motion. "Let me get Grace started on an O.R.," he said. "I expect you'll want to talk to Cap before they take him upstairs."

"Give me a few minutes with him, and I'll meet you in the O.R."

Entering Cap's room, Paul winced at the sight of his father ensnared in numerous tubes and wires. Small devises made sounds and displayed data, while others dripped fluids and hissed gasses. The room glimmered in reflected light from stainless steel and white porcelain under an anemic fluorescent ceiling light. The medicinal odor of alcohol hung thick. A nurse was monitoring the equipment, and Paul wanted her gone. More abrupt than intended, he ordered, "Leave us alone for a few minutes."

She nodded and left.

Cap's exposed chest showed the pattern of men who make their living at sea, with sharp contrast lines between exposed skin and collared shirt. His color had faded to dusky gray. His face, partially covered by an oxygen mask, also attested to a sailor's life. Crease lines caused by constant squinting into reflected sun radiated from his eyes, lending distinction to his agreeable features. His hand, clenched in a fist from the spasms of pain that even morphine couldn't quell, opened to receive Paul's. The cracks and cuts on his fingers, blackened by engine grease, formed a scrimshaw tracery. Despite the cool dampness of Cap's touch, there was an audible scratching sound as the pair's coarsely surfaced hands united.

Paul had to stretch his neck forward to clear the lump that suddenly swelled in his throat. "Hi, Cap. Sorry it took me so long to get here."

"I thought— " His voice echoed under the mask, so he pulled it off.

"You'd better leave that thing on," Paul advised.

Cap waved him off. "I thought I taught you better manners."

"What do you mean?"

"The way you just spoke to the nurse."

Paul remembered that the man never missed a thing. "Don't worry, Cap; they're used to being talked to like that."

"Don't bother trying to rationalize rudeness with me, Skip. Anyway, for a while I thought you forgot about me and took off for a mackerel run."

Paul smirked, acknowledging that he was not above such impulsive behavior and had in the past rescheduled elective surgeries in order to capitalize on fishing and hunting opportunities.

Cap forced a smile, which quickly faded. "What's wrong with me, Skip?"

Cap had had started calling Paul skipper when Paul's biological father had brought him along on snapper fishing trips years earlier. The youngster simply could not be dragged from the helm, regardless of whether the boat was underway or at anchor. The nickname stuck.

"Here's the situation, Cap. It might be something going on with your pancreas, which we ought to be able to deal with, but Cap," he paused. "It could be something pretty bad. We think it's possible that the large artery that carries blood from your heart, the aorta, has a tear in it, and it's kind of ballooning out along some of its length. It may already be seeping some blood. We're waiting for lab results, which will tell us more, but the other doctor you saw earlier feels it indicates an aneurism, and he's pretty good about calling things like this.

"It sounds serious." He sighed, obviously in pain. "And it sure as hell feels that way."

"If it's an aneurism, Cap, I'm going to operate on you and repair the injured section."

Cap stared blankly at him. "Skip, did I just hear right? *You* are going to operate on me? Have you lost your mind?"

"It's not going to be the easiest thing I've ever done, but I can do it, and I won't be alone. Your favorite gun collector will be with me."

"That's not what I meant"

"Cap, I don't trust anyone else to do it."

"And what does Gordy think?"

Paul wanted to lie, but couldn't. "Honestly, Cap, he's not happy about it."

"I see. And how are you going to deal with it if I don't make it?"

"You will."

"You're that sure, are you?"

Cap turned his head and looked away.

There was a page for someone over the intercom. A young child started wailing somewhere down the hall. Two nurses walked by, laughing and drinking coffee.

"I've left everything to you except the truck, and—"

"Do we have to go into this right now?"

"If not now, when?" Cap squawked. "I might be dead in several hours." He grimaced from pain and waited until he recovered sufficiently to speak again. "Let Sheldon and Clorese live on the property until they die."

"Of course I will."

"Is Sheldon still here? I'd like to talk to him."

"I don't know if there's time right now."

"See what you can do." Cap strained, as another stab of pain hit him. "I want you to know, no matter how this turns out . . ." He paused to catch his breath. "I've loved you as I would've my own son. I told your pop I'd take care of you when he left for the war. He didn't have to go, you know, and I'm still angry he went off and left you. But he did the honorable thing and what he felt he had to do."

Paul remembered the day his father sailed out of Virginia for the Pacific. He'd felt alone and abandoned, and Cap, seeing him cry as the ship pulled away from the wharf, felt heartbroken for him and bought him a .22 rifle. Paul's first act with the gun was to shoot a seagull "just for fun," and Cap baked it and made him choke down every fishy bite to teach him a lesson about wanton killing.

From his hospital bed Cap said, "Your dad would be mighty proud that you grew up to be a doctor. Well, I don't think you need taking care of anymore."

After an emotionally trying morning, Paul was at the breaking point. He feared that if he uttered a single word, he'd start crying. There was so much to say, so many reasons to thank this man, but there wasn't time, and he didn't know where to begin anyway. He loved and worshiped Cap and cherished the life they'd spent together. He would show his adoration not in words, he thought, but in action. He simply would not let Cap die, and he really needed to get out of there. "I've got to get things ready, Cap. I'll see you in recovery." He repositioned Cap's oxygen mask, stroked his brow, squeezed his hand, and started to leave.

"Skipper!"

Paul halted in mid-stride, hoping Cap wouldn't drop any more heart-rending bombs on him.

"I don't care if you sell *The Lucky Brake*, but take care of her until you do. Okay?"

"I'm not selling the boat or anything else. They're not mine to sell."

Conferring with Paul and Gordy, Dr. Margolis confirmed Paul's worst fears. "The labs indicate a normal pancreas," he said. "Unless there's something we're missing, I believe you're going to find your father's got a dissecting aneurism."

Turning to Paul, Gordy said, "You still don't want Kevin?"

"No."

"Then I suggest you tell us what you've got in mind here."

"A lot is going to depend on what we find in there. If it is a dissecting aneurism, its location is going to dictate what we can or can't do—" Paul trailed off. He knew if the blood supply were compromised to Cap's kidneys, there would be nothing left but dialysis and its ill effect on Cap's quality of life. Worse, it would eventually mean death from kidney failure, plus with this type of vascular surgery there was also the risk of paralysis. He finally spoke. "By cooling him down we can get six to eight minutes of cardiac cessation."

"That is assuming he doesn't rupture as soon as you cut the pericardium."

"Let me finish, Gordy. Six minutes isn't enough time to graft the aneurysm, but it is enough to place a bypass shunt around it, and then we've got plenty of time to fix the problem."

"It sounds like a sensible plan to me," said Dr. Margolis.

"All right, we'd better get on with it, then," Gordy said, getting himself prepared. "Paul, do you know his blood type?"

"B negative."

"Damn! I was afraid you'd say that. I don't know how much of that, if any, we have on hand, but we're sure to have a couple of units of O negative. Order all you can round up. I've already got Grace moving on O.R. two, and she's piecing together the appropriate team. If you insist on going through with this, we might as well stack the deck as best we can."

Paul attended to the blood-bank request and made sure all the hospital's limited arterial graft supply was procured. He was on his way upstairs when he spotted Sheldon.

"Are you gonna tell me Cap be dead?"

"No, but he's in mighty bad shape. Calm down and listen to me. Cap's problem can be fixed, and I'm going to do it as soon as I get upstairs. Go on home, and I'll let you know when we're finished."

Filled with false hope, Sheldon flashed a broadening, toothy smile that made Paul feel foolish. He couldn't believe he'd just downplayed what was going to be the most difficult surgery he'd ever performed. There could be no turning back now; failure wasn't an option.

Paul climbed the stairs toward the operating room and asked himself, How much more are you going to put at risk? Making a pit stop at the hospital's tiny library, he grabbed *The Atlas of Cardiac Surgery*, and later, while changing out of his sweat-soaked scrubs into a fresh set, he thumbed through the book, reviewing the particulars of the operation. Next came the routine pre-surgical scrub, during which the cuts on Paul's hands stung from the hexachlorophene soap. He had long since gotten used to the deliberate, painstaking pattern of starting at his fingertips and washing each finger ten times, proceeding up each hand, and ending at the elbow. The ten-minute procedure could be agonizing after all the line cuts and scrapes he had sustained while fishing on *The Lucky Brake*. Ignoring the discomfort, he watched the activity inside the OR through the window above the sink.

Dr. Marsh Perdue, the anesthesiologist, had put Cap under, and Paul reflected it would have been appropriate to say a few words, but he wouldn't have been able to handle it emotionally. Gil, Grace, and another nurse, Bonnie Humphrey, were transferring Cap's naked body from a cold water tub to the operating table. Mindful of his father's modesty, Paul hated seeing him so exposed, and Paul looked away. Gordy, already gowned and gloved, was overseeing the preparation, arranging several deep trays of surgical instruments, including extensive abdominal and chest setups.

Dr. Perdue was preparing to use the Bird Mark 7 Respirator while Bonnie used the traditional squeeze bag method. The new mechanical alternative was a substitute for the traditional method of ventilating the unconscious patient by squeezing a rubber bag to force air into the lungs, in essence, breathing for him. Having previously experienced problems with the primitive machine, Paul wanted no part of it during this operation. He poked his head through the OR door and said, "Hey, Marsh, no Bird on this one. I want you to bag him. You know what they say about that contraption, don't you?"

"Yeah, Paul, I know. The stork bringeth, and the Bird taketh away."

"Exactly, so please stow that thing."

Relieved that the device of questionable integrity was out of the equation, Paul looked again at Cap on the operating table, and his mind drifted back to an afternoon shortly after World War Two. Rationing having ended, Cap was able to get fuel for the boat, and he and Paul set off for Bimini. That afternoon Paul hooked and battled a five-hundred-pound giant blue fin tuna. Cap shouted instructions from the bridge while Paul fought the fish. The three-hour battle drained every ounce of energy from his lanky frame. He started to give up several times, but Cap wouldn't let him. Paul's arms and back muscles twitched in spasms and his hands burned from blisters, and almost totally spent from the battle, Paul tried to climb from the fighting chair, but Cap shut down the engines right in the middle of the Gulf Stream gave Paul a lecture on quitting.

After Cap drove the flying gaff into the fish and winched its immense form through the transom tuna door, Cap offered Paul a beer, and Paul savored the deliciously bitter taste for the first time. He was proud to see his giant fish hung on the same North Bimini hoist used by Hemingway, Michael Lerner, and Zane Grey.

Paul also thought about the blustery winter days he had spent in the woods at Riverbend, Cap's 1,600-acre hunting tract in central Georgia. Good friends, fine guns, down-home cooking, the fun of driving the buggy and learning the woods; all of it came back in snippets while soap bubbles dripped off his elbows and he continued to scrub.

Finally he backed through the double doors of the OR, his forearms upraised, and, as the full gravity of the situation hit him, he experienced self-doubt for the first time that morning. With all eyes watching his every move, he questioned his own resolve. All objectivity slipped away with the realization that he was, in fact, in way over his head.

Despite his apprehension, Paul knew better than to show it. "Hi, folks," he said, sounding upbeat and confident.

Bonnie handed him a sterile towel to dry his hands.

"Where are we?"

Gil was the first to speak. "Looks like things is all—"

"Excuse me, son," the anesthesiologist interjected. "We're okay with the vitals. B.P.'s fifty over twenty-two, rate's at twenty-five and dropping quickly. Temp's at thirty-two."

Lying face up, Cap was draped in white sterile sheets that framed his abdomen, which had been shaved. Grace swabbed the exposed skin with an orange iodine disinfectant, the spot where Paul would slice his father open to gain an access leading toward the abdominal aorta.

Grace, who couldn't resist another stab at the orderly, snapped, "Gil, you can go take the linens down to the laundry. When you're done, come right back and stay in the nursing station in case we need something. Is that clear?"

"Yes, ma'am," he replied. "Good luck, Doc."

"No, wait," Paul said. "Grace, I'd like him gowned, just in case we need another pair of hands."

Gil concealed a smile, but his eyes brimmed with gratitude.

"Yes, doctor," Grace muttered. "Don't just stand there, Gilbert, go scrub. Have one of the other nurses watch you do it, and then Bonnie will gown you."

Cap had already been administered Pentothal to induce anesthesia and was being kept there by a gaseous mixture of cyclopropane and oxygen. Intravenous lines were attached to his wrists, one to carry blood to replace volume lost during surgery and the other to carry a balanced saline solution, in case there was a need to restore volume should a precipitous loss occur.

Paul surveyed the setup while Bonnie clothed him in a sterile gown and snapped on his gloves. Droplets of sweat dotted his forehead.

"Marsh, are we good?"

"Yeah, Paul, we're okay at this end."

Paul placed the tip of the scalpel blade below the center of Cap's sternum with a slight tremor in his hands but with no hesitation. He made a deliberate slice from the sternum down to and around Cap's navel and continued to his pubis. Gordy swabbed away the crimson line of blood that followed the knife.

Grace handed Paul a new scalpel, which he used to retrace the incision, going deeper into the thin buttery layer of fat.

Gordy instinctively clamped and tied off several bleeding arteries. This phase of the surgery was routine, so the medical professionals had little need to communicate, but absent was their customary chitchat. None had ever seen a son operate on his father.

At the abdominal wall Paul slowed his pace to trace the exact midline where the cavity's outer fibrous layer, or fascia, originated. After he gently sliced through the fascia, the diaphanous peritoneal sack shrouding the organs bulged slightly.

"It's normal looking—there's no bleeding internally," Paul offered, more for his own benefit than for the others, who already knew how to detect the signs of internal bleeding. "So far, so good, guys."

Snipping a small hole in the peritoneal membrane as an access point and then extending the incision in both directions, Paul laid bare Cap's organs, the surgical light imparting a dreamlike intensity to them. The musty-sweet-metallic odor of living guts wafted up to Paul, establishing immediately that his relationship with Cap would never be the same. It was an unnatural intrusion into another human being's inner workings, especially those of a loved one.

Gordy wrapped the freshly cut edges on the wound in saline-dampened gauze, and before he had the chance to ask for it, Grace handed him a U-shaped metal frame with three adjustable curved blades. He and Paul used it to pull apart and retain the walls of Cap's belly.

Gathering the writhing intestines and drawing them off to the side with another large retractor, the surgeons brought the aneurism into view. They all paused to gaze at the rhythmically pulsing prominence.

"Gordy, it hasn't gotten the renals, but boy, is it close. Look, another quarter of an inch and—" Paul was referring to the renal arteries branching from the aorta just beneath the stomach's main blood supply, the superior mesenteric artery. The renal arteries keep blood flowing to the kidneys, where it is filtered.

"I hope he's got good collateral circulation to the bowel, because the inferior mesenteric looks like it's occluded," Paul observed, cradling the thin collapsed artery with forceps.

"I wouldn't worry too much about that, or anything else, for that matter," Gordy said. "You've got enough to contend with right here." He touched the enlarged purple mass.

"Guys, it's not going to repair itself," Paul said. "We might as well get on with it. Let's isolate the aneurism the best we can and then clamp it right under here, below the right renal. Marsh, is everything okay up there?"

"Looks fine from my end."

"Gordy, we'll save as much of the aorta as possible," Paul said, "and you know what? I think instead of resecting the lesion itself, I'm going to just flap it open, leave it in place, and lay the graft right on top of it. What do you think?"

"Fiddling with it's only going to add time and accomplish nothing. So yes, I'd say that's a pretty good plan."

Within a short time all the neighboring structures had been freed and gently repositioned, leaving clear access to the affected portion.

"Okay Marsh, give him the adenosine, stop ventilating, and have the neostigmine ready."

The anesthesiologist injected the drug into one of the lines and Cap's heart slowed to a stop.

Paul took a large clamp from Grace, slid its jaws across Cap's aorta, and gently squeezed the ratchet-locking handles until they clicked tight enough to cut off the blood flow. He placed another clamp at the other end of the lesion and locked it in place. Working at either end of the clamped aorta, the surgeons worked at breakneck speed to insert the bypass shunt. In several minutes it was sutured in place.

"We're ready here, Marsh; go ahead and defib him and then start bagging," said Paul. "Bonnie, turn on the warming blanket," he added.

Everyone backed away. The anesthesiologist delivered an external shock, and Cap's body arched.

Initially there was no pulse, but then it started weakly and slowly increased. A small amount of blood seeped from around the shunt connections, but everything held.

Gordon, who had been silent during most of the initial surgery, finally spoke. "Nice work, son, but I wouldn't get too excited. We've got a long way to go before Cap sees the Gulf Stream again."

Paul nodded. "Potts," he said, holding out his hand.

Grace handed him a pair of off-angled scissors, which he used to cut crossways into the aorta, forever ending the flow of blood to the lower half of his father's body unless Paul restored it. He repeated the cut at the other end of the lesion. Using the same instrument, he cut the lesion lengthwise and laid the flaps aside, exposing a raw, meaty slab of multicolored ruin. It was like opening the doors to calamity. Paul wondered whether the culprit had been the years of smoking, Clorese's lardy meals, or just bad fortune that had caused such deterioration, and he thought fleetingly and regretfully of his own indulgences.

"Gordy, do you think this is an aberration, or is it going on everywhere?"

"I expect there's more, but I have no interest in finding out." Allowing for a little optimism, Gordy added, "Maybe after the old man recovers he ought to consider taking better care of himself."

Rubbing the terminal end of the intact aorta between his gloved fingers, Paul could feel that it was in no condition to retain sutures. Pathology had left the artery rigid with plaques on a bed of tissue as frail as soggy paper. "I'm going to have to dissect out some of the lumen here, or I'll never get the graft attached to it. It's like jelly. This is going to be rough, Gordy."

"We still may be able to get Kevin if you have doubts," Gordy said. "Nobody's going to hold it against you."

"No, I started this, and I'm going to finish it. I just hadn't expected the tissue to be in such bad shape. I need to get started at this end, so do you think you can take care of the distal stump?"

"That's what I'm here for. I'll do my best, but I sure wish you'd reconsider and let me bring in Kevin."

Paul ignored the comment and began the delicate chore of snipping away the coarse inside layer of the artery. He carried on in silence for some time until he was satisfied that despite being friable, it could be sutured to the graft by using the utmost care. "Bonnie, open all three of those grafts and put them in a basin, but don't put any saline on them."

Gordy raised an eyebrow at the excess of the request, but continued his work without comment. As wasteful as it was, and aware that he was putting in jeopardy any emergency vascular surgeries until the hospital could restock, Paul was not about to be frugal with the supplies. He needed the graft to be close in diameter to the aorta itself, and the only way to check was to try them all. None of the expensive rejected tubes could ever be used again because they would be contaminated.

Placing the grafts one by one against the aorta stump, Paul found one that was only a little larger than the native artery. With some modification, it could be made to fit. "I'm going to need to narrow the diameter of this by taking a little V of material out and sewing it back together. I'm thinking I'll do it all at the same time when I finish the anastomosis to the aorta."

Accordingly, Paul approximated the length of Dacron tube he'd need to span the void left by the resected aneurism and cut it to length, placing it back in the metal basin. "Gordy, draw me about fifty milliliters of blood from one of the smaller arteries and squeeze it in the pan with the graft. This tube's going to leak like a sieve unless we jumpstart it with some of Cap's clotting factors."

As ideal as the newly invented Dacron was, it suffered from the limitation of mesh size, which allowed blood cells to seep through the fiber matrix. By exposing the graft to the recipient's blood, the clotting mechanism of his blood acted as a sealer, in addition to laying down the groundwork for the graft to be assimilated biologically.

"Marsh," Paul said to the anesthesiologist, "where are we?"

"He's used the two units of B neg we had and one of the O neg. I've only got one more, then we're stuck with saline. BP's seventy over fifty; rate's ninety."

"Okay, so far, so good. Let's get old Cap put back together so we can all go home. Bonnie, three-0 silk. Gordy, approximate the graft starting dorsally. Let's get the toughest ones tied first."

Paul ran the needle through the lip of the graft and then took a shallow bite of tissue at the corresponding point of the aorta. When he brought the knot tight, the suture tore out of the tissue. "Oh, my God, is this stuff frail."

"Easy does it, son," Gordy said. "All you need is to approximate it. You try to snug it up too tight, and this is going to wind up being a very long afternoon."

Paul nodded, took a deep breath, pinched another bit of the aorta with a tissue forceps, and hooked it with the curved needle. With the other surgeon holding the graft up against the aorta, Paul delicately drew up the silk thread until the two edges were one. He tied a series of knots in the thread and held it up for Grace to snip the ends. "Well, one down."

"You've got it now, Paul. All we want to do here is get the two ends kissing each other. God will do the rest."

From then on it was a cautious and deliberate advance around the ring of tissue. Several of the sutures pulled free and had to be redone, but in short time all that remained was the V-shaped notch of the final closure.

"It looks like there's going to be a little bunching here when I get this closed," said Paul, pointing at the repair with a needle holder.

"It looks right nice to me, Doc. Them stitches is a mighty pretty sight," Gil chimed in. He'd been standing at the ready and wanted to feel a part of the experience.

Paul had to smile behind his mask at both the compliment and the blessedly uneventful progress they had made.

"If you want my opinion, I say put a couple more ties in and call it quits at that end," Gordy advised. "We've still got the distal to do, and Cap's been under for . . .how long, Marsh?"

"Two hours and fifty minutes."

"Let's not wear out our welcome," Gordy said. "The sooner we can get him closed the better."

Reluctantly Paul, who hated being rushed, moved on to attaching the lower end of the graft, which went quicker, since he'd gotten a feel for it and the tissue hadn't been in deplorable condition, like the other end. Nonetheless, he kept glancing at the proximal repair job.

Twenty minutes later they all stared down into Cap's abdomen, admiring Paul's handiwork.

"Marsh," Paul said, "I'd like you to push the fluids now. I'm going to release the clamp, and there's bound to be some leakage."

"Got it, Paul," he replied, opening up the pinch valves on both intravenous lines.

Paul cautiously squeezed the clamp, disengaging the jaws and opening the vessel. The graft filled with blood and seemed to pop into shape. There was the expected seepage from the suture lines at both ends, which Grace swept clear with a suction tip, but the volume was negligible, compared to the amount coursing through the surrogate vessel.

Gazing in amazement at the results of his labors, Paul said, "Would you look at that, Gordy? Would you just look at that?"

"Very well done, Paul."

"Thank you, Gordy, and I can't thank you enough for your help, and all of you too," he added, addressing the team. "Before we close him, I want to snip that one suture and reposition the tissue first. It's going to bother me to leave it like that. Bonnie, hand me a suture scissor, and load another needle holder. Gordy, this is going to bleed a bit, so keep the suction right on it."

The other surgeon grabbed Paul's hand before the nurse could slap the scissors in it.

"Listen to me. Leave it alone. Perfection is the enemy of good enough, and it's good enough as it is."

"I know, but it looks so pretty except for that one spot. Don't worry. It'll just take a minute."

Gordy's eyes met Paul's, and Gordy held the glare before releasing his hand.

Paul snipped a single suture, causing a pulse of needle-thin streams of blood to shoot at the other surgeon's gown. Both Gordy and Grace placed suction tips at the site, so Paul could visualize it. He bit into the aorta with the needle, which tore through. Relocating the needle, he gently pushed it into the tissue again. Despite two suctions aspirating the leakage, it was in a constant state of submersion because of an upwelling of Cap's blood. The aorta was by then pulsing with each heartbeat, making it a moving target. The needle tore through again, but this time, the closest suture tore free, releasing an even greater flow of blood.

"I'm going to need to clamp the aorta again, Gordy. I just can't see well enough to get a clean bite."

"I wouldn't advise that, son. You don't have any room now without putting too much tension on the suture line, and that's the last damn thing you need to do. You're going to have to work with what you've got."

Paul was getting scared fast, watching Cap's blood being pumped into the hospital's waste bin.

"Give me the aorta clamp," he ordered, and locked it onto its previous spot, not only pulling several more sutures free, but worse, tearing a hole in the compromised aorta, causing even more blood to flow out and obscuring the mounting carnage. Because of the extensive blood loss, Cap's clotting factors had been almost used up, and the potentially catastrophic bleeding continued.

"Gordy, help me here," Paul implored.

"Hey, guys, the pressure is really dropping off, fifty-five over twenty-five," Marsh announced.

Gordy pressed his finger down on the aorta above the kidneys, stanching the flow. "I can hold this for a while, but you've *got* to fix that."

"Guy's, he's fibrillating," Marsh said. "His pressure's bottomed out."

"Marsh," Paul yelled, "defibrillate him, for Christ sake."

"Everyone, stand back," Marsh warned.

Gordon had to release his pressure on the aorta, which caused the residual blood in it to trickle out. Marsh placed the paddle electrodes on Cap's chest and activated the electric device, making Cap's body arch.

"He's still in tachycardia. Stand clear."

Marsh shocked Cap again. Both nurses had stepped back from the table. Grace covered her mask with her bloody gloved hands. Bonnie looked away. Cap's heart, starved of oxygen and contaminated with its own metabolic byproducts, slowed to a quiver and then stopped.

Gordon, shaken and infuriated at his own complicity, snatched the needle holder from Paul's hand and flung it across the room. "He's dead. Goddamn it, Paul, he's dead!"

Paul was paralyzed. He could see Gordon's mouth moving but heard nothing. His head felt as if it could burst and his face was on fire.

"Cap ... what have I done?"

Paul retreated from the table as if it were a nest of rattlesnakes. Stumbling backwards over a stainless steel bucket, he launched soaked and clotted gauze across the tile floor. With the entire surgical team watching, he backpedaled out, stumbled through the swinging door, and vanished.

A man in scrubs holding a mask over his face poked his head in the room. "Hey, I just passed Bennett in the corridor. He looked like he'd seen a ghost."

Gordy motioned him over. "Come here and take a look."

Dr. Kevin Kalen approached the table and viewed the ghastly scene. "What the hell is this?

CHAPTER TWO

Cold Reality

Sprawled on the teak cockpit deck of *The Lucky Brake*, Paul lay with his face pressed hard onto the grainy planks. He dreamed that he was floating on the open ocean atop a black mattress like the kind used to cover the gurneys in the hospital. It was covered in a blood-soaked sheet that despite being awash in seawater, retained its crimson color. Coagulated globs formed at the edges, broke away, and floated aimlessly in the swells around him. A howling wind flattened the wave crests into stinging sprays. Frightened and nauseated from the turbulent seas, he cried out for help, but no sound was emitted. In front of him lay the stern of *The Lucky Brake*, with Cap sitting in the fighting chair, polishing an oversize fishing reel, oblivious to the upheaval.

Paul called out to him, and again no sound was produced. Confused, he scanned the horizon and saw nothing but raging seas. When he spotted the boat again, it had drifted some distance away. This time Gordy, clothed in a suit and long lab coat, had joined Cap. They were both viewing a large x-ray that Gordy held.

His stomach heaving, Paul vomited pieces of bloody graft fabric. He gasped for breath and suddenly felt warmth in his groin. By then the boat was far off, but he could clearly see both men looking at him and slowly shaking their heads. A spray hit Paul, and the image vanished.

The rain spattering his face had awakened him. At eye level were fragments of glass from a broken bottle. The stench of alcohol-laden puke attacked his nostrils. He swallowed hard, suppressing the urge to retch. His pants were still warm from urination.

Straining to find stability on the swaying deck, he pulled himself up using the fighting chair for support. Teetering on rubbery legs, he examined the shards of glass and how they seemed to be one with the rain-slick teak.

"Aw shit! Cap's gonna chew my ass over this," he muttered. It took several seconds until the thought processed, and then reality hit him.

Sheldon watched Paul drop back to the deck. He'd been perched on a dock box by the boat, keeping a silent vigil since the young man had staggered home, bottle in hand, the night before. Bracing for the chore of consoling Paul, Sheldon rose stiffly, and a stream of rainwater poured from the brim of his hat to his oilskin coat as he peered over the gunwale. "Mr. Paul?"

"Go away."

"Come off dat boat, and let ole Sheldon drys you off."

"Just leave me alone."

Sheldon climbed onto the boat and squatted next to him. "Ain't no amount of liq'a gonna bring Cap back," he whispered. "God done took him to par'dise."

"Bullshit. He's dead right now because of me."

"That ain't what Dr. Gordy said. He told us you done the best you could. It was the captain's time to go."

"I promised Cap I'd take care of him, and now look."

Sheldon took off his coat and wrapped it around Paul, who was shaking from a combination of hangover, chill, and anguish. Helping him off the boat, Sheldon led him up the path to the house.

Clorese, a stout, buxom woman in her seventies, had been watching her husband through the panoramic windows facing the dock. She was clutching her Bible as she always did in times of trouble. Opening the door, she ordered Paul, "Get in the tub and gets yo'self washed," addressing him as if he were her own child instead of a thirty-one-year-old surgeon.

He obediently went off to his room, the one he'd lived in since moving in with Cap.

After showering he spent the rest of the day staring out at the rain, alternating between bouts of weeping and nausea as he relived the previous day.

Patty, Cap's English setter, searched from room to room looking for her master, her toenails clicking on the hardwood floors.

Gordy arrived after dark and sat in a sparse leather-and-walnut chair, cattycorner to Paul. "How are you doing, son?"

Without altering his gaze out the window, Paul shrugged.

"You were in pretty rough shape last night."

"So?"

"Look, I'm not here to rub your nose in it, but you were warned this could happen."

"Nobody warned me my carelessness would kill him. I was so fucking close to being done, Gordy."

"Paul, it's when we get a little too self-assured that we get in trouble."

"Yeah, well, I won't have to worry about it anymore. I'm through."

"Over my dead body."

"What, you want me to operate on you too?"

"Cut the self-pity. It doesn't suit you." Gordy was concerned that Paul really intended to quit. "What you need is some time off to get past this. I know you're upset—"

"*Upset?*" shouted Paul, kicking the coffee table and sending glasses and ashtrays flying.

"For all intent and purposes, I just killed my father, and I shouldn't be upset?"

"I suggest you keep that killing business to yourself. You know that a lot of people are going to be wondering about this. I doubt anything will come of it, but I'd keep your mouth shut. Incidentally, the papers have already gotten a hold of it."

"Oh, no! What did they say?"

"Not to worry. Just some nonsense from *The Palm Beach Times* inferring suspicious circumstances, since you're his sole heir. The hospital doesn't see any foul play, so this'll blow over. Just the same, don't fan anyone's fire. Look, Paul, I'm sorry it happened. I know what Cap meant to you, but keep in mind he was a very sick man when he arrived yesterday. His chances were iffy at best. The surgery was not only good, Paul, it was great."

"Yeah, Gordy, the operation was a success but the patient died, right?"

"Enough, Paul. I wouldn't make any big decisions right now, but if you decide not to return, I think it would be a huge mistake, because we will have lost a fine surgeon." He got up and started to leave, but stopped and said, "By the way, the hospital needs to know what to do with, you know . . . Cap."

"Tell them I'll deal with it later, and thanks for coming by."

Gordy let himself out, leaving Paul alone to ponder the sudden changes overtaking him. *The Palm Beach Times* story cinched it. It was just as well he withdrew from surgery since bad publicity was not likely to enhance his referral base. He was certainly going to miss being a doctor, though. He loved the excitement and fulfillment of affecting lives so dramatically. Paul had always displayed a high level of self-confidence in the operating room and took great pride in his mastery of many other skills. His self-confidence, pride, and excellent reputation, however, lay in ruins now.

The memorial service was held the following weekend aboard Cap's beloved boat. His wishes were that he be cremated and his ashes scattered upon the waters of the Gulf Stream. Cap's friends, most of whom were also fishing captains, were all in attendance. One of them, a part-time preacher, conducted the service. The other mourners included Gordy and his wife, Virginia; Grace and Gil from the hospital; Sheldon and Clorese; Paul's one-time girlfriend, Robin, who was accompanied by a man Paul recognized as the current stock car racing champion; and a handsome elderly woman in jewels and designer clothes Paul couldn't place, who was chatting, improbable as it was, with Gil.

The party boarded *The Lucky Brake* on what was promising to be a sweltering Sunday morning. Piloting the boat atop the flying bridge, Paul kept to himself, aside from a few words of forced cordiality, while the others below chatted, sharing their memories of Cap. The rich woman in diamonds and a Chanel suit came up to Paul and introduced herself as Ruth Bliss, the woman whose gall bladder he'd been scheduled to remove the day Cap died.

"I'm so sorry you lost your father, Dr. Bennett," she said. "I wondered why you didn't operate on me that day, and then I read that cruel story in *The Palm Beach Times*. You've done surgery on several of my friends, and they all swear by you, and hope you'll sue *The Times*. I have an excellent lawyer—"

"Thank you, Mrs. Bliss. They weren't there and have no idea what happened. How did your gall bladder surgery go? If you'll excuse my honesty, you still look a bit jaundiced and I'd like to know why, and how you wound up here today."

"Oh, I postponed it and have been enduring until you are available again. When I read the paper about the, you know, I managed to find out about this service. Dr. Bennett, I knew your father. Douglas and I had a thing many, many years ago. I was very taken by him, but it was short-lived. You see, Dr. Bennett, Douglas may have been an authority on brake mechanisms, but there was no stopping *him* when he got started. I think you know what I mean."

Paul had to grin, the first time since the operation. The thought of Cap having been a lady's man was novel to him. "I had no idea, Mrs. Bliss, but I'm sure he would have been pleased to have you here."

"Thank you, and I hope you know how appreciated and respected you are in this community. I wouldn't think of going under the knife unless you—"

"I thank you, ma'am. I really do, but it's impossible. You see, I'm not—"

"Please think about it, doctor. I won't press you here under these sad circumstances. We must allow you to grieve. I'll call your office later on."

She started to return to the cockpit, but he stopped her long enough to extract a promise that if he arranged for Gordy to do the surgery, she would reschedule the operation right away. She agreed, reluctantly. He was grateful to her not prying into his reasons for refusing.

Alone again and surrounded by the aquamarine blue water of the Gulf Stream, Paul throttled back the twin diesel engines and switched them off. The ocean shone like molten lead, an almost imperceptible undulation on its surface causing the boat to rock gently. With *The Lucky Brake* adrift, there was utter silence except for the soft hum of conversation and a faint hiss as a loggerhead turtle surfaced for a breath of air several hundred yards away.

Paul knew that with his piloting duties completed he no longer had any reason to remain isolated from the others. Grudgingly Paul milled about the group of mourners below. Desperate for an out, he asked his recently estranged girlfriend, Robin Casey, to join him on the bridge. Cap had been very fond of her. They'd hit it off the same day that Paul had met her.

"Sorry, I'm with someone," she told Paul, gesturing to Brewster "Brew" Cavanaugh, the race driver. He was standing nearby, basking in the admiration of several Daytona race aficionados.

"Looks like Brew's busy with his fans," she said, thinking better of Paul's invitation to go topside "Sure, let's go."

They'd met one Saturday when Robin's boss, a pale, meaty owner of a Miami advertising agency, had chartered the boat, insisting that Robin and some of the firm's junior partners come along to liven up his cruise. They reluctantly agreed out of concern for their jobs. When the dullard wasn't bellowing in an annoyingly thunderous voice, which he seemed to do without pause, he spent his time guzzling beer until the rough seas compelled him to discharge the contents of his stomach throughout the boat's cabin. While he was incapacitated, Robin, handling the rod like a veteran, caught a sailfish, a wahoo, and two bonito.

Cap was taken by Robin's enthusiasm and how deftly she worked the fish on the line. Paul found her attractive and spent the morning laughing at her put-downs of her boss. As the motors droned on in a harmonious throb, Robin decided she liked Paul's velvety Southern diction. Despite Paul's timidity around women, he sensed she was his for the taking. The deal was sealed when he revealed that he was, in fact, a practicing surgeon and not just a charter boat's mate. They slept together that night.

Standing next to her on the bridge now, he wished he'd paid more attention to her, instead of acting like a selfish prick, as she'd put it during their last fight. Despite the good times they had, Robin finally tired of taking second place to his hobbies and grew sick of waiting for him to return from fishing or hunting trips. Cap tried to encourage him to indulge her more, but the advice had fallen on deaf ears.

"You had no idea how much you needed me," she said, stroking his cheek consolingly.

"I do now."

She glanced down at the crowd on the deck below, where Brew Cavanaugh was beginning to dart anxious looks their way.

Following her gaze, Paul said, "Spending a lot of time in Daytona?"

"His racing team is one of our clients."

From the look in her warm brown eyes, he knew she could still be his if he wanted her, but something stopped him from saying anything. He was in no condition to complicate his life further.

Having at last extricated himself from his admirers, Brew was beginning to make his way to the bridge.

"I have to go," she said. "Be very gentle with yourself. Goodbye, Paul."

The party assembled in the cockpit, so Paul climbed down the teak steps, aware that every eye was on him. He felt suffocated by the confines of the deck and would much rather have viewed the proceedings from the security of the tuna tower twenty feet above. Fortunately his sunglasses made direct eye contact with the guests impossible, affording him at least a thin veil of separation. Cap's sporting pals had always liked Paul and respected his abilities both on and off the ocean, but he could sense a change in their behavior toward him, which had him feeling like the outsider. *Who could blame them, though*, he thought. *I'm the reason they're here.*

They all gathered at the transom of the boat and the proxy minister, Captain Cal De Maria, set the urn holding Cap's ashes on the gunwale and began the eulogy. "Family and friends, we are here today to honor a life and bid farewell to our brother, Doug Hendrix—"

Those words were all it took to set Clorese off. She broke into wrenching sobs, and Sheldon had to guide her to the port gunwale and seat her. The others shifted in discomfort. It was obvious that the fishermen were bothered by the presence of the Negro couple, and their displeasure was deepened by the grief-stricken woman's outburst.

The Atlantic coastal area of Florida, had been and still remained one of the most rigidly segregated regions of the nation. Instead of being celebrated as a vital element in the wresting of the land from harsh wilderness, the descendants of runaway slaves were instead sequestered away and relegated to being second-class citizens. Cap and subsequently Paul viewed things differently.

"Doug Hendrix was a friend to all men," the minister continued. "His kindness and generosity ran as deep as the ocean below us. He lived by a code of honor and values that were an example for us to follow. Doug was not perfect, my friends, but he stood tall among men."

Paul didn't know how much more he could take. The vision of Cap's torn, hemorrhaging vessel was too fresh in his mind. Paul was having trouble breathing. Every cell in his body yearned to scream.

"Each of us is left with our memories of Doug, and these are our own private coves from this storm of loss. Doug saw the best in everyone and gave his best to all. Our sympathy today goes to his beloved son, Dr. Paul Bennett. He adored you, Skip, and was proud of you."

"Sheldon and Clorese were dear to him as well," Paul blurted, surprising himself with the outburst.

Grace wiped her eyes with a tissue and went over to embrace Paul, who turned to gaze out at the water, gripping the gunwale like he wanted to hurl himself overboard and drown. Gil came over and joined them as the eulogist continued.

"And now, as we commit Doug's earthly remains to the sea he loved so much, know that he will be present on the crest of every wave, his voice the sound of every warm ocean breeze. Ashes to ashes, dust to dust. The Lord giveth and the Lord taketh away. We commit your soul to Almighty God." The minister cast Cap's ashes overboard. "May you find eternal peace with God. Amen. Goodbye, Captain Doug Hendrix."

No one moved for almost a minute.

The minister broke the silence. "Paul, would you like to say something?"

Staring off into the emptiness with his back to the group, Paul managed to force a few broken words through a constricted throat. "I would, but I need to be alone . . . for a minute, please." Paul tried to compose something in his mind, but it was no use. Nothing he could say would expiate his guilt. "Thank you all for loving my dad and for coming today to honor Cap's memory."

Clorese sobbed again, and Sheldon, Gil, and Grace quickly encircled her, providing sympathy and hugs in an otherwise cold crowd of segregationists. Gordy and his wife moved to the privacy of the bow, while the rest, with the exclusion of Sheldon, Clorese, and Paul, filed into the cabin for the obligatory toast.

Paul turned back to the transom, leaned over it, and wept, still unable to forgive himself. Digging into his pocket, he pulled out a coin, a twenty-dollar gold piece Cap had given Paul when he graduated from medical school. "I don't deserve this, Cap," he said into the empty sky, and flipped the coin into the water, watching as it flickered down. A small fish darted out from under the boat and followed it into the darkness.

Paul climbed up to the flying bridge and started the engines for the ride home.

CHAPTER THREE

Old Friends

Low gray clouds churned southward, bringing a cold misting rain that slapped at the windows of Paul's sprawling house on the bay. A bewildered, foamy chop had turned the St. Lucie River into a milky cauldron. *The Lucky Brake* heaved at her moorings, giving off a sickening creak as it rubbed hard against the piling bumpers. The weathering craft, idle now for months, pranced like a dog eager to fetch a stick. A velvety green slime grew below her waterline.

Six months had passed since Cap's death, and the shortened winter days added to Paul's discontent. Usually he enjoyed this time of year. In the past it meant deer and bird hunting in Georgia, and despite the invariably awful weather, the fishing was typically good. Sailfish, king mackerel, and wahoo swarmed the offshore depths, while bluefish, mackerel, and pompano migrated down the coast in large schools. None of this knowledge meant anything to Paul now, without Cap at his side.

For Paul, the first Christmas after Cap's funeral was depressing, with Sheldon and Clorese the only ones to share the holidays with him. He'd been in no mood to brave the throngs of grinning Yuletide shoppers with their pretty packages and overzealous enthusiasm.

Gordy and his wife begged him to attend some of the hospital functions.

The hospital, of course, was the last place he wanted to be, having to explain over and over why he'd chosen to "give up such a promising career." He still hadn't returned to the operating room despite Gordy's urging and later, pleading. Money was not an issue since he was Cap's sole surviving heir. Sheldon and his wife were willed a truck, $5,000, and a guarantee of a place to live out their lives.

He'd sat in the lawyer's office after the funeral, repeatedly refusing all rights to Cap's estate. Paul figured that as a murderer he had no rightful claim to his victim's possessions, but the attorney finally appealed to his better judgment. Whether Paul ever fully accepted it or not or practiced surgery again or not, he would be financially set forever. In addition to the riverfront home and its twenty-acre lot, he inherited *The Lucky Brake*, the 1,600-acre Riverbend hunting tract, and a million dollars in savings and stock. On top of that there were the future royalties associated with patents Cap had secured with his innovative brake mechanism, three motor vehicles, one very high-grade English shotgun, nine first-rate American-made shot-guns, seven rifles, six handguns;, a full complement of heavy machine tools, loads of fishing tackle, furniture, an extensive sporting art collection, and one badly damaged but restorable war-surplus Vought f4u Corsair fighter aircraft. The plane was to be Cap's most ambitious project. He'd planned to repair it and then learn to fly it.

Paul would gladly have traded it all for a chance to redo his last op-eration. He'd received unsolicited offers from concerned individuals gener-ously offering to purchase most of the items, but his response was always the same, a terse, "no" followed by a forceful re-allegiance of the phone receiver to its base.

As he sat in the family room mindlessly staring into space and smoking his umpteenth cigarette of the day, a habit he'd renewed after years of ab-stinence, he thought about Robin. He phoned her and intimated they might get together sometime in the future. Although she was no longer with Brew Cavanaugh, she was intimately involved, she informed him, with an archi-tect from Miami. Showing no trace of nastiness, she made it clear by her tone that she was still smarting from the cavalier way he'd treated her. She was right, of course, and he had nobody to blame but himself for her resentment. Robin had come too easily.

He hung up the phone knowing that it would be the last time he'd ever speak to her.

On the verge of wandering out to his workshop hoping to find an antidote to his listlessness, he heard a vehicle pull up. Fearing it might be yet another penitent parasite offering to release him of the burdens of prosperity, he squashed a cigarette into the already overflowing ashtray and sat, ignoring the knock at the door. It opened anyway, just enough for a familiar face to poke through.

"Hey, Doc, I've heard you can make dicks bigger."

"I don't think you need to worry about that, Frank—you're the biggest dick on the planet." He smiled and extended his hand. "How the heck are you?"

"I'm doing okay, Skip. Boy, it's been a while, hasn't it?"

"What, a couple of years?"

"Something like that, maybe more. Jesus, Skip, you look like shit, and what's with the smokes?" He pointed to the little mountain of bent brown tubes in the dish. "That can't be much good for you."

"It passes the time," Paul said, lighting another.

During the period since Cap's death, Paul's healthy tan had given way to an ashen pallor, and what modicum of extra weight he'd carried was gone and then some. Unkempt hair and several days of beard growth, all viewed behind a veil of diaphanous blue cigarette smoke, combined to lend him a haggard visage of a prisoner of war.

Frank Eastman and Paul had been friends since junior high school. They'd met one morning while Paul was trying to land a feisty sixty-pound tarpon from the shore. Frank, who had been on his paper route, stopped and helped drag the petulant oversized herring to the riverbank. The two became fast friends and remained inseparable for years, fishing, hunting quail and rabbits in and around Martin and St Lucie counties, and during the fall months, exploring every inch of Cap's Riverbend hunting land together.

Fond of Frank as a kid, Cap worried about his free-spirited recklessness later on. Frank always found his way into some kind of trouble, first with the school administration and later with the law. His offenses, never criminal, sprang from nonsensical rebellion against authority or spur-of-the-moment mischief. During his later teens, when Frank decided to enter the mullet trade, he seized an opportunity to land some easy money by taking advantage of the huge river's migrating schools of fish, but instead of netting them as was the proven legal method, he chose to cast a five-pound black powder bomb into them from his small boat. The thunderous explosion was heard by beach-going tourists who dutifully passed the information on to the authorities.

Frank was apprehended while dip-netting casualties amid a football-field-sized shoal of dead and dying fish. Cap posted his bail, gave him a proper ass-chewing, and never brought up the episode again.

Frank's father was an abusive drunkard who drove a fuel truck from the port at Palm Beach to stations along the East Coast. He was inclined to arrive home late at night plastered and commence to breaking up the furniture and battering his wife and children. Cap couldn't stand the sight of the burley slob and was always inventing reasons to spirit Frank away from him. Frank was all too happy to reciprocate by standing in as a surrogate guardian for Cap's adoptive son, a godsend to Paul, who was a timid, scrawny teen. No one dared threaten him unless he fancied having his facial features rearranged by the intrepid Frank Eastman.

Early along, Frank's father's abuse took its toll on Frank, who turned to alcohol. The excessive drinking led to schoolyard fights and eventually barroom brawls. It troubled Cap to see him slide down such a slippery slope.

From the start of Paul and Frank's friendship, there had been some sour grapes on the latter's part. After all, Cap was well off financially compared to his own father, and Paul, being the sole recipient of his father's largess, enjoyed a seemingly lavish, sporting lifestyle. It appeared that regardless of the activities the two engaged in, Paul always had the better accouterments. Cap tried to mitigate the imbalance by giving Frank fishing gear, hunting equipment, and guns. Unfortunately Frank wasn't able to enjoy full ownership of some of the items and had to leave them with Paul, lest his father pawn them at the first opportunity, as was his wont.

One asset Frank unquestionably possessed was rugged good looks. He was a handsome, powerfully built man. Girls could resist neither his chiseled features nor his aura of surging virility, and he took full advantage of their weakness for him. His appetite for young women was exceeded only by his inability to sustain any form of continuing relationship. The battered child lived on in him, suspecting something must be terribly wrong with any woman who could love him. Many good ones tried.

When Paul was accepted to college, more bad blood developed between the two boyhood pals. Envious of Paul's academic achievements, Frank wished he had dedicated a little less time to blasting marine life and more time to the books. The two drifted further apart when Paul left for medical school and Frank was drafted into the army. Several years ago they had run into each other in a local gun shop. Frank was showing off photos of a large elk he'd recently bagged in Wyoming. The two conversed for a few minutes and both made insipid offers to reconnect at some point in the near future, but neither intended to follow through.

It was getting dark outside as Paul and Frank sat in the den, overlooking the river. All the trees and shrubs had a homogeneous, dark shadow-less look. *The Lucky Brake* bobbed at the dock, looking lonely and forgotten in the gloomy dusk.

Paul didn't know what his old friend had heard about Cap's death and he dreaded having to address the subject. He didn't have to wait long.

"Where's Cap? I ain't seen the old fart in ages."

"He passed away."

"Don't kid around, Skip," Frank chided. "He out on the boat?"

"He's dead, Frank. He died last summer. You had to have heard about it."

"How come the coon didn't say anything when I came in?"

Paul glanced at the door to see if Sheldon was within earshot and hoping he wasn't. Paul walked over and gently closed the door. "He probably didn't tell you because he knows you have no respect for him. He's been pretty nice to you for a lot of years, Frank."

Shrugging it off, Frank said, "He has his place, I have mine. Anyway, what happened to Cap? I was workin' in Georgia last summer, so I didn't hear nothing."

"He had a problem with his heart."

"Couldn't you help him?"

"It's more complicated than that. Can we change the subject? What were you doing in Georgia?"

Sensing he'd hit a sore spot, Frank backed off. "Get me something to drink, and I'll tell you."

The same old Frank, Paul thought. He could tell by Frank's breath that it wouldn't be his first drink of the day.

Grabbing a bottle of Jim Beam, Paul filled two glasses halfway with ice and water. Frank took a glass from his host, got up from his chair, opened the back door, and threw the ice and water out. "Takes up valuable space," he said, smiling and offering the empty glass to Paul, who filled it with bourbon and then poured himself a scant drink.

Frank took a gulp of his, emptying about half of the glass. His stomach reacted in protest, triggering an involuntary gasp, and he had to suppress regurgitation with a couple of swallows, his eyes watering.

Paul looked at him with distain. "I feel sorry for your liver."

"Fuck my liver. This crap ain't killed my old man yet, so what makes you think it's going to hurt me?"

"How is he, by the way?"

"Alive, unfortunately."

"Your mom doing okay?"

"Yeah, but she's still dealing with that prick. She should have shot him in his sleep years ago."

"Tell her I said hi, will you?"

"Why don't you go visit her? She'd love to see you, and I'd expect she could use a friendly face."

Paul knew he'd never get over to see her. He didn't want to answer any of her questions. "So what's with the earth-moving business?" he asked Frank.

"What can I say? They want to tear up the whole goddamn Southeast Coast, and they need me to do it. I don't have enough equipment and operators to keep up with the demand."

Frank was telling the truth about the unlimited development taking place along the East Coast. What he failed to mention was that his reputation as a dependable contractor had been slipping. For some time his drinking had diminished his capacity to manage the business. Deadlines were missed, bids were submitted late, and the work was substandard. He had trouble keeping employees. The good ones were lost to more dependable employers, so he was forced to use lazy, careless incompetents, and his poorly maintained machines were constantly breaking down. There was so much construction going on, though, that despite losing out on the big, lucrative jobs, he still got work from desperate developers and made a decent living.

"Enough about me. How's the doctoring business?"

"I haven't worked in about six months, Frank."

"What? You're retired already, you lucky bastard?"

"No, I wouldn't say retired. Just done with it."

"What's the difference? You couldn't have made *that* much money already. Wait a minute . . . Cap's estate. Of all the goddamn luck."

"That's not why I quit."

"Sure it is."

Paul didn't like the implication, even though in reality, Frank was right on target. He *was* living off Cap's money. "I did get Cap's estate, but that's not why I gave of surgery. I have my reasons, and that's all I want to say about it."

"Suit yourself, but it looks pretty obvious to me."

"I don't give a damn how it looks to you."

"Calm down. I didn't come here to fight with you about your job or your inheritance. Now how about some more firewater for your old buddy?"

Paul poured a half glassful and corked the bottle.

Frank resented the implication and was about to object, but restrained himself since he had important business to address. "When was the last time you went hunting, Skip?"

"More than two years. Why?"

"Don't you miss it?"

"Not really. I actually like fishing more."

"When was the last time you did that?"

"About six months ago."

"What the hell have you been doing all this time, playing with yourself?"

"Not much—haven't felt like doing anything."

"Well, I've got a proposition for you."

"No, I don't want to sell the boat."

"Who said anything about the boat?"

"I don't want to sell Riverbend either, or anything else for that matter."

"Would you just shut up and listen? Do you remember Scott Cougan?"

It was a name Paul hadn't heard in a long time. Scott had lived close to Frank's house. He was in the same grade as the two friends and shared their interests. Cap had always invited him to come along with Paul and Frank to Riverbend. Frank had pounded poor Scott's head against the hood of a car once, because he'd guzzled the entire half pint of rum that Frank had gone to great lengths to steal from a neighbor's house. If Paul hadn't broken up the fight, Frank would have seriously injured his friend. It took years for Scott to warm back up to him.

"I can't believe he still talks to you."

"You mean the rum thing? Hell, he got over that years ago. We're pretty good friends now. Anyhow, last year Scott and I booked an African safari in Kenya and Tanganyika."

"Africa? Boy, you guys are really into it."

"Yeah, we're scheduled to go in June, with one the best P.H.'s in East Africa."

"P.H.?"

"Professional hunter. They don't like to be called guides over there. The guy's name is Ian Sharpe. Comes highly recommended."

"It sounds swell, Frank. What are you guys hunting?"

"All different kinds of antelope, like gazelle and impala. They got about a dozen different kinds there. Also zebra, warthog—and you're going to love this—dangerous animals. We're going after Cape buffalo, lion, and maybe even rhino and elephant."

"It's going to take forever to shoot all that. How long's the trip?"

"At least six weeks, maybe more."

"I'm impressed. It ought to be a hell of a hunt."

"Here's the kicker, Paul, Scott's wife went and got pregnant, and she's due about the time we're supposed to leave."

"I don't do abortions, Frank."

"No, you asshole. Unless she has a miscarriage or something, he's going to have to back out, and if he does, I don't have a hunting partner. I don't want to go alone, so I need you to go in his place. It's the chance of a lifetime."

"I can't."

"Why not? What else do you have to do but sit around here and smoke butts?"

"I don't know, but it sounds like more than I want to deal with right now."

"All you have to do is write some checks, apply for travel papers, and get some shots in your ass. The rest has already been taken care of."

Paul was astonished how quickly he was warming to the idea. After all, there wasn't anything keeping him in Florida that wouldn't be there when he got back. *Clearing out of here might help me forget all that's happened*, he thought.

"Just how many checks am I going to be writing?"

"Including airfare, Ian's fee, licenses, and whatever, it'll be about ten thousand."

"Ten thousand? Are you crazy?"

"And that's going to break you?"

"Don't start that again," he warned.

"Wake up, Paul. We're talking Africa here, and first class all the way. We'll shoot more in six weeks than we could in a whole lifetime here. I don't know what's been eatin' your ass for so long, but you look like death and probably need to get out and do something fun."

Frank was sounding a little frantic, and Paul picked up on it.

"You're afraid to go alone, aren't you?"

"Yeah, I'm quaking in my boots," Frank said with implied sarcasm.

Paul had hit on the truth, though.

Frank reflected, *What the hell do I know about hunting lions that I didn't get from reading some books? I do know that sometime people don't come back. They're stomped to death by elephants, eaten by crocodiles, or bitten by snakes so venomous that death is a blessing. And how about the people—dark natives with mysterious customs—and fearless white hunters who stare death in the face every day and laugh about it over drinks at night.* He wondered if he'd measure up or soil himself and run away like a frightened child. He desperately needed Paul along for moral support, but he'd never admit it. "I'm going whether you come of not," he boasted, trying to shrug off his own reservations. "I just thought you'd really enjoy it."

He didn't know what to do if Paul refused, short of forfeiting all the money he'd already put out—funds he could ill afford to part with. He'd made a promise to himself that on his return from the trip he'd straighten out his life, give up drinking, and put his business back on track. It was a promise he'd made before, but this time was going to be different. It had to be. He was approaching the bottom with alarming speed. This was going to be his last irresponsible fling.

"Tell me about this guy Sharpe, the P.H.," Paul said. "How did you hear about him?"

Paul was beginning to sell himself on the idea, but the last thing he wanted was to get stuck in darkest Africa with some crazed white hunter, a recluse with a death wish.

"I talked to some guys who hunted with him. One of them is an officer with the Boone and Crockett trophy record club. He said Sharpe's one of the best."

"Did those guys shoot a lot?"

"Got everything they went for. What's even better, because of the game laws over there, if we want to hunt separately, each one of us will have our own P.H. Ian Sharpe said one of his partners will be along if necessary to keep us both hunting as much as possible."

"What kind of guns do we need? They use some pretty big stuff over there, don't they?"

"According to Ian, a heavy thirty or thirty-five caliber is fine. You've still got that Model seventy Winchester three hundred H&H, don't you?"

Paul nodded. It had been Cap's deer rifle. He'd always gone hunting a little over-gunned, and a .300-caliber magnum was a testament to that fact. The obligation of every hunter, he'd said, was to make a clean kill and not leave a wounded animal to suffer and die in agony.

"Ian said to bring a back-up rifle too. Maybe something flat-shooting, like a twenty-five aught six for antelope."

"Anything wrong with my two seventy?"

"You know what that gun expert Jack O'Connor says about the two seventy? He thinks it hung the moon and swears it's the best thing since sliced bread. If it's good enough for him, I'm sure it'll be fine for you. Sharpe said to bring along a shotgun too, since they've got guinea fowl and something called Franklin. He's said they're like grouse."

"What about the big stuff? You know, elephant guns?"

"He has 'em. Double-barrel rifles. He rents 'em out for the trip."

"Did he send you a list of things we'd need to bring, like clothes, boots, and stuff?"

"Yeah, I got it at home. I'll send it to you or bring it by. A company in

New York called Abercrombie and Fitch sells clothes for safaris. I'll get that to you too. If we're missing something, Ian swears there a place in Nairobi that'll make canvas or leather things in a day. I think he's full of shit on that one, but—" Frank held up his glass and smiled. "Fix me up, and I'll tell you some more."

"I hope you don't plan on spending the whole time with your head in a bottle and drunk on your ass," Paul said, doling out another half glass of the amber fluid. He gave himself another small shot. "I'll bet this fellow Sharpe won't stand to have you soused the whole time."

"Are you kidding? Those guys live on booze. It guards them against malaria."

"If that's the case, you can skip the quinine altogether." Mindful of recent news articles he'd read about political turmoil in Africa, Paul inquired, "Did Ian Sharpe say anything about any native problems, an uprising that's going on over there? I think they're calling it The Kenya Emergency."

"No. Why?"

"For a while I've been reading about the natives trying to get rid of the European settlers by banding together and attacking them. The natives call themselves Mu Mu or Mau Mau or something, I think. A lot of them have been killed, and some British settlers too. I'm pretty sure it's still going on in Kenya. You'd better ask Ian about it."

"Who cares if a bunch of natives get killed, and besides, do you really think he'd have us come over there if it wasn't safe?"

Paul shot another glance at the door to make sure Sheldon hadn't heard. "Is anything really safe over there? You're talking about hunting lions, for Christ sake. Just ask Ian, okay?"

There wasn't much else Frank could say, and the bourbon was gone. The two men sat quietly, remembering years of shared experience and contemplating the safari to come. A minute or so passed before Frank spoke.

"You know, it's too bad Cap isn't alive. He'd have loved a trip like this."

Paul remained silent, musing. *Well, at least I've had five minutes without thinking about that.*

Frank got up and swayed a little. The bourbon had made him mellow, and he extended his hand. "I'm glad you're going, Skip. I miss the old times we used to have."

"Thanks for inviting me, Frank. Maybe this is what I need. I'm already starting to look forward to it. Stay in touch, and please get all the info to me. By the way, what day are we supposed to leave?"

"June twenty-sixth out of Miami."

As they walked to the door, Frank said, "Can you do me a favor, Doc? I hurt my knee jumping from a loader a week ago. Do you have anything here for pain?"

"Sure, Frank, hold on," he replied, and went to the hall closet to get his medical bag. Fumbling with some bottles, he finally located a small vial, unscrewed the lid, and took a quick count of the contents. "There's about fifty codeine tablets in here," he said, tossing the bottle to Frank. "Don't take these while you're drinking or running any machines. I mean it."

"Thanks, Doc. I'll be good," he said, folding up his coat collar and stepping out into the cold, damp night. "Talk to you soon, Skip. We're gonna have a blast."

Climbing into his pickup truck, he opened the bottle, poured out three of the white disks, and popped them into his mouth, chasing them with some stale beer he'd left on the seat. He cranked the engine and drove off into darkness.

CHAPTER FOUR

Possessions

The helm seemed heavy and sluggish when Paul negotiated the turns leading to the St. Lucie Inlet's entry to the ocean. The inlet was a treacherous passage even under the best of circumstances. Its shifting sandbars and strong ripping currents challenged the most competent mariners and foundered the unseasoned ones.

He'd navigated the channel many times during day and night and was familiar with its idiosyncrasies. Cap had gone to great lengths to prepare him well for any circumstances involving weather, equipment, and even structural difficulties. He felt as much at ease on the vessel as he did in his own bed.

As the boat twisted through the boiling torrent, he had to fight the helm more than he'd anticipated. In addition, the starboard diesel engine was hesitant every time he nudged the control lever forward. He judged that it was good thing he was on the way to the boatyard as he maneuvered *The Lucky Brake* through the last stretch of turbulent water leading to the open sea.

Once free of the breakwaters, he sensed the strange exhilaration that mariners have experienced for as long as they have put to sea in boats—an elation of absolute freedom coupled with the burdens of self-preservation in this hostile, unforgiving environment. The feeling was enhanced by the fact that for the first time he was in command of his own boat. For *The Lucky Brake*, there weren't going to be any yacht brokers or classified ads, not now or ever.

He'd correctly surmised that the crust of barnacles and algae that had formed on the hull were responsible for the languid response to control. She had been idle for more than eight months, and the signs of neglect were becoming all too apparent. The varnish on the transom and teak toe-rail was cracking and turning cloudy white. Brass fixtures had turned green with corrosion, and the once shiny white decks were dull and dirty. He was ashamed to show up at the boatyard with her looking so run down, particularly since Cap had attended to every detail in her construction at this very boatyard many years earlier.

The news of Cap's passing had long since made its way down to the Pompano Beach boatyard. Its owner, Buddy Murdock, had been most gracious with his condolences on the phone a few day earlier; however, to Paul's consternation, Buddy couldn't resist offering to buy the boat. Paul made it clear, while trying his hardest to keep cool that he only wanted the boat overhauled, not disposed of.

While inspecting the boat recently, Paul had noticed its boot stripe was below the waterline, a foreboding indicator that she'd taken on water, which was cause for immediate alarm. He pulled up the engine hatch and discovered a foot of seawater occupying the bilge. Feeling rotten that he'd failed to perform even the most basic guardianship of what had been Cap's cherished possession, he and Sheldon dedicated the day to pumping it out, replacing the damaged batteries, and removing all the fishing tackle, which was also covered by a film of green corrosion. They would attend to that matter at a later time.

Continuing to cruise down the coast toward Hillsboro Inlet, Paul thought about the upcoming trip to Africa. Frank had delivered, as promised, all the information regarding supplies, vaccinations, and timetables and had kept him abreast of his communications with Ian Sharpe. The departure date was rapidly approaching, and he was getting excited. The anticipation was distracting him from constantly thinking about Cap, but at moments he felt guilty about letting his father slip into the past.

He also had bouts of missing the operating room. Prior to the final surgery that had brought his career to an abrupt end, he'd loved the excitement. What kept him from resuming his work as a doctor was the fear that his confidence was gone and with it his ability to make quick decisions. Perhaps upon his return from Africa he might reconsider.

When he'd told Gordy about the safari, Gordy said he was happy Paul was "going to do something besides hiding out from reality," as he'd bluntly put it. Having exhausted all hope for Paul's return, Gordy had hired another surgeon. Even though it was Paul's own decision that prompted the action, it had seemed impersonal and final. Paul had never expected that being replaced would bother him so much.

As the boat lurched forward through the choppy sea, large surges of water shot from the elegantly flared bow. Paul, standing at the controls atop the tuna tower, admired the craft's graceful lines with a new sense of pride.

The visibility provided by the tower's height allowed him to see an undulating dark mass a short distance ahead. He instantly recognized what it was, as he'd seen the phenomenon many times before. Easing the throttles back, he slowly approached the tightly compacted school of baitfish. Three shadowy figures encircled the school. He watched as one of the sailfish swam away and then turned and charged the mass, slashing its bill back and forth, stunning several of the small fish, which the other sailfish rushed in and consumed. The process was repeated over and over as the sleek predators took turns attacking and feeding. Paul hankered for a rod with a lure or bait on it, since this type of feeding frenzy made the billfish an easy target for a hookup.

He watched the big fish for a while until they tired of the game or got their fill and disappeared into the depths. Having enjoyed the spectacle, he revved the engines and continued his way down the coast.

As Palm Beach slipped past him to the west, he reminisced about earlier lobster hunting trips when Cap took the boys in close to shore. From his vantage up in the tower, Cap would spot rock formations housing the succulent crustaceans. Paul and Frank would dive overboard with masks and coax the wary creatures out of their coral shelters and into waiting nets. They usually did it on calm days, when the fishing was slow. Sheldon would be waiting on the dock when they pulled in at dusk, and he'd skim off some fish and lobster for Clorese to assemble into one of her mouthwatering feasts. While the crew washed the boat and put away the tackle, she'd prepare dinner and set the table. She was an artist with seasoned flour and hot oil. Paul could almost taste the nuggets of fried lobster and fish as he mindlessly cruised along. It had been a long time since the group had enjoyed one of those seafood extravaganzas, and it made him sad that they never would again.

On one occasion the crew had captured a wayward green sea turtle and delivered it alive and flapping to Clorese, who concocted several exquisite meals from its body parts. The thought of food made him hungry, so he lashed down the wheel and went below to scour the pantry for a snack. His selection was limited to provisions with chafed labels and rusty cans, a far cry from one of Clorese's spreads. He grabbed a container of corned beef, an opener, and a spoon and returned to the helm.

Just outside Hillsboro Inlet, he gunned the engines and powered through the breaking waves until he cleared the sand bars and entered the calm harbor. He tried to avoid eye contact with anyone attending to the row of charter boats tied up at the fishing docks because he knew that some of the captains would recognize the boat, and he wasn't yet ready for small talk. He busied himself with a contrived mechanical problem as he waited for the iron turnstile bridge to swing open, allowing him to proceed.

Rounding the last curve in the waterway and in sight of the boat works, he spotted Sheldon squatting on the shore, fishing with a hand line. For someone who had little affection for the open ocean, Sheldon certainly had a passion for fishing, and he was so engrossed in his pastime that he was unaware of *The Lucky Brake* until it was almost abreast. As soon as he recognized the vessel, he stood up and waved excitedly, as if Paul had been at sea for years.

Buddy Murdock was waiting at the dock as Paul masterfully swung the boat around and backed it into the slip without so much as bumping a piling. He could see Buddy was impressed. Switching off the engines, he hopped onto the dock as Buddy cleated the lines.

"Ahoy, Skip, or is it Paul or Dr. Bennett now?"

"Paul's fine."

"You weren't kidding. She looks like crap."

"I'm sorry, Buddy. I just haven't had it in me to care for her like I should've."

"We'll get her straightened out. Any problems on the way down?"

"The starboard engine's a little rough, and as you can see, the bottom's loaded. I don't think all that water in the bilge did anything but ruin the batteries, but check everything out anyway. And as long as she's out of the water, you might as well paint her."

"Same color, I assume. You'll want to teak done too, right?"

"Yep, and look at all the upholstery. If you think its shot, have it replaced in the same material."

"Planning on running up a pretty good tab, aren't you?"

"What else am I going to spend it on, Buddy?"

"Ain't you got a wife yet?"

"Nope."

"That's why you still got a few bucks left. What're you waitin' for?"

Paul shrugged.

"Well, Paul, I gotta ask you one more time. If you change your mind—"

"I'm not selling."

"Okay, okay. It's going to be about three weeks before we can get her hauled and probably a month or more to get all this done."

"Take as much time as you need, Buddy. In fact I don't really want to come get her until August anyway. I won't be back until then."

"Where you off to, Paul?"

"Africa," Paul responded proudly.

"What are you goin' all the way over there for? You takin' old Sheldon here back for a family reunion or something?"

"No." Paul snickered. "I'm going to Kenya on a safari."

"No kidding? Boy, I've always wanted to do that. What are you hunting?"

"Everything, I think."

"Well, be careful over there. I've heard it's a pretty rough place, and I wouldn't want to get *The Lucky Brake* by default."

"I'll bet you wouldn't, Buddy. Just don't pray too hard I get eaten by a lion, okay? Take good care of her for me." He took one last look at the elegant boat that he wasn't absolutely sure he would ever see again.

Paul and Sheldon didn't talk much on the drive back to St. Lucie. Until that moment, Paul hadn't given much thought to the real possibility that he wouldn't make it home from Africa. There were ample ways for someone to meet his end over there. Terrible things could happen just trying to *get* to Africa.

Sheldon hadn't said much about the upcoming trip. He was still getting over the loss of Cap. Losing Paul was incomprehensible and would leave him and Clorese adrift in a hostile world.

"What do you think of me going on this trip?" Paul asked.

The black man stared out the window, deep in thought, until finally he spoke. "Why you got to go halfway round the world to shoot some lion? Ain't Riverbend got good enough huntin'?"

"Sure, but this is a chance of a lifetime. Besides, I need to get out of here for a while. You know, help me clear my head."

"Well, you right 'bout that. If yo' head was right, you wouldn't be goin'. And why go with Frank? He's bad. That boy can't hold his liq'a."

"Aw, he's all right, and I doubt he'll get much of a chance to drink over there," Paul responded, trying to ease his own concerns about Frank's boozing. "I don't know what to tell you other than I want to do this and I think I need to go. If something does happen to me . . ."

"Oh please, Mista Paul, don't even talk like dat. Ole Sheldon gonna cry, you keeps it up."

"Look, we need to talk about this. I'm not planning on dying over there, but I suppose it could happen." He looked over at Sheldon just as a tear streaked down the old man's cheek. Seeing it, Paul decided there was nothing to be gained by discussing it further. He would have to make some sort of arrangement with the attorney and leave it at that.

By the time they arrived at the house, Paul's morale had risen because of the momentum of his progress. He felt buoyed enough to start packing for the trip. He already on hand many of the items on the list of recommended commodities that Ian had provided. Unfortunately some were in and among Cap's personal effects, which Paul had been loath to contend with until now.

```
Sharpe, Weston, and Graham Safaris, Ltd.
Nairobi, Kenya

    For a typical safari, the hunter will
require the following necessities: Four
pairs of heavy canvas long trousers, four
pairs of shorts of a similar material,
five heavy and three light fabric shirts,
undershirts, a suitable jacket and/or
sweater for cool weather. A cotton drill
jacket is recommended for social occasions.
Rubber or oilskin rainwear, wool socks,
underwear, a broad brim hat, a belt, two
pairs of ankle-high boots of good quality,
comfortable shoes for around camp, a full
complement of personal toiletries, personal
medications if needed, a wristwatch,
binoculars, two rifles in proper working
condition, one preferably in a .30 to .35
caliber magnum or larger, the other rifle
to be adequate enough to kill medium to
large non-dangerous game.
    Telescopic sights are optional but are
discouraged because of inconsistencies in
their accuracy. Participants are permitted
to bring a shotgun for wing shooting. A 12
bore is recommended, however 16 or 20 is
acceptable. All guns must be accompanied
```

by five boxes of properly matched rounds. These should be newly acquired. One or more still cameras are recommended and a motion picture camera is permitted if the client chooses to document his safari. An abundance of photographic film is advised. Writing supplies are advocated for those who wish to record their experiences in this manner.

It is also recommended that the participants carry reading material, as there will be some periods of inactivity at intervals during the safari. All foodstuffs will be provided, and items such as liquor and tobacco may be procured at the start and at several points along the route of the trip.

It is advised that all effects are of the highest quality so as not to jeopardize the full experience of the safari. In particular, guns and ammunition MUST BE IN TOP ORDER. Malfunctioning or dilapidated firearms place the hunter as well as the entire party at grave risk and will not be sanctioned for use. It is also advised that the hunter familiarize himself with the firearms of his choosing and therefore be able to demonstrate proficiency with them.

Paul put the document on the desk in front of him and stared at it. He'd perused it the day Frank brought it by and then quickly tossed it into a drawer. This time he read through it, and the Nairobi, Kenya, address on the letterhead seized him. *Why am I trekking half a world away to challenge the planet's most deadly animals?* This was not some fanciful childhood daydream of adventure. It was Paul pitting himself against the raw power and primal instincts of creatures that had for eons considered humans on the basis of their nutritional value alone. Was Frank having the same reaction?

The Abercrombie and Fitch shipping box that had arrived several days earlier contained, among other things, several pairs of khaki pants. "Aw, shit, he muttered when he tried them on. He'd estimated the size based on previous clothing purchases and hadn't taken into account his recent weight loss. He'd have to return the whole lot and hope a properly fitting wardrobe would arrive in time for his departure.

Although leery of violating the sanctity of Cap's closet, Paul needed to gather the guns. He stared at the dusty but formidable gun rack along the wall. Small islands of light rust had formed on some of the guns, which could be removed with an oily rag. Cap had prided himself on his collection but rarely displayed weapons in open view, declaring that keeping guns in fancy cabinets was like "lighting the channel for society's bottom feeders." Paul picked up Cap's Winchester rifle and opened the breech bolt. It was heavier than his own Husqvarna rifle he'd always carried at Riverbend. He closed the bolt, shouldered the Winchester, and envisioned himself leveling at a charging lion. Racking the bolt, he pretended to get off a second shot. He had no idea that there was seldom time for a second shot.

Next was the Husqvarna .270-caliber rifle that Cap had presented to Paul on his sixteenth birthday. The Swedish Mauser had dispatched several deer through the years, including a handsome twelve-point adorning the living room wall. Paul was comfortable with the weapon and knew its limitations.

When it came to choosing a shotgun for the trip, he had no trouble making the decision. If he was going to accompany one of Africa's top professional hunters, he was going to impress him right from the start, and he had just the article. The splendid little English double, one of Cap's prized possessions, had always been Paul's favorite. Not only was the James Woodward and Sons sidelock over-and-under twenty-bore a work of art, it also had an intriguing provenance. Following World War II servicemen returned from Europe with items appropriated from captured enemy soldiers, won in card games, or in a few cases, taken from residents of liberated towns. In the case of the Woodward, an army corporal who helped capture a German village happened upon it in a trunk. How the English-made shotgun had made its way to Germany and how he'd managed to smuggle the recently crafted, magnificently built, elaborately engraved treasure out of Europe and back to America was anyone's guess. Make it to the States it did, however, and the veteran, short on funds and wanting to get a healthy jump on life, sold it to Cap for $2,500, a tidy sum in post-war America.

A masterpiece of prewar gun making, the little shotgun with its richly marbled French walnut stock, perfect wood-to-metal fit, and fitted leather case had long been the darling of dove shoots, quail hunts, and gun-club get-togethers. Every time it debuted, the offers poured in. Paul had spent hours admiring the devotion to detail that the well-balanced firearm possessed. On one occasion, using a magnifying glass, he studied the full-coverage scroll engraving and extensive gold inlays, trying to detect an error in its execution. He came up with nothing more than a greater appreciation for the talents of the engraver.

The shotgun was not part of the standing inventory of the rack. For this distinguished treasure Cap had built a secret closet. Paul retrieved it, and once again admired its splendor. Ian Sharpe was sure to be impressed by this one, he thought, as he readied the gun and the others for travel.

The bosomy waitress was busying herself with Frank's formidable organ. She was doing everything possible to evoke some reaction, somewhat puzzled though far from disappointed by its refusal to acknowledge her endeavors. In any condition, it was, in her estimation, a most satisfactory appendage. "What's the matter, Sugarplum? Don't this feel good?"

"Sure it feels good, baby. I've just got a lot on my mind right now."

He'd stopped for dinner at an Italian restaurant on his way home from work and liked what he saw both on and off the menu. Spotting her as he entered, Frank defaulted to his time-tested routine of strutting confidently straight at her, his eyes locked onto hers until she broke the stalemate, glancing down and smiling submissively, suggesting that she welcomed his approach. He bantered with her and teased her and then switched to an anecdote or story that showed his sensitive side and then downshifted back to banter, amid a constant escalation of intermittent touching. Inspired by a liter of cheap Chianti, following hard on the six-pack of beer he'd consumed en route, Frank worked it until he determined that Wanda Tucker would make satisfactory mattress fodder for the night and propositioned the young woman to join him at the close of her shift, to which she agreed.

The pasta consumed and a map drawn on a napkin, Frank teetered his way out the door.

Wanda arrived at the agreed-upon time, just as he was drifting off. She expressed enthusiasm over the expansiveness of his house, which was a testament to a more fortuitous time. However, any continuity between the dwelling and its contents had been lost during long years of bachelorhood that succeeded in completely extinguishing his desire to establish a home, since there was no one there to appreciate it. The trappings exemplified a total disregard for esthetic intention. What furniture he had was cheap and mismatched, and the place was a wreck. Nothing seemed to be in its proper place, making her wonder if the dwelling had been used for habitation at all. The only area that showed any regard for composition was the trophy display along the living room wall.

Frank had been active with his hunting and obviously successful at it, as evinced by his collection. The display was a Who's Who of deceased ungulates. Game heads from Alaska to the southern reaches of Texas and all points in between graced the partition.

"You catch all them deers?" Wanda asked, kicking off her work shoes and accepted a glass of a sugary-flavored bourbon.

Why do they always have to be so fucking stupid? he wondered, realizing he wasn't in the mood for chitchat or anything else and would appreciate it if she just went away.

"Yes I *shot* them all," he responded, cursing himself for initiating the rendezvous in the first place.

They talked about nothing in particular while her level of sobriety sank to his, at which point they made their way to the bedroom.

She gave up trying to arouse him and slid her nude body up the bed toward his. Reaching over him to get her drink and spilling some of it on the sheets, she pointed to the pile of cases and bags in the corner.

"What's that stuff for? You goin' on some kind of trip?"

Reluctant to take his eyes off the ceiling and more than just a little irritated at having to respond at all, he answered, "I'm going to Africa."

"No kiddin'. I had a uncle that fought in a war there. Whatcha gonna do, shoot a tiger?"

He wanted to reach for the whiskey bottle and smash it against her skull. "Africa has lions. India has tigers," he said. "Look, honey, I've had a rough day, and I'm really tired. Can we just call it quits and maybe give it a shot in the morning?"

Dejected and a little angry, she opted not to make an issue of it. "Sure doll, I can wait a while longer for this," she said, reaching for his groin. She still had a hold of his penis when she dozed off or passed out. He wasn't sure which.

Frank spent several hours awake thinking about the trip. He'd become increasingly more anxious as the departure date neared. The stress of watching his business deteriorate, coupled with rising self-doubt, was wearing him down. He even considered canceling, but deemed it cowardly; besides, how could he ever face Paul again?

Partially sobered up, he motivated himself enough to make another stab at the woman, so he shook her awake. "Hey, Wendy, I think it's time you got a big piece of Frank here."

Groggily she came to. "Who's Wendy?"

"Never mind. Roll over and spread those pretty legs and let me remind you why you're here."

"Don't you want to kiss or fool around a little first?" she half-heartedly protested, rolling onto her back.

"Ain't really necessary, baby. This is what it's all about, right here," he said, mounting her and entering forcefully.

"Hey, Sugarplum, you're hurting me. Take it easy."

Frank ignored her and went at it with gusto until he quickly reached his climax and fell, panting, over to her side.

Hurt, both emotionally and physically, Wanda sat at the corner of the bed sniffling as she put on her work blouse and hose in silence. Gathering her purse and shoes, she walked out, closing the door quietly behind her.

CHAPTER FIVE

The Dud

Jimmy Foust was in a lousy mood. To begin with, he really hated his job. He hated going to work at three in the afternoon and he hated getting off at eleven, when most everything was closed except the bars. Not that he didn't relish having a stiff bourbon or two in the wee hours. It was just that he hardly if ever could find anyone to join him at that time of night. Anyone, that is, who wouldn't mind listening to him bellyache about the Viking Ammunition Company and its narrow-minded management. Most of his coworkers had long since tired of his incessant grumbling about the awkward hours, poor pay, short-sighted superiors, and a host of other failings of his employer of fifteen years. Even the bartenders had heard enough and waited on him with reluctance, knowing full well what the topic of the evening's litany was sure be.

Tonight had been particularly infuriating because of several incidents. First his wife, Mona, had informed him that their kids, Little Jimmy and Molly, needed new clothes for school. He regarded those things as a waste of money, which was always in short supply in the Foust household. Secondly the tune-up on the family Packard, which he'd done himself, not only failed to improve its performance, but it stopped it altogether, leaving him to walk to work. His slovenly six-foot, 260-pound body was soaked with sweat and stank from several days without bathing. Lastly he had just caught wind that because of a reduction in the demand for shotgun ammunition, layoffs were imminent. Since his standing with management had been skidding for some time, he was in serious jeopardy of being unemployed, and he knew it.

He'd come to Viking Ammo after being discharged from the army, where he'd served as a quartermaster in the ordinance division in Europe. His duties were no more complicated than making sure the chain of distribution was maintained so that the soldiers on the frontlines were supplied with the necessary munitions as needed. There was such an overwhelming supply network in place that only at the immediate front line was there any problem with replenishment. When things went wrong, it was usually because Jimmy had failed to do his job.

He had decided while in Europe that upon his return from the war he'd make his fortune developing new and unique forms of ammunition. Upon his return to New Haven, Connecticut, he landed the job, with no small help from his wife's uncle, Calvin Viking, the company's founder. At Viking Ammo, he operated a shotshell-loading machine, a job he viewed as merely a stepping stone to a berth in the research and development branch of the industry. Once employed he embarked on his plan to revolutionize the world of projectile design.

His concepts were extravagant if not totally idiotic. Jimmy's first idea was for an edible shell casing, which, he'd deduced, made perfect sense, considering the fact that frontline combatants often had an abundance of spent rounds and little in the way of rations. His experimentation involved having Mona bake hundreds of small disk-shaped cookies using various recipes while he, milk in hand, tested each one for toughness, uniformity, and flavor. His nutritionally based idea was met with little more than amusement. He was informed that Viking Ammo had little desire to enter the pastry business. It was also brought to his attention that foodstuffs could never be made strong enough to withstand expansion pressures in excess of 30,000 pounds per square inch, a concept he vaguely understood. Discouraged, he moved to his next project, the barbed bullet. This nasty little projectile would give enemy doctors fits trying to remove them from the wounded. The end result would be more causalities or longer recuperation times for enemy soldiers—hence, a smaller opposing force. He brought this idea directly to the superintendent, who'd nearly fired him on the spot, not only for his moral insensitivities, but also for the obvious breech in convention on ethical combat. Convinced that his boss was stealing the idea for himself, he went over the man's head and took the idea directly to the plant manager, who reminded him on no uncertain terms that his position at Viking Ammo did not in any way relate to the refinement of existing technologies. His violating the chain of command did little to endear him to management.

Leaving military endeavors behind, Jimmy turned his attention to the sporting industry in the form of the corkscrew shotshell wad. Not being a shooter himself, he was unfamiliar with the requirement that shotshells maintain the density of pellets at an effective distance. In his mind the more space between pellets, the greater the killing zone, as he called it. His spiral-shaped wad would separate upon leaving the barrel and spread shot in all directions. Jimmy had actually built some crude examples of his invention and had a friend load them into some shells. The end result was a permanently bulged barrel and a shot pattern that an ostrich could have walked through safely at thirty yards without so much as a ruffled feather. He finally gave up and accepted the fact that he was probably never going anywhere but the production line. He could accept the fact, but he didn't have to like it.

His current position involved the final assembly and loading of Viking's super magnum buckshot shells. He started his shift reeking from sweat and seething at all the injustice heaped upon him and worrying about his future. His state of mind did little to bolster his dedication to quality control, a critical facet of ammunition production.

The giant hissing and clanking machine in front of him, a Munurhin rotary shell loader, was simultaneously assimilating and discharging the components needed to produce a loaded shotshell. Its multi-stage process involved forming the cardboard and brass shell casing, placing a primer in the brass base, charging a specified amount of gunpowder into the case, placing a thick cardboard shock wad after the powder, dropping in a specific number of lead pellets, inserting a thin cardboard seal above the shot, and then rolling a crimp at the shell's top to retain all of the components. Its hydraulic appendages moved in jerky articulated rhythms, not unlike the movements of a mighty metallic land crab.

Jimmy's task was to oversee the priming and powder-charging phase of the operation, but in his state of agitation he was slow to notice that the powder-charging aperture had gotten blocked, impeding the flow of gunpowder into the primed casings. Witnessing it, and ignoring strict company directives that mandated a system shutdown, Jimmy rapped on the nozzle with a wrench, prompting the flow to resume. He didn't know how many shells got through without powder, and quite frankly he couldn't have cared less. In any case, he would be the only one aware of the glitch; therefore, in his way of thinking, it hadn't occurred.

He derived a modicum of satisfaction knowing that, at least to a few shooters, the company that had slighted him through the years would be made to look inferior to its competitors. He also chuckled to himself, perversely gloating over furious deer hunters who'd fail to collect another trophy to hang over their mantelpieces. What he failed to recognize was that those same buckshot shells would at some time be called upon for use in law enforcement or in the pursuit of very dangerous game.

CHAPTER SIX

Around the Globe

Paul listened to the distant rumble of thunder, recalling that the forecast had called for scattered showers during most of the morning, with the probability of thunderstorms throughout the day. He didn't know how this type of weather affected air travel, since his exposure to aviation had been limited to several short hops to and from the Bahamas in one of the flying boats that serviced the region from Miami and the one flight home during spring break from medical school.

The thought of weather made him recall that it was about the time of year when the risk of hurricanes increased. He hadn't even considered formulating any plans for Sheldon, in the event one of the massive cyclones threatened the region. What could he do anyway, but board up the house with the shutters that he and Cap had made and move away from the coast for a couple of days? The boat was in reliable hands at the yard, so it wasn't a problem. *I guess there's not much I could do anyway, so why worry*, he concluded.

He was about to get in the shower when the phone rang, and he heard a familiar voice say, "*Jambo, daktari.* That's 'Hello, doctor' in Swahili, Skip."

"I know, Frank, and *jambo* to you. Well, it's now or never, huh?

"Yep. You ready? Oh, you're going to have to get a ride to the airport yourself today."

"What is it now, another quickie before the trip?"

"No it's not another quickie. I took care of that last night with some waitress I met and had her begging for more most of the night. I've just got some business to take care of at the bank, and I don't know if I'll have time to swing by and pick you up when I'm done. I might have to go straight to the airport from there."

Frank did have an appointment with an officer at the First Savings and Loan of Palm Beach. What he failed to mention was that if he was unsuccessful in leaving there with a short-term loan for ten thousand dollars, there wouldn't be an Eastman Excavating Company when he returned from Africa, and he seriously doubted whether he could convince the bank to honor the request. Several years of mismanagement had reduced his business to the point of collapse. His task was to convince the lending institution to ignore the recent decline and instead focus on the assets and potential growth. Fortunately the building boom was in full swing, with no signs of dwindling. He also planned to conceal the fact that he, by the close of the business day, would have departed the country for at least six weeks.

"I guess I can get Sheldon to take me to the airport. How early should I get to the airport, you know, with the luggage and stuff?"

"I'd give yourself at least an hour at the airport."

"All right, I'll meet you there, and you better show up. And try not to get plastered on the way, okay?"

"Yes, Mommy. Oh, one other thing. Ian wrote me that medicines are hard to get there. He asked if you wouldn't mind bringing whatever you could round up."

"Was he specific about what types? That's a pretty broad order."

"I guess stuff like antibiotics, malaria medicine, and painkillers. You know, people get hurt out there in the middle of nowhere. Bring as much of it as you can find."

Paul saw nothing out of the ordinary about the request. What did he know about the availability of medicines in East Africa? "I'll call a couple of pharmacies and see what I can do, and I'll be bringing my bag with me on top of it."

"Thanks, *Bwana*. I guess I'll see you at the airport. I'm so excited I could pee in my pants."

"Just make sure you get there."

"I'll be there, all right. I wouldn't miss it for the world. Bye."

It had been a long time since Paul had any contact with pharmacies, and when he rang a few, the druggist was surprised to hear from him. After some small talk, he explained the situation, and the druggists were more than accommodating. All Paul had to do was go get what he needed.

He spent the rest of the morning organizing his baggage and double-checking everything to make sure it was all there. He then made the rounds of the drug stores and was able to amass a cache of anti-parasite, antibiotic, gastrointestinal, and cardiac drugs. He also secured a large quantity of oral and injectable narcotic pain medications.

As Sheldon toted the luggage to the car, Paul sat in the kitchen and gobbled down a sandwich that Clorese had made for him. He was dressed in one of his new khaki safari outfits. If nothing else he looked the part of the Great White Hunter, replete with cartridge loops, button-down pockets, ankle boots, and a tan fedora. He knew the attire was sure to draw looks at the airport and welcomed the opportunity to explain that he was on safari, should anyone inquire. He wished he could strut into the airport with a double-barrel rifle over his shoulder. The garb had the desired effect on Clorese, who said, "Young man, you look powerful handsome in that getup. Why, I 'spect an elephant to come bustin' through that wall and knock that can of pop right out yo hand."

Paul laughed. He loved Clorese's wit, and more than a cook and housekeeper, she had also been a surrogate parent, one who'd taken exceptionally good care of him over the years. He loved and respected her and was going to miss her. "Aunt Clorese, look after Sheldon while I'm gone, and please don't worry about me, all right?"

"Mr. Paul, I be wishin' you wouldn't go on this trip. I'm scared some-thin' awful's gonna come yo way."

"Naw. I'll be just fine. People do this sort of thing all the time."

"We had enough trag'dy in this he'a house. We don't need no mo'."

"I'll bring you back something real nice from Africa," he promised, ma-neuvering his way out of the kitchen.

"All I wants is yo skinny butt back he'a."

"I've put several hundred dollars in the desk in Cap's study. Use it for whatever you need. All the bills are paid in advance, so you shouldn't have to worry about that. The lawyer knows I'm going to be gone; if you have any problems, call him first. His number is written on a sheet of paper on the desk, and I've asked Doctor Williams to check on things from time to time. I'll try to write, but I doubt there'll be much postal service where we're go-ing." He gave Clorese a big hug and felt a lump in his throat.

"Yo Aunt Clorese gonna worry about you every second. You know dat?"

"I know, and I'll be thinking about you too. You're the only family I've got left."

"Well go on now, befo' I breaks down and cries."

The setter, Patty, was lying on the floor next to Cap's favorite chair. Paul squatted and stroked the smooth soft hair. "Bye-bye, old gal," he muttered as he kissed the little crested part of her head. "It's going to be a while before you see me again, so stay out of trouble and please don't die while I'm gone."

Looking at Paul with sleepy eyes, the dog sighed and sprawled back out on the floor.

Taking a long look around, Paul picked up his day bag and shotgun case and left.

The heat and humidity were oppressive as Paul traveled along the muggy stretch of US1 leading to the international airport in Miami. The auto swept past nebulous patches of tar- smelling steam that arose from the pavement. The interior of the windshield was covered in droplets of condensation that Paul repeatedly tried in vain to remove. Beads of sweat ran down every available stretch of exposed skin, and his damp clothes stuck to the rest of him. He cursed himself for not wearing something lousy that he could throw away when he got to Miami, and then he thought of enduring the damp, stinking garments all the way to New York, which was the first leg of the trip, and resolved to change clothes at the airport.

Apparently unaffected by the weather, Sheldon seemed far away in thought as the scenery passed before him.

When Sheldon approached the town of Pompano Beach, the traffic slowed for what appeared to be an auto accident. Once abreast of the activity, they saw two badly damaged cars at an intersection. A woman holding a bloody towel to her head was sitting on the curb, and several people were attending to her. Next to her was a young girl lying down as others helped her. There were no official vehicles on the scene yet, and Sheldon fully expected Paul to pull over and act like a doctor, as he always had in the past. "Ain't you going to stop and help dem folks?"

Paul was in turmoil. As a physician he was compelled to render care without hesitation, but after Cap's death he'd lost his confidence and his passion. It had been a year since he'd had anything to do with medicine. He knew Cap would've berated him for leaving the scene, but he couldn't bring himself to respond. He looked at his watch and told Sheldon, "I don't have the time to stop." It was a lie. He had more than enough time to take a few minutes and assist. He squirmed in his seat and glanced back at the wrecked cars, and self-disgust engulfed him. The look of disappointment Sheldon gave him didn't help either. "I've got to get to the airport, or I'm going to miss my flight," he declared, grateful for the shielding effect of his sunglasses.

They drove on in silence. Paul lit one cigarette with another, and Sheldon looked out the window. Finally Paul said, "I want you and Clorese to stay around the house as much as possible. With all the civil rights business going on, I don't want you crossing paths with any of those cracker boys in town."

Cap had warned Paul several years back that "the colored folks are getting tired of being crapped on and aren't going to stand for it much longer. Once they start to fight back, all hell's going to break loose." He'd been on target. The tension had been rising steadily since Eisenhower called in the Arkansas National Guard the previous September.

Florida, with its large population of more liberal-minded northern transplants, enjoyed less racial tension than the Deep South but was still plenty itching for a lynching.

"Don't you fret none about ole Sheldon crossin' path with no white boys."

Drenched with sweat, Paul pulled off the road at the airport and changed into a clean safari shirt.

At the airport the porter piled the gun cases and bags on a trolley as the two friends stood facing each other, neither knowing how to say goodbye.

Paul was the first to speak. "I'm going miss having you look after me. I know you've been worried about me since Cap died, and you aren't happy about me going on this trip, but I have to get out of here for a while."

"I know you been sufferin'. You can't turn back time, so if this trip gonna help you get yo head back right, den dat what you gotta do."

"I'm glad you understand. You just make sure you're still around when I return."

Smiling at each other, they shook hands and went their separate ways.

At the airline counter Paul was afraid the international laws would prohibit him from carrying his shotgun aboard the plane and was braced for a fight, since he wasn't about to let the exquisite belonging out of his sight. The polite British-speaking attendant assured him that he was welcome to carry all the gun cases aboard with him if he wanted to.

Since his plane was not scheduled to board for more than an hour, Paul occupied himself by chatting with the amiable woman at the counter. She appeared impressed when he revealed that he was going lion and elephant hunting in Tanganyika. His safari outfit, combined with his newly acquired knowledge from a few books and travel brochures, gave him the appearance of a seasoned African big-game hunter. He supported the masquerade until he turned to leave, revealing a price tag hanging from his shirt collar.

The attendant chuckled as he walked away. "Silly Yank," she mumbled.

Paul walked to the Pan American Airlines building that had served as the airport's main terminal since 1928. The concrete-domed building had enjoyed the distinction of being the first passenger-only facility built in the United States. For many years it had served as the Customs, Immigration, and Public Health Center for departing and arriving passengers. The airy, spacious structure would soon be replaced by a larger modern facility being constructed at the end of the airport, which was unfortunate, since the original building was rich in aviation history. Pioneers such as Lindbergh, Rickenbacker, and Earnhardt had all, at one time or another, passed through its doors.

Outside there was a bustle of activity around a four-engine Eastern Airlines Douglas DC 7. A uniformed man moved from engine to engine carrying a short ladder he stood on to check the propellers and motor components. Another stood on the wing, filling the fuel tanks through a large-diameter hose. Several baggage handlers loaded the storage compartments with cargo from a pull cart. Paul recognized his other gun cases and hoped they'd arrive in Africa with him. He reached down to touch his shotgun case to verify its whereabouts.

An Eastern Airlines Lockheed Constellation roared overhead as it made its approach to the runway. He looked up to see its silver fuselage glisten in the sunlight. It reminded him of the pride he'd felt when during the war the ground shook as waves of military aircraft, including B-17 bombers, rumbled across the sky on their way from Morrison Army Air Field in Palm Beach to bases across Europe. Cap was always moved by the scene and would remove his hat as the squadrons of planes and their crews passed. He knew many of those brave men would never live to see the sunny beaches of Florida again. The spectacle was repeated again in 1951 when more than twenty thousand airmen trained at the same facility—now renamed the

Palm Beach Air Force Base—and then departed for Korea, a less glamorous but nonetheless honorably fought war.

Paul felt a jerk on his collar and turned to see Frank standing there holding the tag by the string.

"Very swanky, *bwana*," he said, glancing at the label.

Judging from his glassy-eyed expression, Paul instantly knew Frank had been drinking. He also noticed to his dismay that Frank was wearing exactly the same outfit, making the two of them resemble a pair of alligator wrestlers from a local Everglades tourist attraction.

"I can't say I'm not happy to see you," Paul remarked, "but did you really have to wear that?"

"How was I supposed to know you'd be in the same thing?" Frank said, pulling up a chair and sitting down at the table. He opened up a small suitcase and pulled out a bottle of beer and an opener.

"Emergency rations," he explained, grinning and shrugging.

"I hope you're going to get this out of you system now, so you don't get over there and make a jackass out of yourself."

"Don't you worry about me, Skippy. Attend to your own ass, and I'll take care of mine."

"Hey, Frank, let's not get this trip off on the wrong foot. I couldn't care less if you drink by the barrel. I'm just saying that there's a time and place for it, and standing forty feet from a charging rhino probably isn't one of them."

Frank didn't respond, and they both focused on the noisy Lockheed Constellation as she taxied up to the Eastern Airlines building and then shut her engines down.

"I've got it," Frank said. "We'll just tell everyone we're scientists from *National Geographic* and they make us wear these clothes."

"That'll work just fine until someone asks you where Borneo is, and you tell them it's in France."

"I'm gonna have to stomp your face before this trip's over. I can see that now."

The cabin interior was an oven when they took their seats directly in front of a young mother with two toddlers. The older, a boy, announced that he just made a poo-poo, which was already glaringly self-evident.

Paul made sure the leather gun case was in full view at his feet. He was wearing his second sweat-soaked shirt, and his undershorts were damp and bunching up in the wrong places. He concluded that the journey was going to be long and arduous.

"Well, buddy boy, here's to the trip of a lifetime," Frank said as the plane roared off the runway. "I may still wind up having to pound you into the ground, but I'm really glad you decided to come."

Paul glanced out the window and got a view of downtown Miami and farther out, Biscayne Bay with its painted shallows and lighter-colored channels. He could see the island chain stretching along the easternmost edge of the bay, and it took him back to one of the trips they made in Cap's boat. "Look, Frank, it's Elliot Key. Remember that trip we made there with Cap?"

Frank strained to see out of the window and was able to catch a glance before the stretch of islands passed behind his view. "Yeah, and all the lobster and the bonefishing. What a place!"

∽⃝   ⃝∾

Paul read an article in *Time Magazine* about Nikita Khrushchev, whom the periodical had honored as Man of The Year and wondered why the publication had chosen him above all others. The Russian president was vehemently committed to the nuclear annihilation the United States and probably would have proceeded with his plan, if he thought he could have pulled it off. Paul judged that perhaps Lunatic of the Year might have been more appropriate.

The pilot announced the descent into Idlewild Airport in New York, and after a short layover, the two men boarded a BOAC Britannia for the flight across the Atlantic.

Again the men were seated in the rear of the plane, away from the four noisy jet-prop engines; however, on this flight their attendant was a creamy-skinned freckled British woman who, by means of her airy, British accent, conjured romantic scenarios in Paul's mind.

For Frank, though, she represented nothing more than another conquest, and he resolved to deal with her at a later time.

Departing New York the two were already feeling the effects of travel. The combination of tobacco smoke, noise, and generalized discomfort made sleep impossible. Frank did what he knew best, which was to ingest alcohol and speculate about the trip.

In desperation, Paul tried Frank's method of sedation, but succeeded in only getting tipsy and inducing a whopping case of heartburn.

During the night as the stewardess was making her rounds, Frank caught her attention and motioned the woman over. She stooped, placing her ear within whispering distance of him.

"Hi, gorgeous. Do you think this tin can has a bed for both of us anywhere?"

Paul was appalled by Frank's comment and turned away in embarrassment, fully expecting the woman to either slap his hunting buddy across the face or worse, report him to the captain.

The woman, having previous experience with passengers of this type, just smiled and proceeded down the aisle.

"Why do you do that?" Paul asked in disgust.

Frank responded, grinning, "I don't give a shit whether they say yes or they say no. It's a game of numbers, plain and simple."

"I could never talk to a woman like that."

"And remind me again, when was it you got laid the last time?"

"You don't really want to know."

"Exactly my point."

Between the change to another Britannia at London's Airport North, Frank dedicated his time to sampling the ambiance and refreshments of a British pub while Paul purchased some imported chocolate and then the men were back in the air for the next leg of the flight. The pair was exhausted, slovenly, and regretting ever having set foot on the boarding ramp in Miami.

CHAPTER SEVEN

Second Thoughts

Frank slapped Paul awake, rousing him from badly needed sleep. "Hey look! It's Kilimanjaro."

Paul had just managed to drop off. His mouth tasted rank, and he knew his breath reeked. He gazed through the window and laid his head along the glass to look out. "I think that's Mount Kenya," he told Frank. "Kilimanjaro's farther south,"

"Are you sure? It looks just like the pictures."

"It doesn't look anything like the pictures, and besides, Mount Kenya's north of Nairobi, and Kilimanjaro's a hundred and fifty miles south of it. Unless the pilot's bringing us here by way of South Africa, there's no way we could see it yet. Here, I'll prove it to you." Paul got the attention of the stewardess who was working in the cabin.

"How can I be of service to you?"

"That mountain up ahead—"

"It's Mount Kenya, sir. Kilimanjaro's about three hundred fifty kilometers south. How did I know that's what you were going to ask? Because I must answer that question about ten times each trip."

"Thank you, and could you please get me some juice?"

"I'll have some juice too," said Frank, "and please spike it with vodka,"

"Straight away, fellows," she said, retreating to the galley.

The men had been in transit for about twenty-two hours. Paul was sporting the stubble of a beard and was considering growing a full one. Frank had freshened up and shaved during a visit to the lavatory. They were sleep deprived, crumpled, and grimy.

Thousands of feet below them stretched the Great Rift Valley, a monstrous fracture in the earth crust extending from Northeast Ethiopia down through Kenya, Tanganyika, and on into Mozambique, terminating in the Indian Ocean. The geological scar represented the cataclysmic migration of continental-sized plates formed tens of millions of years earlier. At the point of the fracture, the earth's crust, thinner and weaker than adjacent landmasses, was unable to resist the upwelling of molten rock from the planet core and bulged up, forming a dome. Similar to a loaf of baking bread, the outermost layer became inflexible to the expansive forces below and tore open, releasing pent-up energy. The absence of land volume at the expanding fissure resulted in a depression, a void that gives the impression that a trench had been gouged throughout the extent of the rift. The dynamic shift in the earth's integument also resulted in volcanic activity, with the resulting formation of Mount Kilimanjaro and Mount Kenya. For millennia the unusual topography of the expanse gave way to genetic diversity found nowhere else on earth. With a multitude of species vying to occupy the same environment, the Great Rift Valley became a region of constant unrelenting struggle, the latest being a native uprising against the British colonizers.

The gouged earth reminded Frank of his business and the mess he left back home and how happy he was to be clear of it. The thought came to him that it wouldn't be so bad to die over here. At least he'd be free of deadlines, bills, and loneliness. Anyhow, he pondered, for the next six weeks his predicament in Palm Beach would just have to fester. As far as he was concerned, Florida was as far away as the moon.

The plane suddenly shook and bounced when the pilot lowered the landing gear and deployed the wing flaps. The stewardesses made one last pass to ensure the cabin was in order for landing. The engines accelerated, slowed, and then accelerated again before slowing a final time. The sparse vegetated ground swept swiftly by as it rose to meet the plane. The two Americans stared ahead, lost in thought. For a moment they both felt alone and desolate. With the soil of Africa only a few feet beneath them, they recognized they had no real idea why they were there.

The aircraft slammed onto the ground at Kenya's Embagazi Airport, the landing, obviously less than the high point of the captain's career. As the plane decelerated, Paul wondered if the aircraft used the braking mechanism Cap had designed years earlier. The notion that the flight could have been initiated, paid for, and brought to a safe termination by circumstances centered around the old man struck him as cruelly ironic.

Frank watched as some shabbily dressed Africans pushed the boarding ladder up to the plane. For some reason they looked fiercer to him than the colored people back home. Perhaps it was because this was their country, and he was the outsider now.

The cabin became a hive of activity as passengers collected their personal effects and advanced toward the exit. Paul smiled and nodded at the captain who leaned wearily against the cockpit door. His apathetic expression seemed to suggest a longing for the glory days in the RAF, where he most likely piloted Spitfires or Lancaster bombers for the honor of king and country.

"Welcome to Kenya, and thank you for allowing BOAC to serve you. Please enjoy your time in East Africa," said the grinning stewardess as the two men debarked.

Squinting as their eyes reacted to the intense equatorial sun, they stepped onto the tarmac, setting foot on the Dark Continent for the first time.

CHAPTER EIGHT

A Change in Plans

"What now?" Paul asked, looking around for direction.

"I don't know," said Frank. "I guess we follow the rest of these folks."

Frank couldn't help noticing the African women, with their handsome features.

"You see Ian Sharpe anywhere?" Paul asked.

"I don't know what the hell he looks like."

"Didn't he give you a description?"

"He said I'd know it when I saw him."

"Well?"

"I don't see him."

Following the others into the building and getting in line, the two men scanned the large open room for what they had preconceived would be a larger-than-life figure of white hunter manliness. All they could see were uniformed British officers, black Africans in bright-colored native outfits, passengers, and airline staff.

"The least this guy could do was be here to meet us," Paul said, struggling to keep his exasperation in check.

"We've been here for only five minutes, Skip. Don't start comin' unglued."

"I'm sorry. It just pisses me off that were stuck—"

A British voice from behind Paul said, "Begging your pardon, young sirs—"

Wheeling around, Paul confronted a short, weather-beaten man in his mid-fifties, thin and sinewy. His fervid green eyes were alive with mischief. Brown hair sweat-pasted to his head bore witness to countless hours spent under the broad-brimmed hat clutched in his left hand. Fresh scratches and bandages traversed his cheek, neck, and right thigh, the latter visible because of the shorts he was sporting. The still-oozing crimson-stained dressings indicated recent wounds of considerable severity.

"Am I correct in assuming you're the two Americans, Eastman and Benson?"

"The name's Bennett," corrected Paul, perhaps a bit too indignantly.

"Hi. I'm Frank Eastman, and this here's Doctor Paul Bennett. Was Ian Sharpe unable to come himself?" Frank extended his hand, hoping the diplomacy of formal introduction would compensate for Paul's bad manners.

"Well, not exactly," the man said, shaking their hands with a muscular grip. "It's a pleasure to make your acquaintance."

"Would you please tell us where we could find Mister Sharpe?" Paul implored, losing what was left of his patience.

"By all means, my American friend," said the man, flopping his broad brim hat on his head. "He's standing right here under my hat."

The lean, battered, and bandaged bushwhacker with twinkling eyes was hardly what they'd expected. Paul rubbed the stubble on his face.

Frank emitted something between a groan and a sigh as he envisioned thousands of dollars, his last, flying south for the winter. "This must be some kind of joke between you locals, isn't it?" he asked.

"Not a bit of it. I can assure you that I'm none other than Ian Sharpe Esquire. No doubt you chaps were expecting your white hunter to be more of the Clarke Gable type. Do allow me to—"

Paul held up his hand to cut him off. "Mr. Sharpe, will you excuse Frank and me for a minute?" Grabbing Frank by the collar, Paul propelled him out of earshot.

The Immigration officer, who knew Ian, looked on with detached amusement.

"What the hell have you gotten us into, Frank? Will you look at him? He needs *me* a hell of a lot more than we need *him*."

"How was I supposed to know he'd turn out to be a basket case?"

"I'm getting right back on that goddamn plane and flying home."

"Hold on. Maybe he's got a plan, like one of his partners is taking over. I say we hear him out, and if it's a line of crap, we leave."

"All right, let's go hear his story. Bet you it has to do with a bar, some drunks, and some other guy's woman."

Ian was clowning around with one of the British army officers stationed at the airport. It eased Paul's mind to know that he obviously had a good rapport with the authorities.

Seeing the men approach, Ian turned and gave them his full attention.

"We'd like to hear your plans, Ian," Frank said, "and we'll decide where to go from there."

"Splendid. I'm sure you'll find the arrangements quite suitable for a most delightful trip."

"What happened to you anyway?" Paul ventured. "Bar-room brawl?"

"No, unfortunately. Had a bit of a row with a rather nasty *chui*."

"Yes, it looks like you've been chewied up, all right," Paul said.

"A *chui* is a leopard, and this particular one took a dislike to having it guts strewn across the bush by a very wretched German marksman. Piss-poor shot he was. Wounded every bloody animal he laid sights to. Anyhow, I had to go into the scrub at dusk to offer my apologies and to cancel the *chui's* plans for any future romance. It's considered bad sportsmanship to leave a wounded animal in the bush, and it makes for a dangerous condition. The next hapless native who strolls by is as good as assured of being attacked." He paused to let that information sink in for a moment before continuing.

"As you can see, the kitty had different ideas, and if it hadn't been for my gun barer, Mchana, God bless his brave soul, I'd be part of Kenya's past."

Impressed by the hunter's nonchalant bravado, Frank inquired, "What did the gunbearer do?"

"Drove a *panga*—that's a knife—into its spine, paralyzing the bloody cat right on the spot.

"Pretty brave guy, huh?" Paul observed.

"Absolutely dauntless. You'll meet him soon; that is, assuming you don't run out on me." Eyeing them for visual clues, Ian added, "Obviously, I got shredded in the rumpus, so I'm out as far as functioning as your P.H.—professional hunter, that is."

"Where does that leave us?" Frank asked.

"Our newest partner is going to handle the safari. I'll be along to attend to minor details. I could use a vacation anyway. Been at it rather stiffly for quite some time."

"And how long has this newest partner been around the business, if you don't mind my asking?" Paul said.

"Let's see . . . twenty-four years, if my memory is correct, and quite a capable P.H., I might add. I'm sure you will be pleased."

"And you'll be along the whole time?"

"Unless these stitches fail and my innards fall out." Ian patted the gauze bandage on his waist.

"Well, Skip," Frank said, "what do you think?"

"It isn't what we'd agreed on, but I guess I'll go with it."

"There then," declared Ian, slapping his hands together. "Let's fetch your belongings and check you through Immigration. Then we'll deposit you at the Norfolk, so you can freshen up a bit before joining me at the local bar for a *gin-i* or two."

Frank liked the sound of that information. He had been craving a drink nonstop throughout the entire exasperating junket. He was starting to enjoy Ian Sharpe's company.

To Frank and Paul's surprise, all their luggage had followed them around the world, and there was little difficulty at Immigration. The only problem arose when the officer asked if either of them wished to declare anything, and Paul said, "I'd love to kill Frank for dragging me to this godforsaken place."

Although Frank was amused, the officer wasn't. Paul had to apologize to the punctilious government agent or risk getting arrested for the cache of drugs in his possession. In addition to making amends for his wisecrack, he pointed to Ian's obvious injuries and flashed his medical license, removing any doubt that he was acting in any other than a professional capacity.

The baggage was piled high in the back of Ian's dilapidated Land Rover, the top of which had been cut away, allowing an open view in all directions. It had a standing gun rack behind the front passenger's seat. Rust, dings, bent metal, welded sections, and an absence of uniform color anywhere along its veneer attested to the vehicle's long service in the rugged African interior.

Ian grimaced in pain as he ascended the two-foot rise to reach the cutaway at the driver's position of the old junker. He resolved to make the best of it, but said it would be a "damned painful safari" for him.

Paul, who knew a thing or two about the severity of abdominal wounds, said, "Are you sure you're up to this, Ian?"

"I was just wondering the same thing myself. It'll be a damned painful safari for me, but not to worry. I'll be tagging along regardless. Now climb in the old gal, and let us nip off and get a drink."

The engine cranked right up, and despite a little heavy smoking, it purred like a cat. Ian engaged the clutch and shifted into gear, each movement provoking another agonizing stab of pain. "A thousand curses on that kraut bastard who did this to me," he grumbled, pulling onto the road.

Because of the Rover's rugged suspension, the ride to the hotel was bone jarring. The two Americans couldn't imagine having to spend all day in the transport, let alone six weeks. Ian, they realized, must have been suffering miserably with every bump, but was still chatty and amiable. At the risk of unduly alarming them, he explained the state of emergency that Kenya had been under since 1952 in response to the native guerilla war for independence known as the Mau Mau Uprising. Numerous colonists had been murdered, and scores of Kikuyu had been killed or imprisoned. Ian had seen it happening, having lived in Kenya for more than fifty years.

Their substitute P.H., Ian explained, was tied up at the moment in Magadi, where a rogue elephant had raided a village, or *shamba*, destroying the Africans' crops and had to be "dispatched," as he put it. In such unfortunate but not uncommon predicaments, the game commission called upon the professional hunting community for help, meaning a well-placed bullet to the brain.

"What will they do with the carcass?" Paul asked, trying to visualize twelve thousand pounds of dead pachyderm rotting in the field.

"The word will spread quickly, and throngs of protein-starved locals will descend on that *tumbo*—elephant—faster than a swarm of blowflies, and Bob's your uncle, there'll be little more than a skeleton for *fisi* to savor."

"*Fisi?*"

"Hyena, vile buggers, they are. You'll see. Come right into your tent at night they will, and tear your face off while you're sleeping. The Africans fear them more than *simba*—that's a lion, to you Yanks."

Ian hung around long enough to see the men registered and settled into their room at the Norfolk, the stately colonial establishment that had been part of Kenya's landscape since 1905, accommodating royalty and commoners alike. Paul and Frank could freshen up, Ian suggested, and he'd meet them later and introduce them to their professional hunter.

An hour later they entered an austere downtown building, pausing at the entrance to give their eyes time to adjust to the darkness. An Indian in a fez and a cotton drill jacket stood behind a fat, heavily varnished mahogany counter. About a dozen small tables with chairs were set about haphazardly. The room was vacant except for a couple of men in khakis, one of whom motioned for Ian to come over.

"Bloody hell, *Umeme*," said a stock, balding man in his late fifties. "Didn't anyone tell you you're supposed to kill the ruddy beast *before* you try to pull him out by the tail? Come over here, you silly little man, and let's have a peek at you."

His tablemate, a tall, slender bloke of roughly the same age, rocked back in his chair, crossing his arms. A thick cigar jutted from the corner of his mouth.

"Come with me, boys," Ian said. "I'd like you to meet a couple of real legends in this business."

"What does *Umeme* mean?" Paul asked.

"Lighting," Ian replied. "I'll explain later," he added, leading them to the men's table, where he introduced them to Jeffery Cosgrove and Victor Ibotson, describing them, to their faces, as two of the biggest cowards in East Africa. "Say hello to my American hunters. They'll be with me for the next month and a half."

Prior to the trip Frank had read a story in *Life Magazine* about the venerable safari company of Cosgrove and Ibotson, depicting Jeffery and Victor as masters of the land and fearless to a fault.

"Ian, you're not going out with them so soon, are you?" Victor asked, examining Ian's blood-caked bandages. "You've got to know you're in no condition for it."

"I'm just going along for the ride. I'll keep an eye on the *campi* and such."

"And who'd you get to chaperone these fine young men, might I ask?"

"The apprentice is going to run things, with me in the wings, just to make sure all goes as planned."

"I see," said Victor, peering out of the corner of his eye at the other man. "Very well then, it ought to make for a glamorous if not productive expedition." He and his friend exchanged a smirk.

Paul caught it and felt their reaction was cause for concern.

Ian knew what Jeffery and Victor were thinking, and even though it was harmless merriment, he took offense at their patronizing demeanor. Eager to spirit his clients away from the two hunters, lest they stir up any unnecessary anxiety, he said, "If you two don't mind, I'd fancy a drink and some time to brief these chaps about the expedition."

"You Yanks listen well to your hunter," Jeffery said, "and you'll be taking some fine trophies back to America."

The pair got up and started to leave. Victor bellowed, "*Kwa heri!* That's goodbye, boys. Good luck to you. We'll be looking to see some record-book heads on your return. And Ian, give my best to *Kizuri*, will you?" He tossed some coins on the table and walked out.

"Ian, what was all that about?" Paul asked, as the three men settled at a table. "I mean, that business about our professional hunter?"

"Oh, that—it was just a bit of harmless repartee between us hunters. Nothing much to it. What will you chaps be drinking?"

"Double bourbon on ice," said Frank.

"I don't know, just some kind of beer, maybe a local one, if there's such a thing."

"*Pombe Ya Tuska*, Tusker Lager. It's made right here in Nairobi. Bloody good, if you're thirsty enough. Wait here, and I'll fetch us some." He rose from his chair like an arthritic martinet and grunted his way across the room.

When Ian was out of earshot, Frank leaned toward Paul and asked, "What do you think so far?"

"I don't know. He seems like a nice enough guy, and he must be pretty well known around here, but did you see Ibotson and Cosgrove's reaction when Ian mentioned the person who's supposed to take us hunting? Like it was some kind of joke."

"He already said they were just messing with him."

"Pretty obnoxious, if you ask me."

"Obnoxious or not, they've killed more dangerous animals than anyone still living."

"Then why aren't we going with them?" Paul asked.

"Booked solid forever, that's why. They take kings and movie actors and shit."

"I just hope for your sake that our guy isn't some kind of flunky misfit."

"I doubt he'd last long if he was. Shh, here he comes."

"Enjoy the killer of pain, boys," Ian said, handing them their drinks. "Oh, by the way, savor the ice. You won't be seeing much of it for quite a spell."

The drinks tasted good to both of them, and the idea of food came to mind. They hadn't eaten since the meal on the plane.

"What do we do about dinner tonight?" Frank asked, savoring his bourbon.

"Perhaps at the Norfolk," Ian said, "unless you just want to snack and then get some *lala*."

"*Lala*?" Paul queried.

"Sleep. You both look a tad overdone, and the morrow promises to be a full day."

"What have you got in store for us?" Frank inquired, eager to start piling up dead animals. "Will we go hunting tomorrow?"

"I don't believe we can attend to all the necessities in just one day. We'll shove off the day after. It's going to take some time to procure the proper documents and check your odds and ends to make sure nothing was left out. Then there's always the task of rounding up the boys, who should be fairly well potted by now."

Paul stiffened in his chair. "I beg your pardon?"

"You see, between trips they lounge about their *bomas*—that's homes— drinking vile-tasting booze called *pombe* that their wives make. It renders them senseless, and it usually takes several days in the bush to undo the effects."

As Ian spoke Paul saw the dark silhouette of a woman against the intense sunlight at the entrance of the bar. She hesitated for a moment and then removed her broad-brimmed hat and brushed off the dust that formed a hazy cloud in the streaming light.

"We'll need to get you over to the bank so you can exchange . . ."

Ian continued speaking, but Paul was too distracted to listen. His gaze was fixed on the young woman, who'd picked up a glass of sherry from the bar and was making her way toward the table.

Frank had also noticed her by then, and both men drew in their collective breaths as she neared. Enjoying the show, Ian pretended not to notice the woman until she was at his side. Frank and Paul were bewitched.

"Hello, Daddy," she said, bending and kissing Ian on the cheek. "How are you feeling?"

"Hi, Kizuri. I'm fine, sweetheart." Turning to Paul and Frank, he said, "I call her Kizuri because it means beautiful in Swahili. Boys, say hello to our company's newest hunter, who also happens to be my daughter, Jean."

Both the men catapulted from their seats

"Jean, I'd like you to meet Dr. Paul Bennett and Mr. Frank Eastman from America."

Both men were in the process of extending their hands when all the pieces fell into place. In an instant Paul recognized what had precipitated the peculiar response from Ibotson and Cosgrove.

"It's a pleasure to meet you," he managed to utter, trying to maintain his composure.

"Delighted to make your acquaintance," Jean Sharpe said, her voice silky and ethereal.

"Same here," Frank added, who was already seeing her as the consummate trophy of the safari. She gave him a friendly nod of acknowledgment and deliberately held her gaze until she looked, to his surprise and chagrin, back to Paul. *Well*, Frank thought, *she'll come around in time. They always do.*

CHAPTER NINE

Goddess of the Hunt

Jean Sharpe wore a loose-fitting khaki shirt tied at the waist and shorts that displayed her shapely five-foot-four-inch figure to advantage, her tan legs sculpted by firm calf and thigh muscles accustomed to hoofing across miles of rough terrain. Twigs and particles of debris were nestled in her long chestnut hair, which was gathered in back by an elastic band. Jean had her father's green eyes, but where Ian's were penetrating, hers were softly inquisitive, expressing that everything she saw was fresh and new to her. Under cheerful wisps of eyebrows, her wide blinking eyes squinted when she smiled, making it difficult not to smile back at her. When she was not talking, her upper lip parted slightly higher in the middle, exposing the edges of her porcelain-white front teeth. A slight cleft in her chin was the terminus of the smoothly angled jaw that intercepted her long slender neck, which was covered by an elegant, rolled-up paisley scarf.

Despite the grime and flecks of what appeared to be dried blood on her face, her skin radiated health, and there was a hint of freckles on her delicate pointy nose. She was, by anyone's standard, a knockout.

Paul was in a quandary. He felt like reaching across the table, pulling Ian up by his collar, and screaming, "Are you out of your fucking mind, you crazy limey gut bag? Is this what you're planning to send us into the jungle with?" But there wasn't any way in the world he was going to make a fuss in front of that goddess. All he could do was smile and pull her chair out for her.

"Thank you so much, *Doktari* Bennett," she breathed.

"Call me Paul, please," he heard himself say as he fantasized about saving her from a charging lion.

Frank was too taken aback to speak, his mind occupied with fantasies of animalistic lust immediately following his saving her from a charging lion.

Ian broke the silence first. "Well, Kuzuri, how did it go in Magadi?"

"Oh, it was the same dreadful story. Elephants! The old *tumbo* bachelor was eating up everything in sight, and what didn't get consumed was trampled into the ground. He just couldn't stay away from the *shamba,* so I walloped him with the four-fifty, and that was the end of it. Nice ivory too, sixty-eight and seventy pounds. One of the *shamba mtotos,* a child of about seven, got a nasty cut on his arm when the *pangas* hacked up the carcass. I drove him and his father to the mission *daktari* at Kajiado. If the cut doesn't become infected, I expect he'll be fine in no time."

Frank was swelling with passion to the bursting point. Not only did the woman excite him, but she also routinely shot elephants as though they were barnyard rodents. *My kind of broad*, he thought.

"Speaking of infections," she said, shifting to a solicitous tone. "When was the last time you changed those bandages, Daddy? They look simply awful."

"I was just going to ask the *daktari* here if he wouldn't mind having a peek at them."

Paul, who no longer thought of himself as a doctor, wanted no part of it, but Ian persisted, saying, "Would you mind?"

Paul replied, "I'd be glad to." He was lying. Doctoring had brought him grief and despair, but hoping it would win him points with the lovely girl he'd just met, he agreed to examine Ian.

Jean fixed him with a look of warm gratitude. In fact she was beginning to take both Paul and Frank as two nice-looking men who were close to her own age. Many of the company's prior clients were typically wrinkled old windbags with overinflated midsections and overinflated opinions of their masculinity, men who could be counted on to make inappropriate advances as soon as the hunting party cleared the limits of Nairobi.

Sizing up the Americans, neither of whom displayed wedding bands or indentations of where they'd been until moments earlier, she figured unwanted advances were undoubtedly forthcoming, but if they did occur, at least they wouldn't be from fat, pasty, balding, philandering rich businessmen.

"We were just discussing tomorrow's plans," Ian told her. "I'm hoping to finish preparations and shove off early the next morning. Your thought, honey?"

"I would think that a reasonable goal. I'll gather up the boys except for Mchana and Jua. They're a little too high-strung for me, so you'd better see to them. The lorry's been fitted with a new axle and should be ready."

Jean was referring to the 2.5-ton army surplus transport truck used for hauling equipment to set up makeshift living quarters wherever they chose to camp. Large enough to carry an ungodly array of materials—everything from welding tanks and spare parts for repairs to china dishes and table-cloths—the truck was an unwieldy, unpredictable relic from the Second World War.

"Barring the unforeseen, we could be prepared in a day," she added.

"What do you folks usually bring along to drink?" asked Frank, examining his near empty glass.

Ian eyed him suspiciously and then glanced at his daughter. They both knew what it meant when the first question a client asked before departing for weeks in the bush was how much booze was aboard.

"We'll bring whatever you'd like," Ian said. "Several villages en route have fairly stocked general stores, called *dukas*, should we need additional supplies." Ian realized he was going to have to watch that guy closely.

"I hate to be rude," Paul said, "but I think I'd better bow out of dinner and hit the sack. The beer's made me groggy. I hope you don't mind."

"Don't give it a thought, "Jean said. "I understand. How about you Frank?"

"I'm raring to go whenever you are," he answered, delighted to get the jump on his friend.

You sneaky bastard, Paul thought.

When Frank staggered in that night, waking Paul up, he was ambiguous about his dinner with the Sharpes. Paul reminded himself that their purpose in coming to Africa was big-game hunting, but the rules of engagement were evolving quickly. He felt a creeping sense of unease.

Frank felt the same. Although he and Jean Sharpe hadn't clicked—she'd proved completely impervious to the cool swaggering ways that reduced most women to putty in his hands—he remained convinced that he'd eventually prevail.

The following day Ian helped Paul and Frank make stops at the bank, game commissioner's office, and clothing-makers' shops, Ian having inspected their wardrobes and singled out safari garb that would be better, locally made. The Americans were skeptical about receiving their finished products in the agreed upon time and were flabbergasted when, just hours later, their garments were ready and waiting.

Paul's cursory medical examination of Ian, performed in the hotel room, was not reassuring. Ian displayed early signs of systemic infection; he was flushed and seemed to be favoring his left side. Paul felt certain he'd caught a whiff of what may have been sepsis. As reluctant as he was to become involved, he felt a professional obligation at least check to Ian's wounds.

Although Ian denied any increase in discomfort, assuring Paul that all had looked well when he'd changed the dressings that morning, he relented and allowed the doctor to administer an injection of penicillin, "to be on the safe side and to keep *Zuri* off my back."

He was proving to be a tough, likeable little banshee, Paul thought, handing him a bottle of antibiotic tablets. Ian then left to track down Jua and Mchana at their *bomas*, instructing Paul and Frank to be ready for an early-morning departure.

Frank and Paul had trouble getting to sleep that night and lay awake talking about hunting, what they'd seen in Nairobi so far, and Ian Sharpe. They didn't mention the girl, but neither Paul nor Frank had been able to shake her from his mind.

It was dawn when the hotel phone rang, and Ian's familiar voice informed Frank that the safari was leaving within the hour, "with or without your pathetic Yankee arses."

Frank thanked him for the wake-up call and hung up, grateful to be rescued from a dream in which he was being court-martialed for dereliction of duty, having failed to service the army bulldozers properly. Frank had served in the army as a heavy equipment mechanic during the Korean War and had performed in an honorable manner, taking his duties seriously and doing the best job he could until his discharge at war's end. Pondering the connection between the nightmare and his business setbacks in Florida, he dressed and joined the others outside.

The hunting party, *their* hunting party, stood waiting as Frank and Paul passed through the doors of the hotel. What a sight it was! The Land Rover was parked in front of a large truck heaped with equipment lashed down under a canvas tarp. Black Africans in wildly varied garb, ranging from ragged threadbare jumpsuits to aboriginal thongs, bustled about in the chill morning air, jabbering in their native tongue. The exotic scene was made even more inviting by the sight of Jean wearing shorts and a bomber jacket, shouting instructions in Swahili. Paul and Frank shivered from the combination of brisk morning air, anticipation, and the image of her.

"Good morning, *bwanas*," she said. "I trust you've had a restful sleep. Would you like me to take that case for you, Paul?"

"Please, but I'd like to keep it close by. It means a lot to me."

"Certainly. I'll just set it in the Rover right here. Come, let us meet the boys."

"Where's your dad?" Frank asked.

"Over there in the *campi* chair. I'm afraid his malaria's acting up something fierce this morning. I pleaded with him to stay behind, but the old stubborn *Bwana* Lightning would have no part of it."

As much as Paul and Frank would have preferred spending the next month and a half in her company without "Daddy" present, good judgment told them, like it or not, Ian was an indispensable asset.

"Wait here for a moment," she said. "I want to have a peek at him, and then we'll meet the boys." She walked over to Ian and knelt beside him.

"You look simply dreadful. Can't we stay in town another day, until you feel a little better?"

"These chaps should be fairly well ready to get on with it, and I don't want to be the one who holds things up."

Still recovering from the horror and outrage over his being savaged by the leopard, she lashed out at him, his persistent disregard for self-preservation having at last pushed her too far. "Do you always have to put everyone before you yourself? Well? Do you really think they'll care if they have to wait an extra day? You know, *Bwana* Lightning, you're not a young man anymore. You know that, don't you? So when are you going to stop acting like a child and give up trying to be such a blasted hero to everyone, you stubborn baboon?"

Ian was embarrassed for the Americans, who had suddenly become intrigued by the local flora a discreet distance away. He tried to diminish the damage to his position, lest they think him as a browbeaten, submissive has-been, cowering from his daughter's fury. "*Kumbe*, my little viper," he commented.

"Yes, that is *so*, Daddy."

"You know what the unwritten rules are that govern this trade, so cut the sermon," he said, using a modicum of restraint. "I'm coming because this is what I do. This is what *we* do. Sure, I'd love to lounge around Nairobi for a while, and maybe that's where I belong, but these fine young men took weeks out of their busy schedules and flew halfway around the world for us. And do you know why? Because I told them to. I promised I'd take them on safari, and whether or not I feel up to it, I bloody well plan to do just that. Now let's get moving, and not another word about it. Here, give us a hand getting out of this *kiti*," he appealed, struggling to wrest himself from the chair.

Jean knew he was right. On several occasions she'd undertaken safaris when a stay at the clinic would have been more appropriate. It was the fear of losing her father that frightened her so. He'd always been there to watch over her. She could not conceive of a world without him.

"Let's get these savages out of here before they try to sneak back to their wives and girlfriends," Ian said, kissing Jean's forehead and patting her bottom. *Njooni upesi*. Come soon," he yelled, clapping his hands, which spurred the ten or so black Africans to gather around at once. *Utakutana na Bwana* Eastman *na Daktari* Bennett. You will meet Mr. Eastman and Dr. Bennett." The introduction was succeeded by protracted handshakes, toothy smiles, a fusillade of *jambos*. The Africans seemed friendly enough and happy to be participating, not only for the income, but also for the chance to escape the monotony of village life. In addition each would enjoy a staple of meat, which was sorely lacking in their diet.

Feeling better after the morning's bout of malaria, Ian went down the line introducing each member, beginning with Mchana and Susani, the gun-bearers, who held the most prestigious positions and were therefore viewed as superiors by white hunters and fellow natives alike. Ian and Mchana reminisced briefly about the accident that had nearly taken Ian's life—Mchana had witnessed it—and the dangers of safari life.

Glancing up and down the line, Ian told Paul, Frank, and Jean, "I love these people for their singleness-of-purpose attitude. To them death is a natural process that they tolerate without trepidation. It never entered this boy's mind," he said, staring into Mchana's eyes, "to retreat from the *chui*, the leopard that did this to me, or to try to save his own skin. Kill the leopard . . . period. Never stop to wonder if you might be mauled or die, just act on absolute pure instinct."

Mchana stood rigidly, staring straight ahead, betraying neither pride nor embarrassment. Although his English was spotty, he sensed the gist of Ian's praise. The gunbearer's reaction was characteristic of his race. While the white man would have expected gratitude for saving someone's life, the stone-faced Turkana tribesman felt he was simply carrying out his duties.

The other bearer, Susani, a native from the Luo tribe, seemed poised and ready to get on with the hunt. His smile revealed a gap of missing teeth—the traditional Luo alternative to circumcision. Several necklaces of hippo teeth and python bones contrasted with his tattered shorts and shirt. His tribe, located around Lake Victoria, had the mixed blessing of sickle-cell anemia, which, while making tribe members less able to sustain vigorous physical activity, also conferred on them a level of immunity to malaria. Next was Jua, a tall, slender, stone-faced Maasai who served as the outfit's game tracker.

During the introductions, Paul's attention was drawn to another member of the group, the cook, Kemoa, whose kind, watery eyes reminded Paul of Sheldon. Indeed, the resemblance was too remarkable to be merely happenstance. Apart from some grotesque scarring on his face, Kemoa was such an uncanny reflection of Sheldon that Paul's spine tingled with intuition that he was in the presence of Sheldon's immediate descendant, and he could almost palpate the bond taking shape between Kemoa and himself. Suddenly overcome by a sense of homesickness and sadness, Paul hoped everything was okay with Sheldon and Clorese and vowed to drop them a letter. Thoughts of Cap came to mind as well, sparking a resurgence of grief, but it had become less painful over time.

Jean, who'd been quietly following Ian's briefing, noticed Paul's interest in Kemoa, who was her favorite camp servant. She always let her father make the introductions, since she was uneasy around the natives and didn't want to expose her anxiety to the new clients. Nervously rearranging her neckerchief, she asked Paul in her soft, caring voice if something was wrong. He told her he was thinking of a black friend back home.

"Is this person close to you?"

"You could say so. He's sort of an extended family member. I mean, him and his wife. Sheldon's the caretaker; Clorese cooks and does the house-work. They raised me." Paul looked back at Kemoa. "The resemblance is incredible. They could be brothers."

"Perhaps they're related by a common ancestor."

"That's what I was wondering."

"Anyhow, I'm sure you and Frank are going to find him to be an excep-tionally good cook. What he can assemble in the bush—well, you'll just have to see for yourself."

Ian was preparing to launch into the attributes of his Dorobo tracker, Jua, when an unkempt, exceedingly drunk native, Nyeusi, staggered around the back of the truck. Ian had given up trying to find him the day before, reckoning the safari would have to do without him. Since Nyeusi's posi-tion as a common camp hand made him expendable, his absence wouldn't have been missed. Now here he was, filthy and teetering from the effects of homemade beer, and Ian scrambled for an exit from the latest snarl, decid-ing humor was his best recourse.

Jean covered her eyes with her hand in a mixture of chagrin and amusement.

"We can be off now," Ian said, "Our driver, Nyeusi, is here."

Two American heads ratcheted, and Jean said, "Daddy! Grow up, will you?"

Before Ian could reply, the intoxicated African beamed a long-toothed grin, belched up a slaver of gray liquid, and collapsed backward, causing his countrymen to cackle with laughter.

Paul made a move toward him, but Ian cut him off.

"Let the bloody devil lay there. The boys will attend to him." He threw his hands in the air. "*Nifanye nini?* What am I to do?"

Once the two *bwanas* were introduced to the rest of the troop, Ian, eager to get going before something else happened, issued the order for everyone to climb aboard for immediate departure. The Africans heaved Nyeusi atop the supply lorry's canvas tarp and climbed aboard, settling anywhere they could find room. Reli, the driver, took the steering wheel and fired up the sputtering ignition.

Grunting and groaning, Ian was ushered by Jean into the back seat of the Rover, where he sat down next to Paul, who hadn't acted quickly enough to capture the front passenger seat, now occupied by the ever-slick Frank Eastman.

Ian's shirt revealed the crimson specks of sustained bleeding, but he tried to conceal them, lest Jean postpone their departure or cancel it altogether. Climbing into the right driver's side, her flaxen chestnut hair flowing from under a panama hat and spilling over the furry collar of her bomber jacket, Jean said, "You chaps ready to go collect some trophies?" She regarded them expectantly over the rims of her surplus aviator sunglasses perched atop the bridge of her gracefully thin nose.

Both Paul and Frank felt a trifle patronized by the awkward reversal of roles, with a female initiating a customarily macho hunting trip. Frank continued to sulk in silence, but for Paul, desire trumped resentment, and he yearned to hold her. He was already beginning to wonder how long he could control himself.

Before the party cleared the limits of Nairobi, Frank, fancying himself the great white hunter, was again enjoying himself, exhilarated by the running commentary of Ian, a consummate tour guide by virtue of having been born and raised in and around the provincial enclave. The route took them from the hotel in the north down through the older parts of town and out to the southwest, toward the green hills of Africa and the plains of Rift Valley. Frank twisted in his seat to face Ian, who was pointing out sights of interest and remarking on the significant characters responsible for wresting the mysterious, uncharitable land from its primitive beginnings. Ian had the good fortune of growing up during Kenya's historic heyday, when British colonials commanded absolute dominance over the native populace, a status in serious question at the current time, because of Kenya's seemingly unstoppable push toward independence from the Crown.

Jean endured the monologue, having heard it ad infinitum. Although her generation was still tied to the land, its members were far removed from the rough-and-tumble days of Kenya's past. She felt privileged that her father had enjoyed personal ties to such luminaries as Delamere, Blixen, and Percival, but she failed to share his admiration for the natives, ill at ease in their presence.

Sitting up front in the Rover, Frank, a recent reader of African hunting lore, basked in hearing it firsthand from a legendary P.H. The five ten-milligram codeine tablets he'd pilfered from Paul's medical kit enhanced his enjoyment. Relying on his memory of names and events garnered from reading several books on East African history, he drilled Ian with questions. His enthusiasm appeared contrived, to Paul and grated on his nerves. Feeling like an ignoramus, he recused himself from the discussion, his knowledge of Africa limited to high-school geography and *Tarzan of the Apes*. He could sense he was losing ground to Frank with regards to Jean and decided to do something about it, saying, "Why don't you give them a break, Frank? Can't you see Ian's off to a shaky start this morning?" Paul did his best to sound like a concerned doctor, rather than what he was—a jealous rival.

"It's quite all right," Ian said. "I'm delighted to spin a little yarn with anyone who pays me a smattering of interest on the subject. Not many folks share your friend's curiosity or have taken the time to learn anything about this place. All they want to do it pull triggers and amass trophies. It's a refreshing change—*Bwana* Eastman has certainly done his homework."

Bwana Eastman is an ass-kissing fraud, Paul thought, recognizing the smug, *How's that, college boy?* expression on his buddy's face. Flicking a cigarette butt to the roadside, Paul resolved to put the brakes on Frank's courtship of Jean as soon as possible. "Why are there so many soldiers around here?" Frank asked. "This all have to do with this Mau Mau thing?"

The question seemed to trouble both of the hosts. Ian gazed off introspectively while Jean assumed a blank stare and fiddled with her scarf.

Ian finally responded, "I'd rather not go into that right now, if you don't mind. We'll talk about it later. However, I can assure you there's nothing you need be alarmed about. Mau Mau terrorism has just about run its course. The Emergency started in fifty-two, and here it is, nineteen fifty-seven, and we Brits are still running Kenya."

Feeling anything but reassured and determined to stake a claim in the conversation and stop losing ground to Frank in their pursuit of Jean, Paul commented on the four green hills they were approaching. "Those mountains up ahead there, are we going over—"

"Those are the Ngong Hills, aren't they?" interrupted Frank. "Isn't this where that lady who wrote *Out of Africa* lived?"

Had Paul know Swahili, he'd have ordered one of the gunbearers to hand up a rifle so he could put it to good use. Instead he held his temper, hoping Ian would rebut Frank's pseudo scholarship.

"You've read it, I assume?" Jean inquired. "A lovely story—and so beautifully written."

"Did you know her?"

"Why, Frank," she tittered. "How old do you think I am?"

"I didn't mean—"

"Well, not that old anyway. Karen Blixen returned to her native Denmark in the early nineteen thirties. I'm sure we would have hit it off. Daddy knew her."

"Yes, Karen was quite a woman indeed," remarked Ian. "I saw her in town from time to time, and she showed up at several gatherings. Lovely woman, she was. Bloody rotten luck with her coffee farm."

"Ngong Hills. What does Ngong mean?" Frank asked.

"It's a Masai word for knuckle," Ian replied. "The peaks of these hills look like knuckles, don't you think?"

The group had traveled some distance south toward Magadi, passing around the edge of the Ngong Hills, where numerous farms skirted the lushly vegetated slopes. By late morning the temperature had risen, because of decrease in altitude. They were dropping slowly into the Rift Valley, along the edge of the Athi Plains. As they descended, the greenery was replaced by grasses, rocky outcroppings, and the occasional Masai *shamba*, or village. Many of the Masai were out tending their cattle and paid little attention to the intrusion of the safari vehicles. To the Americans the spear-wielding Masai looked ferocious in their cloth cloaks. Seeing the primitive people left little question that the Americans really were in darkest Africa.

"Hey, there's some antelope," Frank blurted, prompting everyone to turn for a look. As soon as the words were out of his mouth, he felt silly, sounding more like a schoolboy than a big-game trophy hunter. What he didn't know was that most hunters behaved the same way until they became accustomed to the country. Seeing a wild animal in its natural environment is altogether different from viewing it within the confines of a zoo. Animals in the wild seem larger, more animated, and they tend to materialize unexpectedly. Captive animals appear to have lost the spirit and passion for life that those in the wild radiate.

The bumpy, pockmarked ride was starting to take its toll on Ian, who grimaced at every bounce, clutching his side continually. Paul could see the bloody stain enlarging through his shirt and felt guilty for hiding it from Jean. In good conscience he could sit idly by no longer. "Are you all right, Ian?" he asked.

Ian straightened up in the seat and returned his hand in his lap quickly, before Jean could turn around. "Road's a little nasty on me, but I'll survive," he said.

"Daddy, look at your shirt," Jean shrieked, stomping the brakes and causing the lot of them to lunge forward in a cloud of dust. "That's it. We're going back. Enough is enough. You need medical attention, and you're going to get it."

"Let me have a look at him," said Paul, realizing that it was time to act or face days, possibly weeks, kicking around Nairobi, waiting for Ian to recover.

"With all due respect, Paul, I feel it's better he sees one of the *daktaris* at home."

"Excuse me," Ian interjected. "Do I have a say here? After all, these are my bloody innards we're talking about, yes?"

"Let me guess. All you need is a stiff shot, and everything will be just fine, right, Daddy?"

"No, maybe I'll put you over my knee and paddle your bottom, and you'll remember how to respect your father."

"How sophisticated of you."

The three Africans in the back had no idea what was going on, but they could tell by the tone of voice that it must be something bad. They sat in silent indifference, as they did most of the time.

"We're getting nowhere here," Frank remarked, losing his opiate calm. "Why don't we pull up under that tree over there so my friend, the gifted Doctor Bennett, can take a look and give us his professional opinion?" He pointed to an acacia in the distance. "I'm thirsty and about due for a break anyway."

Paul resented his friend's comment but refrained from responding.

Jean shoved the Rover into gear and drove to the tree, silently conceding that the likelihood of opposing three men was slim, but resenting that her authority as the safari's P.H. was being challenged again. Although granted probationary status as a professional hunter by the game commission, she bristled at the reminder that it was still a man's world.

It had been a year since Paul had done anything more surgically challenging than carve a chicken, and he didn't know if he would be up to it if Ian actually needed surgical attention. The image of that final afternoon loomed fresh, and the same lousy feeling returned. *Maybe they should go back to Nairobi*, he thought. *What if I do something wrong again and hurt this guy in front of his beautiful daughter? Just how much more can I take? Well, nobody's saying I have to actually do anything. I'll just have a look, and if it's bad, we'll go back.*

After the men enjoyed a beer, or three, in Frank's case, Frank decided to explore the surrounding terrain and drifted off unnoticed.

Ian agonizingly removed his shirt, revealing a damp red pad taped to his abdomen. Paul had him stretch out on the bare, dusty ground, using Jean's jacket as a pillow. Jean knelt down opposite Paul, nibbling her lip as Paul snatched the tape free from Ian's skin using two quick jerks. Ian cringed and quivered from the pain. Paul lifted off the bandage exposing a deep six-inch-long, gaping slash in his skin.

"Holy shit, Ian! What a mess!"

"It's bad, is it?"

"Who did this to you, some jungle medicine man?"

"I told you, a *chui*, a damned leopard."

"Not the wound, Ian, the repair job. It's awful."

It was a ghastly sight. Most of the sutures had pulled free or come untied, and the ones that were still intact had the edges of the wound poorly approximated, leaving a rippled seam. The edges of the skin were red from inflammation, and the underlying fatty layer had a brownish-yellow crust. What presented the greatest concern to Paul was the purple marble-sized section of intestine herniating, trying to poke through the tear in the abdominal wall. If left untreated, it would result in the death of that section of intestine, which was already showing signs of oxygen deprivation.

Jean was weakened by the sight but held her composure. "I think we need to go back home, Daddy."

Flies attempted to land on the exposed skin, so Paul quickly covered it. "I know it looks terrible," he said, "but the section of bowel hasn't turned black yet, which means it's alive. I need to free it up, or things *are* going to get bad. Doing it isn't as big a deal as you think, and it's pretty a straightforward job of closure after that."

"Paul, is it really wise to attempt it out here?" Jean asked.

"Of course I'd rather be somewhere a little less, well, remote," he said, sweeping the panorama with his arm, "but as I said, it isn't a complicated job."

Jean and the safari attendants stood waiting for Paul to tell them what to do, and he felt a resurgence of pride for the total faith people have in doctors. "If this is the best that Kenya can offer," he said, "I'd just as soon take care of it myself right here, right now. I've got everything we need with me, but it's in the other truck."

"What if he bleeds to death?" Jean asked.

Why did she have to say that?

"I trust you'll give me something to deaden the senses, huh, *daktari?*" queried Ian, trying not to sound like a sissy.

"You won't feel a thing except the Novocain shots," Paul replied, "and besides, the pain won't be any worse than what you've been dealing with already."

"Then I say let him have a go at it, Zuri. I trust his judgment, and he's right, I can't end up much worse than I am now."

Jean could sense it was futile to argue with them any further. Relenting, she said, "Have it your way, tough guys. It doesn't make any difference what I think anyway. I'm supposed to be running this safari——." Her voice quavering, she leapt up, spun, and stormed off just as the supply truck was pulling up.

Ian and Paul watched her depart, neither knowing how to handle her.

"Well, what do you think of me little girl?" Ian asked.

Paul knew what he wanted to say; she was without a doubt the most ravishing embodiment of female beauty he'd ever laid eyes on, but he decided to be less candid with her father. "She's very pretty," he ventured, and added, "kind of headstrong too."

"I taught her to make decisions and stick with them, a practice I knew she'd need out here if she expects to survive. I really hate to override her on something as silly as this. It's just that the safari's gotten off poorly, and I don't want to muddle it any further," Ian propped himself on his elbow. "Do you think I need to go back to Nairobi?"

"Honestly I'd much rather go hunting than fidget with your innards, but if we can just keep you from damaging your bowel or getting peritonitis, there isn't a reason in the world why we can't take care of it right here. Its small potatoes. Let me go talk to her for a minute. Maybe I can calm her down. Maybe not, but it's worth a try."

"You may be in for hell's own fury, my boy, but have at it. I'll just go check on the truck."

"Why don't you stay right where you are? I don't need any more of your guts poking through that hole. I'll be right back.

Paul found Jean sitting at the edge of a rock outcropping overlooking a sun-parched gully, her arms hugging her bare knees, which were drawn up to her chin. He approached from behind and hesitated, removing his sunglasses. "Jean, can I talk to you?"

A diminutive shrug of the shoulder was all he got.

"Ma'am, I don't want to make trouble between you and your dad, and I sure feel bad about all this."

"Then why don't you help me, and make him go to the *daktari?*"

"He's got a doctor right here, or did you forget about that?"

She turned to him, revealing streaks where tears had washed away grime from the trip.

He felt sorry for her and had to dig his hands in his pockets to keep from scooping her up in his arms. "All right," he said. "You win. We'll go back."

"You don't understand. It's not so much about Daddy's injury—it's the way I'm always being treated like an inexperienced trainee. I saw how disappointed you looked when Daddy introduced us. It's the same with every client. Some people smirk; others protest. We even had a party cancel. Hell, I can shoot rings around most of you, and I've held my ground in any number of charges that would send most men running for their lives, yet I find myself having to justify my position time and again. Daddy should know better than to treat me like such a schoolgirl."

"I'm sure you can see it from our point of view. It's not exactly the line of work you'd expect a woman to be engaged in."

"It's the only thing I know how to do, and it's all I've ever done. I've been with Daddy on safari since before I could read."

"Where's your mother?"

Jean looked away.

"I mean, if you don't mind my asking."

"She moved to England."

"They divorced?"

"No, she couldn't get used to the country and went home. Africa proved too harsh for her."

"Do you see her much?"

She said nothing.

Sensing a taboo subject, he quickly said, "Shouldn't we get a move on, if we're going back to Nairobi?"

Visibly relieved, she replied, "There's no need to rush. I trust you to mend Daddy."

She stood and wiped her face with the free end of her neckerchief. "Just please don't let anything happen to him. I couldn't—"

Ambling up, Frank said, "Hi, guys. What did I miss?"

"Where've you been?" Paul asked.

"Oh, me and the darkies were just discussing the physics behind the atom bomb."

"Very amusing, *Bwana* Wise Guy," Jean said, playfully kicking some gravel at his legs.

"I'm going to patch up Ian," Paul said. "I'll need your help."

"Not me, pal. Not my line of work."

"All right, Frank," Jean said, "if you can busy yourself for a while, I'll help Paul with Daddy."

"You know," Paul said, "we probably ought to spend the night here to give Ian's wound a chance to heal undisturbed. The suspension in that Rover's pretty tough. If I can get his incision closed, I don't want to risk jarring it open again."

"I'll get the boys to pitch camp," Jean said, "and maybe later, as long as we're stopping here, we can shoot the rifles to make sure they're sighted in."

Frank perked up. "Now that's when I go to work."

"All right, then," Jean said, "let's do what we must." She sounded like she was taking command again, briskly summoning the natives, who were sitting by the truck in separate small groups.

One of them, a middle-aged Wakamba tribesman in a cloth robe and wearing a fez jumped up and ran over. "*Unataka nin, memsaab?* What do you wish?" he asked.

"*Nataka na campi kule kwausiku wa leo.* I want to camp here tonight," she replied.

Although he bobbed his head, he gazed at her in confusion; it wasn't customary to set up camp so close to Nairobi or so early in the day.

"I'll need my brown suitcase," Paul said.

"Is there anything else you're going to require, as long as I've got him here?"

"Let's see—some disinfectant or alcohol. Some towels or washcloths. If you don't have clean water, you might get some boiled. That ought to cover it. Oh, yeah, can we get a mosquito net over us to keep out the flies?"

"Yes, all of the tents are equipped with them." She turned to the nodding Wakamba, repeating Paul's requests, and said, "*Tafadhali niende sasa*. Please go now."

He gave a quick dip and hurried off.

The makeshift camp materialized with amazing speed, attesting to the skill and character of the safari team, who erected a latrine, dining tarp, and separate sleeping accommodations for all the white members. Boiling water was sizzling in a five-gallon metal container on the campfire. Frank and Paul's bags were neatly arranged inside their tent, and the dining table glowed with precisely positioned china and flatware. Since no game had been taken thus far, lunch consisted of soup, relishes, cheeses, tinned ham, tinned fruit for dessert, and freshly baked bread, which had been purchased in Nairobi.

Since Ian's condition posed no immediate threat to life, the group decided to relax and enjoy lunch prior to the operation, which was to take place while the rest of the outfit reclined during the heat of the day. Feeling nauseated from pain and his progressive bowel obstruction, Ian said he'd pass on the meal until after Paul and Jean attended to his leaking midriff.

After lunch Frank slouched in a canvas camp chair under the acacia tree and Jean told one of the boys to fix him a glass of bourbon using a few of the remaining ice chips from the cold box.

With his entire existence reduced to watching the serpentine currents of melted ice swirl in the warm bronze liquid and nothing to do but drink and pore over *The Wanderings of an Elephant Hunter* by W. D. M. Bell, Frank felt at peace with the world, a peace he hadn't known in a very long time.

Preparing for surgery, Paul moved the dining table to the edge of the tarp, where the light was better and the heat of the afternoon sun would be less intense. He laid out the meager array of surgical instruments he'd brought for such an emergency: one scalpel, a needle holder, two Kelly-type hemostats, suture scissors, tissue forceps, two glass five-cc syringes with needles, small rolls of catgut and silk suture material, and several suture needles. Barring the unforeseen, the token armamentarium should suffice for Ian's procedure. Jean and her father set up a passible mosquito screen by fastening two small ones together, while Paul scalded his instruments with boiling water and loaded both syringes with Novocain.

"This is a far cry from sterilization," he admitted, pouring hot water from the dish containing his implements. He shook them out into a metal cooking pan and drenched them with alcohol. After scrubbing with an old crescent-shaped sliver of bar soap that Kemoa had found somewhere, Paul sterilized his hands with alcohol and unspooled and cut two lengths of suture material, washed them in a pan of soapy water, and dropped both strands in a dish of alcohol.

"Okay, Ian, it's showtime," he said, hoping to put both his patient and himself at ease.

Despite the simple surgical procedure, Paul was racked by self-doubt. If things didn't turn out well, Ian could be substantially worse off, the safari would be finished, and Jean would hold him responsible. *Some vacation this is turning out to be*, he thought. As Ian climbed onto the shaky metal table and eased himself flat on his back, his pale torso and darkly tanned arms looked hauntingly familiar to Paul, reminding him of Cap.

"I want you both to understand something," he warned. "While this is first-year medical-school stuff, I can't guarantee the outcome."

"That's a fine way to start," Jean snapped.

Cutting her off, Ian told Paul, "Don't you worry about how things turn out, my boy. You just do what's necessary. If by chance my condition sours, we can always return to Nairobi or slip over to Dar es Salaam. But I shouldn't expect that'll be called for."

Paul washed Ian's wound gently, using a soapy towel. In gnawing pain, Ian tensed his abdominal muscles, and Jean held his hand and chewed her lower lip.

After rinsing the site with water and dabbing it dry, Paul tipped the alcohol bottle over the cut and said, "Hold on, Ian. You're going to hate this."

When the solution flooded the cleft, Ian gasped and his eyes squinted under a creased brow. Having been through the same torture less than a week earlier, he knew what was coming next.

Jean looked away as Paul began a series of Novocain injections around the edges of the skin. Ian trembled as small areas of his lacerated abdomen blanched yellow-white from the introduction of anesthetic into the fatty sub-layer of tissue. It gave the flesh a paraffin-like appearance.

Beads of sweat were forming on everybody's forehead.

Paul paused for a second. "I forgot to ask you if you've had a tetanus toxoid shot recently."

Grateful for the break, Ian said, "The chap whose work you're rectifying gave me a booster last week, and I routinely have them every year. You know, always getting scratched up in the bush and such." Looking at Jean, Ian asked, "When was the last time you got one, darling?"

She thought for a few seconds and counted with her free hand. "Three years ago, I think."

Paul continued with the shots until the tissue was uniformly pale and Ian was at his breaking point. "Okay, Ian, that's the worst of it," Paul said, placing the hypodermic into the metal pan. "We'll need to wait a few minutes for this stuff to do its thing. Anyone besides me thirsty?"

"I'd fancy a spot a' gin about now," Ian sheepishly appealed.

"I don't think so, Ian Sharpe," chided his daughter.

"Oh, let him have some, Jean," Paul said. "I think he's earned it."

"Yes, dear," Ian said. "Listen to the *daktari*. He knows what's best. It'll help kill all the nasties down there, won't it, doc?"

"Sure, it's what they used before modern drugs were invented."

Jean could sense a conspiracy in the making. "I can see I'm going to have to watch you delinquents closely." She suppressed a grin, but her playful eyes betrayed her. "I'll trust *you'll* refrain until your work's finished here," she admonished Paul.

"I just want water or a soft drink."

She acquiesced. "All right, then. " She hollered without looking to see if any of the boys were nearby. "*Nitapenda kidogo glasi jjin kwa bwana Umeme, na maji ya limau kwa daktari Bennett.*"

"Since when have you forgotten your manners, young lady?"

"*Tafadhali.* Please," she added, reluctantly.

Within a minute the kowtowing African appeared with a gin and tonic in one hand and in the other, a lemonade. Since Frank had commandeered the last of the ice, the men sipped their drinks tepid.

"Ian," Paul said, "you probably won't want to watch what I'm going to do now." He started to snip and dislodge what was left of the old sutures.

Ian raised his head to take another sip and sneak a peek.

"Can't you hold still for a minute?" Paul asked.

"Yes, Daddy," Jean said, "please stop moving.

To correct the poorly positioned flaps of the wound, which had begun to fuse in healing, Paul had to reopen it with his scalpel. As he severed the partially healed skin, the wound unfolded, exposing more flesh. Small rivulets of blood sprouted from the lacerated walls. Jean kept quiet, but the sight of the bleeding gash terrified her.

"Sponge," said Paul mindlessly.

"I beg your pardon?" Jean asked.

"Oh, I'm sorry. Please dab those bleeding spots with a towel."

She made a tentative blot with the towel.

"No, like this," Paul said, pushing her hand harder into the wound. "Don't worry. He can't feel anything. Can you, Ian?" As he spoke, Paul held Jean's hand a little longer than was necessary. "Just a little pushing," he said. "See?"

When she got the hang of it, he spent the next few minutes carefully slicing away partially healed tissue, while Jean kept the site as dry and clear of blood as she could. He was particularly deliberate with the scalpel around the tiny balloon of intestine; one small nick could introduce a host of problems. As he released the abdominal wall's strangulation of the intestine, the purple color washed out, replaced by a healthy pink hue. "See what I mean?" he proclaimed. "It's better, just like that."

Tired of reading, Frank went searching for something to occupy his time during the operation. He decided to have a closer look at the vehicles and slid himself under the surplus military truck. What he discovered appalled him. The entire undercarriage was a hodgepodge of stopgap and makeshift repairs. Sections of metal were welded to earlier add-ons, some of which were showing the cracks of fatigue. Even the drive shaft had been welded at one time. His experience with heavy equipment told him that under these circumstances, a major mechanical disaster was imminent. It was not a question of if but when the structure would fail. He considered approaching the Sharpes with his concerns but decided it would only serve to delay the safari further. The Sharpes were probably aware of the situation, he thought, opting to freshen up his drink and forget about it.

Paul gingerly tucked the intestine back into the cavity and sewed up the abdominal wall with catgut suture. He tried to pick up speed, because Ian was starting to twitch a little when the needle dug into the meat. Finally he stepped back and stretched. Lifting the gin and tonic from Ian's grasp and winking at Jean, he took a swig.

"*Daktari Bennett*, you should be ashamed of yourself."

"I am, ma'am, terrible ashamed," Paul responded in his smoothest Southern drawl and then took another sip while maintaining eye contact with her, detecting a hint of a blush. He gave the glass back to Ian and started to close the incision with a continuous cross-stitch just under the skin.

Ian was acutely conscious of each stitch but withstood it to the bitter end.

Jean allowed herself to relax, recognizing that the surgery had gone well, and she no longer needed to be apprehensive. "Daddy, take a peek," she said. "It looks lovely."

Elevating himself on his elbows, Ian inspected the job and then smiled up at Paul, raising his near empty glass and saying, "I am forever in your debt, my American friend."

"That goes for me, too," Jean said, moving around the table to give Paul a peck on the cheek.

Beside himself, he was than more a little embarrassed, and his face reddened a bit as he said, "Glad to do it for you." *And for me*, he reflected, for that one little job had been a milestone. Not only had he overcome his fear, but he'd also vaulted past Frank in Jean's affections. *Try to top this one, Frank, old buddy*. He thought.

Ian swung his legs over the edge of the table and winced with a stab of pain.

"Hey, take it easy for a while," Paul cautioned. "It's going to take a couple of weeks for that to heal."

After washing his hands, Paul dug in his suitcase and pulled out the rumpled bag containing the pills. Pausing for a moment, he studied the contents. There seemed to be fewer bottles than he'd packed on leaving the U.S. He shrugged it off, figuring he'd miscounted or in the rush of departure had unwittingly left some at home. Rummaging in the bag, he pulled out a small brown bottle of codeine tablets. "Here, take a couple of these when you need to. I also want you to take these antibiotics for at least a week. The rest of this is stuff Frank said you wanted me to bring."

Ian looked puzzled. He had no recollection of making such a strange request. Drugs were fairly easy to come by, and his small stock was usually ample. *Maybe Frank misinterpreted something I wrote to him*, he concluded.

"Please have someone boil these surgical instruments for about a half hour and bring them back to me while they're still in the water," Paul said, handing the pan to Jean. "I want to wrap them up in case we need them again." He really hoped they wouldn't be needed. He didn't want to push his luck.

CHAPTER TEN

Taken Seriously

Shadows were spreading across the broken, bushy terrain by the time Jean, Paul, and Frank loaded up for their first excursion into the bush. She carefully navigated the Rover through the rocky crags of the *donga*, a ditch formed by erosion. The temperature hadn't dropped much despite the sun's lower pitch on the horizon. It would be several more hours before the baking heat would give way to the evening chill.

Ian had eagerly accepted Paul's recommendations to remain inactive and get some rest. He didn't need to be told twice, since a certain sector of his tummy began sending the same message as soon as the Novocain cleared from the tissues. Jean left him behind in the care of the camp crew while commandeering the two gunbearers and Jua, the Maasai tracker.

"We've got a choice to make here," she said, fighting the wheel as the Rover negotiated a particularly vicious rut. "I don't think we've got time to sight in your rifles *and* collect an antelope for dinner, or *chakula*, as we call it in these parts.

"I thought you said we couldn't hunt until we got into Tanganyika," Frank recalled, though he was itching to get the slaying underway.

"That's right, Frank. *You* may not hunt within the boundaries of Kenya, but we, as representatives of the game commission, are allowed to take game as we see fit."

"Who's going to know who shot what out here in the middle of nowhere?"

Making a quick assessment of Frank's character, she replied, "I will. You don't want to start out by breaking the rules, do you? We'll have ample time to hunt in the weeks to come, so there's little reason to disregard the laws of—"

"*Kuangalia*. Look, Memsaab," said one of the gunbearers from the back, pointing in the distance.

She hit the brakes, and the occupants were thrown forward.

"I wish you'd stop doing that, "Paul said, struggling to right himself in the back seat.

The bearer drew their attention to a scrub-covered slope directly ahead.

Jean said, "Oh, I see. Look over there by that outcropping of rock. Look for a moment, and you'll see a pair of antelope called Grant's gazelle. Not the best for the table, but we won't go hungry."

Stepping out and away from the Rover, she scooped up a handful of dusty ground and then watched as the dust floated down between her fingers, "We're lucky. The wind is coming at us from their direction. I should be able to slip right up within several hundred meters. Anyone care to join me?"

Miffed that Jean, not he, would be making the kill, but accepting the role of spectator as gracefully as he could, Frank said, "Sure would. I'm dying to see how well you handle a rifle."

It was the wrong thing for Frank to have said, Paul concluded, smiling to himself and waiting for Jean to explode.

"You mean," she said, "you're dying to see if this *girl* knows which end the bullet comes out of, right?"

"No, that's not what I—"

"It's exactly what you meant," she hissed, reaching for her Mannlicher bolt action. "I suggest you follow me, and let's just see if I can find the little hook thing you pull to make it go bang."

After instructing the blacks to stay with the Rover until they heard the report of the rifle and then to bring the vehicle to collect the dead animal, she invited her clients to join her on what promised to be a long stalk, since the antelope had covered another hundred yards of so while the group tarried. Guilt over having snapped at Frank overcame her, and she told him, "I'm dreadfully sorry for biting your head off. I just get so weary dealing with the same patronizing remarks again and again. They get irritating after a while."

"No problem," Frank said. "I probably deserved it. I don't have a lot of experience with women who can do much of anything but . . . never mind."

"I see."

Paul gave his friend a scoffing look as if to say, *Keep it up, stupid.*

It didn't take long for the hunched-over posture of the stalk to take its toll on Paul's and Frank's lower backs. The crouched stance didn't seem to disturb Jean, who was traversing the expanse with cat-like grace. The two Americans, on the other hand, were suffering from burning pain in their backs and legs as well as serious oxygen deprivation. Slumping over and panting to catch his breath, Paul dropped back and waved the others on. He could tell that it was going to take some time to adjust to such exertion. *No wonder these trips are a month long*, he thought and decided that his cigarette smoking was, at the very least, going to be lessened, if not cut out altogether.

After his unfortunate faux pas with Jean, Frank wasn't about to give in to his exhaustion. He drew on every bit of strength to keep up with her. She knew he was suffering, and pushed on a little harder, just to teach him a lesson.

The gazelle were on the alert. At least two hundred meters separated the hunters from the nervous animals. Both the young bulls stopped feeding and looked at the approaching humans, who froze in their tracks. Paul watched the whole scene from where he'd floundered, and from the look of things, he expected to be dining on tinned provisions again.

Jean knew they'd advanced as far as they dared. "All right, Frank, where?"

"Where what?" he asked between breaths. "Oh, you mean where are they?"

"No, where do you want me to hit him?"

"I don't . . . care . . . neck."

It seemed they'd hesitated too long. Both the handsome animals simultaneously broke into bounding leaps. Frank was watching the antelope flee when the cracking blast startled him. When he recovered from flinching, a second shot erupted.

Paul, who was quite a way back, could see Jean recoil a fraction of a second before he heard the shots. He was also far enough from the action to hear the separate wet smacking thuds as the bullets hit their mark.

Frank's ears were still ringing when he heard Jean mumble the word *kufa* to herself.

"What was that, Jean?"

"*Kufa*. Dead. Both of them."

"Both? He blurted in disbelief. "No . . . not a chance."

"Come along, then, and let us see."

Paul came puffing up to them. "Nice shooting," he gasped, bending over, his hands on his knees.

"She said she hit both of them."

"I'm pretty sure she did," Paul said between pants and looking up at Frank.

"I'm sorry, I gotta see this for myself."

The Rover pulled up with the gunbearer Susani at the wheel. The other two Africans were standing behind the upright rack. "*Kufa, memsaab,*" Susani observed.

"I know," Jean replied. "Very dead indeed."

They loaded up and sped toward the area where the first gazelle had disappeared from sight and found it crumpled up, still twitching from involuntary muscle activity. Jua hopped off the Rover and quietly wandered off in the direction of the second animal's flight. Mchana, the other gunbearer, jumped from the vehicle and slit the animal's throat.

"What's that all about?" Paul asked.

"Some of the natives are Mohammedans. It's part of their religious customs. Appeases their god, or some such," Jean explained.

It was obvious that the animal met its end by way of a smashing impact to the neck; just below the head a large section of the slender brown promontory was in a state of gory mutilation. Oblivious to Jean's perfect shot placement, Frank was captured by the beauty of the creature before him. The fineness of its sweeping ringed horns and the nobility of the beige, black, and white face made him envious of Jean's coup—a jealousy most hunters feel when someone else secures a trophy animal. He inhaled the clean smell of the gazelle and hungered for the chance to adorn his trophy room with a set of horns. "What a swell lookin' animal," he told Jean. "Is it a pretty good-size one?"

"If you're referring to body weight, it's about average for this type on antelope," she replied, "but you'll see much finer horns, I promise, and you are going to grow fond of eating this chap and his little cousin, the Tommy—Thompson gazelle. Now let's go see if his friend is out there somewhere." She felt confident the other animal was down and that Jua had found it by then.

They hoisted and tied the dead antelope to the front of the Rover and plodded ahead. The coral-streaked western sky was receding in the growing darkness when they finally secured the other antelope, discovered two hundred meters from the first. It too had been brought down with a hit to the neck, the bullet tearing through the base of the neck, severing a major artery and causing massive bleeding and a quick death.

On the way back to camp, though Frank failed to compliment Jean on her marksmanship, she felt certain that from then on, her gender would no longer be an issue.

The two Americans climbed out of the vehicle exhausted and sore after a scant four hours in the bush. Frank headed straightaway for the liquor storage, while Paul ambled feebly over to the roaring fire, where Ian was sagged in a chair, his legs propped up on a wood crate.

Having misjudged the additive effect of the painkillers combined with his evening gin and tonic, Ian felt a bit giddy. "Well, my Yankee friend, what do you make of our splendid country?" he asked Paul. "I trust my little girl made your first foray a productive one."

"She's a hell of a shot. I've never seen anything like it. Two running Grant's, two neck shots, bang, bang, *kufa*,"

"Have a little more faith in her now, do you?"

"I think Frank was more concerned about that than I was, but as long as you asked, our concerns have been put to rest."

"Well then, why don't you have a seat right here and nip a spot 'a gin while the boys throw together some *chakula*?" You've got time to get washed up, if that's your fancy. Just say the word, and I'll have the savages pour a *bathi* for you."

"That sounds more like it, Ian. Let me do that, and I'll join you later. By the way, how's the side feel?"

"Might hurt, might not, can't tell right now," he replied, patting his bandages.

Paul took it as a good sign. Severe pain requires a large amount of analgesics, and Paul could tell that Ian was on a minimal dose, judging by his speech and only slightly drooping eyelids.

Frank plopped himself down in another chair, set his drink on the ground, and began untying his boots. "Some setup you've got here, Ian. No wonder you guys like this business."

"It's a lot more work than you think, but you're right, there are worse ways to fill the coffers. It does have its sticking points, though. Could you believe we have to deal with clients who are stupid enough to think we come out here without knowing how to shoot a rifle?"

"I get the point."

"I bloody well hope you do," he deadpanned, staring at the fire. "If we push hard tomorrow, we should make it to Lake Natron at the edge of Tanganyika, and you boys can start banging away to your heart's content."

"I sure hope so, Ian. I don't think I could stand another afternoon like today."

"Where's Dead Eye Jean?" asked Paul, looking around as he got up from his chair.

"What's that you call her?" Frank asked Ian. "Kosury?"

"*Kizuri.* Beautiful. I would imagine she's soaking the grime from herself about now."

Paul and Frank both willed themselves to stare at the fire instead of reflexively scanning the camp for the naked beauty in a tub.

Dinner was a savory affair involving fresh citrus, tinned sea-turtle soup, fire-roasted yams, salad greens, bread freshly baked in an iron pot, and slabs of sizzling gazelle tenderloin. Dry, musty Bordeaux and any number of bottled condiments rounded out the fare.

Nyeusi, who had recovered sufficiently from the catatonia in which he'd started the trip, was wheeling about the table, making certain everyone had enough to eat. It was a feast that reminded Paul of the post-fishing spreads that Clorese whipped up many years earlier. Both he and Frank ate to the point of bursting, but they consumed a fraction of the meat in comparison to the natives, who returned again and again to the juice-dripping roasted carcasses, hacking off great chunks at a time.

Jean's bright eyes sparkled in reflected firelight as she fielded safari-related questions from her companions. She seemed to have a knack for selecting apparel that highlighted her lovely features. She was wearing a snug white turtleneck sweater and narrow-cut dungarees. Her shiny damp hair was pulled back and broadcast a faint flowery fragrance, which the Americans took in with every breeze. As far as they were concerned, the evening could have carried on forever, but not long after they'd finished their chocolate cake and the brandy bottle had been corked for the last time, Jean rose from the table. "It's been a trying day, fellas, and I really must get some sleep. If you men will excuse me—"

Paul looked at Frank and then roughed up his friend's hair. "Good idea about this trip, old pal. Let's hit the sack."

Paul dozed off, but Frank was in and out of sleep all night. At first it was the humming of bugs, with some cooing from birds, as an annoying backdrop, and then came the insane cackle of the hyena that had gathered to squabble over the skeletal remains of the gazelle. Frank could hear them cracking bones as their powerful jaws reduced the carcasses to splinters. Something coughed or roared or both simultaneously, which to Frank's ears must have been a lion. There was never complete silence throughout the interminable night. Frank started to wake Paul, who snoozed unaware of the cacophony surrounding him, but thought better of it, lest he appear a frightened yellowbelly.

There was a new sound—Elvis Presley crooning "Love Me Tender." It was as familiar to Frank's ears as it was out of place in the desolate safari tent camp. "Hey, Skip, get up," he said. "You gotta hear this. Wake up."

Paul opened his eyes and looked around the confines of the shelter as if trying to ascertain just exactly where he was. "Elvis Presley?"

"Yep. Can you believe it?"

"Must be coming from Jean's portable wind-up phonograph. Boy, she's full of surprises, isn't she?" Throwing his legs over the cot and sitting up, Paul rubbed the stubble on his face. Noting Frank's weary expression, asked, "Did you sleep well?"

"Hardly at all. There was so much noise out there I thought every animal in the whole goddamn world was outside the tent."

"Who did this?" asked Paul, pointing to the clean clothes neatly folded on a small table.

"That drunk darkie from yesterday, Nyeusi. He brought them along with our boots, which are polished, I might add. He also set those basins here and brought coffee."

"I guess he's feeling better. Hey, do you think these natives like Elvis the way the blacks do back home?"

"I don't know, Skip, but Nyeusi wasn't singing along this morning."

"Maybe he just doesn't know the words yet."

The mental image of Nyeusi, with his inch-long teeth and filthy, moth-eaten garb, warbling to the notes of Presley's ballad struck a chord with both of them, and what started as a chuckle quickly matured into howling convulsions. Both of them were long overdue for a good laugh, having traveled thousands of miles only to have their plans turned topsy-turvy upon their arrival. The surprise introduction of the woman followed by Ian's tribulations left them emotionally frayed. They'd started chafing on each other right from the outset, and having survived all the unexpected setbacks, they seized the opportunity to vent their pent-up tension at the expense of the pathetic camp attendant.

It felt good to exit the dank, musty confines of the tent, a night's worth of respiration having left its interior stale and wet. They stepped through the flap only to find the camp nearly dismantled. All that remained was the dining table, some chairs, and heaps of folded canvas. Ian was a short distance away, kneeling and studying the ground.

"Hey, you two, come over and have a peek at this."

"Morning, Ian. What's up?"

"Have any idea what this is?" He pointed to a large paw print in the soft soil.

"It looks like a big bobcat . . . Wait, don't tell me that's a lion track. Here? Right in camp?"

"*Bwana simba*, it was. A lion, and a hefty full-grown bugger, at that."

"I thought I heard a lion roar last night."

"You might have, but it wouldn't have been this one, or you'd still be pissing your knickers. A blast from old *Simba* at this close range would have toppled the tents."

"Why didn't he attack us, Ian?" asked Paul.

"I don't think there's a person alive who can answer that. Nobody knows what makes these beasts tick. Maybe he just meandered through here out of curiosity and didn't like what he smelled or was fresh off a kill and didn't have the tummy space for you or Frank. Who knows? It's common to have beasts show up in camp like this, but it's usually without incident. I've only had to shoot my way out of situations a few times over the years, and we've had only one mishap that ended in tragedy."

"What happened? I mean, if you don't mind my asking?"

"Not at all. Several years ago I had a photographic safari with some chaps doing a piece for a monthly magazine from one of the South American countries—Argentina, if I remember correctly. They were a pleasant lot, but one of them had it in his mind that all of the animals out here were basically tame and sweet on humans and could be safely approached. I'm sure you know the type. The long hair, scrawny, 're-all-nature's-children' variety. There simply wasn't anything I could say or do to convince him otherwise, and several days into the trip, a mother *faru*—a rhino—wandered in at sunup with her calf. I didn't actually see it, but I surmise that our cavilier journalist encountered her as he was making his way to the privy and tried to pet the bloody thing."

Ian stood a moment, shaking his head. "I still can't believe anyone could be that blasted stupid. Mama *faru* are very protective of their young and don't take kindly to being interfered with. I had to shoot her, which I hated to do, and had very little of the photographer to mail home."

Frank thought about the previous night. "I nearly went out to the john last night, but just wound up peeing outside the tent. Ian, are we going to survive this trip?"

"I don't know, son. We try to do everything we can to safeguard you, but this is wild Africa, and there are plenty of ways to buy it here. In fact, did you know that crocodiles eat about twelve Africans a day on this continent? Nonetheless, it's a rare occurrence when a client gets killed, but it does happen. I wouldn't spend too much time brooding over it, though; it'll spoil your time here."

That little piece of advice from the professional hunter didn't lessen

Frank's uneasiness about the whole mortality issue. "Do you let folks keep guns with them at night?"

"Actually we discourage it. The last thing we need is somebody conjuring imaginary menaces and shooting up the *campi*. The young lady and I wouldn't fancy meeting our end with privy paper in hand and our knickers about our ankles."

Paul looked around. "Where is she, anyway?"

"Off on a little hike to clear her head. She likes some free time alone now and then. What say we grab a bite and then get a move on?"

"By the way, how's the side this morning?"

"Top drawer, *daktari*. Changed the bandage this morn, and all's well."

"Keep taking the penicillin, okay?"

"As you wish."

The leopard should have made a kill that night, but had been in no shape to do so. Two nights had passed since the bright flash and searing blow to his leg separated him from his ambushed meal.

It had been easy in the past. The heard of careless languid goats lingering about was too much of a temptation. Even the unfamiliar sounds coming from the nearby building weren't enough to dissuade the reclusive marauder from making the nighttime attack. A leap over the fence, several bounds, and a crunching snap at a hapless beast's neck, and the feast was his to enjoy. He'd done it several times over the previous months and was spending less and less energy pursuing his normal, more difficult quarry of antelope and warthog.

That night was different, however. When the fleeing goats raised a ruckus, the door of the pyrethrum farmer's house flew open, disgorging a moving beam of light that found the leopard crouched over his kill. There wasn't time to react before the .30-caliber bullet from the war-surplus Enfield rifle tore through his right leg, chipping bone. The second crack of the rifle spooked him further, but did no damage, since the impact was many feet behind him, along his path of retreat.

He lay deep in the appropriately dubbed "wait-a-minute" thorn bushes, which grab and won't let go, along a narrow creek bottom in Tanganyika, writhing in pain, his stomach raw from lack of food. His once-powerful 110-pound body, with its shiny spotted golden coat, was matted with filth, his right leg swollen and throbbing. The natural antiseptic quality of saliva, which used to heal his smaller cuts and scrapes, had little effect on the festering wound.

Without a meal in the next several days he was sure to become fodder for his loathsome enemy, the hyena, but if the wound healed enough for him to hunt again, he would recover over time. Because of the crippling leg injury he would be forever limited in his ability to overtake and bring down large, unruly prey, as he'd done in the past. The leopard would have to content himself with sullenly licking his wounded limb until opportunity presented itself anew

CHAPTER ELEVEN

Hard Lessons

Paul took a page out of Frank's playbook and commandeered the front passenger's seat, where he had the delight of watching the Kenyan landscape glide by behind the arresting profile of the female hunter. Frank took it in stride, since he was still smarting from the row of the day before and wanted to give it some time before he attempted a move again.

During lunch break Ian complained of discomfort, but Paul discovered only a trace of bleeding and minimal inflammation of the site. Reassured, Jean proceeded to educate the Americans on the fauna and flora of the region, discharging one of her duties as a tour guide. Next she suggested that Paul and Frank test their guns for accuracy. All the rifles were brought out and fired. Everything seemed to be in order, and there was little need for adjustment of sights.

Frank proved to be a worthy marksman with his new Weatherby .375 magnum, which roared when it discharged. The gun was the latest in high-power sporting rifles and was becoming popular with hunters around the world. It had been purchased with a four-power telescopic sight, which allowed the shooter to fix on the target with greater accuracy at a greater distance. Ian, not a fan of that specific accessory, was pleased to see that Frank had the good judgment to ask a gunsmith to affix a set of sights to the rifle barrel in case the telescope failed, which it was prone to do. The radically styled modern stock felt good in Frank's hands, and with each thundering report, pieces of a thigh-sized tree they were using as a target exploded in splinters. He took extra careful aim, bent on impressing Jean, who was evincing a keen interest.

When it came time for Paul to shoot, all he could do was embarrass himself. He shook, flinched, cursed, and missed. It was not that his shooting was terrible, as all the shots were in the ballpark; it was just that it wasn't good enough to ensure clean kills when the time came. Everybody suggested improvements. Jean told him one thing, and Ian another, but what really galled him was the condescending way Frank instructed him, as if Paul had never held a rifle before, and then he made the crack that the problem was just a "nut loose on the trigger."

Even the natives were laughing and joking among themselves. Paul could only assume that they were discussing the lack of meat they'd get at the hands of the yellow-haired hunter. It was especially humiliating for him to perform so poorly in front of the woman, though she was quite complaisant, telling him not to be concerned and that most of the visiting hunters started out a little shaky. Bruised in both shoulder and ego, he put the rifle away and said a small prayer for divine intervention in the days to come.

Frank asked for a chance to shoot the large-bore double rifles, something he'd longed to do ever since reading about the huge elephant guns years earlier. Ian was happy to accommodate, and shouted for Mchana to bring the *bundouki m'kubwas,* the big ones. Opening the battered leather case, Ian unveiled two partially disassembled and worn, but elegantly crafted, side-by-side English rifles. The stately firearms had survived years of vigorous use, thanks to conscientious care. The checkering on the stocks displayed shiny flat spots from prolonged handling by gritty hands, which had burnished the peaks off the little diamond carvings. An aristocratic patina had emerged where there had once been a rich rainbow of color case-hardened finish.

Ian took one of the rifles and carefully fit the corresponding barrels to it, locking them in place with a crisp snap from the fore-end, the wooden piece that fits under the barrel shaped to fit the shooter's hand during shooting. He handed the Webley and Scott rifle to Frank, who welcomed it with reverence, hefting it to compare it with the weight of the double shotguns he'd used in the past. He tried but couldn't suppress the grin that surfaced as he gazed upon the artfully engraved game scenes on the side plates and underside of the receiver. An elephant figure adorned one side, a rhinoceros the other, and a Cape buffalo the bottom. It was truly an exemplary example of pre-war gun-making mastery.

Ian handed Frank a pair of the cigar-sized .450 number-two cartridges and demonstrated how to stand squarely with the gun, with his right foot bracing him against the recoil. Not knowing what to expect, Frank shouldered the rifle, held his breath, and squeezed the trigger. As soon as he recovered from the bone-jarring ram to his shoulder, he realized several things. It was clearly not a gun he wanted to use on a regular basis, and he couldn't imagine how anyone, particularly Jean, could shoot it frequently. Further, how in the world was he going to fire it without shutting his eyes and jerking in anticipation of the punishing recoil? Lastly, any animal that could take a hit by a .400-grain bullet delivering five thousand pounds of energy and keep coming was a formidable adversary indeed.

Mustering the courage, Frank shouldered the rifle, aimed at a small tree, and fired. That time his hand and jaw buzzed from shock, and his finger bled from a cut caused by the slender metal trigger guard. The tree, which had once stood proudly on the African veldt, was blown to smithereens. Sucking on his cut knuckle, he sheepishly returned the gun to Ian who, fighting to suppress a chuckle, asked him if he'd like to have a crack at the even larger .500/.450 double, to which Frank responded with an emphatic, "No!"

Witnessing the spectacle and still smarting from his own lame target practice, Paul declined when Ian offered him the rifle. He would first have to regain his confidence before discharging the elephant guns.

Once the gun had been oiled and stored and everyone had stuffed themselves with pieces of leftover gazelle, the party got on the road again. As usual the lumbering supply truck fell behind and was soon out of sight.

Reaching into his pocket, Ian withdrew several dusty–looking cigars. "Either of you lads fancy a *sigara?*"

Both Paul and Frank made quick appraisals, deciding that if the purveyor of the strange, roughly hewn cylinders was going to indulge in one, they may as well join him. The cigars were a concoction made from tobacco grown in the western Tanganyika province of Kibondo. The East Africa Tobacco Company supplied the seed, and the natives grew the leaves as a cash crop.

"These things look and smell like dung," Frank said, passing the cigar underneath his nose. "Are you sure this ain't some kind of joke?" He'd grown suspicious of Ian's antic sense of humor.

The white hunter struck a match on the side of the Rover and puffed his reeking cheroot to a cherry glow. The other two lit up and immediately got dizzy from the acrid smoke. Jean wrinkled her nose and drove on, reflecting that her companions, puffing away in the open vehicle as they motored across the African countryside, reminded of the faux pomp of a carload of Nazi SS officers touring the streets of occupied Paris.

Game became more plentiful as they approached Lake Natron. Herds of zebra, gazelle, wildebeest, and oryx and multitudes of other plains game dotted the vast expanses, which appeared to stretch into infinity. Behind them, far off in the distance, the lethargic supply truck whipped up a dust cloud. Ian was about to suggest taking a break so it could catch up, when Jua grabbed his shoulder. "*Simba, Bwana Umeme, simba.*"

"What's that? Oh, yes, lions. Jean, honey, make sure these boys get a closeup of mama *simba* over there."

"Where?" Frank asked. "I don't see anything."

Jean wheeled the Rover toward a baobab tree several hundred yards away. At that distance only a trained eye could distinguish the lioness and her cubs from the tan backdrop of rocks and bushes.

"Look to the left of that termite hill about thirty—"

"Oh, yeah, I see it. Holy shit! Paul, would you look at that?"

Paul sat in anxious silence as the vehicle slowly approached the lioness. She stood up and compelled her cubs to flee into the tall grass behind her.

Frank turned to the gunbearers, expecting to see one of them handing Ian a rifle. When there was no such activity, he tensed with fear. "Ian, is this safe? I mean there's nothing between her and us."

"Not to worry, old boy. This one's strictly a vegetarian. Wouldn't give a thought to chomping your tender bum."

"This isn't funny, Ian," Frank snarled, verging on panic.

"No need for panic, son. As long as we're in the transport, we're perfectly safe. Besides, I'm between you and those nasty teeth, so I'd get it first."

Jean kept quiet as her father conducted his little act, which she'd seen many times before. It had become somewhat of a tradition to scare the pants off newcomers with the lion bluff, which also served the vital purpose of acclimating new hunters to real situations involving dangerous animals.

When the Rover was about a hundred feet from the lioness, she started a dispirited charge, but aborted it after only a few yards, turning away with a roar and glaring at the group with callous defiance. Her rumpled body seemed to hang loosely from powerful shoulders, and her blemished hide twitched from insect bites.

Jean eased the Rover up a bit more, and the beast charged again, stopping some thirty feet away. The two Americans had already had enough and were transfixed by the animal's every move, convinced that for some unfathomable reason, the suicidal lunatics were going to get them eaten alive.

The lioness spun, growled, and advanced again. This time Ian slammed his arm against the side of the Rover, which halted the charge immediately. The big cat retreated a few steps, spun, and lunged, getting to within a few paces of the open vehicle before retreating for good. That charge proved to be more than the newcomers could handle, and they both lurched in the opposite direction with Frank nearly ejecting himself from the Rover.

Jean had expected as much, having seen it countless times, but she caught a glimpse of something she'd never witnessed before, and it disturbed her profoundly. During the last charge, she caught her father flinching—a sure sign that he may have lost his nerve. Was the leopard attack one close call too many, she wondered, or was he just fatigued from his abdominal wound and the trip? There was no way she could know for sure, but, either way, it was a bad omen. As a P.H. on safari, he was expected to stand his ground and shield client-hunters from danger.

Petrified by the lioness, neither Paul nor Frank had seen Ian flinch, but the natives, with their innate capacity for observation, did not miss it, and should they lose faith in their white hunter, disorder and abandonment would inevitably follow. Ian shot a fleeting glance at Jean after the moment had passed, hoping to find her watching the departing lion. Instead he found himself under the watchful eyes of a very disconcerted young woman. As a diversion he looked away, feigned laughter, and slapped his hands together. "Well, my Yankee *bwanas*, what do you think of our style of open-air zoo?"

"Not much, Ian," Paul replied. "That scared the crap out of me."

"Do you do this to all your people?" Frank asked, his voice unsteady. "Or do you just hate us?"

"Guys, I've been doing this for years, and I haven't lost anyone yet. Have I, Zuri?'

A little slower responding than Ian anticipated or appreciated, Jean said, "No, Daddy. You haven't lost anyone yet." She shoved the Rover into gear.

"Yeah, well, I think you guys are nuts," Frank mumbled, his tone suggesting he meant it.

As Jean gunned the Rover, the indignant lioness smoldered at being pestered by the toxic-smelling contraption and its occupants.

Reaching into his shirt pocket for several codeine tablets, Frank was becoming increasingly reliant on the drug to improve his disposition and preoccupied with their whereabouts and remaining numbers. His perspiration had melted the pills into a creamy mass at the bottom of his pocket. Without hesitation he salvaged what he could and sucked it off his fingers like a kid licking cake icing, cursing himself for wasting the bit that remained stuck to the corner of his pocket. Had he been alone he'd have turned his shirt inside out and licked the fabric.

The next several hours in the Rover passed in comparative silence, each person lost in personal thoughts.

With Lake Natron approaching up ahead and the sun sliding lower in the west, Jean brought the Rover to a slow stop and turned to face the men. "Welcome to Tanganyika, fellas. Do either of you fancy collecting some *nyama*—fresh meat—for the larder?"

It took an instant for the question to register, and then a wide grin blossomed across Frank's face. "Yesss, ma'am! Point me in the right direction, and get them cook fires a-roaring, 'cause Sure Shot Eastman's hit town."

Paul found himself contented just to hang around with the woman. "Go ahead, killer, knock 'em dead," he said. *And come back and join us in a month or two*, he thought.

"All right," Jean told Frank. Do you see that tree stump over there?"

"Yeah."

"We're going to motor over to it, and you, Susani, Jua, and I are going to jump out behind it. Paul and Daddy will drive straight away at right angles for several hundred yards and wait for us. That way, those Tommys—Thompson gazelle—over there will watch the Rover while we close in on them from around that line of thorn bushes."

Paul quickly realized that he'd written himself out of the script and made the necessary corrections. "Do you mind if I tag along and watch?"

"Of course not, *daktari*. That is, if Daddy doesn't object to going it alone."

"Pay no mind to me, my little hunters," Ian said with a sweep of his hand. "I'm on holiday, so be off with you."

Frank seized the moment to demonstrate his mastery of safari protocol. "Susani, *toa* Weatherby," he commanded, reaching toward the native and expecting to have the rifle slapped into his hands. Instead the African, who was in fact, Mchana, gave him a blank stare. There was a moment of hesitation by all.

"It's that one right there," Frank prompted, indicating his rifle.

"*Bwana* Eastman," Ian said, "might I suggest you show *Mchana* here just exactly what you're talking about, since judging from his response, I reckon he hasn't the faintest idea what the bloody hell a Weatherby is."

"Oh, I guess he wouldn't know, would he? I just figured he'd remember the rifle from this afternoon."

"Let me give you lesson number one on safari hunting, which is this: until you've been at this for a time, please let Jean or me give the orders and make the decisions. Is that clear? I can certainly understand your urge to get the hunt underway, but getting ahead of yourself will only spawn this type of muddle, which we're trying to avoid. Pace yourself, son. You've got months to hunt."

"Sorry, guys. I'm just excited about this."

"It wouldn't be the first time a client's gotten carried away," Jean said. "Would it, Daddy?"

"Hardly." Ian grunted, maneuvering into the driver's seat and starting the slow advance toward the tree stump. All the stalkers positioned themselves along the right side of the Rover so they could bail out at the same time. Jean addressed Mchana, who was balancing by holding the gun rack for support. *"Toa, bundouki four-oh-four na Bwana* Eastman's *bundouki kwa darbini."* The gunbearer handed Jean her tired-looking Cogswell and Harrison .404 bolt action and passed Frank his rifle with an attached telescope.

Frank forced out a grudging *"Asante*—thanks."

At the prescribed spot, they all fell out in a shuffled mass, Paul landing awkwardly enough to wrench his ankle. As they assembled behind the dead tree, Ian drove away, duping the unsuspecting gazelle. Paul tested his ankle by rotating it. "I must have twisted it when I hit the ground."

"Can you walk on it?" Jean inquired.

"If we have to move like you did yesterday, I doubt it. But don't worry about me. I'm just a spectator."

"Well, Skip," Frank interjected, "don't try to keep up with us if we get to moving too fast for you."

"Yes, Frank. Whatever you say, Frank."

"Hey, I'm just looking out for you."

"I know, and I'm quite touched. Why don't you just worry about yourself, okay?"

"Do you two always carry on like this?" Jean asked.

They both felt sheepish and broke off the hostilities.

Jua, who'd shown little interest in their squabble, had already slipped off in pursuit of the Tommys. Following Jean's lead, the other four fell in a short distance behind Jua. Shouldering both rifles, Susani kept close to Jean, never letting her get more than a step ahead of him. Since the pace was slow and cautious, Paul had little trouble hobbling along with the others. He admired Jua's deliberate movements; the African appeared to glide across the scrubby terrain, his head ceaselessly scanning the surrounding territory for the slightest hint of movement.

Frank, following astride, was uplifted by the promise of erasing his previous transgressions and at the same time winning Jean's respect. By administering one accurately placed bullet he hoped to garner the woman's admiration, thinking, *I may not know much about all this safari mumbo-jumbo, but I can damn sure hit a target when I have to.*

They'd made it only several hundred yards before Jua froze mid-step. Jean halted and grabbed Frank's arm. They all watched, motionless, as Jua gradually and almost imperceptibly crouched down. His fixed stare was a time-honored cue and call to action for Jean. She motioned with her fingers for Susani to hand the guns, which he did with the least possible movement.

Without interrupting his fix on whatever had caught his attention, Jua beckoned the hunters with the subtlest of hand motions, and Jean and Frank started forward. Paul stayed back with the gunbearer.

Frank watched Jean out of the corner of his eye. When his white huntress moved, he moved. When she shifted her rifle, he followed suit. His heart was pounding so fiercely in his ears that he thought it alarm the animals.

Jua opened his hand, and the hunters halted. Jean had a sense that the tracker was watching something other than a couple of gazelle, but because of the intermittent tracts of sense scrub, she couldn't confirm it. The animal, whatever it was, was obscured from view by a thicket at the tracker's immediate left. She eased down and indicated that Frank should do the same. Jua, aware of their proximity behind him, started to back up. When they met, he motioned with a nod of his head and whispered, "*Tendalla*," referring to one of Africa's most magnificent antelope, the kudu.

She looked intently and saw nothing until at last she perceived the vertical lines of the kudu's side seeming to emerge from the tangle of the surrounding bush. "A lovely beast," she murmured, more for her own edification than theirs, "and a respectable *tendalla* it is indeed." More of the kudu came into view with their breathtaking sweep of double curling horns and streamlined, long-stemmed bodies. "Oh, yes, just lovely." She sighed.

The handsome bull had been milling around during the heat of the day until the temperature settled sufficiently for it to abandon the confines of the thick bush and resume feeding on the open veldt. Its dark brownish-red coat contrasted with the various white markings on its sturdy horse-like frame. Adequately graced with long ringed horns, it represented a respectable trophy but most likely fell short of record-book stature.

Frank was feeling like a bridesmaid who missed the bouquet. He had yet to see anything but the locale's uninspiring flora and expressed his frustration in a hushed grouse. "I can't see a damn thing, Jean. What is it?"

Without losing eye contact with the kudu, she tilted her head toward him and whispered, "Focus on the thicket to the left of that acacia with the broken branch. About ten meters from the tree is a lesser kudu."

It didn't help his nerves to know he was in the vicinity of such an awe-inspiring trophy animal or that his ignorance of the metric system left him at a loss as to where he should actually focus. He'd purchased a book with photographic plates of African game animals and had spent several evenings leafing through the pages, admiring the majestic beasts and trying to assign them various places on his imaginary African trophy wall. One of his favorites was now standing less than a hundred yards away, and he couldn't see it. Suddenly his eyes opened like saucers and his mouth dropped. "I got it! I got it! Holy shit! What a beaut."

"Shhhhh."

"Sorry."

He'd seen the photos, but nothing prepared him for the spectacle before him. Even the Wyoming elk he'd taken a few years back paled in comparison to what stood just a short distance away.

"Frank," she whispered, "wait until he steps through the open spot behind that fallen limb. When he's in the open there, put it on his shoulder and wallop him. Okay?"

He nodded but hadn't even been listening to her. Jean and Jua backed away, giving him a clear field.

Frank drew on his experience, sitting on his rump with his left knee bent and his left foot planted on the ground. He braced his elbow in his knee and forced himself to steady his breathing.

Still oblivious to its plight, the kudu drifted into the open as Frank clicked off the safety and drew a deep breath. The shoulder of the animal zigzagged across the aperture in the crosshairs, and Frank's pulse bumped against the rifle's cheek-piece. He waited until the crosshairs passed the vital spot, and he squeezed the trigger.

When he recovered from the recoil, he was secure in the knowledge that his amassing of trophies was well in its way. He knew he was right on. What he didn't know was that when they all jumped from the Rover, Jean's boot had hit the scope and shifted the internal prism out of alignment, so instead of seeing his kudu lying on its side, kicking away its last shred of being, he watched as the graceful creature bounded away through the dense bush.

Jua was the first to come up to him. "*Piga hapana*," he said, while shaking his head.

"I know what you're saying. These animals are tough. The damn thing took a hit to the heart and still tore off."

The austere-looking African didn't understand a word of what Frank had said but was a bit surprised that he could accept a clean miss with such delight.

"I'm sorry to have to tell you this, but *piga hapana* means 'not hit,'" Jean explained. "It looks as though you missed."

"There's no damn way, Jean. That's a dead kudu."

By then Paul and Susani had walked up and gathered around. Jua took off to try to locate any spoor, in the event there had been a hit. Susani stared at the ground and shook his head.

"I couldn't see what you were shooting at," Paul said, "but I'm really sorry you missed."

"I'm telling you guys that shot was dead on."

"I hope you're right, Frank, but I'd prepare yourself for the worst. Jua's fairly reliable on this sort of thing."

With all the doubt floating around, Frank slipped into despondency. Self-lacerating questions swirled in his mind: *How could I have missed such a sure shot? Can't I do anything right? What's going to happen when things get serious? Am I going to be eaten alive because I'm a crappy shot?*

Jean could see that he was really shaken by the missed shot. "As I told the *daktari* yesterday," she said, "it's not uncommon for new hunters to be a little unsteady in the beginning."

Paul couldn't refrain from jibing, "Maybe it was a nut loose on the trigger."

Frank's eyes turned into slits and the muscles in his neck popped up. He stared at Paul and had a fleeting thought that maybe his friend had tampered with the scope in the hopes of leveling the playing field. He scrutinized Paul, trying to detect the slightest hint of contrition and then dismissed the notion. In all the years they'd been friends, Paul had never once displayed so much as a hint of vindictiveness.

Ian came roaring to a stop in the Rover, enveloping them in dust. "I don't like the looks of this. Make a poor shot?"

"It looks that way, Daddy, and it was a fine tendalla bull."

"I don't understand," Frank said. "I might have been shaking a little, Ian, but I was right on."

The seasoned hunter rubbed his chin. "Hand me the rifle."

Frank turned it over to him and watched as Ian pulled a cartridge from a loop in his shirt. He rapped the scope with it, laid the rifle on the door jamb of the vehicle, sighted at a distant tree, and fired. There was no indication of an impact.

"Telescope's out," Ian asserted, handing the rifle back to him. "Hate the bloody contraptions for just that reason. Responsible for countless lost or wounded beasts."

Frank's disposition went from bad to worse. He had been cheated by faulty gear and wanted to sling the rifle into the bush by its barrel. "You got a screwdriver, Ian?"

"Sure do, son," he responded. To Mchana he said, *"Bisibisi tafadhali,"* and the gunbearer opened a tool kit in the back of the Rover, extracting a series of English turnscrews wrapped in a felt bag.

Each ebony-handled implement was a work of art in itself. Frank selected one, and within a few minutes unscrewed the scope and its base from the rifle. He took the greatest pleasure in hurling the optical devise into the bushes with all his might.

Ian and Jean remained silent and let him blow off some steam with his childish behavior.

Jean felt it was important to get the American client back in the saddle. "Now that we've put that behind us, how about attending to the task of securing some good *nyama*—meat—for us and the boys?"

"That sounds fine to me," Frank said, "but I hope you've got some canned stuff just in case."

Although still oozing self-pity, Frank returned to the hunt and scored immediate triumphs. Within minutes the American took a respectable Thompson's gazelle and made an impressively long shot at a wildebeest, which was a clean kill.

CHAPTER TWELVE

Discontent

Although Frank's kills were good, they weren't the most impressive trophies in the world, but no one could have told by the reaction of the natives, who made an inordinately big fuss over them with hooting, hollering, back slapping, and a fusillade of indecipherable phrases. Frank was back in the game, but he longed for the lost kudu.

Paul applauded Frank's minor victories, and at long last found himself itching for a chance to jump into the action and take a trophy, but he'd have to wait, since the daylight was fading fast. The group loaded up and made way for camp.

Jean wasn't sure where the crew had chosen to set up the encampment, but she had a general idea of the location, easing through the darkened landscape as small birds and animals darted across the headlight beams.

Paul couldn't wait to get his boot off and massage his throbbing ankle. He worried that the mishap might prevent him from joining the others over the next several days, which made him uneasy about having Frank and Jean off on their own.

Sweet wood smoke smell hit the group's nostrils shortly before the glow of the campfire came into view, and their spirits lightened at the sight of the roaring blaze in the distance. It meant food, warmth, safety, comfort, and in Frank's case, numbing refreshment. "I could use a drink," he said, "how about you, folks?"

"I was just thinking how a gin and quinine would hit the spot," Ian said.

"As for this *memsaab*, I fancy a hot *bathi*, clean bed sheets, and maybe just a wee glass of *mvinyo*," Jean said, illustrating with her fingers how much sherry she wanted.

The Africans raised a cheer as the game-laden vehicle pulled up, according Frank a hero's welcome.

As the hunters freshened up, Kemoa oversaw the butchering of the tenderloins from the Tommy. Later the venerable native chef grilled the evening's steaks.

Paul stood apart from the others at the natives' separate cook fire, gazing into it and thinking about Sheldon back home.

"Hey, *daktari*, would you care to join us at the table?'

Ian's voice brought him out of a daydream, and he replied, "I'm coming. Just let me get my boot on."

"How's the ankle, Paul?"

"I think it'll be okay. It's just a little sore.

"You were a million miles away just then. I hope you didn't mind the intrusion."

"No, that's all right. I was just thinking about home."

"Yeah," Frank said. "You should see it, the lucky bastard. I'm fixing 'dozers and gettin' greasy, and he lives like a prince. Don't you, Skippy?"

"Knock it off, Frank," Paul cautioned, handling him as gingerly as possible. He could tell by Frank's slurred speech and droopy eyes that he had been guzzling booze.

"Oh, I'm sure they'd love to hear about Cap and how you got so rich so fast."

"Back off, Frank."

"And the yacht, and the—"

Paul sprang from his chair and tackled Frank, spilling him over backwards. He attempted a swing, but Frank blocked it and landed one of his own on Paul's temple. Every native in the camp stopped working and watched with fascination as the white foreigners went at each other.

Jean, embarrassed for the two, chose to remain in her seat and stay out of the fray.

Dazed, Paul felt himself being pulled off the ground by the powerful muscled arms of Kemoa, the first to intervene. Neither Paul nor Frank was a match for the strength of the natives, and they both found themselves dangling in a mid-air bear hug. Despite being disoriented, Paul was astounded by the might of the elderly African cook.

Forcing himself between the two combatants, Ian screamed, "I don't know what the bloody hell this is about, but I . . . will . . . not . . . permit this sort of thing in my camp. Do you understand me? *Bwana* Eastman, if you insist on provoking trouble, I will pack this safari up and make way for Nairobi right this bloody goddamn instant. Do you hear?"

"Yes, sir," Frank murmured.

"If you two can't get along, this trip is done. You need to decide, right bloody now."

"We'll get along," Paul said. "I promise. Won't we, Frank?" Holding his pounding head, Paul looked at his rival, inviting reconciliation. Frank nodded, spun, and retreated to his tent, his head hanging dejectedly.

With the show over, the natives returned to their chores.

"I'm sorry about this, folks," Paul said, returning to his seat. "It's been brewing since we got on the plane in Miami. Maybe now he won't be so angry with me."

"If you don't mind my asking," Jean said, "what on earth did you do to get him so agitated?"

"I guess he's always envied me. Life's been tougher for him.

"I don't want to pry, but who is Cap? A relative?"

Paul didn't want to talk about it, but concluded that it wouldn't hurt to expose a bit of his personal life. "My mother died when I was very young, and my father raised me until the start of the war. He enlisted in the Navy and left me with an old friend of his named Doug Hendrix. Cap is what we called him. Anyway, Dad bought it on the Lexington at Midway, so Cap adopted me and raised me."

"I'm very sorry," Jean said.

"Thank you. Cap was one of those guys who could do about everything. He was a machinist, and he invented some devices that made a good living for him. You know, with royalties and all. He was a pretty shrewd investor and made even more through real estate," he added between bites. "He used to take Frank and me hunting and fishing all the time. He really went out of his way to take good care of Frank, whose father was a worthless drunk— beat up the family all the time."

"I see."

"Cap only had me, Sheldon, and Clorese—no other family."

"You mentioned something about Sheldon the other day. I assume Clorese is his wife?"

"Yeah, they both came to work for Cap as housekeepers a long time ago and have been there ever since." Paul speared another chunk of grilled meat from the platter. "Kemoa and Sheldon look so much alike it's uncanny. They could be brothers. It's like having old Shel along on this trip." Paul drew a breath. "Last summer Cap died, and it's shaken me pretty badly."

"Had he been ill long?"

"For all of five hours," he lamented, looking away.

"Oh, dear, how awful. He must have been proud of your achievements though."

Paul shrugged. "A lot of good it did him."

"What do you mean by that?"

"Never mind. Anyhow, he left most of his estate to me. Sheldon and Clorese got the rest."

Ian said, "I believe I can understand the problem now—with your friend, that is." Turning to his daughter he said, "The solution is for us to get *Bwana* Eastman into the record books during his stay here. That might even things out a trifle." He turned to Paul. "However, that may require you to settle for trophies of a lesser quality."

"Fine by me. It's not that important to me anyway."

"It's settled, then. Frank gets priority—the big buggers are his."

Paul yawned from exhaustion. Both his head and ankle were throbbing. He needed sleep. "If you'll excuse me, I'm going to turn in."

"Do you think it's safe in there with him?" Jean asked.

"If he's even still awake, I doubt he'll give me much trouble now. I think it's out of his system, and I'll bet he feels like an idiot on top of it."

After he drifted off to the tent, Ian observed, "That is some pair, huh, Zuri?"

"They do make for an interesting time."

"I have a feeling there's something buried that the *daktari* hasn't told us."

"What do you mean?"

"I can't explain it, but he's holding something back. The way he was talking, you'd think he feels personally responsible for that bloke's death."

"Perhaps he was just very close to him."

"I don't know, but I wouldn't be surprised if we heard more before this safari's over. Now if you'll excuse me—."

"You just stay right where you are, *Bwana* Lightning. I've got some talking to do with you."

Ian knew what was coming and grappled for a strategy to deal with it. "Yes, honey, what is it?"

"Don't give me that 'yes, honey' baloney. You know bloody well it is."

"If you're referring to that incident with the *simba* this afternoon, think nothing of it."

"Oh, really? Think nothing of it? Like hell, Daddy. You were unnerved, weren't you?"

Realizing that he wasn't about to bluff his way out of it, he changed tactics. "All right, so I flinched. What of it?"

"What of it? How can you protect a client if you doubt yourself?"

"Maybe I'm just a bit frayed from the *chui* business."

"Whatever it is, I don't like it. It spells trouble, and you know it."

"Before you have me cast aside of left for *fisi* I urge you to refrain from making a larger issue of it, especially in front of the boys or the clients. Now, I'm tired and I wish to go to sleep." Getting up and kissing her on the forehead, he added, "Don't stay up too late. I feel tomorrow promises to be a full one. Good night."

CHAPTER THIRTEEN

Scars from the Past

Kilimanjaro loomed massive in the distance, the morning sun illuminating the upper reaches of its snowy summit. The towering expanse served as a backdrop for the grassy plains, broken terrain, and low-lying hills that lay before it. Grazing animals appeared as unsettled flecks on the seemingly endless veldt.

Paul stood against a warm breeze that swept up from the arid valley floor and watched as undulating waves brushed through the stretches of tall grass. From his vantage point on the slope of Mount Gelai, he beheld a panorama that extended from Kilimanjaro to the southeast and to Lake Natron in the northwest. He assumed correctly that it was no accident that the Sharpes had selected the site and was hoping that for a little while, anyway, they would remain there. He got out of bed early and slipped out of the tent without waking Frank. Not knowing what his arousal would bring or how to deal with it, he chose to delay the showdown as long as possible. He understood Frank's resentment of his privileged life and was not particularity peeved at being punched in the head, but he hated any type of confrontation. More importantly he couldn't stand any insinuation that he was delighting in what he felt were ill-gotten gains

There were no footsteps or advance warnings to alert him.

"That's a hell of a sight, isn't it, Skip?"

Paul remained motionless, his gaze fixed on the distant mountain. Adrenaline shot through his system, causing him to tremble. He knew he couldn't ignore Frank, but he really didn't want to deal with him. *Shit,* he thought, *I'm stuck here with this bastard, and he can't leave me alone, can he?*

"I can't blame you for being pissed off," Frank said.

Paul whipped around. "I'm really pleased to hear that, Frank. I was afraid you'd be upset that I thought you were an asshole. Do you have any idea what she—they must think of us after last night?" Paul snarled, pointing toward the camp. "Do you know how close they came to packing up and calling an end to this safari?"

"I was pretty drunk."

"There's a big surprise. How many times are we going to put up with that lame excuse for justifying your idiotic behavior?"

Frank's hand's clenched. "I like to drink, so what?"

"Can't you see what it does to you? Wasn't your old man's boozing tough enough on your family, or did you forget about that?"

"Don't compare me with that piece of shit."

"Why shouldn't I? You're turning into a carbon paper copy of him. Wasn't I beat up by a younger version of him last night?"

"I'm really sorry about that, but you threw the first punch."

"What was I supposed to do, sit there and listen to all that bullshit about Cap's estate? I can't help it if things have been easier for me, and I'm damn sure not going to sit around and let you rub my nose in it."

Gazing toward Kilimanjaro, Frank hesitated before speaking again. "I guess I've always envied you and probably always will."

"Frank, I never knew my mother, and my pop took off and got himself killed in the war. Cap was all I had left, and he's gone now. Just what in the hell is there to envy about that?"

"You had fun as a kid. I lived like a bum and had to put up with that fuck head. You're a doctor, and I haul dirt for a living. And another thing—I can see already that the girl likes you more than me.

"You mean Jean?"

"Do you see any other girls around here?"

"What makes you think she would have any interest in either one of us? The way I see it, she's strictly business. If she wasn't, don't you think she'd already be married?"

"That's the part I can't figure out, but I'll tell you one thing, if anything's going to happen here, I'll lay you odds it involves you, not me."

That was certainly music to Paul's ears. Not for a second did he actually expect his buddy to drop out of the race that easily, but he savored hearing what he'd begun to sense already. He played it down as best he could, telling Frank, "Correct me if I'm wrong, but didn't we come here to hunt?"

"Yeah, but so much has happened since we left Nairobi I'm starting to wonder."

Seizing the opportunity to boost Frank's sagging morale, Paul said, "Last night after you left, some of us talked for a while."

"Talked about me, right?" Frank said, going on the defensive.

"Yes, and Ian said he really wanted to get you in the record books and figured with a little extra effort on their part, they probably could. It would mean I'd have to take a back seat and hunt less, but I don't care."

"That's real nice, Skip, but I don't want you paying all this money and sitting around here watching me shoot everything."

"Look around," Paul said, sweeping his hand across the horizon. "Does it look like there's any shortage of things for me to shoot here? It just means you get first crack at the big stuff. But do me one favor, please. Back off on the bottle and leave Cap out of this. Can't you see it's a sore subject with me? Deal?" He smiled and extended his hand.

"I'm not going to tell you I won't drink, but I'll try to keep it under control."

The two shook hands and the truce was settled.

Paul nodded in the direction of camp. "Let's go get some breakfast and get on with it."

"I'm going to get washed up and ready to hunt," Frank said, leaving for his tent. He was relieved that his old comrade had been understanding, and he resolved to refrain from overindulging again. It shouldn't be all that difficult, he thought; since he had an ample supply of codeine to augment his spirits, should the need arise. Ingesting the little pills elevated his mood without the obnoxious behavior that alcohol induced.

Paul set out to find Ian, feeling the need to let him know that all was well between the two former combatants. He chose a path taking him behind the row of tents before entering the common area, where the dining tarp was erected. The ground was still damp with dew, and his approach went undetected by Jean, who was on one knee, tying her bootlace, her back to him.

"Morning, Jean."

Startled, she spun to face him, her eyes inexplicably full of terror, her hand instinctively flying to her throat, but not before Paul saw the jagged scar traversing it. In her eyes were terror and the fear of discovery. Shocked, he looked away, but it was too late. The damage had been done. She fled to her tent in a state of abject mortification, leaving him dazed and ashamed to have seen her secret disfigurement.

He tried to piece together the circumstances that could explain such brutal, ragged scarring. Could it have been the type of animal attack that recently befell her father? That cause would be the most plausible, but the scar was too adeptly located to have been the result of sheer happenstance. Suicide? Improbable, and the length and position of it made it highly unlikely that the scar had been surgically induced, leaving one other option The mere thought of it made him uneasy at first and then angered. Was it possible that somebody had tried to kill her? Who in the world would have wanted to harm such an innocent creature, and for what reason?

As he walked about the encampment trying to sort through his thoughts, he felt an overwhelming impulse to go to her, but he didn't even know if he could look her in the eye. Instead he sought out Ian, who was working under the hood of the Rover. "Good morning, Ian. How's the side today?"

"Well, top of the morning *daktari*. I trust you've had an uneventful slumber." Wiping grease from his hands, he patted the bandage on his abdomen and said, "Things seem to be improving as expected."

"Good! I had a talk with Frank this morning, and I think we've ironed out some things. There shouldn't be any repeat of last night."

"I hope that's the case, because I'd hate to have Zuri call an end to it and send you chaps back to the States."

"I don't think that'll be necessary."

"That being the case, I suggest we grab some *chamshakinywa* and be on our way again."

"What the hell is that?"

"Breakfast, my American friend," he said, flipping the rag into the Rover and slamming the hood.

"Where are we going after that?"

"We still have another day's drive to reach our first genuine *campi*."

"What's wrong with staying right here for a couple of days? I mean, it's certainly a pleasant enough spot, and there seems to be enough game around here to keep us busy."

"This place is fine, except the game's much thicker elsewhere."

"I don't know, Ian. If it's all the same to you, I'd like to spend some time here."

"Have you discussed it with your companion? I should expect he'd want to be where his chances are best for the records."

"Let me see what he has to say before you have the boys take the tents down."

"It's your safari, *daktari*. We'll go along with whatever you decide."

Paul felt it would do everyone some good to take it easy for a time, and he needed to put some space between the morning's incident with Jean. He wanted to ask Ian about it, but could imagine no discreet way to broach the subject without intruding on what was obviously a very personal and sensitive issue with Jean.

Wanting to maintain a low profile, Frank accepted the change in plans and agreed to hunt around the outlying valleys, admitting that it may actually benefit him to practice stalking and shooting less challenging game in preparation for the trophies he envisaged collecting later.

Jean was conspicuously absent at breakfast. Ian, unaware of what had happened, related her alibi that she was feeling a bit under the weather and would rest in camp.

Paul refrained from offering his medical assistance, which surprised Frank. It would have been the perfect ruse for being alone with her. Frank assumed Jean was probably suffering from the monthly affliction that had, in the past, occasionally thwarted his romantic endeavors. If that were the case, Jean would be in no mood for Paul or anyone else.

Before they left camp for the day's excursion, Ian pulled a pump shotgun from a soft leather case. Both of the Americans recognized it as being a Model 12 Winchester, the preferred choice of a repeater for bird hunters back home. They watched as Ian stuffed several magnum-length shells into the underside loading port of the gun and then carried it inside Jean's tent, emerging empty handed a few seconds later. The two looked at each other. "Must be for snakes and stuff," Frank contended.

CHAPTER FOURTEEN

Melted Chocolate

An hour or so later, in the vast open expanse of the Rift Valley floor, the shot sounded like a thud. Without obstructions for the shock wave to bounce off, there was no echo. The zebra took off with the other ones in the herd but soon lagged behind, and then came to a stop and stood motionless, its head drooping.

"Should we run up to it so I can put another shot in?" Paul asked, feeling sorry for the wounded beast.

"I shouldn't consider it necessary," Ian said. "The poor bloke is already dead, but hasn't realized it yet."

About the time Ian finished his comment, the animal fell over. Paul had made his first African kill. He hadn't expected to feel the way he did. Perhaps it was because the zebra was so similar in appearance to a horse that it didn't register with him as a true game trophy. *Sure, they make nice rugs,* he thought, trying to excite himself. *What am I going to do with it now? Where am I going to put it? On the wall with two spears crossed in front of it, like one of those Hollywood directors whose drinking rooms you see in the magazine?* He smirked at another absurd image that leapt to mind: he was grandiloquently draped in a robe, a cigarette holder clenched between his teeth as he preened in front of his trophy zebra. *Maybe I've outgrown this sort of thing,* he thought. *Well, this is certainly one hell of a time to come to that conclusion.*

As they walked toward the downed animal, Paul was nagged by another, more complex feeling, the same longing sensation he'd felt when Robin stopped calling him, except this time the experience was much more intense. What he longed for was Jean, and despite having known her for a short time, he missed having her by his side, missed her squinty-eyed smiles, and missed her voice complimenting his fine shot. He wanted to watch her as she did anything, everything.

He kept coming back to the image of her looking up at him, frightened and ashamed, trying to veil the physical and emotional scar from some unspeakable horror from her past. The thought of her back at the camp alone, perhaps reliving whatever it had been that had left her marked, erased any pleasure he could have derived from the morning's achievement. *What kind of a god allows things like that to happen?* he asked himself. *The same one who let me kill Cap, I guess.*

With regard to the doctrine of a supreme creator, he'd always taken a middle-of-the-road posture, and recent events did little to change his position. Clorese, a devout woman, had always taken it upon herself to be his spiritual guiding light, forever citing passages from the holy book for his benefit. He'd either argue with her from a secular standpoint or tune her out. She'd become agitated, throw her hands in the air, and beg forgiveness for his heretical soul. Cap, on the other hand, had been a privately religious man who tried to convey his message by action rather than words. "Do unto others as you would have them do unto you" was the sole creed on which he based his conduct. He worked to impart the principle on the young disciple left in his care.

The Rover came zooming up with Frank yelling and waving from the passenger's seat. "Hey Skipper, I see you finally remembered how to shoot. The skin's gonna look great in your living room."

"On the wall with spears in front of it, right?"

"You got it, pal."

Ian noticed Paul's indifference and his general lack of enthusiasm about the kill. It was natural for some clients to experience regret, but Paul's demeanor edged on depression, which Ian considered a bit extreme.

Remorse following a kill was fairly predictable since it meant the taking of a life, which was particularly intense whenever an elephant was taken. Steely indeed was the hunter who did not flinch at the sight of a slain behemoth for which he was responsible. Many a time Ian had busied himself at a distance while his client wept alone out of respect for the noble beast that lay before him. Most of the time the hunter recovered, at peace with the consequences of his actions. However, sometimes plans had to be altered and the safari set on a different, less brutal course. Sightseeing or photographic ventures were recommended for the faint of heart. It was rare that a trip was brought to a halt by the misgivings of the hunter, but it happened from time to time. Ian's technique was to progress slowly, allowing each client to work through his emotions at his own rate and sometimes to offer justification when necessary. "I sense a bit of reservation on your part," Ian said to Paul. "Does the killing upset you?"

Butting in, Frank exclaimed, "Hell no, Ian. Skip's been shootin'—"

The professional hunter held up his hand. "I'd like to hear what the *daktari* has to say."

"I don't know, Ian. I'm really not bothered by it, and Frank's right. I've been hunting since I was a little kid. I guess I'm just overwhelmed by it all, or maybe I've outgrown the sport. I just don't know." *Maybe I just really miss your daughter,* he thought.

"Not to worry, son. We'll carry on, and you just hop in when you're good and ready."

"Thanks, Ian, and don't worry about me. I'll be fine."

They climbed aboard the Rover and drove up to Jua, who was already beside the dead zebra.

The animal had been dead for several minutes, but that fact didn't discourage Mohammed, the skinner, who hopped from the back of the vehicle and slit the zebra's throat. He and his son immediately began to strip the hide from the carcass. The two Americans watched as the two Africans deftly removed the black-and-white banded skin, taking great care not to compromise its beauty or integrity with unwieldy, careless blunders.

Once the hide had been removed, it was salted and carefully rolled up for later attention. Back at camp it would be carefully scraped to remove all remnants of meat that would cause it to rot. The carcass would then feed the natives. Only the bones and some entrails were left for the hyenas and vultures.

A couple of hours later, Frank took his first true trophy animal. The party had been driving through the fairly level but broken terrain when Jua spotted several fringe-eared oryx in the far distance. A plan was mapped out, and a group consisting of Ian, Frank, Jua, Mchana, and Susani were ejected from the rolling vehicle as Reli the driver, Paul, and the two skinners continued at right angles until they were sufficiently far away so as not to alert the prey.

Parked approximately three hundred meters away, Paul warmed his bottom on the scorching hot hood of the Rover, using his knees to support his binoculars. With his sunglasses atop his head and between periodic sips of warm Tusker beer and a pull from his cigarette, he followed the advance of the stalkers. His fellow passengers were cupping their hands against the glare as they watched the event with bare eyes. The visibility was marginal, since turbidity of the hot valley air caused the images to take on a distorted, mirage-like appearance. Paul could barely see the stalkers as they dodged from one obstruction to another, the oryx meandering undisturbed hundreds of meters beyond them. He kept swinging the binoculars from the hunters to the game and back again until he noticed some of the oryx bounding away in alarm. He knew that Frank's moment of opportunity had passed, and they'd have to begin the process all over again. As the image of Frank stabilized in the field of view, he saw him recoil from the shot. A quick shift to the target revealed dust and thrashing legs where the animals had previously been standing. Evidently one of them had gone down. The report of the shot and its impact followed a second later. Reli wasted no time wheeling the Rover around and heading for them.

Frank wasn't just happy; he was ecstatic. He could be seen from the approaching vehicle walking backwards in front of the others, his arms animated as he reenacted the event for their benefit. His elation was because of Ian's suggestion that the animal might have carried enough horn to slip its slayer into the record book.

Breaking away from the others, Frank jogged up to meet them. "Skip, did you see that fuckin shot? Pow! *Kufa*."

"I saw it all in the binocs. For a second I thought they were gone."

"I know. Ian here didn't think I could shoot that well, did you?"

"More than adequate. Considerably more than adequate. In fact, bloody superb."

"Yeah, well, I wouldn't go that far, Ian."

"Like hell! That was as splendid a shot as they come."

Despite Frank's disclaimer, praise was what he wanted and desperately needed to hear. There hadn't been many instances throughout his life when someone he'd respected said something positive to him. Cap had been the frontrunner in that department. He'd always made a point to encourage the young man at every opportunity, to counter the negative influence amply supplied by his father. Frank had such a low opinion of himself that he couldn't even accept Ian's compliment as the genuine article. He liked hearing it but was uncomfortable; deep down he felt he didn't deserve anything.

Sensing Frank's discomfort, Paul chimed in, saying, "I'm really proud of you, pal. I couldn't have done it. How about a beer to celebrate?"

"Stupid question."

Paul, who'd been preparing for the moment by studying Swahili told driver, Reli, "*Mohamad, tafadhali niletee pombe ya Taska kwa Bwana Easton na Bwana Umeme,*"

"When'd you learn that?" queried Frank.

Even Paul himself was surprised when the native produced two bottles of beer from the provision box.

"It appears my services are in the midst of being phased out," Ian said, grinning. He was relieved that things had turned around quickly, for what had been open warfare a short time before had become two friends sharing each other's triumphs with a beer. Regardless of whether the dead oryx carried record-book horns, it was going to make a dandy trophy. While the Americans admired the obtuse-looking black-and-white masked head of the beast, Ian went to get a measuring tape. Having seen countless examples of all the East African species, he suspected this one fell short; however, to give Frank the benefit or the doubt and to interject a little drama, he grabbed the tape and a battered copy of Rowland Ward's *Records of Big Game*. The well-worn volume was out of date by nearly twenty-three years, but it still served as a guide, listing the ranking, in descending order, of the consummate trophies for each species.

Frank stood aside and held his breath while Ian took some quick measurements. "Thirty-one and a quarter. I think we're a mite short." Ian leafed through the book and, noting the cutoff was thirty-two inches, announced the results. "Rotten luck, old boy, I'm afraid we're under by almost an inch."

"Aw, shit!"

Paul, genuinely sorry for the missed opportunity, consoled his friend. "Remember, you didn't come here just to make it into that book, right?

"Well, yeah."

"So what's the problem? This thing's magnificent."

"He's right, Frank. It's all too easy to get caught up in this record-book business and lose sight of the whole affair."

"I know, but for once in my life I'd like to do something really special. Like get into that book."

"Have patience, young man. Glory could await you around the very next *mgeuko*."

"*Mgeuko* meaning turn?"

Ian nodded. "Oh, one other thing. That shot was on par with my little girl's. If you can shoot like that on a regular basis, I do believe she's met her match. Too bad she wasn't here to see it for herself."

"I was just thinking that," Frank said. "I'm sorry she missed it."

Yeah, what a shame, Paul thought. He then got hit with the same empty feeling again. *What's going on here*, he wondered, and the only conclusion he could draw was that he was falling in love with the woman. His mind repeatedly drifted to vignettes of them alone, trading compassionate gazes, his fingers gingerly tracing her delicate features. He wanted to embrace her and never let go. The only problem was that he couldn't even look her in the eye. He made a promise to himself that he would remedy their estrangement as soon as he returned to camp. If he could figure out how.

The hunters spent the rest of the afternoon in the Rover foraging the region in search of other targets, but finding nothing worthy of their efforts. The only interesting prospect was a repulsive-looking warthog. When Ian informed them that the unsightly animals were plentiful throughout the country, they opted to pass it up and take one later in the trip.

Totally wrapped up in the chase, they failed to realize how far from camp the trek had taken them. Wearied, stiff, and hungry from the first day of real hunting, the group bounced and bumped its way back to its starting point. Ian complained about his side but didn't appear to be in any major discomfort. Paul made a mental note to check him over after dinner.

Contented was the only way to describe Frank as he alternated between perusing the landscape and ogling his slain oryx. After all, with only one day of hunting behind them, he'd already taken a fair-sized gazelle, a representative wildebeest, and one very stunning oryx. The bungled kudu still weighed heavily on his mind, but his rapidly mounting tally of successes was taking the sting out of it. Riding in the vehicle, he made a pledge to himself that from that point on he would pace himself and take only exemplary examples of each species. If he were going to return home to financial devastation, at least he'd have an abundance of mementos to show for it.

He reflected on how he'd left matters back in Florida, and it dawned on him how irresponsible he'd been. The fear that potential ruin awaited him at home nearly offset the enjoyment of the day's achievements, and he craved the fallacious tranquility that whiskey and codeine afforded him. On that account Frank knew he'd have to govern himself closely to prevent a recurrence of the previous night's fiasco.

Paul tried to focus on big game stalking, but kept coming back to the girl. He wracked his brain, trying to engineer a suitable reconciliation. He knew he couldn't lie about having seen her scar, or worse, attempt to broach the subject by pretentiously stating medical concerns. That approach was sure to be taken as insincere and pompous. He had to think of something creative.

With the glow of the campfire visible on the plateau ahead, Paul finally devised his plan. It was inane at best, but for lack of anything better he chose to implement the silly little scheme and hoped it would rectify the situation. *The worst that could happen,* he thought, *is that I'll look like an asshole, but she'll still take us hunting, and I'll shoot things over the next month.* The thought depressed him.

There was the typical hoopla when the natives greeted them at camp. Frank took it all in. He felt like he'd caught the winning pass at the football game.

Paul pretended to share in the festivities but had other things on his mind. He'd spotted Jean entering her tent as they pulled in and was eying the drawn canvas flap on the enclosure.

Wanting to handle things as discreetly as possible, he slipped away from the group and made a beeline for his own tent. Once inside he turned up the lamp and rifled through his bag of personal belongings until he ferreted out one of the semi-squashed bars of foreign chocolate that he'd purchased earlier. It was in pitiful condition, having partially melted from the afternoon heat. Seeing it, Paul considered aborting the plan. He handled it as gingerly as if it were a vial of nitroglycerin, not wanting to deform the wrapping any worse. "*What the hell*," he said to himself, and lit out for Jean's tent. "Jean, are you in there?"

"Please, Paul, I'd really rather be alone right now."

"I won't bother you, but will you please just stick your hand out of the tent?"

There was a short delay before she answered. "Perhaps later. For now, I'd just like to——"

"Please, just reach out here; then I'll go away."

He could hear a shuffle as she got up from her cot. Her slender arm emerged reluctantly from the enclosure like a burrowing animal testing the light. He gingerly placed the chocolate in her hand and watched as it withdrew.

After a pause he heard a soft giggle. The tent flap opened, and she stepped out. He shot a quick uncontrollable glimpse at her scarf-swathed neck and then willed himself not to let it happen again, ever.

The sight of her, and the fervor it induced, made him slightly dizzy. Trembling and afraid to speak, he knew his unsteady voice would give him away.

She faced him, her head tipped and slanted slightly. Staring at him from the tops of her eyes, she smiled sheepishly and dug the toe of her sneaker into the ground

Paul felt he had to say something, "I feel terrible——"

She shook her head and lightly placed the tip of her finger against his lips. "Some other time perhaps," was all she said.

He nodded. If she was loath to discuss her scarred throat, he certainly wasn't going to press the issue.

"Thank you for the chocolate. How did you know it was my favorite?"

"It was the only thing I had besides a dead zebra."

"Oh, did you collect one today?"

"Yeah, but now that I've got it, I haven't got a clue what to do with it."

Jean gave him a confused look. "You don't seem very excited by it. What do you mean, you don't know what to do with it?

"I don't know. I just can't see myself tacking it up on a wall at home."

"They do make a lovely throw rug," she offered. "I don't understand. If you feel this way about your first trophy, what's to become of any game heads you might get in the future? That *is* why you went on safari, yes?"

"I'm starting to wonder about that."

"You're not regretting having come here, are you?"

"Oh no, not at all." *I would have made the trip just to look at you,* he thought. "I'm just not that big on flaunting my achievements like other people do."

"Well, you'll have to do something with them. We've always taken a pretty dim view of wanton killing, and you certainly can't expect us to endorse such a thing."

The last thing he needed was her contempt. "You don't have to worry— I won't shoot anything I won't do *something* with." He sounded irresolute, even to himself. "What I mean is, if I decide not to shoot anything else, it won't have any effect on how much fun I have here." *There, that was better,* he thought.

"Yes, but you've spent a frightfully large sum of money to do this."

"I don't think I've wasted a penny coming here."

She smiled at him and shrugged. "How did Frank do today?"

"Oh, he's been stacking dead animals like cord wood. He got a thirty-one-inch oryx and made a hell of a shot to get it. You would have been impressed."

"I'm so happy for him; he needed a boost. I'm afraid he appears so unfulfilled, and this safari seems important to him. Shall we go have a peek?"

CHAPTER FIFTEEN

Close Call

It was not lost on Jean that Paul had placed a highest priority on clearing the air between them. While the others had been celebrating and tending to the animals, he had chosen to call on her and ease the difficulties.

During the day she'd thought about him and had hoped something like this would have happened. She felt she owed him an explanation, lest his curiosity spoil their time together, but it would have to wait for a more appropriate time when she was able to handle it herself.

"Hello, darling." Ian said. "I trust the *daktari* has filled you in on the day's events."

"Most definitely," Jean said, glancing at Frank and then down at the skinner as he trimmed the bits of flesh from the hide of the oryx. "It seems *Bwana* Eastman here is making a name for himself. I can't wait to hear the details."

"How are you feeling, sweetheart?" Ian asked.

"Oh, much better now. And you? How's the side?"

"A trifle sore, but I don't see my guts spilling out on the ground as before. I'll have Paul take a look at it after we eat."

"Speaking of food," Frank said, sipping a diluted tan drink from a clear plastic cup, "are you gonna share that chocolate with us?"

Like hell she is, thought Paul, hoping she would finesse her way out of the question. He couldn't bear the thought of Frank licking the melted goo that he had tendered out of affection to her.

She smiled, subtly slipping it into her shirt pocket. "Unfortunately I neglected to keep it in the shade," she said, shooting Paul a wink. "It's almost ruined,"

Kemoa had outdone himself with the evening meal. The distinct aroma of strong curry hobnobbed with the heavenly bouquet of freshly baked bread. A mountain of a light green mash, which turned out to be canned peas compounded with potatoes and seasonings, filled a wood bowl. Fried bananas, adrift in a candy syrup, invited assault, and bowls of hot peanut soup got things off to a start.

Having rinsed off the day's grime and changed into fresh clothes, the hunters tucked into dinner with a vengeance. The curry, a carryover from the Indian influence of the region, was made with chunks of the previous day's gazelle. It was strongly seasoned, as genuine curry should be, and was fiery hot. Beads of sweat formed on the diners' foreheads, but they couldn't leave the tureen alone. Jean was cognizant of the aftereffects of such a spicy meal. She adored Kemoa's curry, but always paid a high price for it afterward and reasoned that if the others reacted in kind, that night promised to be a busy one at the camp latrine.

The conversation was light with most of the discussion centered on a rehashing of Frank's big day. He was animated with his description of the long-distance-running shot. Although Paul was delighted for him, he quickly wearied of the Frank's exploits as his thoughts turned to Jean. Every time she looked his way, he melted, and as far as he was concerned, they could remain at the table until the end of time. With only three days into it, he was already dreading the completion of the safari.

It may have been wishful thinking on Paul's part, but it did seem as if she were affording him special attention, a detail that wasn't going unnoticed by the other men at the table. Ian, for one, couldn't recall having ever seen her so attentive to a client. It was amusing for him to watch the developing bond between his daughter and the young surgeon. She had never shown much interest in relationships, having grown up under such strange circumstances as a safari apprentice.

Nyeusi gathered the dessert dishes, and Paul leaned toward the hostess. "I want to tell Kemoa I really enjoyed this dinner. What should I say?"

Jean whispered a short phrase, and he repeated it to her. She nodded in approval.

"Kemoa," he called, to the old cook who materialized immediately.

"*Hii chakula ni mzuri kabisi,*" Paul proclaimed as if the dialect were his own.

The chef kowtowed and smiled, making sure the two professional hunters had registered the compliment. "*Asante sana Daktari* Bennett," he said. "*Ilikuwa furaha kwangu.*"

Paul looked to Jean for help. "It was his pleasure," she interpreted for him.

Because of their exhaustion and weariness from battling insects—the pests were in full force by that time—everyone retired for the night.

Jean lay in her tent thinking about the surgeon-hunter. Smiling, she pictured Paul's soft, beckoning eyes and the way his short, disheveled hair seemed to be in a constant state of flux, struggling to find order, and she thought about how his genteel Southern manner had a soothing, disarming effect on her. As she dwelled on his image, she felt an arousal that caught her off guard. Scores of men, both young and old, had been a constant presence throughout her life, but none of them had sparked such a reaction in her. On safari since childhood, she'd daily experienced the spectrum of life-and-death struggles that typify African existence. Protecting royalty and captains of industry from the perils of big-game hunting had lent her an air of authority and competence that people her age group found off-putting. Feeling out of place among her contemporaries, she'd become a loner, listening to Elvis Presley records to fill the void. Even the four years she spent in England

162

attending university had failed to elicit much more than a fleeting interest in dating. She'd been underwhelmed by the antics of puerile male youths and their pointless preoccupations with football, rugby, and social cliques. Even her female classmates had bored her with their incessant primping and silly gossip.

Recently her solitary existence had begun to pall, and she fell asleep wondering what it was about the young *daktari* that made him different from every other man she'd known. Several hours later, fierce abdominal cramps jolted her awake. She dreaded having to abandon the comfort of her bunk to traverse the hundred-foot trek to the privy shelter, but it was a matter of great urgency. Grabbing the lamp and a roll of tissue, she stepped out into the moonlight. She could see the Africans asleep on the ground alongside the transport truck, which was their custom. She made a hasty survey of the grounds and headed for the latrine. Holding the lamp aloft with her right hand, she pushed aside the entrance flap, and the interior was instantly bathed in a ghostly artificial light.

A hissing, fiendish pug face shot out at her, leaving no time for her to protect herself, and she felt a thump to her shoulder. The lamp crashed to the ground, dousing the light, and she fell onto her back in the dirt. She screamed, her body withdrawn into a ball.

Ian exploded from his tent wearing nothing but his skivvies, a flashlight in one hand and the 450 double in the other. The sweeping beam of his flashlight caught the natives surging from their beds. He took off toward the sound of Jean's shrieks. Not knowing the source of the trouble, he hollered to the Americans to stay in their tent. Already darting through the tent flap, Frank did a 180-degree turn and went back inside.

Ian's erratic column of light caught Jean on the ground, sobbing. In an instant he was kneeling beside her. "Jean, honey, what is it?" She continued crying. "What is it, girl? Talk to me."

The raucous bedlam of the natives' shouts, combined with Jean's hysterical sobs, was producing total chaos throughout the camp.

"Jean, you must tell me what's wrong.

Her weeping continued, but she was able to gasp one word, "Mamba."

"Oh, bloody Christ," Ian said. "Where did it get you, baby?"

She motioned toward her shoulder, and Ian, spotting the two wet pinholes, tore her shirt out of the way, expecting to see two matching puncture wounds. He was shaking so badly he dropped the light, fumbled with it, and dropped it again. He felt as if life was passing out of him.

Inside Frank and Paul's tent, Frank was terrified that a lion would rip through the wall at any second or a rhino would come barreling over him. Paul was concerned for the girl. There was no way for him to know whether she was alone, bleeding to death. He wanted to do something, anything other than hide in the tent.

Ian couldn't find any sign of penetration and wanted to get her away from the snake, wherever the hell it was. He and Jua, who was the first to arrive, dragged her off.

"Susani," he bellowed, "*toa bunduki ya marisaa*. The pump shotgun."

They helped her to her feet, and Ian put his arms around her. "Zuri, I can't find any bite. I don't know how, but he missed you."

She was still crying, but nodded her head.

"I think you need to nip off and get washed up, I'll take care of the snake."

During the ordeal she had lost control and was in dire need of sanitizing. Ian said a few words to Nyeusi, who set off to ready a bath. Ian traded the double rifle for the pump shotgun and told Reli to fetch the Americans.

Holding the flashlight in one hand and the Winchester at his shoulder, Ian cautiously crept back to the privy. Using the gun barrel as a rod, he gingerly pushed the tent flap aside and scanned the entire interior with the flashlight, following the beam with the muzzle. There was no sign of the snake. He carefully orbited the structure, paying close attention to the creased canvas floor, and still no black mamba. The only remaining hideout for the deadly reptile, he assumed, was the privy basin itself. Again he slowly re-entered the structure and leveled the muzzle past the seat and pulled the trigger. The noise was deafening inside the confines of the canvas shelter, and his ears rang. He awkwardly pumped the fore-end with his flashlight hand, came in at a different angle, and fired again. A geyser of excrement blew back and covered him. He fought off the urge to retch. Droplets of piss mixed with sweat dripped from his chin. Feeding one more shell into the chamber, he blasted the reservoir again, and another shower erupted. Peering past the seat, he was disheartened by the absence of the dead snake. The serpent had escaped, and now Ian was seriously alarmed.

As Frank and Paul looked on from a distance, Ian and the boys searched the camp and surrounding vicinity without finding so much as a slither trail in the dirt. Giving up, Ian headed for the washbasin, but not before stopping to check on Jean, who was folded up on her bed, clasping her bolt-action rifle.

She had changed into a light turtleneck sweater and shorts. Her nose was red from nonstop sniffling, but she managed to produce something between a laugh and a sob as she beheld her father in his underwear, covered in filth, and toting the Winchester shotgun.

"This is amusing to you?" he asked, simultaneously registering disgust over his offal-smeared body and relief that she'd escaped an agonizing and often fatal bite, while laughing at the absurdity of it all.

"I'm sorry to have frightened you so, Daddy."

"Don't be ridiculous, Zuri, Are you all right now?"

"Just shaken. Did you find that bastard?"

"No, honey, not a trace."

"We have to leave here then. Right away. You know what they do to me."

"I know, honey, just as soon as we can get things packed up."

"Do you think the Americans will mind?"

"With the specter of a mamba crawling around, I seriously doubt there'll be much protest. Besides, we'd only planned to dally here another day anyway. And if you're worried about upsetting the *daktari,* he's so smitten I'd venture he'd follow you into a veritable nest of mambas.

"Oh, Daddy—really?" She hid her face in the pillow before withdrawing it again. "Do you really think so?"

"Come on, Zuri, I'm not blind."

"Well, he is very charming, yes?"

"He appears to be a fine young man, but just the same, make sure you don't let him muddy your judgment. It's dangerous enough out here without you floating off in the clouds somewhere."

"I'll be just fine, thank you," she retorted, a hint of rebellion in her tone.

"Now will you please tell me what happened in the latrine?"

"I can't say much. It all happened so suddenly. The bastard just shot out of the basin at me. I haven't a clue why I wasn't hit."

"Well actually, you were. There's a pair of fang holes in your shirt, and I think I've got a theory as to why you were spared. I want to go back there to have another look."

"Please, Daddy, must you?"

"I just want to have a quick peek, and then I think I'll grab a *bathi*. Do you think I could use one, hmm?"

She had to giggle again at his pitiful appearance and aroma, "Most definitely."

Returning to the privy, he went in with even more caution than before. A quick glance at the lid confirmed his hunch.

The plywood seat had a small v-shaped chunk broken out of it. Ian figured that when the snake had lunged at her, its momentum was arrested when it wedged itself into the crack. He peered into the tank again just to make sure and then ran his fingers around the crack. Sure enough there was a shred of scaly skin stuck to the wood. He shut his eyes and drew a deep breath.

Once the crisis had passed he felt sapped of energy and allowed himself a moment of quiet weeping before returning to his tent. As Ian scrubbed the safari troupe's effluence from his body, he reflected that his precious daughter's life had been spared by a decayed, urine-impregnated, scrap-lumber toilet seat.

Ian harbored few regrets about a life spent in the bush. The adventure and freedom it afforded had, for the most part, been worth the risk. For years the gratification had outweighed the potential daily drudgery and hazards. Now he wasn't so sure. It was sobering enough to have an embittered leopard clawing away at his integument; now his daughter had been put at risk.

For years it had seemed like a practical way to keep an eye on her while teaching her about the land and its many marvels. He was quite surprised and more than a little flattered when she began to show an interest in the safari operation, and it had taken hell's own amount of petitioning for the game commissioners to grant her probationary-licensee status. After the mamba attack, he regretted having allowed her to follow in his footsteps. Perhaps at the end of this safari he would sit down and discuss his feeling and concerns with her.

The stars were beginning to vanish from the eastern sky by the time the boys began toppling the tents and loading the truck. They worked diligently but moved with grave deliberation, mindful that the snake was loose among them. None of them wanted a chance meeting with the wayward serpent, but should it happen, they'd have stoically accepted their fate as the will of God.

Ian reflected on the events of the trip so far, and he didn't like the pattern that had begun to emerge. Too many things had gone wrong. How many more times could he cheat death before he found himself, as so many of his predecessors and contemporaries had, in some lonely remote location, staring up at the African sky, trying to make sense of what had just transpired as eternal darkness engulfed him.

Both Jean and Paul were on edge as she ushered him into her tent on the verge of the troupe's departure. He wasn't quite sure what to do with his hands, but he knew what he wanted to do with them, which was to embrace her and pull her against him. He dug them into his pockets instead. He felt guilty, as if he were peering into some forbidden dominion, like a child clandestinely rummaging through his mother's underwear drawer. Jean was equally self-conscious, unaccustomed to receiving company in her jealously guarded private quarters. Paul couldn't stop himself from surveying the interior, which was sparse and had definite female touches, such as powdery lavender bedsheets on her cot. What especially caught his attention was the curious combination on her bed of a tattered stuffed toy lion and a Cogswell hunting rifle.

"Doesn't the gun make him a little nervous?" he teased, in an attempt to break the ice.

She laughed a bit more than necessary. "Oh, he's gotten adjusted to it by now."

Paul scrambled for something to say. "Does he have a name?" As soon as it left his mouth he realized what a moronic question it was. *She's just escaped near certain death, and you're asking her the name of her goddamn toy.* He couldn't have cared less about the fabric feline anyway, and he was quite sure that she knew it.

He was relieved when she went along with his flirtatious banter, replying, "Promise me you won't laugh. It's Mister Meanie."

He hadn't been ready for that response, and he burst out laughing.

"Paul, you promised!"

"I'm sorry," he managed between cackles.

"I just knew I couldn't trust you, Doctor Bennett," she scolded.

"Are you okay?" he finally asked, out of genuine concern.

"I'm afraid of snakes."

"I'm not real crazy about them myself."

"No, I mean I'm absolutely petrified of them."

"And these mambas, they're pretty bad?"

"The devil himself."

"I guess we'll be leaving here then?"

"We must. I wouldn't have a moment's peace knowing that bastard was out there somewhere."

"You won't get any argument from me. If that thing's got you that riled up, I don't want any part of it."

"It's a bit more complicated than that," she said, lowering her eyes.

Paul wasn't surprised. He was getting used to things being increasingly more convoluted with her. She seemed to be swathed in mystery.

"Do you think Frank will have any objections?"

"Are you kidding me? You just tell him we're going someplace with more to shoot at, and he'll be the first one in the Rover."

"He needn't worry. The veldt between Arusha and Dodoma is stiff with game, and we can hunt the whole way down."

"Do you think we can spend some time in one place? I'm getting a little tired of driving."

"I understand. We're going to motor down to the Pangani River. Once we get there, which is about a day's journey, if the game is plentiful we'll remain in the area for a minimum of a week, maybe two. After that, assuming we've collected some good trophies, we plan to cross over to the Western Province and have a look at the bush around Lake Victoria. It's a beautiful ride. You'll see."

He felt it was time to test the waters. He had to get some sense of her feeling toward him. Mustering his nerve and throwing caution to the wind, he said, "I hope you don't interpret this the wrong way, Jean, but I'd be perfectly content to drive circles around this tent for two weeks, provided you came along for the ride."

Blushing, she seemed unsure how to react. As a client he should be kept at arm's length, as her father had needlessly pointed out. For some time it had been glaringly obvious to her and everyone on the safari that Paul blossomed in her company. She decided to tell the truth. "That's very sweet, Paul. I've found myself feeling the same way about you."

There was his answer. He could breathe again. Not wanting to spoil the moment with any further exchange, he smiled and started to leave. A small, framed photograph atop her locker caught his attention. It showed a young child of perhaps three or four years sitting in a woman's lap. The woman shared the same features as Jean. The little girl was holding the same stuffed animal that was on Jean's cot. Paul started to speak, but recalling how reluctant she'd been to discuss her mother earlier on, he merely smiled again and left.

The campfire was going full blaze, and Paul joined Ian and Frank, who had positioned themselves a comfortable distance from it. Frank shot Paul a furtive glance but kept quiet, refocusing his attention on the blaze. He had dispensed himself a sizable guzzle of his own snake remedy at the end of the ordeal and was starting to achieve some benefit from it. He sat engrossed by the tiny jets of bluish flame hissing from the burning timbers.

Ian seemed restless and on edge, bounding from his seat to worry the coals with a long, leafless branch, and after sitting down, repeatedly running his fingers through his thick brown hair. In the firelight he looked older and more tired, as if the mamba attack on his daughter had robbed him of years. It was obvious that the snake incident rattled him to the core.

Paul reckoned that a little light chatter might help. "You know, Ian, it amazes me. You folks think nothing of teasing lions to within a few feet of yourself, but when it comes to snakes, it's an entirely different ball game.

The hunter rose from his chair again and strode to the fire, appearing to struggle for the right way to respond. Looking up and staring into space, he said, "Jean's mother was killed by a snake." He let that sink in for a moment. "It happened when Jean was about three years. Penny took her for a picnic on the outskirts of our farm. I was busy doing something, fixing a well or some such nonsense." He stirred the coals again and paused before continuing. "I should have been more attentive, but I was caught up in the work and lost track of time."

Neither American moved.

"I don't know what happened, and I could never get it out of Jean. She's blocked it out, and it's probably better that way. Anyhow, I've got a pretty good idea what took place. I can only guess that Penny walked under a low branch and knocked a tree cobra or a boomslang free. It dropped down her back, inside her shirt."

Ian paused again, picturing the horror of the several seconds during which the snake bit his helpless young wife repeatedly, little Jean looking on.

Frank uttered a faint, "Jesus Christ," draining his nearly full cup in one swallow before slumping his head.

Paul relived the anguish he'd felt that day in the operating room, but this time he felt it for Ian and his daughter too.

"When they hadn't returned after several hours, I went looking for them . . . and found both a short distance from the tree where it happened."

Ian tossed a branch into the fire, releasing a billow of sparks. "Little Jean was in tears, trying—" his voice quavered, "trying to wake Penny."

CHAPTER SIXTEEN

Courage

The last detail before breaking camp and leaving was breakfast. Kemoa was setting vessels of food on the table, and the men were alone in their thoughts, trying to regain enough composure to join Jean at the table.

Paul wanted to load up and start off across the valley, longing for the diversion that the backdrop would provide. He more than ever wanted to understand the scar on Jean's neck. Something incredibly brutalizing had happened to her, he thought, and he considered broaching the subject to get it out in the open once and for all. The notion evaporated when she appeared at the table dressed in the day's hunting ensemble.

Everyone was itching to finish the meal and get on with the hunt except Kemoa, who'd prepared the elaborate spread only to watch it go virtually untouched. The despondent old Kikuyu fretted over them, oblivious to the undercurrents. He was aware of Jean's past—how she'd seen her mother killed by a snake—so it was no surprise to him when Jean and her father had all but cracked up during the mamba affair. To Kemoa the whole group seemed to be fragmenting, and he feared the remainder of the safari would be ill fated, or at the very least, unpleasant.

Kemoa and Jean had a bond between them that differed from the typical master-servant relationship, a camaraderie that also transcended color lines.

He'd always gone the extra mile to prepare special meals when she took part in Ian's expeditions, and she favored him over the other laborers. Their alliance struck Paul as not unlike the affinity he'd always felt for Sheldon.

～の　へ～

The day's hunt started out with the usual routine. They ambled slowly across the craggy Rift Valley floor looking for game as debris, dust, and insects assaulted their eyes, got in their mouths, and settled on everything inside the vehicle. The Rover pitched and bucked as Jean fought the wheel, negotiating the jagged terrain. The temperature soared until by late morning, they were all dripping with sweat.

Paul fiddled with his camera, trying to figure out the installation of its telescopic lens. He grew frustrated, finding it impossible to assemble the unit while the Rover was in motion. Giving up, he returned both pieces to the leather bag and directed his attention to the seemingly endless range before him.

Rapport between the hunters began to improve as they distanced themselves from the preceding night. As Jean drove she discussed Masai habit of setting fire to the overgrown vegetation of the grasslands for the purpose of improving the grazing of their cattle. The nomadic Masai derived most, if not all, of their nutrition from drinking a concoction of milk mixed with blood drained from the veins of live animals. They depended heavily on cattle and spent their time attending to them. By burning the grass plains, they accomplished the twofold result of providing fresh, tender shoots for fodder while clearing the cover used by predatory cats that stalked the unwitting livestock. Great billowing clouds of smoke could be seen far off in the distance, suggesting that the area would have to be avoided.

They group had broken free from an expanse of the chest-high grass when Ian calmly addressed his daughter. "Zuri, hold up here, but don't make a sudden stop."

She turned to look at him in the back seat while simultaneously braking the Rover. "What is it, Daddy?"

His gaze was intent on a piece of ground far ahead of their position.

Jua, recognizing what the white hunter had observed, said, "*Kubwa simba upanda mchaka*." His matter-of-fact tone suggested that the large lions under the trees were nothing to be concerned about.

Simultaneously both of the Sharpes raised their binoculars and studied the recumbent beast before planning their assault on the king of the jungle.

"Nasty looking old bugger, huh, Zuri?"

"Uh-huh," she replied without lowering her field glasses.

"Looks as though he's just off a kill."

"Uh-huh."

"Mane's good; must be an older fellow."

"Looks that way."

"Wonder where Momma is," he noted, panning the vicinity.

"I can't see her, but you can bet she's not far off."

Frank remained silent as he glassed the beast with his own set of binoculars. He knew what was coming next, and the demons of self-doubt knocked at his door.

"Mind if I have a peek?" Paul asked. He'd inadvertently left his binoculars on the transport, on its way to the Pangani River.

Jean handed him her binoculars and pointed to the stand of acacias one quarter of a mile away. It took him a while before the scruffy buff-colored lion registered in his brain. "He looks so . . . timid out there."

"You're probably right, Paul. Care to go over there and see if we can pet him?"

"Come on, Ian, don't start that again," Paul remarked. "You know what I mean."

"Sorry, just poking a bit of fun." Ian turned his attention to the other young man in the vehicle. "Well, *Bwana* Eastman, what will it be?"

Acutely conscious that every eye was on him, including those of Jua and the gunbearers, Frank knew he wasn't ready to take on a lion. He been in the country only a few days and was just now becoming acclimated to the terrain and the African style of hunting, but how could he say no and not look like a sissy in front of the whole group? *Ian must figure it's safe, or he wouldn't—* Frank cut himself off in mid-thought, remembering there hadn't been anything safe yet, not even the toilets. He recalled signing the release discharging Ian and Jean's company of any liability "in the event of any unfortunate mishap," as they'd had so delicately put it. Assuming there was no way out of confronting the lion, he plastered a grin on his face. "If you think I can handle it, I'm ready," he announced, hoping Ian would reconsider and call the whole thing off.

"Okay, then," Ian said. "Let's devise our plan."

Lighting one of his smelly little cheroots, Ian paused as the acrid smoke swirled in the imperceptible breeze. The smoke indicated a wind direction that was unfavorable for a near-direct stalk. "You're going to have to circle around from the left in a wide-ranging ark," Ian told Frank. "Because of the terrain, it'll have you emerging from that thorn bush thicket less than seventy-five yards from old bugger. If you don't run afoul of the old boy's girlfriends, and if you're lucky enough to have him stay where he is, you ought to arrive in a good position for a clean shot with little chance for trouble." Ian paused to let his directions sink in and then continued, "I figure it will take at least thirty minutes for you to get around to him. The *daktari* and I will wait here, solve the world's problems, and watch the show unfold from afar. That is, if it's okay with him."

"I'm fine right where I am," Paul said, eying Jean and hoping he wasn't going to have to watch her die from the comfort of the Rover.

Frank climbed out of the Rover and was more than a little uneasy. He fidgeted with the contents of his gear bag, not knowing what to bring along. Jean helped him, but he was so preoccupied that he stumbled on a boulder and nearly fell over backwards. Excusing himself, he went off to urinate and returned with his fly open.

His nervousness didn't concern Ian, whose clients rarely exhibited grace under fire in such situations. "Frank," he said, "I'd like you to use the double for this."

"But I can shoot my Weatherby better."

"I'm well aware of that, but I don't want you fumbling with a bolt if a second shot is necessary. The double is much quicker, and furthermore your shot is certain to be less than fifty yards. You can shoot it *that* far, can't you?"

"I suppose."

"Pardon me, you didn't just say *suppose,* did you?"

"Yes, I can hit with it at fifty yards," he remarked, as if he were addressing a schoolteacher.

"There now, that's more like it," said Ian, softening his tone. "You'll do just fine, son, but make sure you follow Zuri's instructions to the letter. Do you understand?"

"Yes."

"All right then, *Bwana* Eastman, go out and shoot us a *simba,*" He slapped Frank on the back. "And mind you, watch for any lionesses that might be holding back in those thorns."

Paul had been observing Jean, who was quietly arranging herself for the stalk. She took on a different demeanor as she went about checking the rifles and cartridges, the frightened girl of the previous night transformed into a fervently focused P.H. whose life and the lives of those in her care depended upon her ability to make fast, smart decisions. Despite her frailties, which seemed to be unfolding sequentially, he knew that she was the woman for him. Maybe it was *because* of those weaknesses that he was so drawn to her.

The party—consisting of Jua, Susani, Mchana, Frank, Jean, two rifles, and a water bag—departed for the long, sweltering sneak through African low country.

Paul was a little upset that Jean hadn't thought to bid him an individual farewell, but realized she was on duty. He felt embarrassed for being so petty. Once he was alone with Ian, Paul hoped to learn more about Jean, but instead received an east African history lesson.

Going around to the back of the Rover, Ian pulled a small blanket from the supply box, and using it as a cushion, took a position on the hood. After relighting his cigar and glassing the lion again, he told Paul, "You know, you fellows came over here at what will probably be the tail end of safari hunting in this part of the world."

"How do you mean?"

"Things are changing here, and not for the better."

"It doesn't look like there's any shortage of game."

"Oh, that's not the problem, son. The world is changing, and I'm afraid things are going to be quite a bit different around here before too long."

"I don't follow."

"Do you remember when we left Nairobi, you or Frank asked about the number of soldiers in and around the town, and I sort of swept it under the table?"

"Yes, their presence did seem a bit overboard."

"Well, we need them here."

"I assume it has to do with the native uprising?"

"One in the same."

"The papers at home have mentioned that quite a few people have died."

"Fortunately only a handful of Europeans have been killed, but scores of Kikuyu have been wiped out, and plenty more are imprisoned."

"What's it all about?"

Ian set the binoculars on the hood and turned to face Paul. "Real estate's the issue, my American friend. You see, Paul, the natives want their land back, and we don't fancy giving it up."

"Kenya's a big country, and it hasn't looked too overcrowded to me. Neither does this place," Paul added, sweeping his hand across the Tanganyika landscape.

"You know as well as I do that there's good land and piss-poor land, just like in your own country. Two-thirds of Kenya is poor non arable or desert land. The NFD—Northern Frontier District—is wasteland, and the rest of the territory that *is* first class is in white hands, and it needs to remain that way."

"Wasn't it theirs to begin with?"

Ian turned to study the lion. "Blast! He's gotten up." He signaled to suspend the discussion as he glassed the position. "It's okay. The old bloke just needed a stretch. Now what was that?"

"The land's theirs," Paul repeated. "They were here first."

"Of course it was theirs, but Britain wrested it from nothingness and turned it into something usable. Now we're expected to just hand it right back to the bloody savages."

Paul was surprised to hear him refer to the natives in those terms, a departure from the benevolent manner with which he addressed "his" Africans. Paul thought that obviously for Ian, Africans fell into two classes—those who agreed with him and those who didn't. "How about some sort of trade where they're given some good land in exchange for most of what's already in European hands?"

"It won't work. They want all of it *and* total independence to boot. That means we all pack up and hightail it back to jolly old England." Pulling off his hat, Ian ran his fingers through his matted, sweat-dampened hair and gazed at the sky. "You care for a *pombe?*"

"Sure, thanks."

The hunter took a glance at the lion, checked his watch, and went around to the drink box.

"If this *simba* cooperates, your friend will have quite a handsome memento to add to the bunch."

"And if he doesn't cooperate?"

"We'll just have to wait and see."

Dying to bring the girl back into the conversation, Paul ventured, "Aren't you concerned for Jean's safety? I mean we're talking about lions here."

"She's more than capable of taking care of herself," Ian replied, handing Paul the warm Tusker ale. After downing it in two gulps, Paul asked, "I wonder how they're doing out there."

It was slow going as the party fought its way through the high grass and the wait-a-minute thorn bushes, the latter as tenacious as cat claws. Soaked with sweat and bleeding from numerous scratches, they pushed ahead, just out of view from the open veldt that separated them from the dozing cat. Having made it only one-third of the way in fifteen minutes, Jean was vehemently pushing ahead.

The heat was stifling, and Frank's body temperature was so high he felt as if he was radiating more heat than the surroundings. His tongue stuck against the roof of his mouth, and he was unable to accumulate enough saliva to spit. "Jean, I need to stop for a second and get some water."

"We really need to keep moving, Frank."

"It'll just take a sec; my mouth's like sawdust."

Reluctantly she let out a faint whistle to signal Jua, who was advancing slightly ahead of them. He turned in a crouch. Seeing that it was only a break, he knelt down on one knee. The gunbearer following behind them handed Frank the water bag, which he used to slop himself something between a drink and an upper body deluge.

Before he could grab seconds, Jean was off again, gliding through the undergrowth like a phantom. Her reasons for driving hard were twofold. For starters, they had encountered the lion at *the* opportune time, which was right after a meal and during the heat of the day, when the lion was lethargic and inattentive, and the sooner they got into range and settled the score, the better their chances of being around for photos instead of ending up as dessert.

The other and equally important motive behind the push was to get Frank to the lion before he had a chance to consider the showdown and work himself into a dither. The greater his preoccupation with staying up with the group, the less time he'd have to spin grisly scenarios in his mind.

"Where did the term Mau Mau come from?" Paul asked Ian.

Ian fixed him with a hard stare, said nothing, and looked like he wanted to pounce. The question had seemed benign enough to Paul, but to Ian it was an anathema. Finally, in low, temperate tones, he replied, "You'll need some background first before I can answer that."

"If you don't mind."

Picking at one of the small scabs on the palm of his hand, Ian began to recount the events leading up to the horror of the past several years. "Even though we English have been in East Africa for centuries, true British involvement in Kenya started about eighteen ninety-five, with the construction of the railroad. It was originally intended as a means of tapping the riches of Uganda, another British acquisition. We hoped that it would unite Mombasa on the coast with Kampala in Uganda.

"Right from the bloody start, the project was wrought with obstacles. For one, the rail had to ascend from sea level through desert and bush and climb to about seven thousand feet before dropping back to the Rift Valley floor, then climb to eighty-five hundred feet on the other side before descending again, and all this over a distance of just under nine hundred miles."

He paused to check on the lion. "Thirty-two-thousand East Indians were brought in as laborers, since the Africans were essentially useless. Disease wiped out thousands of the Wogs before the lions started on them at Tsavo, killing several hundred more before John Patterson succeeded in dispatching both those bitches. The loss of life was staggering, and so was the financial cost, but it opened the territory up to exploration. Colonists began showing up to take advantage of the opportunities and for adventure. Land grabbing went into full swing, with the British government giving its full blessing. As more Europeans came, more Africans were displaced, with the Kikuyu taking the brunt of it."

Ian struck a match on the Rover hood and relit his cigar. Studying the smoldering tip, he continued, "Now, grant you, I subscribed to the whole affair and still do. The natives weren't using the land for any purposeful reason, and if we hadn't appropriated it, things here would be the same now as they were a thousand years ago. But as you can see, it set up a climate of resentment that intensified over time."

"What happened to all the natives?"

"They were given parcels of land, 'reserves,' so to speak, but not like your Indian reservations in the States. They were districts where whites were not allowed to own land and native rights were ensured. With the mass movement of natives and the natural increase of their population, the reserves were quickly overstuffed. As a result many of them left and went to Nairobi looking for work or became squatters on white-held farms. This was a boon to the settlers, since they depended on native labor anyway. The problem was that we all had throngs of embittered, dispossessed Africans living in our own backyards. The situation became a bloody powder keg waiting to go off."

He looked at his watch and then glassed the horizon. "They should be getting there about now," he commented.

Paul could tell by Ian's agitation that he was worried, but Paul didn't know if it was because of the Mau Mau crisis or the lion stalk.

Continuing to watch from the hood of the Rover, Ian said, "You have to understand that Nairobi became the playground of well-to-do whites, East Indians providing much of the professional, trade, and skilled labor. Africans were simply pushed aside. In nineteen fifty-two all hell broke loose. Started with some murders up at Thompson Falls and spilled over into the rest of the country. I don't think anyone really knows where the name Mau Mau originated or what it means, but one thing's for sure. The mere mention of the words *Mau Mau* stirs up the devil's own terror in most of the whites here."

"Were any of the boys here on the safari part of it?"

"Not on your life," Ian said. "They'd have been very dead by now. Actually we did have one who'd taken the oath. I blew his damned head off."

Paul chuckled, hoping that Ian would break into a grin or wink at him. When he didn't Paul was taken aback. The notion that he, as a physician, was in the presence of a cold-blooded killer unnerved him.

Ian was about to describe the heinous event that resulted in his taking the native's life, which had also been the inauguration of his tenure as a Mau Mau exterminator extraordinaire when he squinted and threw the binoculars up to his eyes. "Look, there they are."

Jean interrupted the stalk before stepping into the open to prepare Frank for the engagement. She could see the double rifle trembling in his hands. "Fire the second barrel as soon as you recover from the recoil, regardless of whether or not *simba* goes down. Reload quickly," she said. She wedged two shells between the fingers of his left hand to ready him for firing two more times.

The two hunters stepped into the open. Jean stood behind Frank and to the left, shifting her eyes from him to the lion. "With any luck, when we clear those hedges we'll have him still sleeping, and you can finish him off straightaway."

At close range the lion looked shabby but no less menacing. In fact in Frank's opinion he looked god-awful huge. What little confidence he'd mustered on the trek vaporized, but it was too late to call off the hunt.

With less than seventy-five yards separating hunter from the hunted, a fat, stinging drop of sweat found its way into Frank's right eye. There was no time to do anything about it, though. The lion, having caught the scent of the hunters, exploded from a dead sleep to a full charge.

Paul froze as he watched the lion close the distance at lightning speed.

Ian's attention was focused on his daughter, who would be the one to thwart the attack should Frank fail. From Ian's point of view, it looked as though Jean were pointing her rifle at Frank's back, the distortion caused by convective air rising from the heated ground.

Through the hazy distance Ian saw Frank's upper body recoil from the force of the powerful double rifle.

The absence of any report and the spectacle of the unwavering lion's advance shook Paul to the core.

The first muffled whump was heard while Frank recoiled again. This time the lion rolled over and went down in a cloud of dust several yards short of the shooter.

"Left! Left! Your left!" Ian shouted in vain when a second lion, a female, churned out of the bushes.

Frank was too preoccupied with reloading, as he'd been told to do, oblivious to the other *simba*, but either Jean or one of the boys caught a glimpse of it, and in the distorted haze, she was seen swinging and recoiling as the lioness also crumpled in a sooty puff.

Paul and Ian watched Jean swing her aim between the two fallen cats and the surrounding thicket. Frank, on the other hand, could be seen falling to his knees and then slumping over backwards in what appeared to be a dead faint.

Ian held his telescopic vigil for a short period before slowly lowering the glasses. "Exhilarating show, wouldn't you say?" He was grinning like a derby spectator as he and Paul climbed into the Rover.

"You think Frank's all right?"

"He'll be fine—when he comes to."

"Is that common? People passing out?"

"Very. At least he didn't run. That's the worst form of cowardice. It makes me sick to my stomach when I see it."

"I don't think I want to shoot a lion."

"That's your choice, son, but if you change your mind and do take one like your friend just did, you'll never have to prove your manhood again. Don't rule it out so early in the game. I think you'd be missing a chance like none other." He cranked the Rover and stomped on the accelerator.

If the shooting of the oryx was cause for celebration, then the lion kill was New Year's Eve at Times Square. The natives were delirious, their jubilation so loud that it could be heard from the vehicle several hundred meters away. It was the relief of having once again survived an encounter, made sweeter by having witnessed the death of two of Africa's most dreaded foes. The only one who didn't appear to be joyous was the shooter himself. Frank was sitting alone, cross-legged, with the rifle across his knees, resembling a sporting-goods mannequin with his far away, fixed gaze.

Ian got out of the Rover and gave his daughter a little peck on her forehead. "Had me a mite uneasy there, lass."

"A trifle close, was it, Daddy?"

"You might say that. Is *Bwana* Eastman okay?"

"I suspect he'll be coming around soon."

Paul ambled over and squatted down in front of him. "Hey, you all right?

Frank turned to him as if roused from a dream, his head moving in tiny uncontrolled jerks. "Huh?"

"That was one hell of a show."

"I just had the livin' shit scared out of me."

"Me too, and I was a quarter of a mile away. I can't even imagine what it must have been like up close."

"Did I do okay?"

Paul looked over at the lifeless cat. "I don't know, why don't you ask him?" He motioned with his head.

"I thought I was a dead man when that second lion came out. That girl is too much."

"I know," said Paul, looking at her.

She and her father had knelt down at the lion's head.

Ian hoisted it up to examine the hide for blemishes. There were many from previous fights with others of its kind. "Oh, *Bwana Simba*-slayer, come have a look at this." Ian beckoned.

Frank lifted himself from the ground as if gravity had increased ten-fold, and he drifted over on unsteady legs. Seeing the lion close up for the first time revealed a mangy and tired creature, hardly the same animal who had moments earlier come at him like a dun-colored missile. He tapped it tentatively, as if expecting it to spring to life and exact revenge.

"Do you always kill your *simbas* with such precision?" razzed Ian, pointing to the seeping void that once housed the lion's right eye.

"Is that where I hit it?"

"Certainly not, *Bwana* Eastman, all *simbas* in this region have bleeding eye sockets. Of course that's where you hit him."

"Where's the first shot?"

"Come see," Jean said, pointing to a long triangular flap of skin that had been torn free from the animal's hip.

Inspecting the wound, Frank felt sad for the lion, knowing it must have suffered excruciating pain.

The natives dragged the other dead lion over and flopped it down next to Frank's. Moving over to it, Ian bent down and pushed on its head, which crunched like a bag of shattered porcelain. There was a small entrance hole above and between the eyes and a ragged crater behind her ear where the bullet exited. He glanced up at his daughter and winked.

The group brought out cameras and snapped photos from nearly every imaginable angle and combination of participants. Ian even managed to have Frank smile for some of them. Finally satisfied that enough had been taken, he instructed the boys to dump the lions in the Rover so the group could take off for a shady spot to eat lunch while Mohammad skinned and prepare the hides.

Before they departed, Ian called Frank aside and dropped a stack of copper coins in his hand.

"What's this for?"

"It's a local custom for a client to reward the boys with a shilling every time a lion is taken. It motivates them and rewards them for their courage."

"It doesn't seem like enough. Is it? I'd be happy to give them more. Let me get my wallet."

"Hold on, son. We don't want to spoil them, do we? A shilling's more than adequate."

"Whatever you say, Ian. You're the boss."

"I'll give you some more when we catch up to the boys at *campi*. Can't leave them out, you know? It'd rouse all sorts of bad blood."

"Just tell me what the total is, and I'll get it back to you."

"My thoughts exactly."

Frank handed each of the natives a coin and received grins, nods, hand-shakes, and a host of strange Swahili accolades and gestures. It was all very exhilarating for him, and he felt like a big shot for a change.

During lunch, while the other's dined on tinned salmon-salad sandwich-es and fruit, Frank's meal consisted of three bottles of lager and six codeine tablets, the latter ingested surreptitiously while he watched the skinning operation. His appetite for food had faded with the lion kill.

Paul was relieved when lunch proved to be a livelier affair after the tense breakfast. "You folks have some pretty weird lives," he said. "I mean its inces-sant challenge."

"Makes you feel alive, doesn't it?" Ian asked.

"I admit it does seem to keep you on your toes," Paul observed. "What do you do when you're not on safari?"

Jean answered first. "Daddy works around the farm trying to fix every-thing that rots while he's away."

"And you?"

"I help out around the farm, but sometimes I like to go down to Mombasa and go fishing."

Paul perked up. "Now you're talking my game," Paul said, bracing to outdo her with his mastery of the subject.

"Oh, you like to fish?"

"I've been doing it all my life."

"Really, what do you fish for?"

Delighted, he pressed on. "Depends on the time of year. We have mar-lin, sailfish—"

"Oh, I caught one of them. It was thirty-two kilos, and I took it on twenty-four thread line."

Thirty-two kilos, he thought. *Shit, that's seventy pounds. Can't I outdo this woman at anything?* His biggest sailfish was only forty-eight pounds.

"That's a heck of a big, sail," he said. "How long did it take to get in?"

"Almost two hours."

"Were you there, Ian?"

"No," Jean interjected. "Poor old Daddy here gets frightfully seasick."

Ian nodded. "Tried it a couple of times, but always tossed me cookies."

"We get tuna," Paul continued, "Giant blue fins that migrate though in the summer. I caught one over five hundred pounds right after the war, when we could get fuel again." *So there*, he thought. *Top that, young lady.*

"You couldn't have been more than a young teen," she said. "However did you get such a mammoth fish in? Did you have help?"

"Cap," he said. "He wouldn't let me give up, but I sure wanted to, about a hundred times. We hung it on the same hoist in Bimini that Hemingway used."

"What a thrill that must have been for you."

"I think about it a lot. Anyhow, there's dolphin, kingfish, wahoo, and several different kinds of smaller tuna."

"We get dolphin and mackerel here also. I could fish every day, if I had the chance," she said.

You might just get the chance, he thought, envisaging the two of them prowling the Gulfstream with her sitting in his lap while he manned the helm and monitored the skipping baits. "I can remember a time when that's all I wanted to do," Paul reflected.

"Did you tire of it?"

"No, I just haven't felt like doing it since Cap . . . but I've started to miss it some." *Much more now, since we started lunch*, he thought.

Ian was starting to feel like a stranger at his own picnic and finally pondered, "I wonder where Frank's off to."

"He's over there with the skinner," Paul said. "I think he's making sure the guy doesn't punch too many holes in his lion skin."

"He should be quite proud of what he did today," said Ian. "Shot like a bloody sniper."

"And what about your daughter? She was amazing."

"I'd expect nothing less from her. Isn't that right, Zuri?"

She gave her squinty smile and shrugged.

Ian looked at his watch and stood up, patting his side. "Almost no pain anymore. What do I owe you for your healing powers?"

"I'll send you a bill at the end of the trip. How's that?"

"Very well. Now how about we shove off. I want to get to the river before dark, if we can."

Mohammad had dispossessed the lions of their coverings and salted the hides for protection until he could attend to the final fleshing, which he'd complete once the party arrived at the permanent camp.

Frank's demeanor had drifted from mute lethargy to the archetypal contrived bravado that accompanied his liquor and opiate intake. He rehashed and modified details of the charge, as if to design and rehearse the perfect story to relate to the guys back home. The part about his post-conquest syncope, Paul speculated, would be edited from the yarn once it crossed the Atlantic. Only those who had experienced the terror of a point-blank lion charge would be in a position to understand the physiology of such an ordeal.

Following lunch Jean rounded up everyone for another hunt, saying they needed fresh meat for supper. Paul's first attempt at attaining a suitable candidate for the larder ended with the group waiting in the sweltering sun as Paul and Jean followed up and terminated the suffering of a small gazelle buck, which Paul had inadvertently shot in the front leg. It would have been an understatement to say that he felt dreadful for wounding the animal, and he cursed himself for shooting like a novice in front of the woman.

More irksome was Frank's hectic, unsolicited coaching and cavalier criticism. Even Ian, who was fairly tolerant, felt it necessary to shut Frank up, employing his subtle, authoritarian manner.

Reluctantly Paul relented to Jean's request that he shoot an additional animal on which the natives could dine. True to form, he belly shot a hartebeest. Once again a protracted stalk and a follow-up shots were necessary, with Paul again feeling remorse and incompetence.

Conciliatory almost to the point of patronization, Jean buttressed Paul with encouragement as they hiked across the scorching, desolate veldt. She was adamant about hustling him along; they needed to dispatch the crippled animal quickly. Like most professional hunters, she could not accept the suffering of or loss of any animal.

They discovered the hartebeest standing alone, as motionless as if it had been stuffed and placed there like a museum display. Paul knelt on one knee and toppled the beast with a single shot to the chest. As he and Jean waited for the Rover to catch up with them, they chatted about fishing again, and he sketched pictures of his boat with a stick, using the crusty soil as a blackboard.

Jean sat on the hartebeest's carcass, trying to picture *The Lucky Brake.*

Poor Jua leaned against his spear, stared down at Paul's etching of *The Lucky Brake*, and tried to comprehend the purpose of the unusual vessel. Studying the outline of the boat with its tuna tower, he failed to see why anyone would be stupid enough to construct a blind atop a floating shelter. White man did peculiar things, and in his mind, this was up there with the best of them.

"Well, Ian Sharpe, nice of you to join us," Jean needled, as her father finally crawled from the Rover. "Come have a look at the *daktari's* angling yacht."

"Very nice," Ian said, fishing being a subject that held little interest for him. "Now can we get this *punda milia* loaded and push off? There's little chance of us making the Pangani at this point. Arusha's about as far as were going to get."

"Geez, Ian," Paul said, "at least you could pretend some interest,"

"As I've indicated before, I'm not much of a mariner."

Obviously Paul's defective shooting had ruined Ian's plans, but Paul didn't care. The fact that Jean could appreciate his boat was sufficient.

They struggled with the hartebeest, finally managing to lift the cumbersome animal into the back of the Rover.

As the receding orange sun settled into the hills, the Rover made its way toward the east.

"I think we'd better plan on spending the night with your Uncle Vince, assuming he's not out in the bush on business," Ian said.

"I'd like that, Daddy," Jean said. "I haven't seen him in ages. You did warn the boys that we may not make it to *campi* tonight, didn't you?"

"They've been instructed not to come looking for us until late tomorrow."

"Who's Uncle Vince?" Paul asked, leaning forward from the back seat.

"Major Vincent Connolly. He isn't really my uncle. I've just called him that forever. Daddy served under him in North Africa, and they've been fast friends since. He's a hoot. You'll love him."

As a veteran and an amateur war buff for many years, Frank perked up. He'd been groggy and emotionally sapped since they had paused for lunch. "I'd like to hear about North Africa when we get some time, Ian."

"Love to tell you about it, son. Maybe Vince and I can chew your ears about it tonight. There's nothing he relishes more than a rehash of his days with the old Sixth Royal Tanks."

"Sixth Royal Tanks? Hey, you guys were in El Alamein, weren't you?"

"Yes, and a few less glamorous campaigns, I might add. If Vince is at home, trust you'll get your fill. In fact we might have to shoot him to shut him up."

CHAPTER SEVENTEEN

The Scotsman

Major Connolly was a first-generation East African whose family had emigrated from Scotland in the late 1880s. He'd always been involved in big game hunting in one form or another, from ivory poaching to shooting meat for the laborers constructing the Mombasa-to-Nairobi railway and everything in between. After the war he settled in Tanganyika and worked as a game ranger, a position he still maintained, if only sporadically.

When the professional hunters and two Americans pulled up at his house, he appeared on the lighted veranda flanked by a pair of fierce-looking Rhodesian ridgeback canines, the hair on their backs in a perpetual state of bristle. Guns had become so commonplace on the trip that Paul and Frank paid no attention to the rifle clasped in the major's hand. They were focused instead on his vast bare chest.

"If yar a louk'n far Naroubi, she's aboot a hun'dred meels tae da narth," he bellowed, stepping down from the landing. Vince Connolly was, if nothing else, a gruff, indelicate nail-keg of a man whose contempt for any design to alter the territory or threaten the traditional provincial customs was exceeded only by the rate at which it had taken place. He'd seen trouble brewing in Kenya years before the 1950s rebellion and had chosen to resettle in neighboring Tanganyika, escaping by several years the disastrous clash between the natives and European settlers.

Because he was of Scottish descent, his squat, stocky, barrel-chested body was covered in a sheathing of sun-sensitive fair skin. As a result of constant exposure, it had become an alternating patchwork of burned, peeling, and healing tissue that seemed to invite pathology. His appearance was topped off with a tempest of unkempt, graying vermilion hair and an obscenely bushy, tobacco-stained mustache. The major's sandals appeared to have been rendered from a pair of old combat boots, his primitive footwear nothing but a set of thick rubber soles from which the leather tops had been cut away, leaving only a band to retain his wide, grimy feet. An even more notable feature of the unusual throwback to a bygone era, which the two American's immediately realized, was his thick Scottish accent.

"Lard, give me strength to endure the be-uty of dis 'ere lassie," he exclaimed, enveloping Jean in an affectionate bear hug.

Paul sat quietly in the Rover as the Scotsman chattered with Jean before turning his attention to her father.

"And you, Ian Sharpe. Ward 'as it you're been offarin' yarself as lepard beet for the cle-ants."

"Got to do what it takes to keep the guests happy. Isn't that what you always told me?"

"Ah, boot yar gettin a mite ould far dis, Ian Sharpe."

"I'm starting to feel that way, Vince. How are you and Stella getting along?"

"Ah! The ould woman's drivin me oup the wall, she is, boot I luve her joust the seem."

"Vince, I'd like you to meet our two hunters from the States. This is Frank Eastman and Paul Bennett from Florida."

Keeping an attentive eye on the dogs, the two slowly climbed out of the Rover and approached the Scotsman.

"Dount fret none aboot the dogs, boys. Theel only trueble ya if yar a darkie. I'm pleased ta meek yar acquaintance." He squeezed their hands firmly. "Ayre ya enjin yarselves sa fars?"

"Yes sir, this is one fantastic country you live in," Frank said.

"No regrets here either," Paul added.

"Weel, goud, then. Have ya had mouch success yet?"

"I got my *simba* today."

"Ah, louvely. Did ya wet yarself in the process? I know I did on me first one." He slapped Frank on the back and winked at Jean..

"No, but I—"

"He passed out," Paul announced

Frank gave him a disgusted glare. "Thanks for bringing that up, Skip."

"Weel, lets jous see what yar bouddy dous when his tarn coums, hu, Frank? New what brings ya to Arusha thes time o' night?"

"We're off to the Pangani," Ian said, "but got slowed up with a couple of wounded beasts."

"Sounds lak some shoddy triggar wark to me."

"It's my fault," Paul confessed, feeling like a dolt.

"Ya moust get bettar at that, me boy. Dis aint no place for pour marksmansheep."

"Yes, I can see that."

"Weel, yar mour than weelcome ta stee da neet. I'd louve the coump'ny. I'll just teel da boys ta threw some *chakula* togethar whilst we doun a bit a quanin and gin."

"We'll have to attend to the animals here," said Jean, pointing to the hartebeest and gazelle.

"Joust leave 'em be. I'll get me boys ta deal with 'em."

He ushered the group upstairs. The dwelling had been constructed from stone and was spacious and airy, the walls plastered with mounted heads and artifacts gathered over the years. The floor was made of heavy planks of jet-black ebony, which highlighted a host of oriental throw rugs. Lion, leopard, and antelope skins covered the massive leather furniture.

It was Frank's concept of a residential Valhalla.

Paul admired the floor, which he surmised must have cost a fortune.

Out of nowhere appeared a tiny yapping dog with large bulging eyes. Its shrill bark, if that's what it could be called, hurt everyone's ears. "Begone with ya, ya blasted paraseet," hollered the major, who shoved as much as kicked the pooch, sending it sliding across the polished floor, leaving in its wake a trickle of urine. The mutt ended up under a chair, where it sat cowering and blinking its protruding eyes in fear.

"Shame on you, Uncle Vince." Jean scolded, wagging a finger at him. "Fancy you picking on something so small."

"Nonsense, missy. When me old lady's aroond, dat leetle basterd rouls da roust."

"Where is Aunt Stella?"

"I'm afreed she ouf to da coust, proubably spendin' me last quid on a set o' pink booties for that mecroscoupic scrap a sheet ovar there," he huffed, pointing to the dog as he walked over to set the rifle on a long wall-mounted rack.

Frank's eyes looked like the dogs when he focused of the shelf. Before him was a seemingly endless procession of long guns. He wasted no time sidling up to the rack to admire the collection, which consisted of about thirty-five rifles and shotguns of various styles and makes, each one bright and glistening with a sheen of oil.

"Are ya a gun man, Frank?"

"Yes, sir."

"Well ave at 'em me boy. Joust dount pull no triggars, mind ya, an weep 'em doun whit dis 'ere rag when yar finished."

"Yes, sir, I will. Thank you."

Frank first walked the length of the rack without handling any of the guns. The diversity and quality of the firearms overwhelmed him. There were quite a few double rifles, some with exposed hammers, some without, and some with incredibly large bores. He couldn't help but wonder about the recoil on the big ones. Recognizing the unusual shape of the single-shot Martini action rifle, he lifted it and nearly dropped the gun when he read the name engraved on the receiver—F. C. Selous, perhaps the greatest of Africa's big game hunters. As the other guests moved off to an immense stone fireplace, Frank remained in front of the gun rack in awe, feeling close to the legendary pioneer of the African veldt.

"So tell me, Mistar Poul Beenut, what lean of wark aer ya involved in?" the major inquired, handing Paul a highball.

"I'm sort of a surgeon, sir."

"Sart ouv? Either ya is are ya isn't. If that's how ya make an introducshon to yar peeshents, no wounder ya got free teem far safari huntin."

"I'm sort of retired from it now."

The major eyed him and was about to make his early retirement an issue but decided against it. "Well then, I'll wager our Ian Sharpe 'ere was please ta 'ave ya on bourd."

"Quite right, Vince. Paul stepped in and un-mucked what the quacks up in the NFD had done to me. My guts were literally pouring out when we shoved off from Nairobi."

"Ah, ya stupid man. Why didn't ya sit this one oot an wait til ya was up ta snuff, an let the lass ere run th' shou?"

"Thank you, Uncle Vince," Jean said, sneering at her father and feeling thoroughly vindicated. "That is exactly what I tried to tell him."

"What difference does it make at this point? Paul took care of it, and that's the long and short of it."

"And hou did the greet Ian Sharpe find himself with da lepard in question?"

"Had a Kraut client . . ."

"Daddy!"

"Oh, hush up, Zuri. As I was saying, this bloke winged every bloody beast he put sights to."

Paul sank into his seat.

"Well, our Jerry wasn't about to go back to his beloved Fatherland without a *chui,* so the boys and I sweated buckets trying to pull one out of the bush for him. Baited trees for weeks, and when we did finally draw one out, our hero couldn't wait and caught it mid-leap between branches." He paused to take a swallow of the drink. "Shot the bloody guts out of it. What else was I to do but head into the thorns after it?"

"Ah, Ian, ya should hang yar head in sheem far gion' inta the bush far a stinkin' square heed."

"Vince, you know I had no choice."

"Ah know, but ah just had ta say that. Cleanses the soul, ya know."

"You don't care much for Germans do you?" asked Frank from across the room.

"Yar carrect me boy. Aye deespises em. It doun't take a whole lot' a seein' yar men shredded ta pieces an roasted aleeve before ya lose yar teest for th' bastards." He turned his attention to Jean. "Are ya sure dis is what ya want ta do for a livin'? I mean, a lass such as yarself aught to be keepin' a home an meekin' babies instead of crawlin' through the bush an' lettin' the bugs pick at yar flesh."

"You as much as anyone should know how this gets in your blood," she replied.

"Tis true, but I've seen many a liter a blood spilt along the way. In fact, I'll wager ya haven't heard aboot Brice, have ya?"

"No, we haven't. He wasn't killed, has he?"

"Not Camaroun, but hees cle-ant were. I picked it oup off the shart weeve yestardey."

"Paul, Cameron Brice is another hunter out of Nairobi," Jean interjected, so he wouldn't feel left out. "Frank, come over here, you may want to hear this. All right, tell us what happened."

"It was anouthar case of a cle-ant failin' ta follow instructions. A wealthy young lad froum Chile, he was. They were doun Tabora way, aftar *tumbo*. That's elephant to you Yanks. Ward 'as it Chile fired before they had a clear shot an' started a stampede right at theirselves. Brice tried ta turn 'em by shootin' the lead bull, and it landed right on toup o' luckless Chile. They was farced to cut the *tumbo* oup joust ta get at Chile, an when they did, he was as flat as a bloody croumpet, he was."

"What will happen to Mr. Brice?" asked Frank, who had joined them on the sofa.

"No more than pour Camaroun havin' ta live whit himself for the rest a hees life an blamin' hiself the whole way."

They sat quietly for a while, all of them conjuring images of what the last few moments must have been like on the Brice safari. Ian and his daughter were more able to visualize the scene, having witnessed seismic elephant stampedes, though without such a fatal finale.

The major's demeanor changed as he turned to address both of the Americans. "Ya lads listen ta yar hunter, if ya aim to see yar loved ones ag'in. Do ya here what I'm sayin' to ya?"

"Yes sir, loud and clear," Frank said.

Paul nodded several times.

"Nou if ya will excuse me, I'll be attendin' to yar boys and those carcasses. I'll also see ta getting' ya somethin' clean ta wear, so Ngana can do yar wash tonight. Drink oup an make yourself ta houme."

Fishing the largest cigar butt from an ashtray full of them, he stuck it under his mustache and took off for another part of the house.

"You were correct, Jean," Paul said. "He's colorful, all right."

"I just love the man. He talks like a big brute, but he's as gentle as a kitten."

"I'll bet that mutt would argue with you about that," Paul said.

"I'm afraid I'd get my fill of the little runt in short time," Jean replied.

"I don't think I'd like to have him catch me on some game violation," Frank commented, pouring himself another drink. "I doubt he's much of a kitten then."

"That's how he came upon that Martini of Selous's you were admiring," said Ian.

"I was going to ask him about that."

"He took it from an ivory poacher he nabbed many years ago. Fined him, sent him off to jail, *and* took his rifle."

"How many tusks did the guy have?"

Ian held up one finger and smiled. "The law's the law. How the poacher happened to possess the rifle is anyone's guess."

"All this injury and death," Frank commented. "I'm starting to get a little spooked."

"We call it big game," Ian responded, "but as you can see, Frank, it isn't a game." The last thing Ian wanted was to have Frank back out. They already had one client who was showing little interest in hunting. Everything would fall apart if the other one lost his mettle.

Sensing the direction of the exchange, Jean told Frank, "You handled the *simba* as well as anyone could have this afternoon."

"I know we survived it, but if you hadn't spotted that other lion, well—"

"Look, Frank, we're not going to force you into doing anything you feel apprehensive about. If you want to restrict the rest of the safari to non-dangerous animals, that's quite acceptable to me, and I'm sure Zuri agrees. Isn't that right, honey?"

"Absolutely."

"However," Ian added, "this may be your one safari. I can't promise you'll ever be able to do it again. With the way things are changing here, this may be your sole opportunity to take some of these animals before the whole enterprise dissolves. Death does occur here, like what happened to Brice's fellow, but it's an isolated instance. Most of the time everybody goes home safe and happy."

"Frank, you've been dreaming about coming here for years," Paul put in. "I remember you talking about it when we were kids up at Riverbend with Cap. You just keep shooting like you've been doing, and you'll be okay."

"But an elephant squashing a guy? Holy shit!"

"That happened because the fellow didn't listen. Period," Jean said.

"Why don't we just go about things and see how they play out?" Ian suggested, getting himself another drink. "Can I get you something, Zuri?"

"Sure, Daddy, I'd fancy a sherry if you can find some. Thank you."

The major attended to all their needs, even managing to scrape together some clothes, baggy as they were, for everyone. Jean was provided with a robe from his wife's closet. He'd made arrangements for their natives to sleep on the veranda and got his helpers to take care of the two dead animals. The lion capes were put in a shed for safekeeping, and all the guns were brought inside after the bearers cleaned and oiled them.

As the cook threw together the impromptu meal, everyone enjoyed a bath. The old Scotsman had been so thorough that he even provided Jean with a clean scarf. The group dined on diminutive quail-sized birds in a sweet wine sauce with yams and salad greens. Paul found the tender birds a refreshing change from the staple of red meat they'd been packing in daily. He was also partial to hunting birds as opposed to larger game animals. "Where did these come from?"

"They're sand grouse. We've millions of 'em round 'ere. Are ye a bird hounter, Paul?"

"Yes sir, mostly quail and dove. Do you hunt them over dogs or just pass shoot them?"

"No man, thee come ta water houles at dusk by the hundreds. Ya can shoot a meal in minutes. Try it while yar here. It's greet spart."

"I'd like that. Do you think we could try it some afternoon?" he asked, directing the question to Jean.

"Whatever you'd like, Paul. This is your trip."

Frank, he knew, would have no interest in the minuscule quarry, preferring to stalk larger game. Paul saw it as a convenient way to slip off and spend some time alone with Jean and do what *he* liked to do.

As could be expected, the mealtime conversation centered around World War II and the tank battles of North Africa. The major was animated with his narration and alternated between bites of food and draws on his cigar as he and Ian recounted specific clashes in vivid detail, while Frank squirmed with delight in attentive fascination.

Jean and Paul shot doting glances at each other, listening to the conversation in comparative silence. When the meal was finished, the two excused themselves and drifted back to the living room. The others remained at the table, drinking brandy as they brought Rommel's Afrika Korps to its knees for a second time.

Seated in front of the fireplace in the living room, Paul told Jean, "After listening to the major and your father, I'm getting the impression that the future's looking pretty bleak for your line of work."

"They've been singing that same sad sonnet for years, and look at us now."

"But it *has* gotten tougher to conduct these kind of trips, hasn't it?" Paul asked. "I mean, you can't even hunt in Kenya anymore. Where's it going to go from there?"

"I don't know, Paul. All I can tell you is that at present, Tanganyika is almost entirely open, and it appears it's going to remain that way in the foreseeable future."

"What would you do if you couldn't run safaris here?"

She pondered Paul's question for a moment. "I honestly can't say. Hunting's the only thing I know."

"An ya got yer popa ta thank far dat," bellowed the major, who'd entered the room on another cigar-rummaging foray. "The id'yot should've chest ya away frum this lean a wark."

"Now that's nasty of you to say, Uncle Vince. I have no regrets, and I adore Daddy for seeing to it that I learned the trade."

"All the seem, tis no place far a woman. Ya aught ta marry a nice fella like the *daktari,* here—"

"Uncle Vince, Please!" she squealed, throwing a pillow at him. "You're embarrassing me."

"Paul, have ya a weef back houme?"

"No, sir."

"Then, there ya have it. Take dis lovely creature aways from 'ere and marry—"

"Oh stop it, Vince Connolly, you . . . delinquent," Jean berated, hiding her face. "Go back and fight your Nazis with Daddy."

Paul wanted to commend the man for airing such an inspirational

200

message on his behalf, but instead he kept mute until the Scotsman plucked a couple of cigars from an inlaid rosewood box, winked at him, and left the room.

"I'm starting to really like that guy," Paul said, "and his point of view."

She wasn't quite sure if he was alluding to the major's notion of her choice of career or the part about her marrying Paul. Not wanting to embarrass herself any further, she said, "Well, he's certainly entitled to his own views; I just wish he'd keep them to himself, the big baboon."

"I thought you liked him."

"I adore him, but he can be incorrigible."

"Have you ever had any interest in seeing America?"

"Oh yes. I'd planned to visit when I graduated university, but when the Emergency began well, my plans . . . ended."

"Ian started telling me about the Mau Mau thing today while you were going after the lion." Paul could see that he'd broached a sensitive subject again when her attitude shifted from relaxed contentment to solemn disquiet. Furrows spread across her forehead, and her bewitching expression faded to a desolate, faraway stare.

His mind raced for some way of distracting her, but the best he could manage was to bound from the couch and pretend to zoom in on one of the many curios the major had collected over the years. The object of his ruse was a Nazi officer's cap with a small hole, perhaps a quarter of an inch in diameter, right under the golden embossed eagle. He was about to comment about the state of its previous owner when he felt a warm surge spread across his neck as the pieces of Jean's story fell into place. He checked the back of his neck to see if it was actually radiating heat. Without thinking, he reacted, saying, "Oh, no, Jean, no."

In an instant he remembered what Ian had said about the Emergency and his steely remarks about blowing an African's head off. Paul thought about Jean and the way she was always alert and edgy whenever the natives were nearby. He pictured the scar across her throat, imagining her clutching her throat as blood poured through her fingers and down her chest. There were gaps in the scene that he couldn't close, but he somehow intuited what had happened. *How much terror has this poor girl been forced to endure?* he wondered. For the third time since they'd met, he'd been presented with a reason and desire to hold and comfort her.

He turned to face the woman, and she looked even more beautiful to him than ever. Paul thought his heart would shatter when he saw tears streak down her cheeks. She was struggling to maintain her composure, and she was losing the battle. They stared at each other until she lowered her eyes and buried her face in her hands and wept.

Paul could stand it no longer. He said a quick prayer that the Third Reich could endure the British onslaught just a little while longer and knelt to his knees before her. Without uttering a sound he placed his arms around her and held her tightly to him. She offered no resistance, allowing herself to cry quietly, her body jerking in silent sobs. He closed his eyes and smelled the subtle fragrance of her hair, and without even realizing it, drew her in even more intimately, until they seemed to meld. The lean muscular build she had achieved through years of physical activity in the African bush did nothing to lessen the delicate feminine quality of her body. The closeness they were sharing reminded him of how lonely he'd been since his days with Robin and how empty life had seemed since Cap's death the year before. Sorrow was welling up in him, and he had to clench his teeth with all the force he could muster to keep himself from coming unglued right along with her.

If someone walks in on us, so be it, Paul thought, but both of them were aware that the growing intensity of their relationship could topple the balance of the safari, not to mention the ill effect it could have on the other participants. As he continued to embrace her, Paul listened vigilantly for any indication of a pause in the table talk in the adjoining room, but he really didn't care.

"I feel just awful about this," she said, sniffling and hesitantly moving to separate from him. Many times she had come to her father for solace, but this was the first time she'd exposed herself to another man, and a comparative stranger at that. Ever since the butchery that had left her scarred physically and emotionally, she'd been wary of men, black or white, and distrustful of their intentions.

"Please, Jean, don't say anything. It's tough enough seeing you like this without having to listen to you defend yourself on top of it."

"I have to deal with the memory every day, and sometimes it's more than I can bear."

He yearned to kiss her, but something told him it wasn't right. "You know I can't take my eyes off of you," he confessed, "and it isn't because of a scar on your neck."

"That's very sweet of you to say," she uttered, forcing a smile.

"If this safari hadn't gone any farther than that place in Nairobi where we met, it would have been worth the trip to get here."

"I hardly think that—"

"It's true, Jean. You're the most beautiful thing I've ever seen. We've got more than a month left to go here, and I'm already dreading the end."

She paused, looking into Paul's eyes. "So am I."

Nothing short of bringing Cap back could have rendered greater joy for him than hearing her speak those three words. He didn't even try to restrain his smile. He hadn't a clue what the remainder of the trip would yield, but at that moment he was sure it wouldn't culminate in simply paying the bill, shaking hands, and saying goodbye. Not trusting his own resolve, he decided to leave it for now and release his embrace. "I think I could hold onto you forever, but . . . if you're okay now, I'd like to get some sleep. It's been a long day."

"Yes, it has been a full one, hasn't it? We'll just say good night to the desert warriors and find out where Uncle Vince has you staying . . . and . . . thank you for . . . you know."

"Jean, please."

They found the three under a haze of cigar smoke. The major and Ian had reconstructed the terrain of El Alamein using some dinner china as props. They were arguing over the location of a certain German armored division when Jean spoke up.

"If you two heroes have no objection, Paul and I would like to get some sleep."

The way she worded the statement caused Frank to snap from his semi-drunken fog. He surveyed the two party poopers with suspicious concern.

Jean picked up on it right away. "Uncle Vince," she said, still staring at Frank, "could you please show Paul to his room? I don't know where you've got him situated."

"Not a problem lassie, I'll be happy ta lead th' way," he said, pushing himself from the table. "If yar poppa here promises not ta muck oup the ba'el feld. He und I have differin' reco'lections as to th' loucations of the Krouts. Poor ould Ian Sharp's miend is a-failin' 'im."

Ian shoved his cigar in his mouth and rolled his eyes.

"Zuri, is th' smoke bothern' yar eyes, little girl?" the major asked, noticing their reddened appearance.

"Why yes, it is a trifle heavy in here."

"Sleep well, you two," Ian said. "We've got another long one ahead of us tomorrow."

"Right, Daddy, and might I suggest that you and Frank keep it short tonight?"

Frank was either too loaded to respond gracefully or he was making a point of his disapproval. Without looking up from the table, he acknowledged Jean's remark with a curt wave of the hand.

Paul and Jean might have hoped for sleep, but they both lay awake in adjacent rooms, thinking about each other.

Staring at the ceiling, Paul wondered if he could bring himself to leave America and relocate in her country. Africa obviously needed doctors, especially surgeons. *I probably wouldn't have to work at* all, he thought. *Jean and I could just have a small farm and raise something like coffee.* He snickered. *Imagine me, who's never planted so much as a single seed, running a plantation in the African highlands.* He knew the safari business was out. Four days into it, and he'd already had his fill.

He thought about Sheldon and his wife and tried to imagine saying goodbye to them. It didn't set well in his mind. *Why does everything have to be so damn complicated?* Remembering that he'd made no contact with Sheldon since arriving in Kenya, he decided to write him a short message before departing for who-knew-where in the morning. He was sure the major would gladly mail the letter for him.

The faint din of chatter still emanated from the dining room as he lay thinking about Jean, yearning to see her lovely face and smell her hair again. *Maybe she'd come home with me*, he thought, *and we could just fish together every day. Sheldon and Clorese would certainly like her.* He remembered Jean's attachment to her father and her responsibility to the enterprise. *More complications*, he thought, *and these are pretty grandiose schemes for someone who hasn't even kissed her yet.* He loved fantasizing about what their first kiss would be like—passionate, for sure, with their souls connected.

In the next room Jean too lay awake, gently running her fingers across her scar and wondering how anyone, particularly Paul, could find her attractive with such a savage disfigurement. She'd never been a particularly vain person. Her interest in the handsome doctor had changed that, and she wondered about surgical correction. She would be willing to undergo it for him, but at the same time, she had to remind herself that any liaison that might develop between them was destined to be short-lived. In little more than a month the safari would end and the beguiling young man would collect his belongings and board a plane for the United States, perhaps never to see her again. She felt an ache of sadness at the prospect and began weeping again, dreading the thought of saying goodbye to Paul and returning to the humdrum routine of preparing for the next trip. She was twenty-eight years old, and for the first time in her life, felt like a tagalong child and a burden to her father. Although she loved the business, the hard work, long, lonely hours, and predictable outcomes left her with a feeling of emptiness that was surfacing for the first time.

She tried to understand what it was about Paul that was stirring such feelings, such an unexpected closeness that she'd never felt for another man. It occurred to her that her entire life had been spent in the company of men who for one reason or another were unwilling or unable to be authentic. She'd come to expect the bravado, made even more palpable by her presence. It was all part of the safari experience. Paul was different. He seemed at ease with his shortcomings. From the acceptance of his poor marksmanship to his hesitancy to perform minor surgery on her father to his legitimate interest in the natives, Paul appeared to be the persona he portrayed. Most intriguing though was his genuine interest in her, which appeared to have little to do with personal conquest. Jean felt a level of comfort and safety with him that she'd never experienced outside of her relationship with her father.

She looked at the doorway, hoping against hope that Paul would cast aside all vestiges of etiquette and come to her in the darkness. After all, who would ever know? Sleep continued to elude her as she imagined how it would feel to have his body entwined with hers.

CHAPTER EIGHTEEN

Breakdown

Frank stared at his bloodshot eyes and pallid skin in the mirror, and the person glaring back horrified him. "You look like shit." He wheezed. Lack of sleep along with cigar smoke, booze, and narcotics were taking their toll. He had to swallow repeatedly to counteract the salivation onset of the heaves. His nostrils rebelled against the dank stench that seemed to permeate the room. A conglomeration of bizarre cooking odors, none of which he could identify, worsened his hangover; however, he knew that if he could hold down the eight or so codeine tablets in his hand, relief would be forthcoming.

The major had charged his cook, Hassan, with preparing a medley of his favorite dishes for the guests, the main course being broiled kippered herring, which accounted for a fair share of the pungent aroma. The venerable army officer also had a penchant for Spam, a canned product that served as a staple for the American troops during World War II. The cook had quantities of the stuff frying with onions in a weighty cast iron skillet. Slabs of orange yams gurgled and spattered in another lard-filled pan, and some oven-baked cinnamon sweet rolls were cooling on the counter. Locally grown tea and coffee rounded out the menu.

Vince Connolly, unlit cigar in mouth, ushered his guests to the table, scorning their sorry state of enthusiasm in light of the promising new day, which in reality was showing signs of being awash in rain.

As promised their clothes had been washed, dried by the heat of a fire, pressed, and laid out for them. Even Ian, who was the first to arrive at the table, was impressed by the spread and was looking no worse for wear, but feeling quite different.

Paul was following right behind him.

Frank, on the other hand, remained abed, his equilibrium dubious at best. Eventually he made it to the table, only to excuse himself and sprint to the washroom. He returned a few minutes later feeling better and looking a bit less wan.

"Can't hold yar liquor, hu, son?"

"I guess not," Frank admitted, feeling the fool.

"Oh, leave him be, Vince," Ian admonished. "He's not the only one who feels like crap this morn,"

"Weel, eat oup; it'll bring life back to ya."

Paul eyed the kippers cautiously. With thoughts of holding Jean closely in the offing, the last thing he wanted to do was risk having his breath smell like a bait pail. He was about to spear some fried K-ration when he heard Jean enter the room. Feeling a jolt of excitement, he turned to greet her, and what he saw stunned him.

She had brushed her hair, giving it a soft fullness, and for the first time had applied lipstick to her already sensual lips and done something to her eyes. For a moment dead silence reigned as each of the men, including her father, took it all in.

Paul rose to get her chair, but she gestured and said, "Please, Paul."

"Zuri, You look smashing this morning," Ian said, unable to recall the last time he'd seen her tarted up in such a fashion. "What's the occasion?"

"Oh, I haven't done anything differently aside from a bit of makeup," she replied, trying not to direct her answer solely at Paul. "With all you handsome men around, a girl has to keep herself presentable. Wouldn't you agree?"

"Bloody weeste, if yer askin' me—takin' souch a feen lass and meekin' 'er plod through th' bush lak a ruddy sleeve," grumbled the major.

Taking her seat next to Paul, she replied, "But I like doing this, Uncle Vince. That's what you don't understand."

"Rubbish, young leedy. This work's not for a be-uty souch as yarself."

"Haven't we already covered this sufficiently?" Ian said, having heard enough of his friend's rhetoric.

"Ah, yer a stubborn leetle man, Ian Sharp," the major countered, taking his own seat.

"Good morning *Bwana* Eastman," said Jean, hoping to temper the hostilities between the two aged warriors. "You seem a trifle peaked this morning. Are you okay?"

"Maybe just a little short on sleep is all."

She was well aware that it was much more than that, but smiled solicitously. "We'll try to make a short day of it so you can catch up."

"Thanks, and by the way, you do look very nice today."

"Why thank you, Frank."

Within seconds and without warning the loud drum of heavy rain was heard coming from the tin roof above. To the visiting Americans it represented little more than a loud distraction. However, to the others, it was an anomaly that could spell disaster, since the rains weren't expected until late October and were usually over by April. They knew if the downpour persisted for long it would mean swollen creeks to cross and the possibility of impassable torrents. Worst of all, it meant mud—miles and miles of slimy, Rover-sticking mud.

"It's a damned good thing we've got the truck and the boys where we need 'em," Ian said. "Oh, blast! The rain jackets are on the truck."

"Not ta worry. Eve got plenty of ponchews for ya. Ye can bring 'em back on yar next teem through."

"Thanks, Vince. Delicious *chamshakinya*. I haven't had kippers in eons."

Jean was also fond of the salted, smoked herrings, but steered clear of them. She and Paul ate quietly, lost in their own personal reflections of the night before.

After consuming only a fraction of the spread, they all rose and preparing to get under way, gathered up the few personal items they'd brought along. The major left to hunt up heavy rubber rainwear for the four of them, leaving the Africans to fend for themselves.

Jean excused herself, ostensibly to go to the loo, but in fact she followed the major and drew him aside for a private word. "First," she said, speaking emphatically, "I need your promise that you won't confront my father with regard to what I'm about to tell you."

"Of carse. Whatever ya say, lassie."

She told him about the incident on the veldt with the lioness they were badgering with the Rover. The major was familiar with the standard pre-safari prank, having performed it many times when he was in the business. When she described her father's response to the lion's charge, the major threatened to question Ian about it, but she reminded him not to make an issue of it at present. The only reason the major relented was because he knew that Ian had been traumatized by the leopard attack, and his psyche could have been temporarily affected. In addition, he was absolutely confident of Jean's capacity to manage the safari with or without Ian's involvement. He warned her that the hunter who'd lost his nerve was sure to be putting the party and himself in danger. Promising to contact him should the situation become worse, she helped him round up the rain gear, and then both joined the others in the living room.

"Many thanks for having us, Vince," Ian said. "It's always a treat to spend some time with you."

"Doun't give 'er a thought. You and the lass are welcoume any teem, and as fer you Yankees, mind yar hunters. I doun't want ta hear no harrour stories."

"Yes sir, and thank you for everything," replied Paul.

"I really enjoyed the conversation last night, sir," Frank said. "I wish we had more time so I could hear more."

"Parhaps on yar next safari," he said, winking at Ian. "And you, precious lass. I expect ta see ya married with herds 'a little ones runnin' aboot. Enough 'a this tomboy safari nonsense fer ya."

"You never give up, do you, Uncle Vince?" she said, giving him a hug and a kiss, leaving a red imprint on his freckled cheek.

"Give our love to Stella, and tell her we're sorry we missed her," said Ian.

"That goes for me too."

"I'll convee the well wishes. Now be off with ya before yer bouys out there run ouf."

There were handshakes all around and another kiss from Jean before the group stepped out into the rain and ran for the vehicle. The natives had affixed the canvas top and were crouched forlornly underneath it.

Frank hopped in the back seat and made a quick search for his lion skin, which was wrapped and tied behind the seat. Jean, whose hair was already clinging together in ropy strands, climbed behind the wheel and hit the starter as Paul ducked under the top beside her. The last to get in, Ian exchanged some words with the natives. They all waved to the major, who was still on the veranda and was lighting a cigar.

Jean shoved the Rover in gear, and it lurched forward, flinging mud and sliding sideways on the slick ground. It was undoubtedly going to be a long and dicey day.

She had plenty to think about. Despite the short-lived downpour, the trail was a muddy morass in places. She had to maintain her focus on the road to keep from sliding into obstacles or drifting into low-lying dips, where standing water could have obscured any number of pitfalls. Not only did she have her father's psyche to worry about, but she was also contemplating her growing attachment to the man sitting next to her. She hadn't fixed herself up that morning just to enliven the gathering, and she knew it. She was falling for the fellow and didn't have a clue how to handle it or proceed.

She wiped a spatter of mud from her face with the back of her hand and carefully negotiated a sloping bend in the trail. When she turned toward Paul to ask him to check a boulder off to the side, he looked at her and burst out laughing. Jean was so startled by his response she misjudged the turn, causing the Rover to careen down the embankment into a muddy ravine.

When the vehicle came to a stop at the bottom, precariously tilting, it jolted awake the two sleeping passengers in the back seat. She turned to check on them, and they also laughed in her face.

"Will somebody please tell me what is so damned amusing about me all of a sudden?"

"I'm afraid your lip dressing's trying to make its way back to Arusha, darling," Ian said. "Here, care to have a peek?" He looked around for the chrome plate they used as a signal mirror.

"No, I would not care to have a peek, and if you feel I've provided enough entertainment for the lot of you, I suggest we endeavor to get us free from here.

She shot a less-than-genial sneer at Paul, who, while offering her a rag, failed to suppress a grin. Her anger quickly faded, and she propelled the used towel back at him, hitting him on his smirking face. Everyone was chuckling as they stepped out into the slimy ooze surrounding the Rover.

If the vehicle had not been equipped with a hand-crank winch, they may never have gotten it unstuck. As it was, it took several miserable, exhausting hours of pushing, grunting, and shoving by all eight of them to get the Rover up the incline and back on the path. Paul felt a strong urge to tackle and frolic with Jean in the muck and would have, had the others not been present.

Within an hour they found a small *kijito*, or river, and stopped long enough to wash off the bulk of the mud before continuing.

"Oh, bloody hell," Jean said, looking off in the distance.

"What is it, Zuri?"

"There's the truck up ahead. They never made it to the Pangani yesterday. I wonder what the problem is now."

"Do you think any of 'em are still alive?" asked Frank, who'd become somewhat of a fatalist about the safari.

"Sure," Ian said, "and they'll probably gripe about being left all night by themselves, but they shouldn't be any worse for the wear."

"I hope it's not something extensive," Jean said. "I don't fancy dallying around here for days waiting for help."

"What would we do if it is a serious problem?" Paul asked.

"Send one of the boys back to Vince's place," Ian replied. "He'd either come for us himself or see if he couldn't raise someone on the short wave. There's apt to be another party in the area somewhere."

"It's always something with that damn lorry," Jean said. "It's nothing but a rolling rubbish pile."

"Now let's not get bitchy, my sweet," countered her father.

"Well, I don't know why you insist on keeping the thing. It's simply worn out."

It was true. The old army-surplus transport was long past its prime and could be counted on to break down at least one time per trip, but for sentimental reasons, Ian couldn't bring himself to part with it. He'd had it since his first foray into the safari business. "All it needs is a few new rivets and a polish job, and it'll be fine," Ian responded, winking at Frank.

"I'm warning you, you old loon," Jean said. "One of these days that precious truck is going to leave you in a lurch that you can't get out of, or it's going to get somebody hurt. You mark my words."

"Yes, honey. Thank you for the warning."

Pulling up beside the truck, they could see that the rear drive shaft had separated from the differential housing and was hanging toward the ground. Frank knew right away that the universal joint had failed. It would likely be a simple repair job, if they had a replacement part.

The natives, who were all talking at once and all reenacting the lorry's breakdown, besieged Ian. It was a relief, but no surprise, to see that everyone was present, unharmed, and sober, the latter a sure indicator that the liquor supply was safe. Even Nyeusi appeared lucid as he gave his take on the mishap.

More concerned with the repairs than listening to a bunch of Swahili jabber, Frank slid under the truck. It was immediately obvious to him that the driver had miscalculated the ground clearance and hit the drive shaft and the differential on a boulder, breaking the universal joint and denting the differential housing.

"Hey, Ian, take a look at this," he shouted. "We've got serious problems here."

Within seconds the hunter was lying face up beside him, the others on their hand and knees, looking in from the sides.

"Do you carry extra U-joints, Ian? This one's had it."

"Absolutely, and a box of needle bearings to go with it. I told you we're prepared for any event."

"I hope you are, because if this housing's bent into the bull gear, you're going to need a new one of them too. Look at this ding. It could spell real trouble if the bull gear's bent inside there. I'll bet you don't have a spare one of them, do you?"

"Ah . . . no."

"Well, keep your fingers crossed that the dent didn't push into it."

"What's say we just drain it and have us a peek?" Ian suggested.

"It's dripping oil too," Frank said. "Did it always do that?"

Deciding to add her two cents, Jean said, "Everything drips from this wreck."

"Hush up, Zuri," Ian said. "It's always had a little seepage from the seal, but maybe it's a trifle worse now."

Addressing Frank, Paul, who was no stranger to the inner workings of four-wheel-drive vehicles, said, "Can't we just disconnect the rear shaft and keep going, using the front drive train?"

Frank wanted to tell him, "Listen pal, you might be able to sew the girl's father up nice and pretty, but why don't you just shut up and let me take care of this one?" Instead he replied, "No, we can't *just* use the front drive train, because there's too much of a load for the front end to handle. It'd just tear up the transfer case, which is probably about shot as it is."

"Well, it was just an idea."

"Yeah, well, it wouldn't work for long. Ian, you might as well have the boys unload us and find the parts. We'll also need to jack up the rear end. I need to spin the wheels to check it."

"As good as done," Ian said, scooting out from under the truck.

214

Taking another look at the chassis, Frank shook his head over the wretched condition of the structure. There seemed to be as much welded repair work as there was original frame. *Amazing that it's held up this long,* he thought.

The natives made short work of the offloading, and within a half hour a mountain of cargo was piled behind the truck with Frank and Ian went back underneath the truck again working on the drive shaft. It was the type of job that Ian or his daughter could have easily undertaken themselves, but as long as an expert was present, they let him run the show.

Paul and Jean would have just as soon gone off on a sightseeing stroll, but instead they made themselves available to hand tools to Frank and Ian.

As the two mechanics struggled with the tenaciously bound-up hardware, they got greasy to their elbows. During a break they nibbled sandwiches thrown together by Kemoa and enjoyed cold beer provided by Major Connolly, who had seen to refilling their ice container that morning.

With the new joint in place, Frank turned his attention to the differential housing. Removing the drain plug, he expected oil to pour out into a cook pot he was using as a catch basin. Instead of the anticipated stream, he watched as a gush of molasses-like fluid quickly diminished to a slender shiny strand. "Nice oil level, Ian. When was the last time you checked it?"

"Should have been attended to just before we left Nairobi."

"Don't you check these things yourself?

"Ordinarily yes, but with the *chui* ordeal and all—"

Frank turned his attention to Jean, putting her on the defensive. "He's right; you couldn't have expected him to climb under here in his condition. Don't you look at these things too? I mean this is supposed to be your safari."

Despite the fact she hadn't thought to check the fluid levels, having assumed it had been taken care of, she resented Frank's tone. "I really don't think you're in the position to make appraisals regarding our preparedness for this trip," she told him.

Lying beside her under the truck, Paul immediately realized, with a sense of relief, that Frank no longer presented any threat to his amorous designs.

"Look," Frank said, annoying her further, "all I'm pointin' out is that either this thing's been allowed to leak slowly over time without being refilled or it's leaking like a sieve now. Since there isn't a puddle under it, my guess is you guys haven't filled it. Either way, it wouldn't have taken much longer before the goddamn thing locked up. Then we'd have had a real mess on our hands."

Sensing it was time to change the subject, Ian grabbed a spanner and started to loosen the ring of bolts on the housing. "Frank, why don't you set the jacks? Zuri, you and the *daktari* chock the tires with some stones. Get the boys to bring a few larger ones over here."

Jean and Frank exchanged hard glances and then climbed out from under the truck.

Paul didn't know whose side to take. His impulse was to defend the girl, but Frank was right—the deplorable condition of the truck was unacceptable, and the oversight could have caused the trip to be waylaid for days.

As it turned out the dent had not affected the inner workings, and within another hour the travelers were reloaded and on their way to the Pangani River. Following the truck in the Rover, all four passengers watched the truck pitch and sway perilously in the rutted trail. With each lurch the truck tried its best to fling aloft the clinging natives atop the load. Frank expected the transport to topple at any moment. At last the troublesome journey ended hours later, and the group established a river campsite.

It was immediately apparent that the insects, specifically the biting ones, were especially fond of the river, and who could blame them? The setting was, from what Frank could discern in the radiant firelight, idyllic. He stood on the elevated bank watching the flickering fire illuminate the canopy of trees overhead and listened to the hiss and gurgle of the Pangani behind him. The drone of the bugs and the occasional unidentifiable animal sounds echoed down the river, lending an aura of surrealism. Despite having to squash yet another mosquito against his neck, he permitted himself a moment of deep satisfaction. This was the life he'd always fantasized, and here it was, at last.

His brief moment of bliss was quickly replaced by foreboding as he remembered what lay ahead once the safari was over. He'd be forced to return to—*to what?* He'd run from his obligations, leaving his affairs in such disarray that there was sure to be little back home other than nasty letters from banks, idle rusting equipment, angry clients, and little hope for reclamation. Kneeling under the vast African sky, he was overcome by a feeling of failure, total and absolute defeat. His participation on this trip, with all its implied prestige, was nothing more than a masquerade, one last fling before a ruinous end. In a strange way he hoped that something would happen to him here, something that would come suddenly, without warning, and save him from the unbearable specter of losing what little dignity still remained. *Who gives a damn if an elephant tramples me? Paul will just go back to his inheritance and live happily ever after. My dad won't give a shit either. That horse's ass will probably think it's funny—give him something to laugh about at the local bar.* The image of the bar revived him a bit. *At least I've got that to count on.* Suddenly he wanted a drink more than anything else in the world and wasted no time getting one as soon as he was called to dinner.

"What are we gonna do tomorrow, Ian?" Frank asked an hour later, mopping up the last of the gravy from his plate with a chunk of bread. He was intentionally ignoring Jean, although the decision of what to do the following day was hers, as head of the safari.

Mindful that Jean was in charge, Ian replied, "Zuri and I think we ought to collect some leopard baits, a couple of warthog or *tomis*, and get them hung in trees. They need to get a bit ripe to attract the cats. Then we'll build the blinds and leave the whole lot alone for a day or two."

"I read somewhere," Frank said, "that you can hang a live dog or goat in a cage and it'll work better."

"I'm from the old school, Frank. I . . . we don't buy into that sort of rubbish. Fair play in this camp, my American friend, or no play at all."

Paul asked, "If we're not going to hunt the afternoon tomorrow, do you think we can look around for a place to shoot some of those grouse we talked about last night?"

"Jesus, Paul, we're on a safari," Frank scolded. "Why waste time on pigeons?"

Ignoring him, Paul continued, "Major Connolly said they come into water holes at dusk. I'd really like to take a crack at them—I mean if you don't mind 'wasting time' with it."

"I'd love to have a wing shoot for a change," Jean said. "Grouse are tasty little buggers, aren't they? All this red meat tends to strain one's palate after a while. Wouldn't you agree, Paul?"

"I know exactly what you mean," he replied.

Envious of their cozy rapport, Frank pointedly ignored them and continued to shoot questions at Ian. "What do you think we can pick up around here?"

"We've always been able to pull at least one *chui* out of the bush along the river, and there's a good chance of running up on *faro or tumbo*. This is also fine ground for kudu. I'd like to see you get another shot at one, sort of take the sting out of one you botched the other day."

"Daddy!"

"Sorry, bad choice of words."

"Yeah, Ian," Frank said. "I don't think it's fair to say I botched it. It wasn't my fault. It was the goddamn scope."

"Okay, okay, I stand corrected. Anyhow, we've taken some fine *mbogo*, or buffalo, from here in the past, but the grass was shorter then. They're tough to locate when it's as high as it is now. I'm afraid, if you've got your heart set on taking a *mbogo*, you're apt to have to wait until we get over to the Western Province."

"You find me a leopard," Frank said, "and there won't be any bitchin' out 'a me about buffalo."

"Oh, you'll get your *chui*, all right; you just make bloody sure it hits the ground dead."

218

"You still don't trust my shooting, do you?"

"Frank, there's something about a leopard that affects a person. Maybe those fervent green eyes staring down at you—I don't know. All I can tell you is this: I've seen some of the best marksmen around miss a shot clean at meters. I simply can't explain it."

"He's right, Frank," Jean added. "Once old *chui* peers down on you from the branches, it chills you to the depths of your soul."

"It's a lousy cat, for cryin' out loud! And besides, it's only about half the size of that lion I shot yesterday. I think you folks have been out in the jungle to long."

Neither of the professionals was about to argue with Frank. It was late, they were both worn out, and it would be a lesson he would have to learn for himself.

CHAPTER NINETEEN

Baiting the Traps

Paul and Frank sat on their cots, putting on the clothes Nyeusi had laid out for them. The early hours, long days, physical demands, harsh travel, and having to share sparse quarters did nothing to fortify their strained friendship.

Paul was about to shove his foot into a boot when Frank reminded him to shake it out first. He would have ignored the warning just to annoy his bunkmate, but something, perhaps the recollection of Jean's toilet serpent, made him withdraw his toes. Turning the shoe upside down, he shook out a black centipede. The five-inch critter hit the floor squirming, and the two men sat and stared at it, Paul chewing his cheek.

Frank finally got up and ground his boot into the demonic-looking worm, sending juice squirting in all directions. "Told ya so."

"How did you know it was in there?"

"I didn't, but I'm getting to the point where I expect that sort of thing. This place is nuts."

"Thanks for the warning. I suppose that thing was probably the 'Pangani Worm of Death."

"Or maybe it's the Tanganyikan Boot Eel of Pain and Sorrow. Either way, it didn't look too friendly."

Frank grabbed his hat and was about to leave, but paused at the doorway. "Hey, Skip?"

"Yeah?"

"Have you noticed that Jean's always got something around her neck, like she's tryin' to hide something?"

"She is, Frank. She's got a bad scar there. I saw it the first morning we were in camp."

"Really? Do you know what happened?"

"Not the details. It's a sore subject with both of them. All I know is that it had to do with the native uprising. I suspect a Mau Mau got her. That's it."

"Holy shit!"

"Please don't say anything. She's sensitive about it."

"What, do you think I'm an idiot?"

Paul smiled and said nothing.

"Screw you, asshole," Frank said, storming out of the tent.

Frank had been worrying about his pill supply. As the group bounced and jostled through the scrubby bush country, he kept running the numbers through his head, trying to calculate how many more days he could squeeze out of the thirty-seven tablets. Even if he cut back, he'd still have only enough for four or five days at best, and then what? There was plenty of booze, but it wasn't the same. Liquor made him act like a jerk, and he'd done more than enough of that already. Codeine made him feel good without the drawbacks of the alcohol. Frank knew what he'd be in for when the pills ran out. He'd been there before, experiencing a miserable antsy feeling and the depression that came on as the drug left his system. He ruminated over the ten or so pills he'd thrown up the morning at the major's house and regretted he'd lacked the guts to salvage the partially dissolved tablets in his puke. *What a waste*, he thought. He figured he could always sneak into Ian's first aid kit and pinch some of his supply, but what hell he'd pay if he got caught. It wasn't worth the risk. Yet.

It was late morning before the hunters stopped at a trail crossing the road. Jean confirmed that it was a warthog path, one that revealed recent traffic. When she suggested they follow it on foot, everyone objected, pointing out the mosquitoes and flies were horrendous and their only relief was to keep ahead of them in the Rover.

Scraping a layer of bugs from his arms, Frank said, "How about if we keep on moving and hope we run into something on the road?"

"*Bwana* Eastman," Jean remarked with a hint of distain, "no warthog, no *chui*."

"I get the point," Frank conceded.

"I knew you'd see it my way," she said. "Just cover yourself with this repellent and come along. We mustn't dawdle. Paul, are you coming?"

"If you don't mind," he replied, "I think I'll just stay here and keep your old man company."

"Don't you two juveniles get into any mischief while we're away," she said, tossing Paul the can of repellent.

After Jean and Frank took off with bearers and tracker in tow, Paul seized the opportunity to pump Ian for a detailed account of Jean's injury at the hands of a Mau Mau terrorist, trying to slip into the subject as subtly as possible. "Ian, what was Jean like as a child? She's different from most women I've known. Was she always unconventional? Not that I think there's anything wrong with that."

Ian snickered and spoke into the hat that was covering his face. "She was a bloody handful, all right, from the start."

"What do you mean?"

Straightening up in his seat, Ian said, "Do you know how toddlers will have a favorite blanket that they carry for security?"

"Yep, I had a flannel one."

"Zuri's was a leopard skin. She was never without it, and it got so foul from the smell of pee and spittle that I could hardly stand to be in the same room with it. About a year after Penny died, when Zuri about four, I came home and found her wandering across a field, dragging my four-fifty number-two double and carrying a sack of cookies. When I asked her what in the bloody hell she was doing, she looked up at me with those little crinkly eyes of hers and announced without a hint of reservation, 'Why Daddy, I'm on safari.' That little excursion of hers ended with her bottom being warmed and my rifle needing some extensive refinishing, but it took all the restraint I could muster not to laugh myself silly. She repeated the same stunt several years later and showed up back at the house with a rather nice gazelle. One of the boys carried it back for her. In fact the head of it was on the wall of that bar in Nairobi where we all met. She's somewhat of a legend there because of it." Ian beamed at the memory of that day. "It was then that I knew she was destined to follow in my footsteps."

"She doesn't seem to have much in the way of friends."

"She never did. Always the loner, she was—and still is. Her limited social associations used to bother me, but now, with the damned Emergency, I'd prefer to have her around so I can keep my eyes on her."

That was the opening Paul had been waiting for. "You never told me exactly what happened, but I'd understand if you didn't want to talk about it."

Ian fanned himself with his hat before beginning. "It was shortly after she returned home from university. There had already been some incidents in volving Kikuyus murdering some of their own leaders, leaders who gave no credence to the Mau Mau movement. Then several Europeans were killed and the whole thing exploded. You couldn't tell on the face of it which natives were loyal to whom, and we were left to defend ourselves for the most part. Only later were British troops and the RAF called in, and they've been here since. A home guard was established too. Throw me that bug dope, please."

After spreading some of the liquid on his arms and face and drying his hands on the front of his shirt, he continued. "As I said, it was anybody's guess who was faithful to us Brits and who had taken the oath."

"What oath is that?"

"To swear loyalty to the movement, these animals had secret ceremonies where they ate blood and sheep dung and performed all forms of perverse acts. It's too bloody vile to go into. We had a house boy at the time, a nice Kikuyu kid of twenty. Never heard a peep out of him . . . until he caught

Jean in the chicken house and—" He paused to light a cigar. "Care for one?" he asked, holding it out for Paul.

Paul was tense with dread and anticipation. He watched as Ian's eyes grew cold and his jaw muscles flexed.

"He crept up behind her and knocked her out with a board. Then the son of a bitch cut her throat with a *panga,* but not deep enough to kill her, thank God. Then he ripped off her clothing and smeared her with chicken droppings and her own blood. He was standing over her, urinating on her and preparing to violate her before he killed her. Fortunately Kemoa, bless his soul, came out there and saw what was happening. He snuck up and cracked a shovel handle over the bastard's head."

Paul tightened up. "Who took care of Jean?"

"Another house boy ran to a neighbor's house, and they in turn called for the *daktari.* I was in town and showed up about two hours after it happened. By then the *daktari* had stopped the bleeding and had sewed the wound. He'd given her something to make her sleep."

Paul's mind was in chaos, stunned by the nightmarish vision of Jean's naked, bleeding body. A surge of vengeful lust rose in him. "Did you have the native arrested?"

"No," Ian said, "but he paid for the crime. I went out to where Kemoa had tied him up."

"What did you say to him?"

"Nothing. I stuck the barrels of the Webley in his mouth and pulled the triggers."

At that instant, the deep thunder of a rifle report echoed through the trees, adding audio to Paul's vison of Ian's execution-style murder. To conceal his dismay, Paul said, "That must be Frank nailing something."

Ian shrugged and went on. "We dragged him out and left his detestable carcass for *fisi.* They polished him off," Ian added. "And that was that."

"What did Jean say when you told her you killed the guy?"

"We never discussed it and never will. Paul, there's a war going on over here. Our way of life is at stake, and I'm not about to get sentimental over a dead Kikuyu who maimed my little girl. If I have to obliterate half the Mau Mau in Kenya with my bare hands, I'm prepared to do it."

Paul had already heard more than he cared to. "Do you think we ought to go pick them up and get a move on?"

Ian nodded and started the Rover. "I apologize for erupting, but I think you can understand."

"I understand, but it's still a little tough to swallow. How do you think this uprising is going to play out?"

Spinning the vehicle around, slinging dirt and rocks, and propelling the Rover into the bush, Ian said, "They're going to get their goddamned independence *and* this beautiful country, and maybe the whole of Africa is going to revert to God knows what."

After finding Jean and Frank, Paul looked down at their kill. The warthog was almost comical, its head and dentition grossly out of proportion to its squat body. "Christ, they're ugly, aren't they?"

"Yeah, and they're just as stupid as the hogs back home," replied Frank, who was studying the animal's oversized rapier-like cuspids. "I wish I could keep the head for the wall."

"I think you might as well give this one up, Frank," Ian said. "We need it for bait, and there'll be more opportunities. *Ngiri*, wild boar, are fairly plentiful throughout the country, and besides, this one here really isn't anything to boast about. Now we'll need to get another or a gazelle or something for the second blind, and we need to get busy constructing them, and they need to be first rate, because *chui* isn't stupid. We're going to split up into two teams, and each will have his own blind, got it?" Ian swatted his neck and added, "Unless you fancy being fodder for all these blasted flies, I suggest we load this beast and shove off."

The others didn't have to be asked twice; they were all ready for a reprieve from the swarms. Within seconds they had the warthog loaded and were on their way again.

In less than an hour a second boar of equal proportion was adding volume to the large pool of congealed blood in the back of the Rover. Frank took it on the rare occasion that Jean allowed him to step out of the vehicle and shoot without having to stalk through the bush after the game. The bugs had taken such a toll on her that she permitted the shortcut.

Ian chose two sites about a half a mile from each other and close to the river. With effortless agility Susani shimmied to the middle branches of an acacia tree, rope in hand, and secured the dead warthog bait that the others hauled up to him, repeating the exercise at the other blind. With that accomplished to the Sharpes' satisfaction, the group members all scavenged about, collecting fallen branches, cutting new ones, and piling them such that as they lay in wait, they'd be hidden from view.

Jean attended to the building of each blind, while her father oversaw the operation and offered suggestions here and there on how to improve the setup. Paul went through the motions of helping, but his thoughts were still consumed with conflicting images of rape and execution—Jean's offal-defiled body and butchered throat, and Ian's shoving the double rifle into the African's mouth and blasting his head into fragments. Paul didn't know where he stood anymore about anything.

The blinds were positioned about fifty meters from the baited trees. Careful attention was paid to the field of view, with emphasis on having an unobstructed line between the rifle rest and the baited limb. Only a tiny opening was left through which the rifle barrel could protrude. One of the blinds had an outcropping of rock behind it, which provided a cave-like setting.

With everything in place, the areas around the setups were swept with branches to remove any sign of human activity and were abandoned to allow a day or so for the warthogs to ripen and things to settle down.

On the way back to camp Paul spotted a water hole that looked like a possibility for an afternoon bird hunt and pointed it out to Jean. With her ordeal fresh and raw in his mind and heart, his voice took on a new tenderness as he asked, "Do you have any interest in coming back here later and trying a little bird shooting?"

"I think I might be able to avail myself," she responded, winking at him.

Paul felt obligated to ask Frank to join them, but hoped he'd decline. "How about you, Frank, care to give it a try?"

Frank shook his head. Big game hunters couldn't be bothered with the humdrum sport of grouse hunting, and the relationship that had sprung between Paul and Jean made it futile for him to try to woo the girl any longer. With nothing to do for the rest of the day, Frank settled into a camp chair with a glass of bourbon while he watched Paul and Jean ready themselves for the sunset grouse shoot. He raised an eyebrow when he saw Jean take a bottle of wine from Kemoa and place it in the Rover, and he'd have been kidding himself if he hadn't felt more than a twinge of envy for his friend's good fortune. Before the whiskey had a chance to work its magic, feelings of emptiness and inadequacy assailed him. He attempted to comfort himself by focusing on the safari, but it was getting harder to ignore the unpleasant details of his woeful existence. Nonetheless, he gave Paul and Jean an artificial smile as they pulled away. As soon as they were out of sight, he got up to search for some diversion. It came quickly and in a form he could never have imagined.

CHAPTER TWENTY

The Last Straw

A small African boy of perhaps seven years of age wandered into camp and strode up to Frank. The child may have been older, but it was hard to tell, since he was clearly malnourished and was as thin as a twig. His head seemed too large for his diminutive torso, as were the scratched and dirty feet attached to spindly legs sticking from his threadbare hand-me-down shorts. The sight of him tugged at Frank's jaded heartstrings. His first thought was that the child was an orphan, but he couldn't imagine how the waif had survived on his own in the bush. The only plausible conclusion was that he must have wandered over from a nearby village when he saw the expedition arrive.

Towering above the child, Frank looked down at him and smiled. "Hi, little guy."

There was no reply, only an expression of bewilderment from his large blueish-white eyes.

"What's your name?"

Again, no response.

"We're going to get nowhere fast. You don't know what the hell I'm sayin', do you?"

The child held up a carved baseball-sized wooden ball he'd been holding.

"Did you make this?" Frank took the rough-hewn sphere from him, and throwing it up, caught it with his free hand.

The boy held out his hand for the ball, and Frank promptly returned it, whereupon the tiny African tossed it up slightly and caught it on the top of his head, balancing it there.

"Hey, that's pretty good, kid. Let me try that."

The enormous white man took the ball and tossed it up higher than it needed to go. When it came down on his head, it did so with an audible thud and bounced off. "Ow!" cried Frank, which set the child off in an outburst of giggles. Even Frank had to laugh at himself over that one. "Come with me," he said, motioning with his hand. "Let's go find a translator."

The child retrieved his ball and followed Frank to the truck where Ian was working.

"Hey, Ian, look what I found."

Ian stuck his head out from under the hood. "Well, aren't you a lucky fellow?"

"Can you find out where he came from?"

The hunter climbed down from his perch on the truck fender and fired a volley of Swahili at the youngster, who responded in kind. "He's a Bondei from a village about two miles from here. His name is Dando. I'll send him off."

"No, he can stay as long as he wants to, as far as I'm concerned."

"Beware he doesn't steal you blind and vanish."

"Aw he wouldn't do that, would he?"

"In a minute," said Ian, eying the child.

"Aren't his parents afraid something will happen to him, wandering alone out here like this?"

"I told you before—to these people, death is the will of God."

"Ask him if his folks know where he is."

There was another exchange between the two, and Ian shook his head. "His father just drinks and beats him and his mother. He's very afraid he'll beat them to death one day in a blind rage. He says his mother is very beautiful."

Instinctively, Frank felt himself bonding with the tyke.

Dondo spoke to Ian again, prompting a smirk on the hunter's face.

"What did he say then?" Frank possessively placed his hand on the Dondo's head.

"He wants to know if you will be his father. He thinks a man of your size must have much land and many goats and could surely provide for one more small *mtoto*. He also wants you to marry his mother."

Frank didn't know how to respond. "What the hell is a *mtoto?*"

" A child"

"So what am I supposed to say to him?"

Ian thought for a moment. "How about I tell him that in your village, you are a poor man with few goats who wouldn't be able to care for him."

Frank didn't think the child would buy the story, but it *was* the truth. He probably was going to be poor when he returned to his village in America. Taking a swig of his drink, he said, "Go ahead and tell him that."

Ian spoke, and the child's head sagged.

Frank felt a stab of empathy. "Please tell him I'm sorry, but he can stay around here for a while—that is, as long as you don't mind."

"I have no objection as long as he doesn't get underfoot, or if things don't start disappearing. If that happens, he's a goner, get it?"

"Fair enough."

Ian spoke again, and the child's spirits revived.

"Can I get him something to eat? The poor kid looks like he's starving."

"If you'll give me a minute, I have Kemoa throw something together."

"Thanks, Ian. I'll keep him out of everyone's way," said Frank, leading the boy away with him.

Paul couldn't remember the last time he'd felt as excited. He and Jean were alone, setting up a picnic at an idyllic spot they found underneath a spreading shade tree. He was so excited by the possibilities of intimacy that he nearly forgot his shotgun back at camp. The only reason he remembered to bring it at all was to impress Jean with his taste in exquisitely built double-barrel shotguns. Otherwise he definitely would have left it behind, which would have impressed her only with his ineptitude, since hunters don't typically forget to bring their guns.

He waited in the Rover until she assembled her twelve-bore double and rested against the tree beside her rifle before he unveiled the Woodward over and under. Gingerly locking the barrels in place, he snapped the fore-grip on before leaving the vehicle.

Even the constant nuisance of flies and mosquitoes didn't dampen his spirits as he helped Jean set up the collapsible chairs. Here he was, alone with the woman whose mere presence altered his normal physiology. He could feel the surge in his heart rate and breathing, and all he'd done was stand close to her.

Jean had set some plastic cups on a squat canvas-and-wood table and was opening the wine when she noticed the gun, and she literally leapt with excitement. "Paul, how on earth did you come upon that?"

"Oh, you like it, do you?" he said, as if he hadn't anticipated the reaction.

"Like it? It's magnificent! May I?" She held out her hands.

He placed it in her hands and watched as she ogled the perfect craftsmanship. "Cap bought it from some G.I. who'd smuggled it out of Europe. You know, the spoils of war."

"It looks like something a king would own."

"It might have been, but today it's going to be used by a princess."

"Oh, Paul, how sweet."

He was gathering the courage to take her into his arms when the flutter of wings signaled the first flight of birds dropping to the bank of the water hole, ruining the moment.

Over the next half hour Jean proved to be as nimble with a shotgun as she had been with a rifle. Nearly every time the sleek double went to her shoulder, a pair of sand grouse tumbled from the sky.

Paul was also in top form, despite having to use her cumbersome double twelve bore. He kept pace with her shooting and made some impressive shots on a few faraway birds.

Between flights the couple sipped wine from plastic cups while scanning the skyline for incoming birds, making small talk, and taking turns darting out from the tree to pick up dead grouse.

It was great fun for both of them, but finally, with the pile of birds mounting and darkness making the remaining birds tough to see, they called it quits, packed up their gear, and headed back to camp.

Lost in his own thoughts as they rode along in the darkness, Paul was convinced it was going to be difficult, if not impossible, to leave the country without Jean.

Jean, on the other hand, was disappointed that he'd had failed to make good use of their time alone. Was he attracted to her but repulsed by her mutilation? Her hand went to her neck again.

Back at camp Jean switched off the Rover. "It appears that *Bwana* Eastman has found himself a new friend," she said, pointing to Frank, who was staggering toward them with delighted Dondo astride his beefy shoulders.

"I wonder what that's all about," Paul responded as the unlikely pair approached.

"I'll wager the *mtoto* belongs to one of the itinerant game rangers," Jean replied. "Word spreads quickly out here when a safari shows up. Anybody who's seen or thinks they've seen some beast will show up to report it. If it proves to be true, we usually tip them. It makes our work easier."

By the way Frank weaved it was apparent that he'd been hard at the booze and that the child could hardly have found a more precarious perch.

"Hi guys," Frank slurred, sliding Dondo from his shoulders. "Say hi to my buddy, Dodo, or Dombo, or somethin' like that. Cute little fellow, ain't he?"

"*Hujambo, rafiki*. How are you?" Jean said to the boy. "*Jina lako nani?* What's your name?"

"*Dondo, memsaab.*"

"His name is Dondo, Frank. Did he come here with his father?" She surveyed the camp looking around for any strangers.

"No, his father's an asshole who beats him up, so he asked me to be his new daddy. Isn't that swell?

"Shouldn't we just run him back to his village?" Paul asked.

"We're not going to run him anywhere, Skip." Frank asserted. "He's staying right here."

Dondo intuitively reached for Frank's hand.

"Not so fast," Jean said. "He belongs with his people. What does Daddy have to say?" Jean asked.

"As long as he stays out of trouble, he stays right here."

"And what will become of him when we move to another spot?"

"I don't know. We'll cross that bridge when we get to it."

"Frank, why don't you listen to her and take the kid—"

"Shut the hell up, Skip. It doesn't concern you."

"Like hell it doesn't! Things are finally settling down here, and now you want to stir it back up again. This kid isn't some kind of pet you can keep for just a week or two. He needs to go home. Now!"

"He'll go home when I goddamn say he goes home."

"Yeah, well, when you sober up, we'll see about that." Grabbing his gun case out of the Rover, Paul gave Frank a burning glare and left for the tent.

"I feel sorry for this kid, Jean. Don't you understand?"

"I can appreciate that, but this is a mistake. If he stays any length of time here, it's going to send him the wrong message. He'll expect you to take him with us. His mother is probably frantic right now."

"Right now his mother is probably being beat up by his father. That's why he ran away."

Jean looked down at the child. "Can we discuss this some other time, Frank? I need to get washed up."

The tension at dinner was palpable, and there was scant conversation. Frank managed to behave himself, but it was obvious that the simple task of eating was a challenge. Dondo sat cross-legged on the ground outside the dining enclosure, his presence making everyone at the table feel uncomfortable and guilty for the lavishness of the provisions before them.

Ian was obviously so apprehensive about the state of the safari that the possibility of cancellation was intensifying. At his wit's end with *Bwana* Eastman, Ian sat at the table pondering Frank's excessive drinking and decided it had to cease, and furthermore the child was to be returned to his village—and soon. It was tough enough to oversee the safari without adding superfluous baggage.

Even the natives appeared edgy. Kemoa and Nyeusi bickered over the placement of the forks and the cleanliness of plates. They expressed their disdain for the uninvited visitor by ignoring Dondo altogether.

Having eaten, the group couldn't depart from the table fast enough, except for Paul, who made a point of thanking Jean for the afternoon bird shoot.

Inside his tent, Paul found Frank passed out, with Dondo curled up at the foot of his cot, which infuriated him even further. Even as an outsider unfamiliar with the local protocol, Paul knew it was way over the line.

Stretched out on his cot, Paul took stock of the situation and concluded that the safari had gone totally sour. He couldn't imagine another month of it. That afternoon at the waterhole with Jean was exciting, but ultimately it went nowhere when his courage failed him. Jean was a huge prize, and any form of rejection by her would have been too much to handle. Disgusted by his own spinelessness, he swore to himself that if given the chance, he would redeem himself with her. He drifted off, fantasizing of what *could* have happened that evening at the water hole.

CHAPTER TWENTY-ONE

Darkness Falls

"Morning, Ian," Frank said, as if nothing had happened. Dondo was standing beside him, lost inside of an oversized shirt of Frank's.

Wrapped in a blanket, shivering in front of the fire, and suffering from a recurrence of malaria, Ian didn't even bother to acknowledge Frank. Finally, in a shuddering voice, he asked, "Did you fancy our *chakula* last night?" Or do you even remember it?"

Oh boy, here we go, Frank thought, prepared to defend himself, and then deciding it was hopeless. Instead he settled into a chair next to Ian and waited to take his punishment, which was not long in coming.

"In case it's not fresh in your mind," Ian said, "let me revive your memory. Dinner last night was like a bloody goddamn wake. Camp morale's at an all-time low. Less than a week we've been out in the bush, and we're at such a point that I'd just as soon call it quits, refund your money, and bid you farewell."

"Ian, I—"

"Let me finish. I don't think that's what you want, and neither do I. So let me tell you what the rules are going to be."

"I think I've got a pretty good idea already."

"Let me spell them out for you anyway, so there's no misunderstanding.

The boozing is finished as of right now. I don't mind if a client has a *gin-i* or two after a long day, but I won't play wet nurse to a sot. I'm getting too old for it."

"Ian, I don't intend to get plastered; it just creeps up on me."

Ian's eyes blazed in reflected firelight as he said, "Perhaps you need to do something about that."

Frank looked away. He knew it was the truth. His drinking had finally caught up with him and could no longer be passed off as merriment. It was a dependency, and it was ruining him. That the criticism came from a professional hunter, a group not known for temperance, was especially galling.

"You're a fine young man, Frank, but you're pissing your life away with booze."

It's a good thing he doesn't know about the codeine, he thought, *or the shit would really hit the fan.* The problem was there was no way for him to stop drinking as long as liquor was available, and he wasn't about to tell Ian to dump the stuff out. He came to Africa to enjoy himself, and drinking was an essential part of it.

"The other issue is the *mtoto.* He goes back to his people today . . . this morning."

"I was just trying to let the little kid have a break from his old man," he said, rubbing the bristly fuzz on the child's head.

"That's very noble of you, I'm sure," Ian responded, his tone implying indifference. "But this is no place for him, and I don't care to be responsible for anybody beyond the party we left Nairobi with."

"All right, Ian, I'll take him back. But can't it wait until after dinner tonight?"

"No. It's just going to prolong the inevitable and make it tougher on him."

"I know, but at least he'll get another decent meal before havin' to go back to . . . who knows what."

Shivering a bit, Ian said in deference, "Very well.

"Thanks. The kid really means something to me."

Looking down at Dondo, Frank tried to figure out how break the news to him, but decided to put it off until later. *After all*, he thought, *why spoil the kid's day?*

They wandered off together to the cook's tent, where Frank intended to scrounge up some food for the child.

Ian watched them walk off before reluctantly getting up and leaving the warmth of the fire. *Every trip, it's something new*, he thought, shaking his head. *This is getting old.*

When Paul wandered out to the campfire, he found Jean having her tea and took the opportunity to explain his behavior of the previous evening. "Things were pretty tense last night," he began, "and I didn't get the chance to tell you how much it meant to me to spend the afternoon with you. It was the nicest time I've had in, well . . . a very long time."

Jean's reaction was restrained. Plain and simple, she was hurt by his perceived ambivalence. She had gambled on her feelings for him and had nothing to show for it. "I'm glad you enjoyed it," she said. "So few of our clients take advantage of the wing-shooting opportunities we have here."

Registering the chill in her response, Paul realized nothing short of sweeping her up right then and there, which he wasn't about to do, could mitigate the situation. He was at a loss. "What do you have in store for us today?"

"Daddy and I thought we'd have a look around for a respectable *pongo* or perhaps we'll take a drive out west and try to find some *mbunju*."

"And those would be . . .?"

"Bushbuck and eland—big antelope. There's also a spattering of *faru* in this region, so we might happen onto one of them."

"Rhino, right?"

She nodded. "Will you hunt today, or more sightseeing?"

"I don't know. I'll play it by ear. I think you know by now how I feel about shooting the big stuff."

"Even so, I think you should take some of these animals . . . I mean as long as you're here. Now if you'll excuse me, I've got a few things to attend to before breakfast."

"Sure, go ahead. I won't hold you up."

Her contrite smile suggested that he'd squandered the only opportunity he was going to get. A hollow feeling of despair gnawed away at him as she walked away.

Frank conjured up a better mood with about a third of his remaining painkillers and was raring to go at whatever Tanganyika could throw at him. As the hunters departed the camp for the day's hunt, he was still bothered by how he was going to part with his little buddy and deal with his estrangement from Paul, who was preoccupied with planning his next move with the girl.

Nyeusi wasn't thrilled about being told to keep an eye on Dondo in Frank's absence, but he was in no position to question Ian's orders. He had concluded that the pretense of goodwill toward the boy ought to be worth an extra pound sterling at the end of the trip, so he showed a semblance of compassion toward the boy until the Rover was out of sight. Afterward he essentially told him to get lost until the party returned later in the day.

The safari took to the trail of a rhino that had recently passed through the area. Jua had spotted the tracks as the Rover passed over them. It was a considerable feat of observation, since Jua found the tracks in an area of rocky terrain. Paul didn't feel like joining the stalk, but Ian assured him that because of the nature of the beast, the pursuit could take hours, and he might find himself sitting alone until dark. They walked for miles, Jua alternately losing and reestablishing the trail. At one point they were within a hundred meters of the rhino, catching a glimpse of its massive hindquarters through thick vegetation. Jean and Frank, both carrying double rifles, followed the tracker as he started the cautious approach toward the animal. When they closed the gap to seventy-five meters, they still couldn't get a good look at the rhino's head, and when the wind shifted, the great beast scented them and thundered off, cracking limbs and knocking down small trees.

Frustrated, sweaty, and tired, the advance group retreated and joined the others, starting the process all over. Two hours later they were slipping up on the behemoth again, only to discover that it was a female with negligible horns.

"Rotten luck, Frank. Sorry," Jean offered. "She isn't worth taking. That's how it goes here."

"That's all right," Frank said. "It was exciting anyway. Those things are huge. I can't even imagine what an elephant must look like up close."

"Very intimidating, indeed," she said, grinning at him. "We'd better start back if we're to reach the Rover by dark."

"Lead the way, *memsaab*. I'm exhausted."

After Jean and Frank joined with the others, the group wasted no time setting out for the vehicle. Thanks to their veteran tracker's skill, they were able to follow their own tracks and arrived before dark, hastening toward camp to close the distance before darkness fell. A rough high-speed ride put them in sight of the campfire as absolute darkness set in.

To everyone's chagrin except Frank's, Dondo was the first to greet the group as the Rover skidded to a stop. The child took Frank's hand as he dislodged his stiff, tired body from the vehicle.

While the others departed for their pre-meal de-griming, Frank squatted to his knees and said, "Hi, junior. Wa'cha been up to today?"

"*Kifu o-ote?*" asked the boy as he stood on his tiptoes, trying to peer over the back of the Rover.

"*Kifu?*" asked Frank. "Oh yeah, dead. No, there isn't anything dead back there." He picked the child up to show him, and Dondo frowned, slowly shaking his head. Laughing, Frank asked, "Bet you think I'm a dud as a big game hunter, don't you?"

Dondo let fly with a stream of Swahili and pointed toward Nyeusi.

"Did that guy give you a hard time while I was gone?"

There was another round of native jabber from the child, followed by a pause.

"How about if I shoot him after *chakula* and leave him out there for the hyena?"

Repeating the word *chakula*, Dondo rubbed his belly.

"Hungry, are you? Let me see what I can do."

With boy in tow, Frank strode over to the cook tent, and using panto-mime, instructed Kemoa to feed Dondo without further delay. The cook's contempt was obvious, but he laid out a meal, and Frank left to wash up for dinner. He skipped his bath and settled for rinsing in the washbasin, his nervous system crying out for a drink the whole time. He thought about how good it would taste and how its heat would rekindle his spirits. He salivated thinking about the caramel-charcoal essence of the whiskey burning the inside of his mouth; however, having one drink would end his safari, and he resolved to steer clear of booze for a while, if it was even possible.

At dinner, struggling to keep his mind off of the uncorked bottles of wine on the table, Frank focused instead on his bantam protégé, Dondo, who was running around the cook fire, oblivious to the annoyance of the adults. The mosquito netting that enclosed the dining tent imparted a filmy quality to the already murky camping area. Frank had to squint against the intense light from the gas lamps above the table to keep track of Dondo. The rest of the diners ignored the playful child and ate in weary silence.

Frank hoped Ian would shelve the idea of taking Dondo home after dinner. At the very least it would give Frank more time to prepare for the boy's inevitable protest.

Dondo appeared to be perfectly contented at the camp and in no hurry to be reunited with his people.

Ian looked up from his plate when he heard Nyeusi griping to the other natives.

"You know, Zuri, we really should have brought back a *tomi* or two for the boys," he said, spitting out a piece of birdshot from the chunk of grouse breast he was chewing on. "I don't think they fancy Kemoa's cuisine."

It was true. The natives were serving themselves from a kettle, grumbling to each other as they clanked the ladle onto their bowls in protest. They hated the watery meat and barley soup the cook had thrown together for them. What they wanted was meat and lots of it, not gruel concocted from leftovers, of which they'd already had their fill back home.

"I suspect we'll have a throng of very poor sports tomorrow if we fail to return with sufficient measure of *nyama*. They want meat."

"I shouldn't expect it will kill them to do without for one night," Jean countered, talking through a mouthful of the livery-tasting fried grouse.

"What was that you said, Miss Antoinette? I couldn't understand you, with so much in your mouth?"

Jean gave her father a sheepish little shrug. "I guess that was a trifle bourgeois, wasn't it?"

"You remember what happened to the queen? She got——" Ian cut himself off, seeing Jean's hand on her scarf, adjusting it.

Paul's eyes met hers and quickly returned to his plate.

"Frank, me-boy, do you have any interest in shooting a crocodile?"

At that instant, Dondo lit out across the open area with Nyeusi in hot pursuit, hollering and swinging a stick at him. Frank jumped up from the table but was anchored by a scene that was so bizarre, so surreal that his brain couldn't make sense of it. All he could do was stand transfixed as a leopard leapt from the darkness, slamming into the child.

An eerie stillness fell over the camp. It may have lasted for a second or a minute or an hour, as far as Frank's overloaded senses could comprehend.

The only sound was the crunching noise of Dondo's neck breaking as the leopard chomped down, killing him instantly.

Ian looked over his shoulder in time to see the cat bolt into the darkness with the child's limp body in its mouth.

"Oh, bloody Christ!" Ian exhaled something between a groan and a whimper. *"Toa, bunduki ya marisaa na tochi, sasa,* sasa. Get me a gun, now, now*!"* he screamed. Shifting into action, he launched himself from the table, hitting it with his knee, dumping glasses and clattering plates. "Stay here," he said to the others, tearing off toward the supply tent, his daughter one step behind him.

By then pandemonium reigned among the natives. Yelling in Swahili, dark bodies were running in all directions. The gunbearers dived into the tent to retrieve the shotguns and load them. Others were shining flashlights into the bush where the leopard had withdrawn, leaving a trail of the Dondo's blood in its wake.

The two Americans were speechless. Disobeying orders, they walked to the stained earth where the boy had met his end. Paul was speechless. Saying "Sorry your little buddy got eaten by a leopard" seemed inappropriate.

Still shaky, Frank hadn't yet grasped the reality of what had happened. His only clear thought was that he needed a drink more than he ever had in his life.

Out in the thicket Ian and Jean's flashlights furnished a narrow, wavering tunnel of light.

All perception of depth was lost, and Ian knew it was dangerous—and probably pointless—to proceed. "We'll get nowhere with this tonight, Zuri. We have to wait until the morning. I knew no good would come of this— just *knew* something like this would happen. I hope *Bwana* Eastman is satisfied with the outcome."

"I don't think you can hold him responsible, Daddy. I agree, the child should not have been allowed to stay, but this could have happened to any of us."

She was right. With a man-eating leopard nearby, everyone was in danger, and it was only a matter of who would be next.

"I implore you to go easy on him. He's miserable enough already."

"He bloody well should be." Ian handed his shotgun to Susani and stomped back to camp.

Frank saw him coming and knew he was in for it, but having fortified himself with a healthy slug of bourbon, he asked, "Did you find him?"

The two professional hunters ignored the question and swept past him.

"I think I'm entitled to an answer," Frank declared.

Ian stopped dead in his tracks, clenching his fists and spinning around.

Sensing a confrontation, Jean headed directly toward Paul, who was staring into the campfire.

Ian closed in on Frank until his face was near enough to smell the drunk's liquor-laden breath, which infuriated him even further. Ian's eyes were slits of rage, and it took all of his self-restraint not to belt Frank. "What you're entitled to, my American friend, is the knowledge that the blood of that child is on your hands, not mine." He was deliberately trying to provoke a reaction in Frank that would justify smacking him.

Frank wasn't intimidated by the thought of tangling with the smaller, older Brit, but the need for discretion at the moment sealed his lips.

When Frank failed to respond, Ian backed away and stormed off to his tent.

With Ian out of the picture, Frank walked to the campfire, slumping into a chair opposite Paul.

Jean said, "Paul, if you'll excuse me, I'll be heading off to bed. I fear tomorrow is destined to be a long, unpleasant day."

"Sure, go ahead. I'm going to stay up with Frank for a while. Good night."

Paul watched her depart and then asked Frank if he was okay.

"Ian said it was my fault the kid's dead," Frank replied. "Is that what you think?"

"I don't think it's anybody's fault, and neither does Jean, but you have to admit he'd probably still be alive if you hadn't encouraged him to stay here."

"Shit, Skip, I was just trying to give the little kid a break from whatever they call a life here. Now Ian doesn't want to have a goddamn thing to do with me anymore."

Paul was surprised to see a tear rolling down Frank's cheek. "Aw, Frank, he'll settle down in a couple of days, but you'd better lay off the booze."

"Don't start that crap again."

"It's the truth. It's getting in the way of everything."

Frank took a deep breath. "Can't you see, Skip? I can't."

"Yes, you can. You just need to have some willpower."

"Willpower's got nothing to do with it. I don't want to talk about it right now. Just leave me alone."

Paul had no choice. If Frank didn't want to talk it out, there was little point in staying up with him. "Have it your way, but if you change your mind, just get me up."

"I'll be all right. See you in the morning."

"I'm sorry things are turning out like this. I know what this trip meant to you."

"No, Skip, I don't think you do."

Paul stared at him for a moment, expecting more. When it didn't come, he turned and left for bed.

Frank threw a couple of branches onto what was left of the fire and watched as flames grew along the underside of the wood. He thought about getting a drink or some pills or both, but deemed it a waste of time since he was beyond caring about improving his mood. What he wanted was for the leopard to return, which would take care of his drinking problem his Ian problem, and almost everything else wrong with his wreck of a life. *Here I am, you bastard. Come and get me*, he thought, trying to imagine what it would feel like—that one last instant—and what could be said about him at the funeral back home. *Friends, we're here to bury what's left of Frank Eastman, a fuck-up who managed to piss people off all the way to the jungles of East Africa.*

What would Ian say? Frank had wanted so much for the hunter to regard him as one of the best shots to set foot in the Rift Valley. That possibility had disintegrated. *Christ*, he thought, *the guy won't even talk to me. I'll bet he hates me more than that kraut client who got him mangled.* Several times Frank had to fight down the lump in his throat. He wasn't going to give in to it. No, he was going to take what he deserved, like a man.

Early the next morning, Frank awoke—still outside—to the sound of a log hitting the ground. "Go get washed up, Frank," Ian said, easing himself into a chair. "We've got to get going."

Rubbing his itching face and discovering several new hard bumps from insect bites, Frank gazed at the dim light spreading across the eastern sky. He was damp and shivering from being out all night. "Do you mind if I warm up a bit? I'm freezing."

Ian nodded and took a sip of tea. They both sat in silence, watching as the fire crackled and popped back to life.

Afraid Ian was going to kick him off the safari, Frank decided to beat him to the punch. "Do you want me to go home?" Frank asked.

"That's up to you, but I think you know how I feel."

"I've looked forward to this trip my whole life, but now that I'm here, I can't enjoy it."

"I can tell you why, but you won't want to hear it."

"That's only part of it, Ian. There's a reason why I drink so much."

"There's always a reason, isn't there?"

"If you knew the half if it, you'd understand."

"My job is to take people like you on safari, not to function as a bloody shrink and solve personal problems. I have to keep everyone safe from the type of thing that happened last night. You've made it nearly impossible to maintain order around here, and you can see the end result."

"How was I supposed to know that was going to happen? And besides, if it hadn't happened to the kid, somebody else would've gotten it. Maybe even you."

"You're right, but the point is that I didn't have to be responsible for one more soul until you made it so."

"I don't know what to tell you. If you want me to leave, do what you have to do. It really doesn't matter to me at this point."

"We need to find Dondo first, and then we'll decide what to do next. Now you better get ready, and by the way, I trust you won't mind if we forego breakfast this morning. If we find him, you'll not want to have a full stomach.

The search party was on its way before the sun cleared the horizon. Paul, Jean, Jua and Susani followed the trail on foot while Ian, Frank, Mchana, and Mohammad covered as much ground and checked as many trees as possible from the Rover.

Jua hadn't gone far before he stopped and spoke to Jean, pointing to a track on some soft earth.

"Well, that would explain it," she mumbled to herself.

"What did he say?" Paul inquired.

"This leopard's got a lame leg, which would account for its having become a man-eater. See how the pug mark turns out here?" She used her open hand to characterize the leopard's impairment.

Paul nodded, but he didn't see anything but a large cat footprint and a drop or two of dried blood.

"If the injury is severe enough in an animal like this, it has to substitute its normal diet with whatever it can catch. Humans, especially children, make exceedingly irresistible targets."

"How do you suppose it got hurt?"

"Could have been any number of ways. A fight with another beast, a native's spear, even a horn stab from one of its victims. If you study most man-eaters you'll usually find they've had some injury that sent them off in that direction. You can understand why it's essential that we find and kill this animal."

"This thing's not going to jump out on us, is it?" Paul darted his eyes around, fully expecting to see the feline crouched under the very next bush.

"I can't answer that. Shall we press on?"

"Lead the way," he replied, still scanning and praying they wouldn't encounter the killer.

There were several places along the trail where the sandy dark stains were extensive, indicating a pause in the leopard's progress, but on two occasions they lost the trail altogether, forcing Jua to move out in progressively larger orbits until he picked it up again.

By late morning, because of a restless night's sleep, Paul was drifting off. As a result he was badly jolted by the sight of the Dondo's torso barely twenty feet above him, in the crotch of a large acacia tree. Paul wasn't sickened as much as grieved by the sight of the partially eaten child amid a cloud of flies.

Jean had to step away from the tree several times and take deep breaths to keep from gagging. When she recovered sufficiently, she sent Jua to find her father. Without hesitation the African took off running.

"Why don't you go sit down somewhere?" Paul told Jean. "Susani and I'll get him down."

"No, we mustn't move him. Not if we want to have a shot at the *chui*."

"We're going to use the boy as bait? You can't be serious. It's barbaric!"

"It also happens to be the only way to draw the animal into range."

"It's sick!"

"I'm sorry you feel that way, but we've no choice."

"This is nuts! Human bait for leopard hunting? What's next, Jean, cannibalism?"

"With all due respect, there's no time to debate morality. We must leave the body as it is and construct a blind. Otherwise we risk missing our only opportunity. If you don't want to help, it's understandable, but Susani and I need to get busy."

"Of course I'm going to help you, but Jesus, what an irreverent way to deal with the dead."

"Better this than waiting for another victim."

Susani had already wandered off, *panga* in hand, to chop branches. Jean made a quick appraisal of the area. "We'll want to construct it right over there by that fallen tree. At least our backs will be protected."

"Protected? From what?"

"A leopard that eats people."

Ian swung the Rover close to the second baited tree. The first baited tree they'd checked hadn't produced any takers, despite the fact that the bloated, rotting warthog could be smelled a quarter mile away. The second bait was different.

"Look, one of our friends has paid a visit to this one. See, the rump has been chewed," he said, pointing up at the reeking carcass. "This one has promise."

Frank was relieved to hear something out of the Englishman. The whole morning had been spent driving around in silence. If it hadn't been for about half of his remaining painkillers, he couldn't have endured the tension. "Do you think it's the same one that killed Dondo—"

"Can't say," Ian replied. "We'll just have to sit it out this evening and hope for the best."

"If we nail it, do you have to turn the skin in?"

"I'll need to report the incident to Vince and let him handle the report. Trust me, I don't relish that one whit. I'm never going to hear the end of it. As for the hide, I figure to give it to the child's father."

Frank didn't like that thought at all, being that it was likely to be his only chance to pin down a leopard. *Maybe he'll feel sorry for me and let me keep it as kind of a going-away present.* The thought depressed him, not for what he would miss, but for what he had to return to.

"We may as well go chase down some *tomis* for the boys and come back later," said Ian, easing away from the tree.

Jean erected her blind out of branches and thorn bushes, hoping to afford an additional measure of protection for Paul and herself. The only opening in the vegetation was a small, unobstructed portal in which she placed a forked limb to serve as a rifle rest for Paul. Satisfied at last that the blind was as good as it could be, she and Susani swept their tracks away and backed out of the area while Jean worked at getting a splinter out of her hand. "It's not a perfect blind, but it should suffice," she mumbled. She nibbled at the thorn as she studied her handiwork. Turning to Paul, she observed, "Since we have several hours to wait, we might as well put it to good use. Feel like taking a walk and trying to scare up some game?"

"Is it safe? I mean, with the leopard—?"

"As long as we stay out in the open, there shouldn't be a problem."

"What happened last night was out in the open, remember?"

Jean gave him a timid shrug before heading off into the sparse scrub, delighted to place some distance between herself and the remains of the child.

Paul couldn't keep himself from glancing back at the tree until the gruesome sight was out of view.

With a bolt action over each shoulder and a shotgun slung over his back, not to mention a water bag and another leather bag of miscellany, Susani resembled a one-man munitions depot. Despite his burden and its potential for clatter, there wasn't so much as a rustle, not even a footfall from the bearer.

Paul tipped his head, whispering to Jean, "Don't you think we should offer to carry the guns ourselves? The poor guy's got a load back there."

"No, it's a pride thing with them. If you took the guns, he would take it as an insult, as if we were implying he wasn't capable of handling them himself. They're very peculiar about that sort of thing."

"They seem to really like and respect Ian."

"That's because Daddy's always been fair with them—demanding, mind you, but fair. He won't put up with much static from the boys, but he never asks them to do anything he wouldn't be prepared to do himself."

"How can he be so bitter on one hand yet have such respect for these guys?"

"He's made sure he could trust them. Right after my . . . incident, Daddy was literally insane with rage. Darting her eyes at the gunbearer, she continued, "I remember Daddy rounding all of them up on the veranda. He was screaming like a demon that he'd shoot them in their *shambas*, their homes, in front of their wives, if he caught wind of any involvement in the Mau Mau. I was in bed with my neck in bandages. It was all very frightening."

"Aren't there some laws against that sort of thing?"

"Now, yes, but then it was accepted, in fact, encouraged. There was even a head-hunting contest with prizes, but that was frowned upon by London and has long since passed."

Paul thought of Sheldon and what the coloreds were facing back home. "You know, we've got Negro problems starting in America. They want equal treatment in schools, voting, and things. Christ, I hope it doesn't end up like this."

Jean shook her head. "I hope for your sake it doesn't. It's been ghastly." Without waiting for a response, Jean gave a little tug on his sleeve. "Come on, let's keep moving."

Paul interpreted the touch as a positive sign and continued walking.

They were just coming up out of a fetid-smelling, muddy bottom along the feeble remnant of a creek, with their heads barely poking up from the depression, when Jean froze. Paul watched her eyes squint and understood that her jubilant grin meant that his marksmanship was about to be called into action. "What is it?" he whispered.

She kept her concentration, and without a blink, she whispered, "*Daktari*, you may be one shot away from being inducted into the family of Africa's esteemed record holders. Just before us is an absolutely monstrous reedbuck."

Paul turned, expecting to see some tremendous stallion with towering spiraled antlers. He scanned the distance, his eyes darting back and forth in anticipation of the majestic creature that was soon to be his, but he couldn't make visual contact with anything except a runty, inconsequential antelope with stubby horns grazing forlornly by itself. "I can't see it, Jean," he said, frustrated by his own ineptitude.

"You can't be serious. It's the only thing there, and it's right out in the open."

"You mean that puny little thing? *That's* going to bring me fame and glory? Are you kidding?"

Susani crept up to them and eased his arm around Paul, shoving the rifle into his chest.

Jean whispered, "Trust me, Paul, take the gun and don't miss this chance."

Sliding the rifle over the edge of the ravine, he flipped off the safety, and in one effortless squeeze of the trigger had bested a century of record seekers before him. Looking up from the sights, he said, "That was pretty tough. Now where's my prize?"

She scampered out of the gulch, kicking dirt all over him in the process. Arriving at the downed animal, she made a swift measurement using the width of her hand as a ruler. When Paul and the bearer caught up, she was already squealing with delight and bouncing around the antelope.

"Paul, do you know what we've done?" she shrieked, throwing her arms around him.

"If I'd have known that was going to be your reaction, I would've started shooting things days ago."

She gave him a reticent smile, explaining, "This isn't just any old dead antelope. We've just taken what may be the largest reedbuck ever recorded."

Even Susani, who rarely displayed emotion, beamed and gave him the peculiar two-handed African handshake.

"It certainly isn't a very glamorous thing," Paul said, squatting to examine the stubby antlers.

"I think its ruddy splendid," she enthused. "We just need to figure out what to do with it until Daddy can collect it tonight. We can't just leave it here, or *fisi* will rip it to tatters."

Pointing a thumb at Susani, Paul suggested, "How about having him carry it back to the blind?"

"I don't think it's wise to have it in the blind with us, for obvious reasons."

"Can we just leave it under the tree where the body is?"

Jean shook her head, "That would surely raise the *chui's* suspicion. No, I'm afraid it's going to stay here."

"If that's the case, how about a fire?"

"Not unless there's someone here to keep it burning into the evening, and I don't want to be without Susani if we need him."

"If we can't take care of the damn thing, why did you have me shoot it?"

It was a question she couldn't answer, or more precisely didn't want to. She desperately needed the trophy to prop up her position with the other hunters. Her competency had been an issue around Nairobi ever since her ingress into the business, and the record-setting kill would mitigate it. Under the guise of being misunderstood, and playing on his tender side, she tried to weasel her way out. "I thought you'd be pleased to have one prominent trophy to take home."

"Oh, come on, Jean. You're the one who wanted it, not me. Don't get me wrong, if it benefits you in any way, I'm delighted to do my part, but it was for you, not me."

"No, that's not it at all—"

"Look, it isn't important, is it? Getting it out of here in one piece is. Maybe Susani has some bright idea. Why don't you ask him?"

The solution was to cover the animal with thorn bushes. It wasn't foolproof, but under the circumstances it had to suffice.

"Not again with the thorns!" Paul protested, looking at the collection of scabbing scratches he'd gotten during the blind project.

"I'm afraid so. Sorry"

Once again they fanned out and reluctantly gathered an assortment of the sticking, poking, and scratching limbs, piling them on top of the carcass until it was undetectable to the eye. If the barrier fulfilled its intended purpose, it would prove to be too painful for the hyenas to reach the morsel.

"There's not much more we can do," Jean said, "so I suggest we make way for the blind."

Paul licked a trickle of blood on his forearm. "Are you sure we can't find more uses for these plants? I mean they're so much fun to play with."

"Come along, Paul; we've got work to do."

CHAPTER TWENTY-TWO

Antithesis

Jua caught up with the Rover and informed Ian that Dondo's corpse had been found in a tree and that Jean was building a blind to cover it, should the leopard return.

Ian stuffed five Viking Super Magnum buckshot shells into the belly of his Winchester pump gun and directed the tracker and Mchana to park the Rover somewhere midway between where he and Frank would be and where Jean had discovered the child. That position would put the two natives about twenty minutes away from either party. He instructed them to wait for the sound of a rifle report before proceeding to its origin.

After Ian and Frank entered the confines of the blind, Ian started lecturing Frank about staying perfectly still and absolutely quiet.

To Frank Ian seemed more squirmy than he had reason to be.

First Ian fidgeted with the contents of his *chui kitunda*, or leopard bag, laying out its contents, which consisted of leather-and-sheet-metal neck and arm bindings and a buckle-laden leather corset, all of which would be worn, reluctantly, in the event a wounded leopard required retrieval. He shifted and peered from the blind numerous times, not to mention incessant rehashing of directions. Obviously his psychic and physical injuries from the leopard attack had affected him more than even he realized, and whether he would overcome them in time remained uncertain. "Let's go over this one more time," he told Frank, "so there are no mistakes, all right?"

"I don't think that's really necessary, Ian. I'm not stupid."

"Your stupidity is not the problem. Your instinct to shoot the *chui* at the first opportunity is, and unless I drill it into your thick head not to do it, you will. Don't do it! Wait until it makes it to the bait up there. It's going to be as dark as a spinster's heart when that cat arrives—if it arrives at all—and you must make your shot count. There won't be a second chance. Wait until it hits that top branch with the bait, pick a rosette on its shoulder, and fire."

"What if—"

"No what if's, Frank. Just do as I say."

This guy can really be a prick when he wants to be, Frank thought. *How did he get such a terrific reputation?*

About an hour into the wait, with the shadows sliding across the chalky, sterile landscape, Ian settled down.

The mosquitoes started feeding on them, filling their little guts to the point of bursting, while the two men were powerless to thwart the fueling process. The men couldn't risk swatting the pests and revealing themselves to the leopard or any of the other creatures converging on the site. Monkeys screeched and chattered, small birds fluttered about, and the buzz of insects intensified as each agonizingly minute wore on.

Frank studied the tree with an intensity that he hadn't exercised since the days he and Paul had watched the baits behind Cap's boat. They'd both lie on the deck of the flying bridge and stare at the skipping mullet, eagerly awaiting the dark apparitions of rising game fish that would swell the water behind them and crash the baits, popping the lines free from the outrigger clips. They did it for hours or until their eyes burned from the strain.

His gaze fixed on the tree, Frank massaged the trigger of his Weatherby in anticipation of the moment he'd squeeze it.

With Susani holed up in a tree several hundred yards away, Paul and Jean arranged themselves in the blind and caught the first fleeting whiff of Dondo's putrefying body. Jean wrinkled her nose, and despite the fume of death, Paul couldn't help thinking how cute she looked. He was ashamed of himself for even having such a degenerate thought, but regardless of circumstances, she always seemed to have an aura of radiance around her, a glow that even morbidly couldn't quell.

He contemplated leaning over and whispering in her ear, but couldn't think of anything to say. The dead child in the tree, the fear of the leopard's return, his attraction to her; there were too many contradictory emotions at play.

Sensing both his confusion and desire to touch her, Jean took the initiative and whispered, "Paul, why did you abandon your profession?"

The question caught him off guard.

Jean watched as his brow furrowed and she knew she'd hit a nerve. His vision seemed to turn inward as he transported himself back to the previous summer. She watched him and waited, but he remained mute so long she assumed that he had no intention of responding.

She was about to return her attention to the baited tree, when he emitted, almost inaudibly, "I let him down."

"Excuse me?"

"Cap came to me for help, and I let him down."

"I don't understand."

Paul drew a long breath and stared off into the oblivion. "Last summer he came into the hospital while I was on duty. It was a Saturday." He shifted his eyes to her. "Do you really want to hear this?"

"I can see that it's upsetting you, so if you'd rather not—"

"I haven't talked about it in a long time. I couldn't."

"And you don't have to now."

Paul considered it for a moment, snapped a thorn from one of the branches, held it cigarette-style between his fingers, and tested the point with his thumb. He pressed his thumb harder against the thorn until the tip disappeared into the digit's dirt-smudged covering, causing him to flinch in pain and then he pressed it even harder. "It was a perfect surgery," he hissed.

Jean watched until she could stand it no more. "Paul, please stop that. You're making me uncomfortable."

He ignored her and stared intently as his thumb took another thrust of the lance.

"Enough, Paul!" she commanded, forcing his fingers apart and removing the thorn, but not before he had a chance to drive it to the bone. "What's the matter with you?" she shrieked, striking him soundly on the shoulder with a balled fist. "Have you lost your mind?"

Being wary of humans and sensitive to the slightest stir or sound, any leopard within earshot would have abruptly departed the area. Her outburst effectively ended the hunt. Jean was livid. She rose, exposing herself through the top branches of the blind. "I don't understand why you're punishing yourself because one of your patients didn't make it through an operation." She was talking down to him as he remained on the blind's dirt floor, his head slumped. "I'm very sorry your father passed away, but—"

"He didn't pass away," he said, his voice quavering on the edge of tears. "I killed him. I had to show everyone what a goddamn hero I was."

"So you took on more than you could handle, made a bad decision. It was a painful lesson but—"

Paul leapt to his feet, dropping the rifle, which thudded on the dirt. "Listen to me!" he screamed, startling her. "I accidentally tore his fucking sutures apart trying to prove what a great surgeon I was. He was the only person who gave a crap about me, and I thanked him by draining his blood and using his money to go to Africa so I could hunt for leopard using dead children for bait." The absurdity gripped him. Dropping to his knees as a year's inventory of pain and remorse came to a head, he burst into tears.

Nothing in Jean's experience had prepared her for the moment, but she recalled what he'd done for her at the major's home and eased down and put her arms around him.

As the two of them kneeled and embraced, Jean's grief surfaced as Paul's loss of Cap brought back the sadness of her mother's death, and she dissolved into tears. She cried over her slit and scarred throat. She cried over the death of the child. She cried over her unfulfilled needs, mainly to be loved by someone besides her father, someone who added some meaning to her desolate existence. Tear-streaked and drained, the two held each other.

Paul reluctantly released his hold on Jean and moved to pull apart, but she clung to him. His lips found hers, and they tasted salty from tears. Her breathing grew shallow and erratic the moment their mouths met, and he felt her quiver. The timing seemed all wrong, even blasphemous, but he didn't want to stop, and she couldn't. Suddenly they were all over each other. Their cramped quarters and pebbles that dug into their skin did nothing to deter them. Only when he tried to remove her scarf from her neck did she protest.

"Please, Paul, no," she whispered as his hand moved to untie the knot.

"I don't care about the scar."

"I don't want you to touch it. It's . . . repulsive."

"No, it's not. It's just another part of you, and *you* are the only one who cares about it."

"Paul, that's not true. I saw the way you looked. Why would you want to touch it? How could you—"

"Shhhh," he cut her off, kissing her on the chin.

She stiffened as he removed the silk neckerchief, and her hand started toward her throat, only to be blocked by his. As gingerly as he could, he gently kissed a path along her jaw and down her neck until he felt the texture of the scar on his lips.

Jean held her breath as his soft kisses traversed the length of the blemish. She tried to turn away, but his hand gently brought her face back to his.

"Jean, it's just another part of you. You're the only one who's making a big deal about it."

She stared at him for a long time, her bright eyes surveying his every feature. Just before she put her hand on his cheek, she had a fleeting thought that her lonesome, empty days in East Africa were coming to an end. She squinted into one of her bewitching smiles and joined her mouth with his in an embrace of total surrender.

With the western sky veiled in coral hues and the backdrop of death in plain view, and as the creatures of the jungle went about their own clamorous sundown activities, Jean and Paul found—and made—love.

CHAPTER TWENTY-THREE

Settling the Score

Frank was dozing off when the symphony of jungle peeps, screeches, and barks came to an abrupt and eerie halt. Ian perked up and squeezed Frank's thigh so hard the poor man nearly yelped in pain. The hunter motioned toward the tree with a nod of his head and then pointed at the rifle with a twitch of his finger.

Darkness having taken most of the colors from the landscape, visibility was reduced to shades of gray. Frank strained to see the bait as he mounted his rifle. Ian's mantra, *Don't shoot until the leopard hits the baited branch*, played over and over in his head. He could feel his breathing accelerate and then spike when he heard the cat grappling for a hold along the upper trunk of the tree, its claws making an ungodly racket as they dug against the bark. His heart pounded so loudly he was sure the leopard could hear it.

The animal had positioned itself on the first branch and slowly turned, staring directly at the blind. Frank couldn't restrain himself. In a fraction of a second he forgot everything he'd ever learned about shooting and anything Ian tried to bore into his head. He put the sight on the leopard's body without aiming at a specific spot, and he jerked, instead of squeezed, the trigger.

Before the echo had quit reverberating through the bush, Ian was in Frank's face, screaming at him. "Jesus bloody Christ, I *knew* you were going to muck it up. Why didn't you listen to me? Why? Don't you think I know what I'm doing, Frank? Damn it, boy, can't you get anything right?"

"What are you talkin' about, Ian? That leopard's dead as a doormat. I heard it hit the ground."

The hunter spun on his heels. "That leopard is not dead. Not one bloody bit dead. It's out there with a hole blown through its guts. And do you know whose job it is to go fetch it?"

"I think you're wrong, Ian. I'm pretty sure we'll find it at the base of that tree."

"Wrong, am I? Well, let's go have us a peek, shall we?"

Grabbing Frank by the arm, Ian shoved him through the opening in the blind.

Outside, staring in total bafflement at the lighted disk of empty ground, Frank said, "I don't understand. I know I made a good shot."

Too angry to speak, Ian knelt and blotted the earth with his fingers. A quick sniff confirmed his suspicion. The blood had the distinctive odor of feces. He shoved his hand up to Frank's nose. "What does this smell like to you?"

"Shit," Frank mumbled.

"Not much here to send to the taxidermist, is there, Frank?"

The American felt totally dispirited. "No, I guess not."

"That being the case, take yourself back to the blind and wait for me there. I've got work to do."

"No, Ian. I'm going in there with you."

"Like hell you are."

"You need me in there."

"To do what, shoot me in the back? No thanks. Your kind of assistance I can do without."

Ian tromped off toward the blind to get the necessary equipment.

Calling after him, Frank said, "That's not fair, Ian. My shooting's been damn good until now, hasn't it?"

"I don't have time to argue with you, Frank," he answered over his shoulder.

"Wait a minute," Frank insisted, spinning the hunter around by his arm. "I know you're pissed off with me about a lot of things, and I don't know why I missed that shot. Maybe I got too excited. I don't know. You said yourself—leopards have that effect on people. All right, I'm sorry I missed. But that doesn't mean I can't back you up in there, and you know it."

He was right. Another pair of eyes and another shooter could make all the difference, and it was true, Frank wasn't the first to flub a shot at one of those animals. Maybe it wouldn't be so bad to be shot in the back anyway, Ian thought. At least he wouldn't have to face this nightmare again, and it *was* a nightmare for him. He was plenty scared. The last mauling had shaken him to the core. He cursed his misfortune by not having Jean or one of the boys with him, but there wasn't time to wait. If the cat recovered from the shock, it would slip away and present a serious menace to the natives. They didn't need what could be two man-eaters roaming around the area. A gut-shot leopard could survive for days, and anyone hapless enough to run into it was sure to be done for. Never mind the awful suffering of the animal itself.

"All right, Frank, you want to come? That's fine, but I want you to know this. You're taking your life in your own hands. There's a solid chance that one or both of us won't make it out of those bushes alive."

Frank was remarkably calm, and Ian's warning didn't faze him in the least, perhaps because he'd be spared the trouble he was facing back in the States if he didn't make it out. "Just tell me what you want me to do, and I'll do it."

Ian stared at Frank's outline in the darkness. He couldn't see his eyes, but his voice was level and unwaveringly assertive, which Ian took as a good sign. "Put another round in the chamber and then help me put these things on."

Ian's getup looked like a bad costume for a medieval ball and would have been laughable had the implication not been so grave. The garments also restricted his motion, conferring a robotic rigidity to his movements. Checking to make sure the buckshot load was in the chamber of his shotgun and then picking up the blood trail, he reluctantly followed the flashlight's feeble stream into the dense growth, Frank bringing up the rear.

Each step Ian took was a calculated move. Rolling from the balls of his feet to his toes, he inched through the underbrush without cracking a single twig. It was not an attempt to sneak up on the animal, which he knew to be virtually impossible. It was more to enable all of his senses to operate at peak level.

If the leopard was still alive, and there was no reason to believe otherwise, his only chance to walk out of the bush unscathed was to detect the beast before it had the chance to blindside him. The hunter was bug-eyed from straining to get as much vision as the darkness would permit. His eyes burned from strain and lack of moisture. He dared not blink and miss a lightning-quick leopard leap. He was a frayed cable ready to snap, so when Frank whispered his name, it elicited a backward kick like a surly mule.

Frank got the point and kept his mouth shut.

Ian cursed his misfortune when he heard the distant drone of the Rover. Ignorant of Ian's predicament, the driver and some natives were threading their way through the darkness. Ian took one more step and froze. His ears perceived the wet, raspy heave of the leopard.

Ian's flashlight shifted so quickly that Frank couldn't follow it, nor was he attuned enough to identify the sound. Ian's reaction, however, was enough to make Frank flip the rifle safety and level his gun ahead and to the side of Ian's head.

The light beam and Ian's shotgun were one as he panned the undergrowth around them. At the end of a sweep of the flashlight to their right, the glowing-eyed gaze of the poised leopard startled them.

Ian's firing pin struck the primer, but instead of an explosion, there was an insipid thud of a primer-only discharge. Jimmy Foust's incompetence at the Viking Ammunition Plant had claimed its first victim.

Ian's mind slipped its mooring and drifted away. Time seemed to slow as the streak of gold and brown catapulted toward him. "Wait," he yelled, holding up a hand like a traffic cop, as if to persuade the beast to reconsider. It didn't, and it slammed into him with the force of a locomotive. The impact was so numbing that Ian never saw or heard the discharge of the Weatherby. Frank fired the instant he saw the leopard go airborne.

The men were shrouded in a darkness thoroughly devoid of sound, the rifle report having stifled all of the fauna. Even the insects got quiet. The pungent odor of burned gunpowder hung in the claustrophobic stillness. The release of tension seemed to hiss away like a leaking boiler pipe.

"Ian? Hey, Ian, you okay?"

When no response came, Frank felt a surge of dread, fearing that his shot had killed Ian.

"Hey, say something," Frank appealed, imagining how Jean was going to react. "Oh, God, please. Ian I didn't mean —"

"Yes, yes, I'm sure," Ian muttered, his mouth puffing dust as he lay face to the ground. "Now would you kindly get this spiteful bastard off of me? But tell me, did I have a misfire, or did I imagine it?"

"You mean you're not shot?"

Frank's voice sounded faint and distant. Ian's right ear had been close to the muzzle when Frank blasted the brainstem of the airborne feline. He was almost too sapped of strength to respond. "Not in the sense you're speaking of. Now, answer my question."

"The gun made a funny noise, like there wasn't any powder in the shell."

"Rotten bit of luck, wouldn't you say?"

Pleased to see the old man coming back to life, Frank asked, "Do you think this thing's safe to touch?"

"Trust me, *Bwana* Eastman, if old *chui* here wasn't dead, we'd be. Now pull it off of me, will you? I think I've had enough for one day."

Frank groped around, grabbed a handful of warm leopard hide, and pulled the animal aside.

Ian rose to all fours. "Let me stay here for a minute until my ears stop ringing."

"Take your time, Ian. You've earned it."

The Rover arrived, and Ian and Frank dragged the cat from the dense bush. Jua examined the dead animal, looked up, and announced in Swahili that it was the leopard that killed Dondo.

"You killed the man-eater," Ian said, gazing at Frank with a respect that Frank hadn't seen before.

Jean had been stretched out next to a small fire, her head in Paul's lap, when the second shot rang out. She bolted upright. "I don't like the sound of that," she said. "That second shot means Daddy had to go into the bush after another *chui*. Blast, I hope this isn't a repeat."

"He's probably fine," Paul said. "I doubt anybody could be that unlucky twice in a row."

"I haven't wanted to say anything, but Daddy's been affected since his injury. I think he's lost his nerve, and that's a serious problem."

"Maybe it's time for him, and for you, to give all this up."

"I don't know what else we could do."

"How about game control, like Major Connolly?" *As for you*, he thought, *come with me to Florida, and you wouldn't have to worry about doing anything.*

As if reading his mind, she said, "I love this country, Paul. I don't see myself leaving it."

He didn't like the sound of that, but it wasn't the time or place to go into it.

"Just hold me, Skip," she said. "Isn't that what Frank calls you?"

"Well, well, look at what we have here," Ian announced when the headlights found Paul and Jean standing and holding hands.

Frank smiled when he saw them, too elated by his coup to be jealous of their intimacy.

Jean was relieved to see her father step out of the Rover intact. "You had to go in after another one, didn't you?"

The weary Englishman nodded. "And you have *Bwana* Eastman to thank for seeing to it that I made it back out, because I nearly didn't. Of course he's the reason—aw, the hell with it. One thing's for sure, Zuri, it's the man-eater, and his career is over. Something was different about his daughter, and then it hit him. She wasn't wearing the scarf. He looked at Paul and then back at Jean, and a light seemed to shine from within him. He put his arms around the two. "Come see our newly departed friend."

"I've got a surprise for you too, Daddy."

"I can already see, honey."

She was confused for a moment and then remembered her neck. "Oh, not that. Paul took a reedbuck earlier in the day, and I venture to say it's the record."

"Where is it?"

"We didn't want to chance having it around the blind, so we buried it under a mound of thorns. Susani can take us to it on the way back to camp."

"It looks as though this trip may be taking a turn for the better," said Ian. "Except, that is, for the *mtoto*. We really should get him down and return him to his village. I can't see any point in doing it tonight. Unless anyone objects, I'll come back with the boys and deal with it in the morning."

The news of the exceptional reedbuck failed to get a rise out of Frank. He was civil and even congratulatory about Paul's trophy as he and the others headed for the reedbuck. In his mind, it was small time compared to his prize. With one sweep he'd settled the score with Dondo's killer, bagged an apex predator, and saved Ian's life.

As the Rover approached the area where Jean and Paul had concealed the reedbuck, Jean's hopes for record-book recognition were dashed when a dozen or so pairs of eyes glowed back at them like the devil's army. Before the vehicle had come to a full stop, she was out, shotgun in hand, cursing at the top of her lungs, her shotgun lighting up the night with bursts of yellow-orange. Hyenas yelped, snarled, and bit at their pellet wounds as she fired shot after shot. She would have minced them to pieces had Ian not slapped the barrel down.

"Zuri, what's gotten into you?" Ian said, yanking the pump gun from her hands.

"Look what these bastards have done to my reedbuck," she replied.

"*Whose* reedbuck, Zuri?"

"You know what I mean. Oh, just look at this bloody mess." She lifted a strip of tattered carrion from which one broken horn dangled, flung it to the ground, and stormed off.

"If you didn't want them to get it," Ian blurted, "you shouldn't have rung the dinner bell for them."

Paul caught up to her and tried to minimize the loss. "Jean, it's not that important. One deer is the same as another to me."

"You don't understand. Chances like this are rare, and I wanted it, Paul, I wanted it badly, for both of us."

"Forget about the lousy antelope. It's just another dead animal." Before she had a chance to object, he kissed her forehead.

She beamed up at him, laughed, snatched his hat off, and swatted him with it.

CHAPTER TWENTY-FOUR

Facing the Truth

Although Frank was accorded a hero's welcome when the hunters returned to camp, he grabbed a bottle of whiskey and headed for his tent. He had plenty to think about and wanted some room to do it.

Ian, meanwhile, harbored mixed feelings about the intimacy between his daughter and the *daktari*. He realized he didn't know where their relationship was headed, and he prayed that his daughter wasn't being set up for heartache.

Paul waited until he was certain Ian was fast asleep and then slipped into Jean's tent. He returned to his own quarters in the wee hours. He found Frank still awake. Glancing at the bourbon bottle, Paul was surprised to see it hardly touched.

"I'm glad you're back, Skip," Frank said, "I need to talk to you."

"Can't it wait until sunup?" Paul asked, lying down fully dressed and pulling the covers to his neck. "I really need to get a few hours of sleep."

"No, I don't think so. I need to talk to you now."

Paul grudgingly pulled the covers back down and swung his legs over the edge of the cot. He lit the gas lantern, which hissed and bathed the interior in a dim glow. "Fire away."

"I'm goin' back to Florida. Soon, maybe even today."

"Hold on, Frank. Regardless of what's happened, I think we can work something out with Ian."

"That's not the problem," he replied. "I need to get back, not that there's anything for me to go back to."

"I don't follow."

"I haven't been straight with you." Frank drew a deep breath. "When we left to come here, my business was about demolished, and I think . . . no, I'm sure I'm bankrupt."

Paul stiffened. "How the hell did that happen? You were on top."

Frank response was a single nod at the whiskey bottle.

"Jesus, Frank. Why?"

Frank didn't answer; he didn't have to. The problem had been self-evident the day he'd shown up at the house with the safari plan, but Paul didn't want to see it. Now he had to. He was looking at a different Frank, the real one, a deflated, beaten man whose life had unwound.

"What are you going to do?"

He shrugged. "It gets worse."

Paul sat silently and chewed his cheek.

"You know those pain pills? I've been takin' them a long time, and I'm stuck on them too."

All of a sudden things became clear to Paul. The strange request for drugs before they'd left Florida. The missing bottles and the rapid mood changes. Paul was furious with himself for not recognizing the warning signs. "Boy, you sure know how to mess up in grand style."

"I didn't intend to wind up this way, and now I don't know how to get out of it. What's worse is I used up the last of them this morning, and I think I'm in for a couple of really shitty days."

Paul got up, walked to the tent opening, and spit. He stood for a while with his back to his friend and then slowly turned around. "Sit down, Frank."

Frank complied, with the demeanor of a child about to be scolded for shoplifting.

"You and I go way back, Frank," he began. "We've been like brothers from day one."

Frank nodded.

"And Cap always did his best to treat you like one of the family. Don't you agree?"

Frank nodded again.

"I can't see any reason why that should stop just because he isn't around anymore. And by the way, just so you'll know, he isn't around anymore because of me. I made a mistake when I operated on him. A mistake that didn't need to happen, and he died right there with me watching him bleed to death."

Frank looked down and rubbed his brow, having just gotten a full load of what the past year must have been like for his friend. He realized why Paul had been so dispassionate from the outset.

"As you well know, Cap left me a bunch of money, along with all the other stuff, and it's a white elephant, as far as I'm concerned. I think you can understand that. So listen—" He sat down on his bunk across from Frank. "There are people who can deal with your drinking problem. Groups of people. Some are in hospitals or sanitariums, and they can help you. There's also a group in the Northeast that works by having people like you help others stay off the stuff. I don't know much about it, but I've seen some folks who were pretty bad off get their lives back in order. You need to involve yourself with those people. I don't care how you get sober, as long you stay with it. Do that, and I'll give you whatever you need to get back on your feet. Cap would have wanted it that way."

Frank was afraid to speak. He was being granted clemency, and the relief was overwhelming.

Paul waited for his response. It took a moment, but slowly, very slowly, Frank's hand traversed the rift between the two lifelong friends. Their hands met, and they spontaneously rose and hugged one another. Paul could feel Frank's body heave.

"A couple of weeks one way or the other isn't going to make any difference," Paul offered, "so why don't you stay?"

Stepping back, Frank rubbed his reddened nose and shook his head. "No. The sooner I get things straightened out, the better. Besides, I've already had enough of this place. I did what I wanted to do. I've seen enough." He walked over and picked up the bottle, torn between his vulnerability and his desire to keep his word. He needed a drink.

Paul knew it. "Go ahead. At this point it won't make any difference," Paul offered.

Frank pulled the cork from the bottle, pausing to look ahead for a moment. He set the bottle back down uncorked and walked away from it with the cork clenched in his fist. "What are *you* going to do once I leave?"

"I don't know," Paul said, looking in the direction of Jean's tent. "I'm certainly not in any hurry to leave Jean. In fact I don't think I can."

"She's some kind 'a doll," he said, smiling for the first time that morning.

"I'm in love with her, Frank."

"That's just the way things have always turned out for us. You get the diamond mine, and I get the shaft."

"You're going to get a chance to turn everything around."

"What am I supposed to do about the pain pills?" Franks asked, remembering the misery of his last withdrawal.

"Either way, you're going to have to get them out of your system, and it's going to be unpleasant, but I don't want you turning your guts inside out twenty thousand feet over Ethiopia. Let me talk to Ian. He's got some in his medical kit."

"Don't drag him into it. The guy already thinks I'm an asshole."

"I wonder why. Face it, Frank. He's going to want to know what the hell's going on here, and we need to be straight with him."

"Can you at least keep Jean out of it?"

"I'll do my best, but no promises."

"Not that it matters, but do you think they'll give me any sort of refund for leaving early?"

"You're right, Frank, it doesn't matter, and I damn sure wouldn't ask for one. Forget about the money. I'm going to write a note to Marvin Silver at

First National of Palm Beach. That's where my account is. You'll need to go see him personally. How much do you need right away?"

"Ten thousand ought to call off the dogs for a while."

"I'm going to warn you, just so there's no misunderstanding. If you stay drunk and piss the money away, forget you ever knew me. Understand?"

"I want to straighten my life out, Paul. The last few years have been living hell."

"Well, here's your chance. Don't screw it up."

"I won't . . . and thanks. I don't know how to—"

Paul waved him off. "Like I told you. Cap would have wanted it this way. End of story. Oh, and one other thing. When you get back, please go check on Sheldon and Clorese. Bring them up to date on what's going on over here, and tell them I'll be home in a couple of weeks."

"You got it."

"All right. Let's get cleaned up, and I'll talk to Ian."

"That young man is a bloody mess!"

"I know," Paul agreed, "but he had a crappy childhood and a boozing slob for a father."

"Now I'm sorry I was so hard on him."

"Don't be, Ian. He's responsible for what he brought on himself here. You were just doing what you had to do."

"I'll give him enough codeine to make it back to the States, but I feel like I'm helping him with his habit."

"You're just buying him a little time, that's all."

"What are *your* plans? You're not leaving too, I trust."

Grinning from ear to ear, Paul replied, "Ahh, no, Ian. I don't think so."

Ian shot him a cockeyed little glare. "I hope you know what you're doing. I won't stand to have Zuri hurt."

"I have no intention of hurting her, sir." The memory of Ian's reaction to the last person who harmed his daughter flashed in his mind. "I just haven't figured it all out yet."

"Hmmm," he said, rubbing the stubble on his chin. "I can take Frank to Tanga and put him on a plane to Nairobi. He can fly home from there. I'll have someone meet him and see to it that all the necessary arrangements are made. The trip will have me away for two, maybe three days tops. You'll be without transportation for that time. That is, unless you want to hunt from the truck."

"No thanks."

"I see. Well, what say we go have a chat with our *chui* slayer?"

Jean, Ian, and Paul found Frank packing a suitcase in his tent. Ian was as diplomatic as he was understanding, and made no attempt to chastise or denigrate Frank, who was down enough already.

"I should be tied up, dealing with the child for most of the morning, so if you'll assemble your effects, we can shove off for Tanga as soon as I return. Your skins will catch up with you in about a half a year, barring the unforeseen."

"Is there something I can do for Dondo's father?" Frank asked. "If it weren't for me he'd probably still be alive."

"The gift of money would be acceptable, if not appropriate."

Frank dug out his wallet. "I might as well take care of the boys too while I'm at it. Here, take it all" he said, holding out a stack of bills.

Ian looked at the pile of currency. "That might be overkill, Frank. There's about two hundred American dollars there."

"They had to put up with me. They earned it. Go ahead and give it to them. Maybe now they'll remember me."

"It wasn't so bad for them or us. Isn't that right, Zuri?"

"I wish you would reconsider and finish the trip," Jean said, "or at least stay for another week or two."

"I'd love to, Jean, but I gotta go."

Several hours later the group convened at the Rover, which still bore the stench of Dondo's remains, to bid Frank farewell.

Paul reaffirmed their agreement, shaking on it, reminding him to look in on Sheldon and handing him an envelope containing a note to the banker.

Frank could feel a clump at the bottom of the envelope and realized that Ian had supplied enough pills for his return flight. Stuffing the envelope in his shirt pocket, he hoped Jean didn't know about the tablets, which would have only worsened his desolation at the moment.

Jean delivered a peck to his cheek and promised to take great care of his trophies until they could be forwarded to him in America.

Studying her beauty one last time, he sank further.

The farewell gathering also included the natives, who, upon having received the inordinately large gratuity, converged on him as if he were Mickey Mantle in Yankee Stadium. It helped a little, but he needed to get out of there. Taking one last look around the camp, he yearned for a drink to ease the pain. He had dreamed of his own safari since boyhood. Stretched out on the cold cement floor in the elementary school library he had skimmed the musty pages of Roosevelt's *African Game Trails* and imagined an expedition with his own tent, natives, and professional hunter. Here it was within his grasp, only to be taken away by a past that wouldn't let him go.

Despite all the conflicts that had surfaced since the pair boarded the plane in Miami, Paul knew he was going to miss his friend. Not wanting to be the last image Frank had before ending his safari, Paul spun about, and retreated to his tent, where he sat on his bunk opening and folding the temples of his sunglasses until the drone of the Rover had faded in the distance.

With Ian and Frank gone, Paul and Jean had the camp to themselves, apart from the natives, and turned it into their private quasi honeymoon resort, dancing to scratchy Buddy Holly records, taking a moonlight walk, and finally pulling their chairs beside the fire and sitting in reflective silence.

Eventually Jean rose, placed her hand on his shoulder, and parted for her tent. He hesitated a moment to savor the moment then followed her to her quarters.

For the next two days they were inseparable, leaving her tent late in the morning and spending the day going for long hikes through the bush. They were always accompanied be at least two Africans, who carried their guns. Jean and Paul each shot a gazelle the first afternoon to keep the larder stocked, and they ended the day at the water hole. The birds came in as expected, but this time the couple made fewer shots than kisses.

When Ian returned late in the afternoon on the second day, he was surprised to find his daughter and Paul frolicking in the river like a couple of newlyweds on a beach in Bermuda.

Wading from the water bare-chested, Paul worried about the conservative Englishman's reaction to the evolution of his relationship with Jean and braced himself for the worst.

"Don't you know, there are crocs as big around as fever trees in that river," he groused, taking off his hat and combing his hair back with his fingers.

"Yes, sir," Paul said. "We have Jua and Mchana keeping an eye out." He pointed to the two men stationed on the bank.

"And what are they supposed to do if a crocodile slips up underwater? Zuri, you should know better than that."

"Oh, Daddy, don't be such an old maid."

"Listen, young lady. I don't want to spoil your merriment, but haven't we been through enough already?

Paul apologized, confessing the swim was his idea.

Ian said, "I don't mind you two having a good time together. I just happen to regard this as the wrong place to do it."

"We'll stay clear of it from now on," Paul promised. "Did you get Frank taken care of?"

"By this time tomorrow he'll be well on his way back home. Fine young man he is. I had the chance to talk with him at length. Got me wishing he'd stayed." Ian was backing up the bank, his boots sinking in the damp sand, as

Jean and Paul followed him, hand in hand. "Poor fellow needs to dry out and arrange his priorities, and he'll be fine," Ian continued. "I commend you for largess on his behalf. That was a very noble gesture."

"I'd like to think it will make a difference, and besides, it was as much for my benefit as his."

"Nonetheless, it was admirable. Reli tells me things got a tad raucous around here the other night, with you two dancing. I'm sorry I wasn't here to see it."

"Believe me, Ian, you were better off," Paul said. "It wasn't a pretty sight."

"Nonsense!" Jean said. "You're a splendid dancer, Paul Bennett."

"Don't listen to her. The only thing that was missing was a bone through my nose and a spear in my hand."

"The next thing you know, she'll have *me* convulsing like that bumpkin, what's his name?"

"Elvis Presley," Jean said.

"Yes, that's the fellow. Quite indecent, wouldn't you say?"

Paul didn't want to come off as too much of a square, but he also wanted to play it safe. "Aw, he's okay. This new music just takes some getting used to."

"I daresay," Ian muttered. "Have you two given any thought to the itinerary for the next month?"

"I'm fine with just seeing the country," Paul replied. "Maybe shoot enough to keep everyone fat and happy. How about you, Jean?"

Taking his hand, she said, "It's your safari, Paul. Whatever you wish."

"I can promise you one thing," Ian said. "There'll be no more leopard hunts on this trip. I've done my last one of them for a while."

With the effort to amass dead game a thing of the past, the pace of the safari slowed dramatically. Ian, when he wasn't tagging along for lack of anything better to do, hung around the campsite and read, puffing away on his foul little cigars. Jean showed her boyfriend around the Tanganyika countryside, and on more than one occasion they suspended their jaunt, leaving the African chaperones to guard the Rover while they vanished for hours, emerging disheveled and blissful. Despite her protestations that "Daddy won't care," Paul chose to maintain his own tent, and only under the cloak of darkness slipped over to hers.

The eventual outcome of their relationship began to concern him. Either she'd abandon ties to her homeland and accompany him to America or he'd take up residence with her in Kenya after disposing of his U.S. properties. For both of them, seismic changes would be in order. Others would be affected. What would he do, for instance, about Sheldon and Clorese? One thing he knew for certain. He couldn't stand to be apart from Jean more than a few hours, let alone climb into a plane and leave forever. Sooner or later he was going to have to address the issue with the Sharpes.

Before dinner one evening, Ian tossed a thigh-sized log on the fire, sending up barrage of tiny sparks, and told Jean and Paul, "I think we might shove off for Dodoma tomorrow. I trust we've fairly well beaten the bushes around here for all they're worth. Any objections?"

"I was hoping you'd propose something like that," Paul commented. "What's to do in Dodoma?"

"The area's pretty stiff with big *tandala,* and if you choose to give it a chance, there's no shortage of *faro.* The hunting's tough because the bush is so dense. I think we should plan to tarry there for only a short time—use it as a jumping-off point for the ride to the Southern Highlands, where we should *really* see some game. It would be a crime not to take some of these animals while we're down there."

"I didn't say I wasn't going to hunt. I'm just not going to kill myself—or Jean—in the process. But even if I don't shoot another thing," he said, taking Jean's hand, "this trip has changed my life."

"Yes," Ian said. "I think we'll want to discuss that very soon."

"Oh, Daddy, don't put the poor boy on the spot."

"I have no intentions of putting anybody on the spot, Zuri, but this safari isn't going to last forever, and then what?"

"Please, let's not go into it now," Jean pleaded.

"If not now, when?"

Paul sensed that Ian's patience was wearing thin, and that he expected some answers. Realizing that he had to state his intentions—and soon, Paul said, "How about if the three of us talk about this when we get to Dodoma?"

Ian's tongue worked at a piece of gazelle that was stuck between his teeth while he eyed Paul. Ian finally gave one nod, which Paul interpreted as a brief reprieve.

To be on the safe side, the lovers stayed in their own tents that night. The danger of Ian catching them *in flagrante delicto* was too great.

When the order came to take down the tents, the natives, who'd been getting restive, sprang into action, eager to move on. As usual the Rover occupants quickly found themselves miles ahead of the transport; however, this time it was Paul's driving. He reasoned that as long as he was moving toward being one of the family, he might as well share in some of the duties. He did so to everyone's annoyance, though. Despite Jean's incessant coaching and an almost endless stream of bitching from the back seat, Paul managed to approach every obstacle incorrectly, battering the occupants senseless. By the time he halted for lunch, the riders fell out of, as much as climbed from, the Rover. The natives, drained from the hours of hanging on for dear life, shot hateful looks at him as they clustered among themselves.

"What's their problem?" asked Paul, oblivious to any difference between his driving and Jean's.

"You know, *daktari,* those fellows aren't above indulging in a little cannibalism, and they're especially partial to impetuous American drivers."

"Aw, c'mon, my driving's no worse than hers," he said, poking Jean in the ribs.

She whacked him on the hand. "I beg your pardon."

Lunch was a catch-as-catch-can affair held beneath the canopy of an immense acacia, a can of this and a chunk of that, followed by a warm Tusker beer—spartan, but adequate on safari. Ian was mid-guzzle, when something caught his attention and he moaned. "Aw, shit! What is it now?"

Paul and Jean twisted around to see Reli bounding toward them from a distance. As he approached they could see his khaki pants were discolored. Assuming it was oil, Ian dragged himself up so he could confront the latest crisis. His mood changed when he realized that the stains on Reli's pants were blood. As Reli recounted what had happened, Ian's face took on the same deflated, ashen cast it had the night of Jean's black mamba attack.

Paul couldn't understand the exchange, but he did pick up the names of their camp hands, Nyeusi and Kemoa, as well as the work *kufa*, meaning dead. He'd heard that one before and judging by the reactions of the Sharpes, Paul knew they were in serious trouble.

Ian handed his beer to Reli and took off for the Rover, hurdling into the driver's seat and pounded the wheel impatiently while the others flung themselves in from all sides.

"Will somebody fill me in?" Paul asked, his head jerking back from the wrenching departure.

"The big truck rolled over, killing Nyeusi, and Kemoa's injured badly."

Paul felt the transformation from vacationing tourist to physician. His brain pulled medical procedures from memory. Check and maintain airway, locate all sites of blood loss, check for punctures to the chest, perform a thorough exam, and don't overlook anything. All these thoughts shot through his head while he bounced along in the Rover in anxious silence. He didn't know what he could do for Kemoa, with only the barest of medical supplies on hand, but regardless of the African's condition, Paul was fervent about keeping him alive, if not for the native's sake, then for Jean's.

He had an opportunity to right the past, everyone's past. Regardless of what Paul had to do, if the man was still alive when the Rover reached him, he was going to stay that way. Paul recalled that he'd made a similar proclamation previously, and the costs were so great that he was barely starting to recover. *No*, he thought, *I'm going to do what I've been trained to do, and if the man dies, then he dies, and that will be the end of it.* The rationality gave him a sense of empowerment and calm, allowing him to take command as soon as the Rover pulled up to the wreck.

As Frank had predicted, the rear end of the truck had dropped into a depression, causing the undercarriage to give way. Fatigued from a conglomeration of repairs, the frame couldn't absorb the jolt and had cracked under the shifting weight. The vehicle then rolled over and came to rest on its side like a huge, dead, rust-colored pachyderm. The natives had jacked it up with a pair of scissor jacks so they could extricate the men from underneath.

All the injured, and nearly everyone was in some degree, were stoic, sitting in silence and holding blood-sodden rags against themselves.

Reli took the doctor to the canvas tarp covering what was left of Nyeusi. The ill-fated camp hand had made the mistake of jumping from the top of the load as the truck went over and had been underneath and folded double by the falling tonnage.

Ian lifted the shroud, took a fleeting look, and quickly dropped it again. "He's finished," he announced, his voice lacking emotion. "Let's see about Kemoa."

Jean had gone directly to Kemoa and was kneeling by his still body. "I think he's dead already," she said, sniffling. She had a tight squeeze on her cook's arm.

"Move over, Jean, and let me take a look."

Either she was so wrapped up in thought that she didn't hear him or she didn't want to leave her beloved cook's side. In either event, she resolutely stayed put.

"Please, Jean, I can't help him with you in the way."

Ian instructed, "Zuri! Give the *daktari* some room, and go see what you can do for the others."

She stood up unsteadily and backed away.

"Jean," Paul said, attempting to jolt her out of her daze, "get the bandages out of the first aid box and give them to anyone who's bleeding. If they're bleeding really bad, put some pressure on the wound, and I'll get there in a minute."

When he was satisfied that she was all right and distracted, he turned his attention to the cook, who did in fact appear deceased. His eyes looked dull and rolled back. He'd been bleeding from numerous places and was soaked. Paul felt Kemoa's neck for a pulse. "He's not dead, Ian," he said, tearing the native's shirt open. His chest was moving slightly, and foam bubbles were sprouting from his mouth. Paul made a quick check for breaks in his skin. "Help me roll him over. I want to check his back."

The two pushed the man onto his side. When they did, he produced a gurgling hiss.

"Just what I thought. He's got a pneumothorax. Give me one of those bandages and find some wax paper or foil, and make it snappy. He's not going to stick around forever."

While Ian dug through the heap of scattered supplies, Paul swept his fingers inside Kemoa's mouth and checked him over for more signs on injury. "C'mon Ian, we're running out of time here."

Although Paul would have never admitted it to anyone, he was enjoying himself. The excitement and the challenge were taking a hold of him once again.

"How's this?" Ian asked, handing him some tin foil.

Paul slapped it on the puncture and covered it with gauze and tape. Almost instantly the native's breathing improved. Next Paul turned his attention to another crisis point in the form of a deep slash in the man's groin. There was no way to know how much blood he'd lost from the cut in his femoral artery, but the bleeding had to be stopped, or he'd bleed to death in a short time. Paul tried in vain to apply a tourniquet to the spot, but its location made it impossible. "We're going to have to keep direct pressure on this until we can get to a hospital. There *is* a hospital somewhere nearby, isn't there?"

By then Jean had reappeared. "There's a small dispensary at Hedaru. It's the closest thing," Relieved to find Kemoa still alive, she knelt, gave the native a smile, and squeezed his arm again. She looked up at her boyfriend, who had an I-do-this-all-the-time air about him.

"How long will it take to get there?" Paul asked.

"Three to four hours, tops."

"Do you think they've got anything there besides aspirin and bedpans?"

"I couldn't say, but some of those places are fairly well equipped."

"I hope so, for his sake. He's going to need surgery *if* he makes it there."

Ian said, "Then might I suggest you shove off? I'll stay back here with the boys. Zuri, does anyone else need to go along?"

"No, Daddy. There are some minor cuts and scrapes, but nothing serious."

"Well, then, let's get him loaded. When you get to Hedaru, get a message to Vince, and let him know where we are. You might ask him to round up some trucks and come fetch us. I'll just leave the old gal here for good."

"You're not actually going to retire that scrap heap, are you, Daddy?"

"In view of this," he said with a sweep of his hand, "I think it's time."

"All right. I'll send help as soon as I can."

"Thanks, darling. Now run along and don't let Paul drive."

"Thanks, Ian," Paul said. "We'll have someone to pick you up around Christmas. Now give me a hand getting Kemoa up."

The natives and Paul positioned Kemoa so Paul could ride with him and keep pressure on the wound. He wanted to be able to regulate the force so he could intermittently allow some circulation to the leg.

Reli took the wheel and they left Ian and his crew to bury Nyeusi and watch over the cargo.

The dispensary was an unassuming little stone structure staffed by a frail-looking German doctor with a thick accent and scraggly goatee. He had the pallor of a corpse but was amiable, putting his facility at Paul's disposal when Paul introduced himself as a visiting American surgeon. As soon as Paul got to work he was appalled by the dearth of supplies, but he was in no position to be finicky, since the trip had taken an additional toll on his patient, who was by then hypovolemic and listless.

While Paul ironed out the specifics, Jean got on the facility's short-wave radio and in short time made contact with Major Connolly. Between the hissing and cracking of the connection, she was able to relate what had happened and where her father could be found. Following a most profane monologue during which the major verbally pared her father's backside, he assured her that he would take it upon himself to attend to the team's retrieval.

In the treatment room she found Paul conversing with the German doctor.

"I'm going to need to put him under. What anesthetic do you have here?"

"I have ethea. Zat is all I have."

"Can you deliver it?"

"I ave been trained to do so, *ya*."

"What about instruments and sterility? Do you have an autoclave?"

"Paul," Jean interjected, "the doctor is nice enough to let you use his clinic. How about showing him a little courtesy?"

He paused. "I'm sorry. It's just that if I don't get Kemoa on the table here, and soon, it's not going to matter."

"Docta Bennett, I am quite certain zat you vill have the necessary implements and zat they vill be appropriately dizinvected."

"I know it's too much to expect you to have blood, but do you keep any fluids here?"

"I can offer izotonic vater vis glucose."

"Fantastic! Let's get him knocked out and see what we can do."

The light was inferior, and the supply of instruments was a fraction of what he once had back home, but with the German delivering the ether drops and Jean doing what she could, the three of them managed to close Kemoa's puncture wound and arrest the bleeding artery in his groin.

Signs of gangrene would not appear for more than a day if Kemoa's leg had been inadequately supplied with blood during the trip. If infection was going to take hold, however, it would become obvious soon enough.

Paul and Jean slept together on a cot adjacent to Kemoa's bed. On the following day they pitched in and helped the German doctor with the daily routine at the dispensary. Paul set a broken leg, stitched up a nasty dog bite, and extracted a decayed tooth—the latter a first for him. He also got an education on tropical skin conditions and learned how to make a delicious *hasenpfeffer* using guinea fowl instead of rabbit. The real high point of the undertaking, however, was the time he spent with Jean. She was proving to be skillful companion—quick, calm, capable, multilingual, and cut out for nursing—and he realized he'd better start convincing her to leave East Africa, or he'd better become accustomed to living in the bush, because there was no way he was about to be separated from her. Not even for a day.

Kemoa started running a fever on the second day, so they upped his penicillin injections, and Jean stepped up her sponge baths. His leg seemed to be responding, and with no sign of gangrene evident, Paul determined that the worse was behind them.

CHAPTER TWENTY-FIVE

Loose Ends

Paul and Jean could hear the trucks at a distance, clambering up the main road, and went outside to greet them.

Ian was the first to disembark, and with almost three day's worth of beard and no bath, he had the face of a skid-row bum. He'd been wearing the same outfit for days, and judging from the bags under his eyes, Paul surmised he'd caught little or no sleep. Jean threw her arms around him and kissed him anyway.

"Hello, little girl," he breathed. "Kemoa still with us?"

"Not only is he still with us, he—"

"Are ye gonna just ignore yar Uncle Vince?" bellowed a familiar voice. "What kind 'a upbringing do ye call this?"

"Hello, Uncle Vince," she said, letting him bear hug her until the air was squeezed out of her lungs. "Thank you for getting Daddy," she wheezed.

"Aw, I should've left 'm out in the boush for *fisi* ta have their wee with."

"Hi, Ian," Paul said. "Nice to see you again, Major."

"Quite a tale you'll have ta spin back at yer country cloub, hu, *daktari?*"

If Paul hadn't had prior experience with the rancorous major, he'd have taken offense. Instead he laughed it off and commented, "It's been an ordeal."

"Where's Reli?" Ian inquired. "Vince wants to head back to Arusha, and we need him to drive the other truck."

"You're not heading back right now," Jean protested.

"'Fraid so, missy," the major said, "Got wark ta do. Now go fetch yar boy so I can poush off."

"I hope you recognize that the safari's finished," Ian told Paul.

"I figured it was done for when the truck went over."

"I hope you aren't too disappointed."

"No, Ian. I've had the chance to think about a lot of things these past two days. Things we need to talk about. No, I'm really fine with calling it quits."

After wresting some clothes and personal items from the trucks, Vince climbed aboard one truck and drove off, Reli following behind in the other.

Jean, Paul, and Ian dined with the German doctor that evening. Ian tried to worm his way out, but Jean would have no part of it. Despite harboring resentment, Ian was civil and gracious, thanking the doctor for his assistance during Kemoa's crisis.

The next morning after breakfast, Jean excused herself to check on Kemoa. The three men sat around and made small talk for a few minutes before Paul and Ian set off for the clinic.

On the way along the road Paul stopped in his tracks. "Ian?" He swallowed hard. "I want Jean to come back to Florida with me."

Ian hesitated, letting it sink in, and finally asked, "Have you discussed it with her?"

"No, sir. I wanted to talk to you first."

"What makes you think she'd go?"

"You've seen what's been going on between us."

Ian stared at Paul long and hard before he spoke. "America's a long way from here. If she did leave, I would never see her again."

"With air travel you would be about two days away."

"You might just find she's opposed to it. Jean loves this country, and I don't know if she'll leave."

"All I can do is ask her to come with me for a visit. If she likes it and wants to stay, then we go from there."

285

"And if she doesn't?"

"I'd rather not think about that right now."

"It's a distinct possibility."

"I suppose."

"What about your career? What are you going to do? I know you have money, but the two of you can't just sit around doing nothing."

"I'm going back to work."

"When did you decide that?"

"When I dealt with Kemoa."

"I'm certainly glad to hear it. You're a bloody good sawbones."

"So I have your approval?"

"Don't' ever do anything to hurt her, or you'll find that the Atlantic Ocean isn't wide enough. Do you get my meaning?"

"Loud and clear."

"Then I suggest we go and see if this conversation was for naught."

Paul found Jean with Kemoa, and she could sense Paul and her father were up to something from the way they looked at each other and the fact that Paul appeared to be a million miles away as he pretended to examine Kemoa, who was recovering satisfactorily.

"Jean, could we have a word with you, outside?" Paul whispered.

After following the pair out the door, she said, "You two, what scheme are you concocting now?"

"I want you to come with me to America."

Jean put her hand to her mouth and turned her back to them.

Paul moved to her side. "It can't be *that* bad."

"Oh, Paul, I would dearly love to go with you, but you know I could never leave Daddy here alone. I'd worry myself sick over him."

Ian spoke up. "Maybe I can help you with that, Zuri."

"What do you mean?"

"You won't have to worry about me, because I won't do safaris anymore. This was my last one."

Jean's eyes opened wide. "I beg your pardon?"

"I've had enough for one lifetime. I might be a slow learner, but this trip has shown me it's probably time to get out. Too many close calls."

"What on earth are you going to do with yourself?"

"For starters I might move back to England."

"Are you insane?" Jean asked, her voice rising. "Sell the farm and leave, just like that?"

Paul asked, "You're not doing it on my account, are you?"

"Don't flatter yourself, lad. I'm doing it because Kenya is going get her native independence, and that's going to start the largest land grab since the California gold rush. We Brits may find ourselves out on our ears. I'm going to get a jump on it and clear out of Kenya with a couple of quid in my pocket and the skin on my back."

"Why can't you move here, to Tanganyika, like Uncle Vince?"

"When Kenya goes, Zuri, Tanganyika won't be far behind."

She stopped to ponder the epochal events bearing down on them. "If Paul and I . . . you know . . ."

"I'll come to visit you. You needn't fret over that."

She gave out something between a sob and a laugh and hugged Paul and her father at the same time. "Daddy, do you think we can start back today?"

"I think that's up to the *daktari* here."

"I'll get started on Kemoa's discharge papers right away," Paul said.

The three thanked the German physician, and Paul gave him a sizable donation. Ian even dug out a couple of pounds for the clinic, all the while swearing Paul to secrecy. "If you ever tell Vince I did this, I'll have your guts for garters," he said, jabbing him in the side with his elbow.

Within a few days the former hunters were back in Nairobi, sorting through the mountains of gear and dealing with a host of post-safari details. There were also airline reservations to be amended and government paperwork to be completed.

Ian paid another grim visits to a nearby *boma,* this time the one belonging to Nyeusi. He went through all the customary routine of presenting the widow with the deceased's effects and gave her his pay, plus some additional money. He offered condolences, which were accepted quietly and with dignity.

Word of the ill-fated trip had gotten out, and a constant stream of friends, curiosity-seekers, and plain gossipmongers flooded Ian's office.

Paul stayed with Ian and Jean at their unpretentious but well-adorned home replete with trophies from a lifetime of hunting. He spent one afternoon on a walking tour of the farm with Jean. He was saddened to think of their charming plantation in the greedy hands of real-estate lawyers.

Much to Paul's disappointment, Jean had reverted to covering her neck with scarves, and he resolved to address the problem when they got to the States. He wondered how Sheldon and his wife would react to her and her to them, but he was confident they would meld well together. *The Lucky Brake* was also very much on Paul's mind. He hoped that Buddy had at least begun to overhaul the boat and crossed his fingers that a hurricane hadn't hit while he was away. He wanted Jean to see his boat gently rocking at the dock, her decks and trim and glistening in the morning sun. Again he envisaged plying the Gulfstream with Jean in search of marlin and tuna, but this time it wasn't just a dream. It really was going to happen.

He realized he was excited about life again and looked forward to getting back to the operating room. He also was eager to see that Frank was sticking to his word.

On the morning of the flight, Paul left Jean alone with her father and went for a walk by himself. When he returned he found them huddled together on the sofa, their eyes watery and noses pink. He made himself scarce again, and a while later, they came to ask if he was interested in having a drink at the bar where they'd first met.

Over cocktails Paul poked at his ice cubes and let Jean and Ian do most of the talking. He couldn't help thinking how lovely she looked in the powder blue turtleneck and white skirt, and he fell in love with her a little more, right then.

Looking up at the stuffed animal heads on the wall, Jean pointed to her cobweb-covered gazelle, the Tommy that had brought her such notoriety as a child, and Paul listened to the story again, but with more enjoyment and connection that he'd had the first time

Later, as Paul and Jean prepared to board the plane, there wasn't a dry eye in the group, save Jua, who had insisted on being there for their departure. Even Kemoa, who stood proudly, propped by a crutch, had streaks across his dark, wrinkled face.

Jean gave her father one last long hug and backed away, unable to utter a sound. Paul shook the natives' hands first, giving them respectful nods. When he got to Kemoa, the old man handed him a bracelet made of the hair of an elephant's tail. By the look on Ian's face, the gesture must have been a supreme compliment. Paul trembled from within and could do nothing but grasp the man arm and stare into his watery eyes in kind.

When Paul got to Ian, he didn't know what to say or do.

Sensing Paul's dilemma, Ian liberated him with one small remark. "Go on, son, go take my daughter to the plane."

Paul nodded, turned slowly, and took Jean's arm. She glanced back once, right before they walked up the ramp. Her father was wiping his eyes.

Looking small through the aircraft window, the whole ragtag lot of them were lined up, hoping to get one more glimpse at the departing couple.

Kemoa pointed when he saw Jean's face appear in the oval porthole. Paul leaned over her and looked down at them, his head next to hers. He noticed Jua, who hadn't so much as batted and eye or changed an expression throughout the entire trip, was smiling. As the two men stared at each other, Jua extended his hand and pointed a finger up toward the sky and then nodded at Paul, indicating that all would be good in the heavens.

With the sound of the first starter motors winding up to speed, Paul eased back in his seat, took a deep breath, and closed his eyes. His thoughts went to that day when Cap demanded he fight the giant tuna to the end. Paul felt peace in knowing that despite having his world turned upside down, Cap's message had never left him.

The End

CPSIA information can be obtained
at www.ICGtesting.com
Printed in the USA
LVHW010149100221
678885LV00002B/152